THE LAST BUFFALO HUNTER

The Last
BUFFALO
HUNTER

a novel by

Jake Mosher

DAVID R. GODINE
PUBLISHER
BOSTON

First edition published in 2001 by

David R. Godine, *Publisher*
Post Office Box 450
Jaffrey, New Hampshire 03452

www.godine.com

LIBRARY OF CONGRESS CATALOGING-IN-PUBLICATION DATA

Mosher, Jake.
  The last buffalo hunter : a novel / by Jake Mosher.—1st ed.
    p. cm.
  ISBN: 1–56792–146–9 (hardcover : alk paper)
    1. Teenage boys—Fiction. 2. Grandfathers—Fiction.
    3. Montana—Fiction. I. Title.
  PS3563.088442 L3 2000
  813'.6–dc21   00–060999

First Edition

Printed in the United States of America

For my parents,
Howard and Phillis,
and my friend,
Tom Hahn.

For my parents,
Howard and Phillis,
and my friend,
Tom Hahn.

THE LAST BUFFALO HUNTER

CHAPTER 1

M ONTANA. It took up two pages in my father's atlas. He said we could fit three New Yorks in it, that it took a full day to drive from one end to the other, and if its mountains were flattened out it would be larger than Texas. He said the sky did look bigger, that the fly fishing was beyond compare, and the views, snow-capped mountains, golden prairies, and meadows over-flowing with wildflowers, would take a man's breath away. I would ask him then, every night, if they had taken his breath away, and he would say, "yes," even though he'd seen them every day during his childhood. I would ask him if there were real cowboys, saloons with swinging doors, and ghost towns where tumble weeds blew down Main Street and buildings were pocked with bullet holes from shootouts with outlaws. I would ask him if there were still streams to pan for gold, if there were herds of buffalo, and if the bugle of a wild bull elk was the greatest sound on earth. And he would always answer, "yes." I'd make him take my hand and pull the way the five-pound brown he'd caught in the Jefferson River had, laughing when he lifted me half out of bed. I'd make him go through the picture book he and my mother bought me for Christmas, usually cover to cover, listening to him go on about how the photos of Glacier didn't do it justice, how the elk in Yellowstone were so tame they were hardly worth photographing, how the bulls of the Pintler Mountains were the true elk of Montana, and how the sunset pictures should show the eastern sky because due to some inexplicable twist of na-ture it was the sky opposite the sun that often had better color.

Growing up outside Syracuse, in the central New York corn belt, where

3

the biggest mountains were little more than swells in the rolling landscape, it was hard for me to imagine everything my father told me about Montana. Partly because it was difficult to believe such a place existed, despite the pictures, which, though they offered two-dimensional proof, weren't tangible evidence, and partly because a boy's imagination, one that creates everything from dinosaurs behind the house in cornfields, to monsters under his bed, must provide him with some notion of what unseen places look like, Montana for me had a special meaning that ran far deeper than its physical attributes. From a very early age, when I would sneak through head-high corn with a bow made from a limber black-walnut limb, hunting herds of buffalo, to my years in grade school when writing assignments invariably revolved around a frontier-era Montana, for me that western state was freedom, lawlessness, independence, ruggedness, pure wilderness. Personified, it was what every boy dreams of being. It was a man. And not the effete, deskbound, hen-pecked type. It was a big, strong, tough man who would turn its residents into the same or send them away with their chins on their chests as unworthy to live there. For as long as I can remember, I wanted to go to Montana. I wanted to throw myself headlong into its lifestyle, soaking it up in my soul until it coursed through my body as the Big Hole River does through the landscape when it crests its banks in the spring, swollen with snowmelt and rain, as unstoppable as anything in the world.

I thought about Montana the night before my fourteenth birthday, one day after graduating from the eighth grade, at the height of the spring lilac season in early June. I shot a basketball through a rusted hoop on the front of our garage for most of the evening, listening to a cock pheasant cackle from the hedgerow of ash and locust trees that separated our side lawn from the neighbor's cornfield. As the sun went down, I watched a turkey buzzard cruise overhead, grudgingly flapping his wings in the absence of a breeze, and when the peeper frogs began ushering in the arrival of night with their chorus of high-pitched chirps, I opened the garage door enough to send the basketball skipping inside and headed for the house.

I hurried upstairs, bounced onto my bed, and stared at the picture of a decaying covered wagon with a mountain chain behind it that I'd found in an antique store outside Boston on a trip to the ocean a few years earlier. I didn't know if it was Montana, but I liked to think it was. But there was something haunting about it, something more than fact that it was black and white. If I stared at it long enough, I thought I could see the gray, weathered bones of a skeleton lying half buried in the sage under the wagon. I tried to show my mother once, and she looked hard, but she said she didn't see them. It was a disconcerting image, more so because I couldn't see it all the time, and I wondered if it was something the photographer had intended or if I really was the only one who could see it. The night before my fourteenth birthday it looked quite plain. The skull was lying behind one of the wooden-spoked front wheels, and a curl of ribs was visible jutting from the earth in front of a clump of sage. I could see it clearly, and decided it was there. It left me with an uneasy feeling, not necessarily about Montana, but about the wilderness in general. It seemed to be saying something about man's assault on some of the world's wilder places. Places that beckoned to men with souls brave enough to go, places that used harsh beauty and the lure of un-seen sights like the Siren's song to lure them from civilization only to trans-form them into skeletons lying under the vehicles in which they came. I fell asleep that night thinking about the picture and what, if anything, it meant, and when I dreamed, I dreamed of grassy plains covered with buffalo, a hill-side dotted with elk, and a circle of tepees, smoke curling from their center, curling into a high, wide, Montana sky, and perhaps above the sky into time itself where it floated forever. In the morning, when I woke up, I was four-teen, and when I looked at the picture I saw only a fallen-in wagon.

I always opened my presents before breakfast. I'd sit on the living room couch while my parents brought them to me one at a time from various closets, cupboards, and the other places which had served as hiding places, sometimes for nearly a year. It rained the day I turned fourteen. I sat on the couch and watched drops, propelled by gusting winds, splatter against the window before me, washing silky strands of spider web down the glass. Outside, in a cornfield of more than twenty acres, the rain was magically pulling tiny green sprouts from the dark soil. The corn had come up liter-ally overnight, the new plants leaving their loamy home to search for day-light, taking their first drink together, rising to mark the progression of spring into summer.

My mother handed my a large box wrapped in fancy, silver paper.

"This is from your grandmother Richards."

Grandma Richards. She was my father's mother. She lived in Glouces-ter, Massachusetts, and I knew what to expect. Her taste in finery, one she claimed to have inherited from her southern, plantation-based ancestors, dictated that she always buy me some expensive, hideously impractical ar-ticle of clothing. I tore the paper off the box and broke one end of it open. This time she'd sent me a Woolrich sweater, drab green, tightly knit, with a simple checkered pattern. It had disproportionately large brown wooden buttons, and an oversized front pocket perfect for holding a pair of bifocals. I held it up and forced a smile.

"What the hell is that, Kyle?" My father set his coffee down to examine the sweater more closely. He always made fun of her presents, rarely with the complete approval of my mother. He took it from me and fished his hand around in the pocket. I heard something crinkle, and from the depths of the abyss he retrieved a fifty dollar bill. "Not a complete waste after all." My mother shot him a quick glance of something less than total affection, and we both laughed.

"Okay, hurrying right along. . ." My father drew an envelope from the back pocket of his jeans. "This is from your mother and me."

It felt too heavy to be money, and its irregular corners didn't line up the way bills would have. I peeled the envelope open from the front, sliding my fingers under the flap, breaking the bond of glue, still sticky from where it had been licked, pinched the sides, shook it gently, and let a map of the United States fall into my lap. It had been folded several times, leaving central New York face up. There was a dark red line beginning in Syracuse, small arrows drawn in along Interstate 90, leading west across the paper to the first fold. I held the map in front of me, eyes fixed on the red line, hardly daring to see where it went.

"Don't you want to see where you're going?" My mother sat down beside me. "Come on, open it up."

Slowly, an inch at a time, I began to unfold the map. The line ran west through Buffalo, out into Ohio, past Cleveland, on into Illinois, by Chicago to the Mississippi in Minnesota, all the way across South Dakota, up to Wyoming, over to Montana, through Billings, Bozeman, and Butte, turned south along Interstate 15 to Divide, jackknifed west again along the Big Hole River, and ended in a red circle at Mistake.

I was shaking. Mistake, Montana. The Big Hole River, the Pioneer Mountains, bull elk, cowboys, cutthroats, and Cole Richards, my grandfather. A logger, trapper, bar fighter, ex-bullrider, and half a dozen other things that all embodied the spirit of Montana, the west, and a modern frontier, Cole — and the stories I'd heard about him — seemed more like legends than family history. As I sat on the couch holding the map, I vividly remembered our only meeting. He'd come east for Christmas the year I was four and when introduced had picked me up to eye level, stared intently at me for some time, then set me down with a slap on my behind and, somewhat surprised, and maybe somewhat pleased, said, "Well, son-of-a-bitch."

In the instant my father asked if I'd like to spend the summer with him, the phone calls, the photos of bull elk and heavy stringers of trout, the presents of arrowheads and petrified wood, everything that had kept my grandfather and me as close as half a continent would permit, everything that until then had seemed like objects that appear at the end of a fairy tale to lend credence to a fantastic story, suddenly seemed real.

I lay awake a long time that night. I'd gone to bed earlier than usual, hoping sleep would come quickly, taking me into that blissful state of unconsciousness where time passes without comprehension and dreams replace thoughts. But I had too much on my mind to sleep. Too many questions that I couldn't begin to answer until I was in Montana. Questions about the country, the people, the woods, waters, and wildlife, and questions about my grandfather. But along with more excitement than I'd ever felt was a touch of apprehension. My mother did not like my grandfather, and she made no bones about it. She said he was a womanizing adolescent whose soul would remain seventeen no matter how long his body lasted, and, given how much he drank, she didn't figure it would be much longer. I didn't completely understand her resentment, or all the things she said he was, so I rarely talked to her about him. Even my father was careful not to make his boyhood experiences in Montana a topic of conversation in her presence, and I have no idea how he got her to agree to let me spend that summer in Mistake.

My uneasiness was not a product of my mother's feelings, however. It stemmed more from an inner fear that I would not measure up to my grandfather's standards. There was a tiny part of me that wondered if my reserved personality, one that led me more toward observing deer and pheasants than hunting them, the way my grandfather did, would clash with his. I didn't know everything about him, but I could easily piece enough together to realize he was outspoken, abrasive, widely known, not widely liked, and the last thing in the world he would concern himself with was what others thought of him. In the late hours of my birthday, I believe it was this sprig of doubt that eventually allowed me to sleep. Without it, had I only felt the excitement of the upcoming trip, my eyes never would have closed.

CHAPTER 2

THE SYRACUSE bus station was crowded. I stood beside my parents before a line of more than half a dozen Greyhounds, parked under a giant cement awning, in various stages of loading and unloading. My father held a large, burgundy suitcase jammed full of everything from clothes to fly reels, and I had both hands wrapped tightly around the straps of my backpack. Inside were candy bars, a couple of cans of soda, my wallet with the traveler's checks, a small pillow, a radio headset, and my picture book of Montana. Orange lights recessed into the concrete above us gave a surreal appearance to the scene of suited businessmen arriving late from Cleveland, picking their way through an obstacle course of bums, many of whom still wore their heavy, army-issue winter coats. I fidgeted with the book of tickets in my shirt pocket, sure I was forgetting something, not sure what it was.

A man's voice boomed out over a loudspeaker announcing the first call to board the midnight bound for Chicago. I looked at my father and he motioned with his free hand toward a bus two down from where we were standing. Above the driver's side of the windshield, in bold, green letters, the city was spelled out.

My mother put a hand on my shoulder, opened her arms for a hug, and held me a long time. She was wearing scented soap, the same brand she had used forever, and immersed in its fragrance, I suddenly knew how much my home meant to me, and for the first time in my life I felt homesick. An emptiness between hunger and nausea welled up in my stomach, and I pressed my face into her shoulder, letting one hot tear blot on her blue sweater. When I lifted my head my eyes were dry, and a single, determined stride took me to the stairs of the bus. My father shook my hand, reminded me not to be afraid to ask for help, told me to call him when I got there, and walked away without looking back.

Sleep was unthinkable. I tuned my headset to Syracuse's largest rock station, screwed on the little overhead light above my seat, and opened the picture book. I knew every page of it as well as my own hands. The sunrise in Glacier, followed by a winter print of buffalo in Yellowstone, then a page cut into quarters by seasonal pictures of a waterfall near the Idaho border. There were nearly three hundred pictures, all familiar. There were two I especially liked. One was of the Big Hole, ice-bound and quiet, where it flows through a wide valley dotted with cone-shaped hay stacks. My father said the picture, taken from the air, was just above Mistake, near Wisdom or Jackson. The other picture I liked so much, filling page ninety-one, was also a winter shot. Taken around the turn of the century, it showed a trapper's cabin in the Bitterroot Mountains. The logs, banked high with snow, were covered with pelts. There were beaver, pine martin, wolf, fox, and coyote. In front of the door, stuck into a snow bank more than five feet high, was a grizzly trap fastened to a chunk of fir sporting more than a dozen long spikes. The door was open, and through a haze of smoke seeping from inside I could see the trapper, and if a tougher-looking man ever walked the face of the earth I didn't know who it was or when it had been. The badger hat he wore, complete with the animal's head, jumping from his own like a grotesque growth, was pulled nearly to his eyebrows. He had a buffalo coat, pants from the same, and beaver mittens, one of which cradled a short-barreled rifle, while the other gripped the handle of a Bowie knife wedged without a sheath into his belt. The picture's title, "A Rough Customer," was nothing short of the truth.

The bus stopped in Rochester and again in Buffalo, and before it crossed the Pennsylvania line I was fighting to keep my eyes open. I woke up in Cleveland an hour before sunrise with a stiff neck a cramp in my right leg. I turned toward the aisle to stretch, but sometime while I was sleeping a woman had taken the seat next to me. The bus was only a little more than half full, and I was irritated that she hadn't sat by herself.

"Good morning." She sounded pleasant.

"Hi."

She was my mother's age, give or take a couple of years, and well dressed.

"Traveling all by yourself?"

I nodded.

"Let me guess. Going to see relatives in Wisconsin?"

"Montana."

"Montana? You've got a long ways to go then, don't you?" She leaned back and closed her eyes.

I eased closer to the window. Outside, the stark fronts of Cleveland's downtown office buildings loomed up from the concrete sidewalks.

"We'll be here an hour or more." The woman had positioned herself sideways in her seat to face me. "No point staying on the bus. Especially not for you. Got too far to go to get cramped up this early. I'll buy you a coffee and doughnut in the station if you want."

"I can get my own."

"No doubt, but when a lady offers to pay, you'd better take her up on it. Doesn't happen that often. Especially not with me." She laughed when she said it, poked me in the side, and looked surprised when my expression didn't change. "Don't get it, do you?"

She stood up, wedged her brown carry-on between me and window and reached for my hand, an act which served to get me up as well.

The inside of the bus station seemed larger than the whole building looked from the outside. A dirty tile floor spread out from the revolving doors we entered through toward a counter with several bank-like teller booths set into it. There was a small yellow cart in one corner with a couple of coffee pots and round glass container full of doughnuts of it. A tired-looking Black man stood behind it, fiddling with the brim of his Orioles hat.

"Two coffees, cream and sugar in both, and two doughnuts. The frosted ones right there." The woman turned to me and nodded rapidly as if we were about to receive a steak from New York City's finest restaurant.

"I don't think I've introduced myself," she said as soon as I'd taken the last bite of my doughnut. "I'm Florence. Everybody calls me Flo, though."

I took a long drink from my coffee cup.

"And you are?"

"Kyle."

"Nice to meet you, Kyle." She extended her hand and I shook it. She had a good, firm grip. "Ever been to Montana before, Kyle?"

"No."

"Me either. Stayed a while in Denver once. Nice city . . . not much business there . . . not like Reno or Vegas . . . but pretty. The mountains are beautiful. Does your grandfather live near the mountains?"

"Yeah."

"Oh, you're lucky. You know, that's what I'd like some day. A little place up in the mountains. Log cabin, fireplace. . ." She closed her eyes and rocked back and forth. "Wouldn't like the Indians probably."

"Indians?"

"Oh, yes. West's full of them. Like these." She pointed at the bums. "Boozers. Never have any money. Should have seen them in Denver. Always trying to get it for free."

"Free?"

"Oh, just an expression. Rude people, Kyle. I guess I'm not one to talk though, am I?"

I shrugged, finished my coffee, and stood up.

"Are you embarrassed?"

"What?"

"Does it bother you?"

"What bother me?"

"You really don't know, do you?"

"Know what?"

"What I do. Who you're sitting with."

"I guess not."

"Well, that's a relief to me in some ways. Sad, too. But in a good way. You know what escort women do, Kyle?"

I had an idea. The pieces were beginning to fall together, and I blushed.

"That's right. You get it now. Probably think I'm awful."

I shook my head.

"Well, that's sweet. We'd better get back on the bus."

To my immense relief, Flo fell asleep almost as soon as she sat down. It was only then that I dared look closely at her. She was wearing a lot of makeup. Heavy rouge on her cheeks, dark eye-liner, and nail polish that matched her lipstick. Her legs were thin and pale; two slender limbs protruding from a cotton skirt. The leather dress shoes she wore had seen their share of mileage. The brass eyelets were tarnished and the laces had faded from black to brown. Everything about her looked as though it had faded. Her makeup was vibrant, but she was not. I was homesick again.

We stopped for lunch at some enormous truck stop on the Indiana border. Flo disappeared into the women's room, emerged ten minutes later, her face wet, her shirt tucked neatly into her skirt, her shoes clicking with new vigor across the floor. She didn't notice me in the high-backed orange booth I sat in, half-heartedly picking away at a cheeseburger, and when she walked through a side door toward a line of trucks stacked up across the parking lot, I didn't see her again.

I had two seats to myself all the way to Chicago. I found that by sprawling out over them and pretending to be asleep I was able to avoid sharing with another passenger. We didn't arrive in Chicago until after dark, and I waited on the bus instead of going into the terminal.

Crossing the Mississippi ten hours later, the natural barrier between the east and west, was thrilling. The river, murky with spring run-off, churned along exactly as it had one hundred and fifty years earlier when it was forded by covered wagons instead of spanned by steel and cement. On the other side, half way across Minnesota, short-grass prairie stretched away from the highway as far as I could see. It was as if the landscape suddenly decided to shuck off all semblance of the rolling, eastern farmland, and begin assuming the shape of the west. We passed into South Dakota before noon, and I fully expected to make Montana before nightfall.

A day later, after stopping at every spot in the road between Sioux Falls and Sheridan, Wyoming, we did roll across the border into Montana. We dropped down into a gully, came up the other side, and at the top of a knoll, red rock outcroppings poking their heads above ground to break up the monotony of the prairie, we entered Montana, and it didn't look a bit different than Wyoming. I hadn't slept at all the night before, and was growing sick to my stomach. I glanced down at my backpack, thought about looking at my picture book again, but couldn't bring myself to haul it out.

Billings was hot. Heat waves slithered across the street and the tangy odor of tar filled the air. The air conditioning had broken down in the bus station, and building's large, glass windows magnified the sun's rays. I was too hot to eat. I bought a can of soda and sat on a bench with my back to the sun. There were Indians in the station. Lots of them. Many were carrying more than they could comfortably hold. A woman with two boys sat down next to me, resting the garbage bag she'd been lugging on the floor. Brightly colored clothes spilled out, and the boys were snapped at for stepping on them. The woman was joined shortly by an older man in a brown cowboy

hat, the sides turned up sharply, the brim pulled down over his forehead. His skin looked tough. There was no hair on his face, and he squinted even when he looked away from the light. The silver duct tape he'd wrapped around the toe of his left boot had begun to wear, much as the leather beneath it had. He was heavy. His black T-shirt had said something at one time, but all that remained of the writing was a tattered B. A pewter belt buckle, large enough to partially obscure his open fly, had a running buffalo on it. As soon as he sat down, he was asleep. I remembered what Flo told me about Indians. With the addition of a winter coat, the man would have fit in nicely at the Syracuse station. I could smell alcohol, either on his breath or his clothes, and a thin line of saliva leaked from his mouth as his head tipped forward in search of his chest.

I returned to the bus and waited for what seemed like three hours before it started.

The Bridgers were the first snow-caps I saw. For ten or fifteen miles, I'd mistaken their peaks for clouds. Between Livingston and Bozeman, looking straight up at them in the late afternoon sunlight, I knew that the place I'd come to was entirely different than the one I'd left. Rock slides half a mile long reached down from their summits into the dense coniferous forests that blanketed their lower slopes. I had a good view from the station in Bozeman, running north away from the Yellowstone River, leaping up into the Montana sky, which, just as my father had told me, really was bigger than anything I'd ever seen.

When we left Bozeman, I moved to the front of the bus and took a single seat across from the driver so I could look out the windshield. Twilight faded quickly to night; faster, I thought, than back home. We slowed to less than thirty miles an hour while we climbed a pass west of Whitehall, and at the top, on an overpass, hung a sign whose reflective letters read, "Continental Divide. Elevation 6939." A second later, in the Pacific Ocean's watershed, we rounded a bend and I got my first look at Butte. It looked as big as Chicago. Each of its thousands of lights stood out sharply in the dry night air. It was enormous and at the same time self-contained. Where the city ended, country began. There were no suburbs or scattered lights outside the streets. The mountains ringing the city were dark.

My grandfather was picking me up at the bus station, and I made sure I was the first one off. It was chilly, colder than it had been since March in New York. And he wasn't there. I dragged my large suitcase out of the hold, and jerked it to the side of the terminal. There were no benches outside, so I sat on it, my arms wrapped around my chest for warmth, shivering in part from the cold, in part from excitement. Half an hour later, the bus left, bound for Seattle. It was getting colder, approaching midnight, and I was the only one there. Despite the temperature, I was falling asleep. Jet lag and the loss of adrenaline that had built up in me over the trip hit all at once. I summoned enough strength to walk inside the station, not much larger than the bus, sat back down on my suitcase, and immediately drifted off.

CHAPTER 3

WAKE UP, Kyle, we've got a situation."

A giant hairy hand rested on my shoulder, and as my eyes focused, taking longer than usual, my head spinning from my untimely awakening, I saw my grandfather — his heavy black beard, tattered felt hat, torn wool pants, and hunting knife, drawn from its sheath, the shiny blade held close to my legs — bending over me. He smelled like the woods, a strong odor of dirt and leaves that reminded me of the hedgerow along my neighbor's cornfield in the spring when the snow melts and the ground turns to mud.

"These pants expensive?" He gestured at the loose-fitting slacks I was wearing with his knife. "Doesn't matter. They won't do out here. Not where we're going." He knelt, one knee on the floor, the other sticking up into my chest, jerked my left leg out straight, pulling the pant leg all the way down over my sneaker. "Too long. Be tripping on it."

He sounded serious. I heard the knife poke through the cotton even with my ankle, and in one smooth motion my grandfather circumcised my slacks, tossing the extra fabric onto the floor. He set my leg down hard and reached for the other.

"There." He stuck the knife back into its sheath on his belt and picked up my suitcase. The door swung out away from him, reached the extent of its hinges and came back fast, before he was all the way out. My grandfather's right hand shot up from his side, palm open, and struck the glass, bowing it in its frame, sending the door open again.

"Son of a bitch!" His voice was deep. A growl from the back of his throat.

15

I stood up, my legs moving of their own accord, and followed him. I didn't know what else to do. Our introduction thus far had been everything but what I'd expected. Outside, the air felt too cold to be a dream, but I was so tired I didn't see how I could be awake. I was quite certain that at any moment my legs would go out from under me, and I knew if they did I'd never feel myself hit the concrete.

A pickup started up across the street, louder than bus when it climbed the divide.

"Come on." My grandfather stuck a hand out the passenger window and waved to me.

I crossed the street toward the truck, its bed filled with the biggest tire I'd ever seen, holes the size of softballs rusted through the fenders, something hanging down from its midsection an inch or two off the pavement, a tangle of wire holding the hood closed, carpet dripping from the ceiling of the cab like a partition between the driver and passenger, the exhaust bellowing like the dirt-track racers' back in Oswego. There was no handle on my door.

"Reach in and get her from in here." My grandfather pointed under the carpet at the door.

I fumbled with the handle, a slim piece of metal, sharp on the underside, and pulled. The door creaked, fighting against me, then opened enough to let me in. I tried to position my backpack on the floor at my feet, but a mountain of Styrofoam cups, sandwich wrappers, some still holding crust, and beer bottles prevented it. I held it on my lap, reached for the seatbelt that wasn't there, and stopped my head just before it connected with the back window as my grandfather popped the clutch, lurching the truck into the street inches in front of a slow-moving car. The driver honked his horn, flipped his lights up on high, and sped up.

"Hang on." My grandfather's instructions were followed immediately by the screeching of tires and the grinding of metal on metal as he stomped on the brake. The truck bucked to a stop, stalled in gear, the car almost running into us. In an instant, my grandfather was out, taking long strides back to the car, opening the driver's door, his right fist cocked behind his head. Through the dirty glass behind me, I watched him, his features blurred by the dust, his voice booming off the buildings on either side of us.

"Outta there, tough man," he screamed. "You're fucking with a logger now, and shortly you'll regret it." He stepped back away from the door, dropping his fist. No one got out. "No?" He shrugged. "Sorry son-of-a-bitch. You remember this the next time you're thinking those things between your legs belong to an elephant."

The car backed up, turned around, and very slowly accelerated away. My grandfather was supporting himself with the help of the tailgate, coughing violently. He spat twice, cleared his throat, and climbed back in.

"No one wants any part of a logger anymore, Kyle. Not even in Butte." He sighed. "So, how was your trip? Long bus ride, isn't it?"

"Yes."

"Who'd you meet? Anyone interesting? Usually do on the bus."

"A woman named Flo."

"Flo!" My grandfather slapped the steering wheel and began to laugh. "Now there's a whore for you if ever a whore there was. Tell me, am I wrong?"

I didn't answer.

"That a boy, Kyle. Tell me, did she come onto you?" We were roaring up an interstate ramp, the muffler, or lack thereof, so loud I had to shout.

"What?"

"Did she come on to you? Try to get you to fuck her? Take you into the restroom for a quickie?"

The conversation was overwhelming. Coupled with the near fist fight, the custom tailoring of my slacks, and the speed at which we were going, at least half again as fast as the bus, it was more than I could comprehend. I was rapidly coming to the conclusion that my grandfather was a raving lunatic, a realization that would have been quite troubling had I not been so tired. As it was, I was able, in the state of complacent shock I was entering — like a drowning man who ceases to struggle and lets the water enter his lungs for relief — to sit quietly, unemotional, ready to except whoever my grandfather was and whatever we were doing.

"I take it that's a no." He sounded disappointed. "No matter. Be soon enough, Kyle. Now, the business at hand. Here's the deal. Fishtrappers, big Indian family in Mistake, they're running low on meat. Didn't lay in enough game last fall. Little Darla, big as a bull moose," he winked, the white of his eye vanishing into the dark forest of hair on his face, "she's been clamoring for fresh meat. Said she'd trade me for it."

I hadn't noticed the rifle between us until my grandfather tapped its stock.

"Going to do that very thing. Going to kill two birds with one stone, too, Kyle. There's a son-of-a-bitch rancher down here who likes to think he owns all of southwest Montana. Won't let anyone hunt on his place, keeps her all locked up, just bitches about everybody. You've heard the expression the closer the bone the sweeter the meat?"

I hadn't, but I nodded anyway.

"Well, I've got a little take-off on that. I say the bigger the asshole, the greater the thrill; the sweeter the taste of the meat on the grill. Ha! You see what I'm saying?"

I nodded again.

"This rancher's name is Tipton. Bruce Tipton. Owns land all over God's green hills. Owns a bit of it right in back of my place. Inherited it all from his old man. He was a hard worker, and fair, too. Got along good with him. But his boy, he's one of these new-age bastards thinks the sun rises and sets in the crack of his ass. Rude, Kyle. Very rude. And that's something I refuse to tolerate. So tonight Mr. Bruce Tipton is going to make a donation to the Indian community. And when he wakes up tomorrow morning and feels all bubbly inside, happy as the day is long, he won't know why, but you and I will, won't we? Be because he's done something good. Helped instead of hindered for a change. That seem reasonable to you?"

"I guess."

"Good, then you can shoot. You know how to shoot a high-powered rifle, Kyle? Can't believe your dad has forgotten everything about his up-bringing. Must have some sense of the west still in him. Can't have fully cas-trated himself. You do know how to shoot, don't you?"

I'd shot a .22, in fact I had one of my own, and I wasn't a bad shot. At least not at the soda cans I set up at the base of a large ash tree in our side yard. But I didn't hunt, and the golden cartridge lying in the half-open ac-tion of the rifle beside me was longer and bigger around than my middle fin-ger. I didn't want any part of it.

"Not as bad as she looks. Just an ought-six. Big bullet, little kick. You can handle it. Think it over anyway."

We rode in silence for the next ten minutes. Driving south on Interstate 15, we crossed back over the divide, hurtling over a set of rolling hills, and got off at the Divide exit where the Big Hole pushes through a canyon, swinging in beside the road. It was up even with its banks, ripping along louder than the pickup. In the moonlight, it looked silver: an icy torrent bearing away a winter's worth of snow from the mountains rising sharply on either side of us.

"Not far now, Kyle."

There was a noticeable tone of excitement in my grandfather's voice. He held the wheel with both hands, yanking the truck through the turns at a dizzying rate of speed, my body, limp with fatigue, banging off the door, leaning over onto the rifle, lurching forward into the clutter in front of my seat. Ten miles up river we suddenly exited the canyon, breaking out of the dark gorge into gentler country, sage-covered ridges stretching away from us toward a line of distant snow-caps, outlined against the stars more than twenty miles away. We dropped into a gully winding out of the sage toward the river, and my grandfather shut the lights off and hit the brakes. He cut the wheel hard and we skidded to a stop, sideways in the road, facing up the gully.

"That gate there. Get out and open her up. Let me drive through, then close it."

There was a barb wire gate strung across a narrow, two-track trail leading up the gully away from the road.

"Hurry up. Bad place for someone to come along. Probably couldn't stop in time."

I whacked my door open, fearful that at any moment a vehicle would crest one of the rises and descend upon us. A loop of wire held the gate closed, and it took all my strength to lift it over the post, allowing the fence to go slack. I hauled it out of the way, four strands of barb wire catching on the sage between the tire tracks, jerking at my shoulders. As soon as there was room for the truck, my grandfather gunned it through. It was all I could do to refasten the gate. My lungs felt as though they'd collapsed in the thin air. Every breath was difficult, but if my grandfather noticed my heavy breathing, he didn't mention it.

"Well done." He slammed the bolt home on the rifle, checked the safety, and sped up the road, his lights still off. "Old Bruce would shit himself if he knew we were up here after his pets. Likely give his hands orders to shoot to kill. Bullets whizzing all around us, you returning fire out the window, me all hunkered down behind the wheel going like a raped ape. Be something to talk about for sure."

I didn't find the prospect of being shot at, one I was quick to believe could and would occur, probably momentarily, as humorous as my grandfather. I looked nervously over my shoulder, convinced I would see head-lights, praying I would not have to shoot anyone. I'd been in Montana less than a day, and the thought of killing a man, even in the wild west where I understood such a thing wasn't out of the question, didn't sit well with me.

We pounded over a stone, the spinning front wheels sending it up into the undercarriage like a shotgun blast. I clutched at the dash and closed my eyes, sure it was over, wondering what the bullet would feel like. The truck slowed, and I figured they must have hit my grandfather. We coasted to a stop, and I held my breath, not daring to look, until I felt him shift in his seat and open the door. He put a finger to his lips as a sign for me to keep quiet, a gesture that was quite unnecessary, and pointed at the rifle.

"Bring it out here, Kyle," he whispered. "Careful with your door, too. Go ahead and leave it open."

The rifle was heavy. Far heavier than the twenty gauge shotgun my father owned. The stock was smooth, the trigger guard cold, and the barrel looked as long as a pool cue. I kept it pointed away from me and offered it to my grandfather as soon as I was outside. He shook his head.

"See that ridge up there?"

I did. It loomed up from the two-track, now little more than a cattle path, a few hundred yards ahead of us.

"That's where the cows like to bed. It's steep just off the back side. Open sage country. Good spot to catch up with them. What do you say we creep up there and ruin one's night? You can give 'em hell with the six."

Cows. So that's what it was. We were going rustling. I'd come the better part of three thousand miles to be hanged for cattle rustling. That was if I wasn't gunned down by a hired hand.

The last thing in the world I wanted was to follow my grandfather up that ridge, but I found my feet moving numbly over the rocky ground be-hind him. We went a few yards, stopped and he reached back with his right hand without turning around.

"Rifle," he said.

I was all too happy to hand it to him. He brought it to his shoulder, held it a long time, then lowered it.

"Mule deer."

I took another step toward him and heard something clatter away.

"Looked like a buck, too. No matter, we've got bigger fish to fry."

My grandfather carried the rifle the rest of the way to the top of the ridge, moving slowly, skirting the sage, pausing frequently to cough into his jacket. Near the top, he dropped to his knees, motioning me down as well. We crept forward, an inch at a time, until we could peek over the edge. My grandfather looked first, shook his head, then moved to the side to give me a view. There were half a dozen horses lying down fifty yards away, their heads resting a couple of feet off the ground, dark against the light sage. I didn't see any cows.

"Look for one without a calf."

Until he said it, I hadn't noticed the smaller, darker animals lying next to their mothers, but they didn't look like any calves I'd ever seen. More like colts.

"Darla ain't picky. She'll take an older one a bit past its prime. Don't want to orphan one of the little ones if I can help it."

The moon came out from behind a small cloud, lighting the ground, aiding our eyes. A little further down the hill I saw another clump of horses, three together, one by itself.

"There we go." My grandfather eased the rifle in my direction. "The one all alone down there, Kyle. Aim for the neck and touch it off."

I quailed away from the gun. Shooting a cow was bad enough. A horse was unthinkable.

"Go ahead, it's alright. She's all yours."

I moved further away.

"No? Okay, you can do it next time."

Next time. Did my grandfather make a habit of shooting cows and horses? I wondered, quite seriously, if he did, desperately searching for some rationale in it, my mind whirling a million miles an hour, trying to make enough sense of what we were doing to believe it was real.

The jet of orange flame blowing out the barrel and the explosion of the gun a few inches from my left ear dispelled all question of whether or not it was real. Seconds later, my grandfather was up, running down the hill, his footsteps mingling with the galloping horses', the echo of the blast bouncing off every mountain around us, coming full circle to surround me, just as the posse of armed men I was sure the shot would summon would soon be doing.

Since we'd gotten out of the truck, I'd been smelling sage. The pungent odor, similar in some ways to cedar, but more acrid, filled the night air as thickly as the scent of ripening corn in my neighbor's field back home. I pressed my face into a brushy clump of it, in part to hide, in part to increase its aroma, and watched my grandfather move away. In less than a minute, I could no longer hear his footsteps. I was cold. I wasn't wearing a jacket and it felt like it would frost before morning. The cold seemed to amplify the odor of sage, and lying there on that ridge, far away from everything that was familiar to me, breathing deeply to suck it into my lungs, wondering where it was I'd come, I was calm. The last reverberations of the shot had died away, and it was so quiet that I could hear the blood coursing through my ears as though I was holding a sea shell to them.

"Down here, Kyle." My grandfather's voice sounded far off. "Come on."

I pushed myself up and began walking, my head reeling, my back beginning to ache from the cold.

"Down here," he whispered. He was kneeling, his back moving up and down, breathing hard after his run. "Might have hit her a little far back. Have a look."

He pointed to the ground. Shiny liquid — blood — glistened on the light brown soil. He ran a finger through it and held it to my nose. It smelled like a barn — cow and horse urine with a touch of something wilder, probably from living outside.

"Track her." My grandfather pointed down the hill, and I looked to be sure I'd heard him correctly. "Follow the blood and tracks. See?" His bloody finger traced a depression in the ground, darker than the bits or rock around it. "Don't look for them too close together. She was running. Shittin' and gettin'. Go on now."

I'd followed fox tracks in the winter in New York, and once a set of turkey tracks, long and pointed, through the soft muck of a cornfield, but that was the extent of my tracking experience. But I didn't argue, and it was easier than I expected. The blood showed up well under the moon, especially where it had dripped onto the pea-green sage, and the line of running tracks was clear. I took my time, moving slowly but steadily, afraid of what I'd find at the end of the trail, unable to stop myself. I came to a flattened clump of sage, its dead undergrowth strewn over the ground, its leaves drenched with blood.

"Fell here ... bubbles in the blood. Might have lunged her after all. Won't be far now I don't reckon."

My grandfather was right. Another twenty yards brought me to her; neck outstretched, legs splayed apart, gruesome yellowing teeth protruding from a curled upper lip, the spot of blood on her side darker than her shaggy mane.

"Grab a hind leg so I can get her guts out. Hurry up."

I reached for the hoof, relieved there wasn't a shoe on it. Perhaps she was past her prime and wouldn't be missed. My grandfather's knife was flashing for the second time since my arrival, performing an equally odd task as the first. I heard air rush out of the incision, and when the stench hit me, sickly sweet, stronger than the sage, it was too much. I dropped the leg and began to retch, falling to my knees, the tiny bit of food in my stomach sliding up my throat onto the Montana earth.

"More of your mother in you than I thought." My grandfather laughed without looking up. "Be all right, though. Try not to think about it. A man gets used to it quick. Muckle hold of her stomach, right here." He slapped the gray sack protruding from his cut. "Won't puke again, trust me."

The stomach was slippery, warm and wet. I dug my fingers into it and leaned back. It came out hard and was heavy enough so I couldn't pull it completely free.

"That's good. Let's go get the truck."

He was up without another word, wiping his hands on his pants, cutting across the side of the ridge back toward where we were parked. I couldn't keep up, and heard the engine start a hundred yards ahead of me. Then I heard him coming, sage breaking under the front bumper, the springs squalling as the tires hit rocks, the rumble of the exhaust rising and falling as he worked the gas. He waved as he sped past, his white smile as big as if he'd won the lottery, crashed over a twisted sage bush approaching tree size, locking the brakes just before he collided with the horse. I retraced my steps, dragging my feet, once more feeling that before the night was over I'd become acquainted with the hangman's noose.

"Quartered and ready," my grandfather announced. He held a meat saw in one hand, the horse's head in the other, the dismembered chunks lying around him. A nightmarish scene. He tossed the head aside, squatted, wrapped his arms around part of the torso, hiked it into the air, and deposited it in the center of the tire in the back of the truck, a procedure he repeated four more times He pulled a dusty piece of olive canvas over the tire, secured the four corners with odd chunks of iron he dug out of the bed, slapped his hands together, and climbed back into the cab. As soon as I got in, he handed me the rifle.

"Safety's on the top, and she's loaded."

I didn't think a rougher ride than the one we had up the draw, as my grandfather called it, was possible. I was wrong. I could feel the sage tearing at the underpinning beneath my seat, and half the rocks we hit were large enough to throw us off course. We were bucking and spinning, sliding and jumping so erratically that Bruce Tipton's hired hands, the men I still feared would soon be in pursuit, would have had to have been extraordinary shots to nail us.

We were almost to the main road before we stopped. My grandfather looked over his shoulder, back behind him into the night, then popped the clutch and I heard the accelerator greet the floor.

"Here they come, Kyle! Here they come!'

We skidded around a bend, missing a cottonwood by less than a foot. Ahead of us I could see the outline of the gate.

"Tight grip on the rifle, now. She's our bread and butter. Hold strong and make the ride!" He had one hand on the wheel, the other raised above his head bull-rider style. I couldn't see any headlights behind us. No muzzle flashes from the posse. No mounted range riders. But I wasn't about to argue. I was expecting my grandfather to stop so I could open the gate and had begun groping for the door handle.

"No time, Kyle."

We hit the gate head-on going almost thirty miles an hour. The barb wire came screeching up over the hood, a fence post shattered, my head slammed down on the dash, ricocheted over against the side window and snapped back against the seat. And then we were in the road, tires bawling on tar, careening sideways toward the ditch, catching just before we went over the edge, and rocketing up away from the draw.

"Good run for rainbow trout over there," my grandfather said as he adjusted his hat and pointed across a meadow to the Big Hole. "You and I, we'll find out all about them soon enough."

I fully expected to find out about the long arm of the law, or worse yet, lack thereof, well before any rainbows. I crouched low in my seat, my breath coming irregularly, waiting for my grandfather to give the "fire at will" order. It was five or six miles before I could speak.

"Grandpa?"

"Christ, Kyle, don't call me that. Makes me feel old. Name's Cole, okay?"

"Yeah." I was ready to agree to anything. "Cole, what do you think will happen when they find out?"

"About what?"

"About tonight."

"About tonight? What makes you think anybody will find out? Coyotes and magpies will have those bones picked clean in three days. Then they'll just be bones. Shit, mountains are full of bones out here. Ground's so dry they last forever. Bones can't talk."

"I mean the men. The ones who were after us."

"Oh yes, that band of gentlemen." He raised the carpet between us so I could see his smile. "I wouldn't go worrying about them any too much. Dumb as mud. Type of men who couldn't find their asses using both hands."

"But they were behind us, weren't they?"

"Certainly. You bet. At least it looked it to me." He winked. "Kyle, you and I are going to have a time of it this summer. I can tell already. You and I, we're going to do great things. A couple of wild mountain men like us, and there's no telling what hell we'll raise. Jesus, I'm glad you're here."

I'd never thought of myself as a wild mountain man, but then, I'd never considered myself a horse killer, and was, at least an accessory to, just that. If I was going to kill horses, I might as well be a wild mountain man, too.

"We need to celebrate!" My grandfather said it with enthusiasm; as though he'd suddenly arrived at the answer to a difficult question. "Yes, sir, we need to celebrate. Celebrate your arrival, Tipton's donation, and Robin Hooding the Fishtrapper's meat. Kyle, you'll like this."

In my opinion, fitting celebration would have been a good night's sleep. Maybe in the morning I'd wake up on the bus and would find the night's events were part of a long, drawn-out dream. I could cross into the Montana I'd pictured, meet my grandfather instead of Cole the horse killer, and begin a summer I'd truly enjoy.

"Here we are." We whipped past a small green and white road sign, spattered by birdshot, that read, "Mistake." There were a handful of buildings, short, fat, and close to the road. A flourescent light illuminated a set of old gas pumps in front of a store with a false front, there was a one-room school house with a large cupola, and fly shop sporting a wall-length mural of a green fish rising for a rainbow-colored fly. We pulled into a dirt parking lot next to several other vehicles, most similar in condition to my grandfather's. He pointed at the building in front of us. It had a large set of double doors, a wooden porch supported by rough-hewn timbers, and the Big Hole for a back yard. "There she is. Home away from home. The Six Point Saloon."

My grandfather got out and didn't lock his door. When he reached the stairs leading up onto the porch he looked back and motioned for me. I followed, one step at a time, listening to the steady beat of a country song emanating from inside that grew louder and louder. My grandfather pulled the doors open and let me in first.

The bar ran the length of the floor, high and made of polished wood. There were fifteen stools along it, most occupied, and several tables scattered along the walls. An oversized juke box was positioned in one corner, its neon lights pulsing to the beat. Above the door, lying on a mantle made especially for the purpose, was the largest elk antler I'd ever seen. It was white, pitted from the weather, and one of its massive tines had been shortened slightly by mice. Its base was as big as a man's calf, and it was more than four feet long.

"The Six Point," my grandfather said as he stepped around me toward the bar.

A huge woman with long black hair and a stained San Francisco 49ers sweatshirt slid off her stool and met him half way. He threw open his arms to receive her, barely able to clasp his hands behind her back.

"Darla, my dear, how are you? Looking lovely as ever."

She pulled free and plucked a hair from his jacket. Her dark eyes glistened as she held it to her nose and smiled.

"Yes, we have returned triumphant."

She hugged him, longer than he had her, then pointed at me.

"Come here, Kyle." My grandfather's voice was louder than the music. "Kyle, meet Darla Fishtrapper. The best-looking Sioux in all Montana. Darla, this is Kyle Richards. The best rifle shot I've ever seen. You can thank him for your elk."

I extended my hand and she wrapped hers around it. "Your grandfather?" she asked, gesturing with her head.

I nodded.

"You look alike." She dropped my hand and turned toward the bar. As soon as she looked away, I grabbed the corner of my grandfather's jacket.

"Elk?"

"What's that? Speak up. Damn music's so loud I can't hear myself think."

"You told her I shot an elk."

"Sure. Nothing but the truth, right?"

"Won't she know the difference?"

"How the hell will she know? She wasn't there to see who shot it."

"Can't she tell by the way it tastes?"

"The way it tastes?"

"Yeah, the horse." I stood on my toes to speak close to his ear.

"Horse?"

"The one in the truck. The one you shot. Mr. Tipton's pet."

"What the . . . I don't . . . Holy shit!" He broke into violent laughter, then a coughing spell that lasted well into the next song. He grabbed Darla, seated back on her stool, and whispered something to her. Then she began to laugh, and he started up again. I failed to see the humor in it. In my eyes, it was a serious offense.

"Kyle Richards, haven't you ever seen a cow elk?" He had his hands on my shoulders, pressing down hard. "Christ almighty!"

The only pictures of elk I'd seen were the bulls he'd shot and the ones in my picture book. I never thought about what the cows looked like.

"My boy, a poacher I am, and a damn good one at that. But a horse slayer, although I've never been in love with them, I am not. And neither are you. Jesus, did you really think . . ." He was coughing again. "Did you really think . . . explains how quiet you were I suppose. Holy shit! Well, now that we've got that straightened out, I guess I can have a drink. Son of a bitch, I need a drink."

I was too relieved to be embarrassed.

"Laurie!" My grandfather had wedged himself in between Darla and an equally big woman beside her and was hollering at the bartender. A girl in her late twenties looked up from where she'd been toweling off a spilled beer further down the bar. "Laurie, the ladies and I want to cross the border tonight. Head on down to old Mexico. Three shots of Mr. Quervo, please, and," he turned to me, "what will you take, Kyle?"

I wasn't thirsty. All I wanted to do was sleep.

"And a glass of pop, too."

Laurie brought him the drinks, smiled a tired smile, snapping the one he gave her for a tip into a large front pocket on the skirt she wore, and went back to wiping the beer.

"Darla, Dell, here you go, Kyle," he said handing me my glass. "Bourbon and Coke for you tonight."

"Bourbon and Coke, my ass. Boy probably don't have hair on his balls yet." The comment came from down near Laurie. There was a man sitting sideways on his stool facing me wearing a clean black cowboy hat and faded jeans. My grandfather moved a step away from the bar and shot him a cold stare, narrowing his eyes so his thick brows touched his eyelashes.

"Pete Lewis, don't start." He turned his back on the man and bent over me. "Don't worry about that asshole. He's pissed off that there ain't a whole flock of women on him. No, don't let it bother you. He'll find out that I've got something for him if he wants to keep it up." My grandfather pointed to my drink. "It's just Coke."

"Thanks."

"You bet." He patted me on the back. "And now a toast. A toast to Kyle Richards. May he find fun, fucking, and fine fishing all summer long. And to Darla and Dell Fishtrapper. May they help me find the same."

They emptied their glasses, and I took a sip from mine. It was warm. I looked down at the wooden floor where a quarter rested under Darla's stool. I would have picked it up, but I was too tired.

The Six Point didn't start to empty out until the clock, mounted to varnished slab of pine behind the bar, said almost three. Half an hour later, only the four of us remained. My grandfather and the Indian women had been drinking steadily since we got there, and if they weren't in Mexico, they were on the border. The juke box had fallen silent, but my ears still rang. I had my head resting in my hands on the bar about to fall asleep.

"You're going to have to get them out of here," Laurie said, pointing with a mop at Darla and her sister. "I'm done serving."

My grandfather reached into his wallet, shook his head, and retrieved a ten. It was his last bill.

"Laurie, Laurie, Laurie." His voice was as loud as ever but about three speeds slower. "Laurie, one more round and you keep the rest. You're beautiful, Laurie."

She frowned, then emptied the last of the Tequila into two glasses.

"That's it, Cole. No more tonight."

"Oh, Laurie, you mean you won't give me any yourself?" She rolled her eyes. "Maybe she'll give you some, Kyle. That be alright with you? Go home with her for a little rodeo?"

Laurie didn't look up. If she had, I couldn't have made eye contact. It was bad enough that my grandfather was insane, but he didn't need to involve me.

"Come on, grandpa, let's go." I tugged at a tear in the side of his coat.

"Easy, Kyle, don't rush me. And fuck all, quit calling me that." He swallowed his shot. "What do you say, ladies, are we ready?"

Darla plopped off her stool, but Dell shook her head.

"No, Dell? Not up for it this evening? Well, give me a peek at those bombs of yours before we go."

Darla pushed him. "These aren't good enough for you?" She wrapped her hands around her breasts.

"They're just lovely, Darla, but you've got to admit your sister's can't be beat. Please, Dell, just a quick peek."

Laurie banged on the bar with the empty tequila bottle. "Outta here, Cole, and I mean it."

"Yes, my dear, we're on our way." He staggered toward the door, looked back to make sure Darla and I were coming, then plunged outside. He got in the passenger side of the truck. "You drive, Kyle."

My father let me drive our car a little, but it was an automatic. I'd never tried a standard.

"I can't."

"Nonsense. There's nothing to it. Here, Darla, you sit on my lap."

The cab was barely big enough for two people, and Darla accounted for at least that. I don't know how they fit in, but they did, and I found myself jammed between them and the driver's door. I turned the key without stepping on the clutch and the truck jumped forward.

"Jesus Christ." Darla began laughing. "Push the clutch."

It went down hard, and I couldn't reach the floor.

"Try it now."

The engine turned over and I revved it up.

"Easy now, let it out slow."

I released the clutch too fast and it stalled.

"Slower, okay?"

I tried again, and we were off. My grandfather motioned up the road, and I cranked the wheel. I knew I had to shift, but had no idea where the gears were, and Darla's eyes had closed.

"Grandpa?" He didn't answer. "Grandpa!" I began to panic. He grunted a little, wiggled under Darla, and started snoring.

I drove a few hundred yards, crossed the Wise River on a narrow bridge, then coasted to a stop in a pull-off next to the Big Hole letting the truck stall. I had no more idea where my grandfather lived than how to drive his truck. I wished I was home, and I wanted to cry. I stared out the windshield, spider webbed with a hundred cracks, at the river. It was cold and high, a far cry from the tranquil Big Hole of my picture book. Its motion was hypnotizing, and I couldn't look away. I was overtired, entering a state of semi-consciousness, trying to understand everything that had gone on, coming back again and again to the conclusion that my grandfather was crazy. He was vulgar beyond vulgar, seemed to have as little regard for the law as he did his own health, and somehow he thought I was the same. He was not the man I thought he was, and it appeared my conceptions of Montana were equally off base. Disappointment turned into discouragement, then depression. And then all I could think about was home and how far away I was, and how difficult it would be to get back there but how determined I was to do just that. In my decision to leave, I found enough comfort to allow me to sleep.

CHAPTER 4

OW ABOUT some breakfast, Kyle?" My grandfather's words sounded far away. "What do you want in your coffee?"

I opened my eyes enough to take in some of my surroundings without letting in the full force of the day. I was lying on a brown couch covered with a sleeping bag. A small table in front of me held a bowl of cereal and a glass of juice. I sensed more than saw my grandfather moving in a room behind me, his shadow spreading across the wooden floor, flicking back and forth over the coffee table. I sat up.

"Cream, sugar, both?" He was standing in the doorway to what I assumed was the kitchen.

"Both." I looked around for a phone. I had to call my parents, and none of the resolve to go home I'd felt the night before had faded. I tried to stand up but my lower back hurt too much. I slumped back down on the couch.

"Quite a night of it last night, wasn't it?" My grandfather handed me a chipped mug with a peeling picture of a deer on it. "Got the horse all taken care of." He winked. "Darla wanted me to tell you how much she appreciates it. She said she wants to fix you up with her daughter, too. She's about your age. Maybe a year or so older. Good looker to boot. We'll look into it if you want. Go ahead and eat your breakfast. You can get changed over there." He pointed to a closed door, crooked and cracked, beside a gun cabinet bristling with ordinance. I could see the barrels of more than seven guns. "That'll be your room. I put your suitcase and backpack in on your bed. I've got to go outside and get a few things ready."

"Grandpa?" He didn't turn around. "Cole?"

"That's better. What?"

"Can I use the phone?"

"Already took care of that. Your mom and dad send their love. Said they'll call in a day or so." He stepped outside through a screen door in the kitchen.

I wondered how he knew what I wanted the phone for, and if he suspected what I was going to tell my parents. It didn't take long for me to eat, and I was still hungry when I finished. I opened the door to my room and was greeted by a moose head on the far wall, its skull polished white, its dark antlers rising almost to the ceiling. A heap of shed antlers rested in one corner, and a small, unfinished dresser with three wooden legs and one made from stacked red bricks stood in the other. My suitcase and backpack lay on a single bed with a sleeping bag comforter. There was a large, square window in one wall with a red wool blanket hanging from two nails down over it. I peeled a corner of it back and looked outside. It was bright. The sun had been up quite a while, and the view was lovely enough to momentarily make me forget about planning my escape. A field of sage stretched out six hundred yards toward a line of softwoods, dark and unbroken, at the base of a mountain. Beyond the trees were more mountains, many of them white near their peaks. It looked a lot more like the Montana I'd seen pictures of. I opened the suitcase, traded my crudely altered slacks for a pair of clean Levis, and found a light button-down shirt. My feet had a little more room in my leather boots than they did in my sneakers, and if felt good to put them on. My legs, however, were stiff, and I heard my knees pop as I walked outside.

My grandfather was sitting on a block of wood looking intently down at a chainsaw between his legs. There was a ratchet stuck in the ground beside him and half a dozen sockets lay scattered around it.

"Son-of-a-bitch won't run," he said without looking up. "Just sputters and farts. Won't cut worth a damn. Figured it was a gas problem, but now I don't know. Sometimes I think it's doing it on purpose. You know, just to piss me off." He kicked it over onto its side. "Take that." He shook his head and looked up at me. "Haven't you got any shitty old clothes? You can't hardly be a logger looking like a Philadelphia lawyer. You'll have those ruined in under an hour. See if you can find something a little more suited to working outside. Save those for Darla's daughter."

"They're all I've got."

"What, only one pair of pants?"

"I mean they all look like this."

"Not for long they won't. After today, you'll have no trouble telling them from the rest. You ready to go to work? I figure we should. Try to get a little something done before the sun goes down."

I shrugged.

"Good. I've packed us a lunch, and we'll stop down to the store for a drink if you want. And this piece of shit," he kicked the saw again, "can stay right here and think about whether it wants to run or if it's ready for the parts pile."

The tire was gone from the back of truck. It lay on its side near the wadded-up piece of canvas that had been used to conceal the elk the night before and an overturned fiberglass canoe.

"Goes to the skidder." My grandfather saw me looking at it. "Worn down pretty good now. Started going flat every couple of weeks. They wanted to charge me twenty dollars to dump it in the landfill. That's America for you. Make you buy it, make you pay to get rid of it, too. I'll take the damn thing out back and burn it some night. Twenty dollars!" He yanked his door open, cringed when the hinges squalled, and shut it gently. "You can hoe some of that shit outta there at the store if you want." He pointed to the garbage at my feet, which, when seen in the light, amounted to even more than I thought had been there. A beer bottle lay on its side near the top of the heap, and as we backed up I watched an ounce or two still trapped inside wash back and forth.

My grandfather's driveway was more than half a mile long. It twisted through a sage flat, crossed a tiny creek bridged by heavy logs woven together with a thick cable, then ascended to the main road. For some reason, I thought Mistake was to our right, and when we turned left I put a hand on the dash and stared in the opposite direction.

"Know where we are?" my grandfather asked.

"No, not really."

"Then how'd you find your way out here last night?"

"What?"

"I forgot I hadn't told you where I live. Must be Darla directed you. She's been there more than a few times."

"Grandpa, I fell asleep by the river."

"Oh yeah? Must have been homing instinct. Like a pigeon."

"Darla was drunk." I wasn't in the mood for his game.

"Not drunk, Kyle. That's a rather harsh word, don't you think? No, she and I were in Mazatlan. She was waiting with supper ready on a long, sandy beach. I was going to be late. The marlin hadn't hit until midafternoon, and he was a whopper."

I folded my hands on my lap and closed my eyes. Maybe there would be a pay phone at the store.

"Okay, okay. So we were a bit intoxicated. Don't be too hard on us. It all worked out all right, didn't it? Hey, see that?"

I opened my eyes. A monstrous bird was perched on a bloated deer lying broken and dead in the ditch. It was hunched over, tearing the hide from the neck, its wicked hooked beak shearing through the skin.

"Golden eagle. Got lots of them out here. Sheep ranchers aren't too fond of them." He swerved at the bird and it flapped up onto a fence post, glaring angrily at us. "Keep your eyes open while you're out here, and you might find a feather."

We crossed the Wise River on the outskirts of Mistake, smaller than the Big Hole, fast and lined with cottonwoods.

"Got a lot of snow in her from the Pioneers," my grandfather said. "Not bad fishing early, but then it gets hit pretty hard. Thirty years ago it was better. Back before half the country decided to start playing Norman MacLean."

There hadn't been many lights on when we'd come through Mistake in the dark, and I'd assumed there was more to the town than what I'd seen. There wasn't. There was the Six Point, the school, a couple of houses, and Pioneer Mercantile, where we stopped for gas.

"Yes, sir! A dollar fuck-me-forty a gallon. A hop skip and a jump from the interstate and they still want to grab everyone by the balls." My grandfather punched his door, all compassion for his truck gone.

The gas pumps were ancient. The price dial inside the glass had broken on thirty-five cents a gallon, and numbers on the pay dial turned slowly, even when my grandfather clamped the handle on the pump all the way down. It took the better part of five minutes to fill the truck.

Inside, a woman with a sharp nose that reminded me of the golden eagle's beak stood behind the register, staring blankly at the rows of groceries.

"Hello, Helen," my grandfather said as we walked in. She acted as if she didn't hear him. "I've got eleven in gas, and my grandson wants a pop."

Helen punched at her register, took my grandfather's money without speaking, and we walked out.

"California bitch," my grandfather said as soon as we were back on the road. "Moved out here from Los Angeles with her husband for a change of pace. Guess she found it. Winter will likely give her more than she bargained for. Hope so, anyway. Should see how she treats the Indians. Rude. Saw her follow Darla's mother around the store with a bottle of air freshener one day."

We crossed back over the Wise River and continued past the turn to my grandfather's house, paralleling the Big Hole. The road curved through a gorge, not as long as the one between Mistake and Divide, but steeper and narrower. Where there was shade there were still waist-high banks of dirty snow.

"Quite a set of rapids, isn't it?" My grandfather slowed down. "A mile and half of the wildest water in Montana. Nobody floats it. Not when it's up like this. There was an Olympic kayaker from Quebec came out and ran it a few years ago. Nearly did him in. Got upside down in an eddy and busted himself against a big stone. Somehow he managed to right himself and get to shore, but he left a good chunk of scalp in the river. Before they blasted out a path for the road, this canyon was impassable. Had to put out around it."

It looked mean and powerful. I couldn't imagine anyone, including the kayaker, trying to float it. "Has anyone ever done it? I mean made it through?"

"Not in a long time. Maybe not ever. There's a legend says a couple of Indians did it more than a hundred years ago."

"Really?"

"Well, so the story goes. There was a medicine man in a canoe, and supposedly he went through standing up and the water in front of him turned as smooth as if he was on a lake early in the morning before the wind comes up."

"Do you believe it?" I didn't.

"Kyle, this is Montana. A man will sell himself short if he's too rigid in his beliefs out here. And that was Montana more than a hundred years ago. What do you think?"

I looked out my window at the Big Hole and frowned. I didn't see how it could be possible. "I don't know."

"Well, I don't either. But I wasn't there to say one way or the other, so I try to keep an open mind."

"But standing up?" I could picture the medicine man bedecked with feathers and an ornate chest plate of wolf ribs cruising down the rapids. "I don't see how."

"Yeah, He couldn't have done it alone."

"Who was with him?"

"I mean he had some help. Some extra powers."

"Magic?"

"No, magic is tricks. I reckon this would have had to have been real enough. You follow?"

"No. What do you mean powers?"

"I mean . . . I don't know . . . maybe he didn't have any powers. Or maybe he did and it was because he believed so strongly . . . didn't limit his mind to what he felt was possible the way everyone does now. Or maybe none of it ever happened. Maybe it's just a story. It's a good one, though, huh?"

We left the canyon and turned up a dirt lane bordered by straight lodgepole pines. I was still thinking about the medicine man when we stopped.

"Here we are. Not much left to do. We can finish most of it up today if we push."

We got out in a circular clearing some fifty feet across. A deeply-rutted skid road led away into the forest, and all around the truck lay evidence of cutting. Broken limbs, some draped with orange clumps of dead needles from last fall, jutted up from the ground in every direction. Wood chips, thick and damp, gave the earth a spongy quality that made walking difficult, like loose sand along Lake Ontario. They clung to my boots, working their way over the tops, down against my socks. Empty oil jugs, some partially buried, their labels peeling, their sides caved in, and their screw-on tops long gone, were scattered throughout the clearing, and there were several fire-blackened ovals along either side of the skid road. The trees along the edge of the opening stood out sharply against the sky behind them. They were tall and slender; pencil-shaped and limbless except for the cluster of branches near their tops.

"Grab the saw and we'll get to it." My grandfather had his battered cooler with our lunches in one hand and two milk jugs, the gas and oil, in the other.

The saw was heavy. The bar didn't weigh enough to offset the motor, and I had to use both hands to carry it. I followed my grandfather up the skid road, walking between the tire tracks, trying to keep up. I could feel the pressure of the thin air on my chest, much as I had the night before, and in the woods where the sun hadn't fully penetrated it was still cool. Something the size of a bumble bee whirred past my head, circled, and made for my grandfather. It landed on his back and a split second later he dropped the cooler to swat at it.

"Goddamn it! If it's not the mud, it's the horse flies, and if it ain't the horse flies it's the heat." He picked the crushed fly off the ground and worked it into a black paste between his fingers. "Then there's the cold . . . and the snow . . . but if a man can put up with it, provided he doesn't starve to death, he'll damn sure live longer. Got to look at it that way. How you doing? That saw too much for you?"

I shifted it between my hands and shook my head.

"Good. You'll make a logger. Wait and see. Do a lot of people good to pick up a saw and work for a living."

It wasn't far to the skidder, but I was happy to see it. My shoulders ached and I was having trouble with each breath.

"The yellow beast." My grandfather slung the gas and oil up onto its seat. "Will you start for me this morning, honey?" He patted the front tire. "Just set the saw down there for a minute. Might need you to hose her down with ether."

He climbed up a rickety-looking set of chain link stairs and sat down on a piece of foam lying loose on the metal seat. He pulled a couple of switches, fiddled with a cracked control panel in front of him, and the engine turned over, thumping like an oversized partridge drumming in the spring. It didn't start.

"Come on, now. Don't get ornery with me. Too nice a day for that." He tried again. Nothing. "Why you stubborn bitch, I won't put up with this." His fist crashed down onto the wheel, and I backed up a step. "You won't win this game."

My grandfather jumped to the ground, tripped on a branch and fell into a water-filled rut. He came up gasping for air, a vein as big around as a night crawler bulging between his eyes. He snatched a piece of wood three feet long and several inches through up out of the rut and swung it with all his might. It bounced off the skidder's tire with a hollow thud, springing back into his face, knocking him down. Blood began trickling from a cut above his right eye, running down into his beard. He wiped at it with the back of his hand, then laughed. I backed up some more, again feeling the need to get home.

"Never pays to strike a lady, Kyle. Why don't you run back to the truck.

Got a first aid kit behind the seat. Just bring a couple of band aids. Something to close up the cut. I'll mess around with the skidder. She'll probably go now. Done her best to lay me low for today I reckon." His laughter turned to coughing, and he pushed himself to his feet.

I found the first aid kit, a wad of dusty medical supplies leaking out of a plastic tackle box. I grabbed a couple of large band aids and headed back up the trail. I hadn't gotten far when I heard the skidder fire up. The rumble filled the woods, and I could see the black column of smoke rise above the trees. The cut on my grandfather's head had stopped bleeding, and he waved off the band aids as he helped me up onto the chain stairs.

"Hang on good now. Here we go."

I dug my fingers into the heavy-gauge wire cage of the cab, scared to look down. We chugged up the road, my feet swinging to every bounce, certain before long I'd slip and go under the massive rear tire that was churning along behind me, throwing mud onto my jeans, breaking unseen branches with startling snaps, and rotating faster as my grandfather gunned it up a rise. At the top, he stopped and pointed across a large clear cut to a square of thirty trees standing conspicuously by themselves.

"That's it. They're the last of them." He shut the skidder off and smiled. "Enjoy the ride?"

I slowly relinquished my grip and hopped down.

"You can drive it out if you want. Be something to tell your folks. Or maybe not." He got out on the other side of the cab. "Ready to go logging?"

I looked at the trees on the far edge of the cut. They swayed back and forth in the first breeze of the day, moving in unison, undulating in hypnotic synchronization.

My grandfather took the saw this time. He carried it on his right shoulder, effortlessly, the bar sticking up above his head where it caught the sun's rays and sent a bright beam of light onto his face. A mule deer and her fawn broke out of the trees as we approached. They hopped toward the woods, their hooves striking the earth together, their comical, bouncing gait carrying them away deceptively fast.

"Do they always run that way?" I asked.

"Damn near all the time. They can really get with it, too. Got one fatal habit, though. Like to stop and look back after they run a bit. See?"

The deer had stopped just inside the woods. They stood broadside to us, the doe looking over the back of her fawn in our direction.

"See how white their asses are?" My grandfather was walking again. "Antelope, elk, sheep, and mule deer all have those light rumps. Makes it easy to see them on bare ground."

I stood still and watched them, listening to my grandfather's voice fade as he neared the trees, losing his words altogether when he started the saw. It wasn't until he revved it up that the deer ran again.

I didn't come much closer to where he was cutting. I found a suitable stump to sit on, one with enough pitch to give the seat of my pants a sticky coating, bringing them a little closer to the color of my grandfather's. I looked at the clean blue fabric on their knees and thought about how long I would have to work before they would acquire the dirty-green appearance of his. I knew it would be a very long time, and thinking about the days, weeks, perhaps months it would take once more turned my thoughts to home, and how long it would be before I slept in my own bed. I looked up at the sky, blue and big, trying to find some comfort in the fact that my parents saw the same sky, but it seemed the only thing we had in common, and it wasn't enough.

"Kyle. Kyle!" My grandfather had turned the saw off. "Come on over here. There's something I want to show you."

I picked my way around the brush piles, dragging my feet, looking down at the ground.

"Come on, you'll like this." He was smiling; the look that in the short time I'd known him characterized him. "This is my favorite part of all this."

The saw was wedged into a cut in a tree a foot through and more than one hundred feet tall. He'd cut a triangular notch opposite it, exposing the white flesh of the pine.

"Push her over, Kyle." He slapped the bark a couple of feet above the saw. "I'll pull the saw out when she starts to go over, then you step back and enjoy the show. Oh, here, use these." He pulled a pair of orange, fuzzy gloves out of a back pocket. I had to pull them well past my wrists before my fingers found the tips. "Push good and hard then get the hell out of the way. Most trees don't resent you cutting them, but every once in a while you'll get some cantankerous old bitch who'll try to kill you for it. Spring up and send her ass at you like a locomotive. Come on now, give her hell."

I braced myself and heaved against the tree, in the back of my mind hoping "she" wouldn't hold it against me, surprised by how easily I moved it. It tilted slowly, the cut opening wide enough so my grandfather was able to withdraw the saw, then began to fall faster, the wind accelerating through the crown of limbs high above me. I stepped back, my eyes glued to the pine, oblivious to everything else around me. Halfway down it broke free of the stump, seemed for an instant to hang suspended above the earth, then slammed down with a tremendous crash that I felt throughout my body. And then it was quiet. As quiet as it had been the night before, after my grandfather had shot the elk and moved down the hill away from me.

"Something else, isn't it?" He flipped a stick toward the tree. "I never get tired of it. Seen it thousands of times, and I like it every bit as much now as I did when I was a young man. What do you think?"

I nodded.

"All right. My boy's a logger! I knew it!" He pulled the saw to life, knocked down four more trees in line with the first, then limbed them, lifting the saw from one side of the trunk to the other, working the throttle as he moved up the trees so it sounded as though the saw was talking to him. When he cut the last top off, he stopped.

"Pile up the brush, now. Heap it up so I can burn it this winter. If those tops are too heavy for you, I'll cut them in half. I'll go over and start on the other end. Won't need to worry about a tree landing on you that way."

The tops were heavy. It seemed as if they had deliberately buried themselves under anything they could find on the forest floor to make moving them more difficult. They hung up on the smallest of sticks, jerking my arms painfully back as I dragged them, lighting a fire in my calves, pointing out muscles in my back I didn't know were there. By the time we stopped for lunch, two or three hours later, I'd been made well aware of those muscles and many more besides. My whole body ached.

"How you doing?" my grandfather asked, his mouth full of the ham sandwich he was eating.

"Not bad."

"Sore?"

"A little."

"Gets you back here, huh?" He tapped the small of his back.

"Yeah."

"Well, you're doing a good job. A hell of a good job. I didn't figure you'd be this tough. Shit, most men would be whining and ready to quit. They don't realize that every day you spend working in the woods adds one on to your life. Of course most of 'em don't have squat to live for. Go all year hunched over a desk so they can spend two weeks where you and I work every day."

Every day. I was quite sure I'd be crippled in less than a week. But my grandfather had called me tough, and there was no doubt in my mind he knew what he was talking about.

"What about your dad? He ever gonna get out here for a visit, or has your mom pretty well collared him to New York?"

"I think he'd like to."

"Bet he would. He was a good worker, too, Kyle. Strong . . . like you." My grandfather sighed.

My father never talked much about working in the woods. I knew he had, but the Montana we discussed was closer to my picture book. I knew he missed it, and I didn't feel completely comfortable talking about it.

It didn't take me long to eat. The sandwich, orange, and brownie went down fast. My soda was warm, but it was wet, and I hadn't realized how thirsty I was. The air was drier than back home. I'd worked hard, probably harder than ever before, but hadn't sweat.

Sometime in the middle of the afternoon, when the sun had warmed the air sufficiently to bring out an entire regiment of horseflies, all capable of biting through my shirt, my grandfather cut the last tree. The clear cut was complete: the unnatural opening in the forest would remain long after my grandfather, and probably myself, were gone and a tiny sliver of sadness mixed with the sense of accomplishment.

"Be a good place for elk to feed now. Give them a little patch of grass." My grandfather sat down on the ground and looked up at me. "Don't feel bad about it. Ain't like New York where all that's left are patches of woods. This don't hurt a bit."

I don't know how he knew what I was thinking. Perhaps he felt the same way and said it to assure himself as much as me, or maybe the smile on my face wasn't totally convincing. Either way, I was glad to hear him say it.

"You want to drive the skidder out?" He stood up, then bent over while a spasm of coughs shook his upper body.

"Are you okay?" It sounded more serious than a cold. It came from deep in his chest and was muffled my the fluid he spit when he finished.

"Right as rain. Now, you want to drive, or you want me to?"

"Go ahead."

"What's the matter, worn out?"

"I'm tired."

"Not too tired to look for moose before we go home, are you?"

"Moose?"

"Yeah, we'll take a drive along the river up toward Wisdom and see if we can scout some up. What do you say?"

I wanted to see the upper Big Hole more than I did a moose. I wanted to see something that I knew would look the way I pictured it. I wanted to see the Montana I'd been obsessed with.

"Are you up for it?"

"Sure."

"Good. Help this old man out of here then, will you? No, kick him in the ass and tell him to move. I'm not that old. Look at this, I can still carry the saw, gas, and oil."

"Want me to take something?"

"Yeah, your time walking out of here so I can keep up. Ready?"

We left the skidder parked on the edge of the clear cut and walked all the way down to the truck. The seat felt heavenly. Before we hit the main road, I was sleeping, dreaming of the medicine man going through the rapids we'd seen earlier. I was with him, in his canoe, sitting calmly, watching as he rose in his seat, the water becoming as gentle as a swimming pool.

"They really did it," I said as I woke up. We were parked on the shoulder of the road, a cow and calf moose feeding in a hay meadow less than a hundred yards away.

"Really did what?" My grandfather didn't take his eyes off them.

"I was dreaming."

"Dreaming about what?"

"The Indians going down the rapids." I felt stupid talking about it.

"And you were with them, right?"

"How did you know?" I was beginning to think he could read my mind.

"I've had the same dream. Weren't scared a bit I bet, either, were you?"

"No."

"Neither was I." He put his arm around me and pointed to the moose. "Funny looking critters, aren't they?

"Yeah."

"Leggy sons of bitches. Stubborn, too. Don't know how to go around anything. Just over or through. Watch." He opened his door and hollered at them, laughing as they lumbered away, breaking into a dense stand of willows along the river. "No, won't turn for nothing. What do you think, could you have hit that cow when she was standing there?" He looked at me now, no longer laughing, and I glanced between us to make sure I hadn't over-looked the rifle.

"Probably."

"Yeah, I bet you could have. Big as a barn door, wasn't she?"

The sun was setting, dropping behind the Pintlers, the mountains of my picture book, when we turned around and headed back toward Mistake. I had slept longer than I realized. It took forty-five minutes to reach the gorge I'd dreamed about, and an eerie feeling, somewhere between déjà vu and a premonition of something to come swamped me as the river had the kyaker. My grandfather was quiet, too, and we didn't look at each other. In the darkness that overtook us before we reached his house, the western dark-ness that does such a perfect job of covering so large a land, I decided to stay for the summer, but in doing so I felt more homesick than I had since my bus left the Syracuse station. And when I saw my grandfather's house in the headlights, the rough-log siding soaking up the beams rather than re-flecting them, the ghostly set of elk horns sticking up above the door, it took every ounce of fortitude I could summon not to cry. I was overtired and scared. Scared because so little I'd found was as I expected, and scared even more because I knew I would stay.

"Supper time," my grandfather said as he shut the truck off and let it coast to a stop near the skidder tire. "I'm hungry enough to eat the balls off a brass monkey and tongue the tin dick off a metal mule. Got some elk back-strap that might be a bit fresher than the game wardens say it ought to be. Bet I can cook it so you won't need a knife. Be so tender your fork will slide through it like a hot knife in soft butter. Sound good?"

It did. I was tired, but I was hungry.

"You can take a shower while I get her going if you want."

"That's all right." I didn't want to be alone, even one room away from my grandfather.

"Suit yourself."

We walked into the kitchen, lit by a bare light bulb hanging from the ceil-ing. My grandfather selected a cast iron skillet from the assortment of pots and pans stacked next to the old-fashioned gas stove and broke a stick of butter in half, letting one end fall into it. He turned the heat on full bore under the pan and retrieved a bloody hunk of meat from a humming refrigerator near the door. He slapped it down on the table, a homemade contraption sporting stains of every shape, and with his hunting knife he sliced half a dozen pieces from it. I looked around the room, studying the house, thinking the wooden walls couldn't be too far removed from the trapper's cabin in my picture book.

The meat hissed when it hit the skillet, and my grandfather jumped away from the stove. He let it cook four or five minutes a side, then plopped three big pieces down a plate for me.

"Hope you don't mind meat by itself. Too lazy to fix anything to go with it. Put a lot of salt on it. Brings out the flavor."

It was good, and I could cut it with my fork. We sat at the table, across from each other, eating rapidly, pausing our chewing just long enough to sip from our glasses of milk.

"Are we going to work, tomorrow?" I asked, fearful that I knew the answer.

"You bet. But not in the woods. Going to work for Darla's mother, Sarah. She needs some brook trout, and I figure you and I are just the pair to get them for her. Think you can handle that?"

I was anxious to fish. My father had taken me into the Adirondacks for a week every year since I'd been old enough to hold a rod, and unlike hunting, which intimidated me, I loved to catch trout.

"We'll give Cow Crick a try. Be a lot of snow in it yet, but if your father's half the man he was, you know how to handle a rod, and we'll nail a good mess. Now, there ain't no dessert tonight. Have to have Darla bake us up some pretty quick. Hey, you want to see if she and her daughter want to come tomorrow?"

"I guess."

"We don't have to."

"No, it doesn't matter."

"Well, maybe we'll have them over to eat when we get back. How's that sound?"

"Fine." I didn't want them to come. I'd waited a long time to fish with my grandfather and wanted it to be something for just the two of us.

"Good. You tired?"

"Yeah."

"Ready for bed?"

"I think so."

"Okay, you know where your room is. Mine's back there." He pointed to a door opposite my room. "If you need anything in the night, just holler." He stood up, rubbed his knees, and pulled a bottle of whiskey out of a cupboard, and, after filling his milk glass, took a long drink.

I could see the yellow light of the kitchen through the crack under my bedroom door. In the time it took me to fall asleep, I heard the cupboard open and close three more times, heard my grandfather have two bad bouts of coughing, then fell asleep to his laughter filling the house, seeping into the sleeping bag I pulled over my head, ringing in my ears. I heard it in my sleep, too. Not from the kitchen but from further away. In another time it seemed. Closer to when the Indians floated the rapids. It came from the trees and rocks around me as I stood beside the river, loud and unbroken, larger than the sky above me, more penetrating than the cold running up my legs from the frigid ground.

CHAPTER 5

I n New York, mornings in mid-March before the sun comes up, when
the air is still and cold and birds haven't awakened to sing in the new day,
have a rejuvenating quality about them. The level of light, if not the temperature, works its way deep into a person's soul: infallible evidence that winter will end, spring will come, the earth will bloom, and the cycle of life will
begin again for everything from the crocus to the robin. In Montana, my
grandfather said the spring-dawn phenomena that reaffirms one's vitality
and gives him strength to see out the rest of the winter isn't confined to a
specific time of year. That's why he got me up at four o'clock for our day of
fishing. So we could sit together behind his house, shivering both from the
cold and the excitement of a new day and what we were about to do. We sat
side by side in the kitchen chairs, carried outside to face the sun rise, and
neither one of us said a word. Coyotes bid farewell to the night from some
meadow on the mountain across the sage flat, their voices rising and falling
without rhythm but still together. Frost from the ground imparted a chill to
the air that numbed my feet and accelerated my heart beat. I wasn't as tired
as I had been the past couple of days, and Montana didn't seem as foreign.
I looked over my shoulder to the western sky, in transition from gray to
pink, and an uncontrollable smile spread across my face. The sage smelled
strong, its scent hanging in the air all around us, so thick I expected to see it
much as I would the fog on an early spring morning back home. The sun
appeared suddenly, a yellow ball of fire over the mountains east of Mistake,
and an eagle screamed above us. My grandfather stood up, tucked his chair

46

under his arm, and went inside. I waited several minutes before following, but the spell was gone. Inside I could smell coffee and more backstrap cooking.

"Good day for a limit of trout, Kyle. Gonna warm up nice." My grandfather flipped the pieces of elk and poured us each a cup of coffee. "I remember fishing Cow Crick when I was a lot younger than you. Went with your great grandfather. Used flies then. Flies and a little spinner." He sat down across from me at the table. "Remember taking your dad, too. He loved to go. Ever tell you about the first time he went by himself?"

"No."

"He was seven. Couldn't for the life of me think where in hell he was at. Worried about him most of the day. About supper time he came strutting in with a big stringer of trout. Didn't know whether to tan his ass or pat him on the back. Think I decided on the latter."

The elk began popping vigorously, and my grandfather stood up.

"Jesus Christ! Gone and burned it. Nothing I hate worse than to ruin a fine piece of meat. Ought to be bull whipped for this." He tipped the backstrap out of the pan onto a plate, scraping the charred sections with a fork. "If it ain't edible, just fling it out the door, Kyle."

It was edible. In fact, it was almost as good as the night before, and I think he knew it would be. I finished before him and asked where he dug his worms. It was a ritual I enjoyed nearly as much as fishing. The excitement of breaking apart a shovelful of soil in search of worms was surpassed only by the tug of a trout on my line.

"Worms? Oh, of course. You're used to living where you can find the things most anywhere. No, out here the soil ain't fit for them. Too rocky. There ain't but two, maybe three nights of the year when I can pick up crawlers. I don't where they go after that. We'll just buy a couple of packs down at the store. You bring anything besides a fly rod with you?"

"No."

"Well, I got a couple of old reels with monofilament on them. You want to use your shortest rod. Crick's so narrow that a long one's nothing more than a pain in the ass. Why don't you get your work clothes on, and I'll be right with you."

The two fly rods I had were both seven and a half feet long, a length which my grandfather said was good for "poking at rattlers" but wasn't worth a "flying fuck" on a stream. I was becoming accustomed to his foul mouth, but I wondered how he and my father could be so different. But then, I didn't see how anyone could be like my grandfather.

I waited in the truck while he went in Pioneer Mercantile for the crawlers. An Indian wearing a Seattle Mariners ball cap walked past, turned around, and came back to the truck. He stuck his head in the driver's side window and looked at me. When he smiled, he revealed a less-than-full set of teeth.

"I'm Badger," he sat as he thrust his hand inside.

I shook it and he held on a long time, looking intently at me.

"And you are?" He was still holding my hand.

"Kyle. I'm Cole's grandson."

"You look a lot alike, you know it?"

I looked down at the floor. I could smell alcohol on him.

"I'm Darla's brother. You met her the other night, huh?"

"Yeah."

"She knows your grandfather real good. Real good." Badger smiled again. "Says you got her an elk the other night. That right?"

"My grandfather did."

"She says it was you. I won't tell her different." Badger's long hair drifted over his shoulders into the cab. It was black. Blacker than mine and looked sleek. His face was weathered like the Indian's I'd seen in Billings, and he was tall but not heavy. He'd cut the sleeves off a denim coat to expose his arms. They were long and slender, the veins close to the surface. "What are you up to today? Cole taking you logging? He did me once. Made me pile brush and stack wood. Had all I wanted in an hour. Lay down and went to sleep. That made him pretty mad."

"No, we're going fishing."

"Where?"

"Cow Creek, I think."

"Uh-huh. Good place. Think I can get your grandfather to buy me a drink when he comes out?"

"I don't know."

"Bet I can. You know what he'll say?"

"What?"

Badger stepped away from the truck, deepened his voice, and did a good impression of my grandfather. "Jesus Christ, Badger! It's not even ten and you want a drink? Son of a bitch."

"There, now you've saved me the speech." My grandfather had come out unnoticed. I expected Badger to be embarrassed but he wasn't, and he and my grandfather began laughing.

"Met your grandson." Badger pointed at me.

"What'd you think of him? Is there any hope or has the east ruined him?"

"I think he hadn't ought to hang around you. What do they call it? Corrupting a minor?"

"I hope to do just that. Now, in order for us to get out of here I expect it's going to cost me. Probably a beer, huh?"

"Just one?" Badger sounded dejected.

"Well, Christ, Badger, I'm a poor logger. What, you think I'm made of money?"

"Got more than I do."

"Okay, here's a couple bucks. Go crazy."

Badger was still laughing when he walked into the store.

"Why do you buy them beer?" I asked as soon as my grandfather was in the truck.

"Why not?"

"He's drunk."

"So?"

I wasn't in the mood to argue. I nodded, thinking to myself that Flo's interpretation of Indians was right on the money. My grandfather looked at me a long time. Finally, I looked away from him, out my window, and he turned the key.

Cow Creek ran for half a mile, the entire width of the Big Hole valley, through flat sage country before crossing the main highway less than two hundred yards east of Mistake. We parked by the culvert, and I looked up at the Pioneers, searching for the break in the trees where the stream ran out. A lone clump of willows sitting tight to the softwoods marked its exit. It looked a long way away.

"Up for the walk?" My grandfather was stringing my rod. I hadn't gotten out of the truck. "Not much point in starting below the woods. Crick's too flat. No good pools. Have to walk up a bit to where it drops."

I got out and stared down into the culvert pool on the other side of the highway. The water rushed under the road hard enough to carry a current through the pool. It was the same slate-gray color as the Big Hole.

My grandfather had crossed a fence and was heading upstream. I jogged

49

fifty feet through the sage, stepping over dry heaps of cow manure, breathing hard by the time I caught up with him. He handed me my rod.

"You're not fishing?" I asked. My grandfather wasn't carrying another rod.

"Nope. Not unless you're completely incapable of catching them. I've caught thousands ... probably tens of thousands. Besides, I want to see what your father has taught you. Find out if I have to disown him or not."

We started fishing at the edge of the woods. My grandfather opened a white Styrofoam container of night crawlers, commented on how "snarly" they were, broke an inch off the end of one and baited my hook. He pointed to an eddy where the stream swirled around a boulder. I flipped the line underhand, landing it even with the stone. The current swept it away immediately, and I threw it farther upstream. As the bait drifted by the rock, it hesitated and I felt the fish. He came quickly, hit hard, and I lifted ten inches of flopping trout onto the back, and for an instant everything was perfect. There was me, the trout, the stream, and nothing more.

"You've got a good knack for locating fish," my grandfather said. "That's something that can't be taught. It's instinct. Like knowing when to shoot at a flying grouse or how long to sit on a stand for deer. Glad to see it hasn't been washed out by the civilized world."

Several times over the course of the morning I asked if he'd like to catch a trout, and each time he waved off the question before I finished. Toward noon we reached a section of brook where the water fell sharply and the distance in pools increased three fold to more than one hundred yards. At the base of a waterfalls, where Cow Creek thundered over a wall of silky granite twenty feet high, we stopped.

"Let your grandfather sit down a minute. These trout are heavy." He was carrying them on a forked fir bough which he set in the pool at the base of the falls. He drove the straight end of the stick into the bank, and I watched the fish undulate in the current. Once in a while one would appear to twitch. He had close to twenty, all between seven and twelve inches. It was easily the best mess of brook trout I'd ever caught.

A pine squirrel began chattering from a nearby lodgepole, flicking its tail back and forth, its front feet drawn into its chest.

"Doesn't like us here." It's what my father told me when we flushed a noisy kingfisher out of a sand bank on the upper Hudson.

"No, I reckon not." My grandfather tossed a stone in its direction and it went tearing off, bounding like a miniature deer. "What do you think, Kyle? Will you always enjoy doing this type of thing?"

"Fishing?"

"Yeah, fishing. And just getting outside. Seeing country that's still country."

"I think so." It wasn't something I thought about often, but many of my happiest childhood memories involved fishing with my father or cross-country skiing with him through the woods around our house in the winter.

"I hope you do. Some young men lose interest in it after a while. Get into cars and women and drinking . . . not that there isn't something to be said for all that, too, but when you're my age it seems what you remember the most are days like these. I can't tell you what the best piece of ass I ever got was, but I can tell you that on November 5, 1951, I killed a six-point elk. And I can't remember much about Christmas in 1960 . . . don't know what I got your dad or how much snow we had, but I know the night before I caught a lynx in a number 4 Victor leg-hold trap. I guess it's all what a man places worth on." He lifted his hands and gestured around him. "Me, this is it for me. You know, I've lived through a number of wars. Wars I saw some of my friends go off to and not come back. All fighting for their country. And I can admire that. Would have done the same thing myself if I perceived any immediate threat to this." His hands were still up. "But I didn't. Never figured what was going on half way around the world would fuck up my fishing or logging, or that the Vietcong would keep me from shooting an elk. If I had, it would have been different. I'd die for this in a heartbeat. Like to think I wouldn't go quietly, either."

The conversation was becoming too profound for me. I didn't like to think about dying period, and I didn't like hearing my grandfather talk about it.

"What's above the falls?" I asked enthusiastically.

"What's that?" My grandfather blinked and rubbed his eyes.

"Above the falls. What's up there?"

"Lake Firewater if you go far enough. It's above where my legs feel like carrying me today. Probably all iced in yet. We'll hike up there sometime this summer. Good place for big cutthroat. Maybe camp there." He started coughing, leaned forward, and spit into the water. A shiny drop of blood, brighter than the red spots on the trout below it, spun in tight circles, then was whisked downstream. "Let's get out of here," he said.

51

It didn't seem possible, but we'd fished more than a mile of the creek. By the time we broke out of the woods, still a long haul from the truck, I knew I'd been walking, and when we finished cleaning the trout at the upstream end of the culvert, I was ready to sit down.

"Sarah will be pretty tickled to get these trout," my grandfather said as he deposited them into a plastic bag he retrieved from behind his seat. "She doesn't much care for the browns and rainbows, but these brook trout . . . she loves these brookies. We'll give her ten and keep the rest for ourselves. Cook them up with some elk tonight for the girls. You still want to ask them over?"

"You can if you want."

"You know I want to. That's not what I asked, though. Do you want to?"

"Sure."

"Good. You ain't shy, are you?"

"No." I was lying, and he knew it.

"Hey, don't worry. Ain't like a big date or anything. If you don't have a good time, I'll tell Darla you just aren't comfortable around women. Course then she might figure you for a queer. Wouldn't want that, would we? Not a grandson of mine." He lifted the carpet on the roof to see if I was smiling. "Damn it, Kyle, lighten up. Old Cole's gonna line you up with a piece of ass. Believe it or not, it won't kill you. Shit, if she's half as good as her mother she'll strap one on you you'll never forget."

The thought of it scared me to death. If she was half as big as her mother, she'd squash me. At fourteen, the physical features of girls, notably breasts, thighs, and hair, were all that attracted me. If she bore any resemblance to her mother, I wanted nothing to do with her. Then there was a nagging question I had to broach to my grandfather concerning who her father was. It crossed my mind that we might be far too closely related to engage in anything but the most platonic brother/sister relationship. I decided I'd ease into the question.

"Grandpa . . . Cole, what's her name? Darla's daughter. I don't even know her name."

"Her name's Katrina."

"Do you know . . . I mean . . . who's her father?"

"Shit, Kyle, is her family heritage all that important? We're talking about fucking here, not walking down the aisle."

"You don't know?"

We turned into a dirt drive across from the Six Point and slowed down. My grandfather was quiet for a few seconds then began laughing.

"Don't worry about that. Ain't no chance of that. After your grandmother left I got my nuts cut. Wanted to avoid this very thing. This and a few others. No, don't trouble yourself over that. Good Christ, what you must think of me!"

I wasn't exactly sure what my grandfather meant when he said he'd had his nuts cut. It sounded painful to me, but I felt confident we were on the same wavelength concerning my genetic distance from Katrina. Even so, more than a little of me hoped they couldn't make it for dinner.

Sarah lived in an upstairs apartment of a newer-looking duplex. I wanted to wait in the truck while my grandfather took her the trout, but he wouldn't hear of it.

"I didn't catch a damn one of them. Now come on. It ain't gonna take long and I want you to meet her," he said.

Sarah was half, maybe only a third as large as either of her daughters. Her hair, long and combed back away from her face, was going gray, but slowly. Along the middle of her back where it was thick, it was still the same color as Badger's. She had a pleasant smile and spoke politely to my grandfather.

"Come in, Cole. Who's this you have with you?"

"Sarah, this is my grandson, Kyle. He's from New York, but don't hold that against him. He caught you these trout." My grandfather handed her the bag of fish and she held them up to the light. The apartment was dark. Blankets hung over the two windows I could see, and the bulb in the ceiling wasn't very powerful.

"Kyle, you said?" She was still looking at the trout.

"Yes." My grandfather spoke louder.

"Well, Kyle, thank you." She lowered the bag and looked at me. "What do you think of Montana?"

"I like it I guess. Only been here a couple of days."

"And your grandfather hasn't gotten you into any trouble?" There was a quality about her eyes that made them sparkle even in low light.

"No."

"Well, give him time." She elbowed my grandfather in the side and he pretended that it hurt. "Introduced you to my daughters, has he?"

"I met Darla and Dell."

"I'll bet you did. And Badger and Little Elk? Seen them?"

"I met Badger this morning."

"What about Katrina? She's about your age."

"I haven't met her yet."

"We're having her and her mother over for supper tonight, aren't we, Kyle?" My grandfather winked at Sarah. "See how much Richards the boy has in him."

I edged toward the door.

"Can you stay and have a drink? Beer's cold." Sarah headed into another room and I heard water running.

"We could probably have one, couldn't we, Kyle? No place you need to get to right off, huh?"

I didn't want to stay. I feared one drink would turn into one dozen, and I didn't think I could deal with my grandfather if he got drunk this early in the day. I sat down in a sky-blue recliner and stared at the wall. There was a picture of a buffalo made from brightly colored thread strung between pins which traced the animal's outline, and a painting of an Indian chief that looked like something offered at the dart throwing booth of a fair. Sarah emerged with a beer for my grandfather, one she'd been nursing herself, and a full bottle for me. My grandfather didn't act surprised, nor did he say anything when she handed it to me. I tried to catch his eye and he deliberately looked away.

My first swallow of Rainier went down hard. I didn't like the bitter flavor, and the aftertaste hung in my mouth like sharp cheese. I felt obligated to take another sip, then slid the bottle down onto the floor, close to my chair where Sarah couldn't see it. She and my grandfather talked about the weather, work, and her daughters, and I stared at the chief and buffalo. When their conversation turned to elk, I paid more attention.

"Easy winter for them," my grandfather said. He could speak clearly with a mouthful of beer. "Be lots of them around this fall. Make sure and get your tag. I'll keep on Badger and we'll get his driver's license renewed so he can get one, too. Don't need anyone running out again. Had Kyle take care of Darla's problem the other night. Worked out real good."

"What about Allen's bull?" Sarah was leaning to the edge of her chair. "Is there anything you can do about that? The auction's the day after tomorrow, isn't it?"

"It is. I've got something cooking, too. Haven't told Kyle about that." He turned to me, drained his bottle, and pushed the brim of his hat up. "Little

Elk's boy, Allen, lost a nice bull to the wardens last year. Shot it on some of Tipton's land and the son of a bitch had it confiscated. Real bad deal. The boy's what, ten? Eleven?"

Sarah nodded.

"Took his elk, his rifle, and fined his dad, too. Yeah, real bad deal. Land wasn't even posted. Not like the bastard's gonna miss one bull, either. Anyway, the fish and game's having an auction of all their confiscated game up in Missoula this weekend. Fucking warden told Allen that if he wanted his bull head he could go up and bid on it. Self-righteous cock-sucker!" The vein was sticking out on his forehead. "Imagine that. Telling the boy he could go bid on it. Well, he's going to. In fact, maybe we'd better head home, Kyle. Got some final phone calls to make about this. Thanks for the drink. Kyle, grab yours and I'll finish it off for you."

He drank it on the way down the stairs and threw the empty bottle into the bed of his truck. I heard it shatter, but he didn't inspect the damage. He slammed his door, swearing to himself, and spun the wheels into the road. It was a quiet ride back to his house.

I fixed myself a peanut butter and jelly sandwich while my grandfather talked on the phone. Occasionally I'd hear a "you're goddamned right we will," or a "be a fucking mistake if they try," but other than the fact that he was mad, I didn't know what was going on. He made a lot of calls. More than I wanted to try to listen to. I walked around the house, not bored, just acquainting myself with it. There were five rooms. The kitchen, the living room, our bedrooms, and a tiny bathroom. There was a wood stove in a corner of the living room, and the floor in front of it was charred from where a log had rolled out of the fire. It looked like it had been allowed to burn there for quite a while. The bed in my grandfather's room took up most of the floor space. It was a queen or king with a high wooden headboard. It looked like something my grandmother would buy, and I suspected she had. An elk head hung from one wall, dusty and decked with spider webs, and across from it were six sets of mule deer antlers nailed fast through their skull plates. Below them on a rusty hook hung eight leather belts, all with oversized buckles. I lifted one, rubbed the dust off it, and looked at the engraved scene. It was a bull, all four hooves off the ground, twisting so sharply it appeared to be trying to fold itself in half. A cowboy hung onto his back with one hand, while the other reached high above him. The place and date of the rodeo where it was won had been worn smooth.

In the center of my grandfather's room, over the middle of his bed, was a trap door in the ceiling. It didn't look like it had been opened in a long time. I stood on the bed, tried to reach it, but wasn't tall enough. I walked back into the living room, could still hear him on the phone, and headed outside. It was hot. Not as hot as it would get in July and August in New York, but the sun felt more intense. In the thin, clear air, its rays were scorching. I looked across the sage toward the woods, trying to imagine my father looking at them when he was my age. I knew somewhere up there he'd killed his first elk, spent his first night alone in the forest, and taken my mother for walks when she came home with him on the weekends while there were in college.

My grandfather left to pick up Darla and Katrina shortly after six, and when I heard his pickup pounding back down the driveway half an hour later I retreated to my room. I was going to make myself scarce. I lay on my bed and listened to them in the kitchen. Darla's voice had as much resonance as my grandfather's, and eventually, she raised the inevitable question concerning my whereabouts.

"Kyle, you around here?" my grandfather called. "He's probably cowering in his room. His appetite will get the better of his shyness before too long." I heard a hunk of butter hit a hot skillet. "Damn kid is still like a pup in a new house, but he'll get over it. Katrina, how are you?"

I had almost tricked myself into believing Darla had come alone.

"You can take a walk outside if you want. Supper will be ready shortly, but you don't need to wait in here."

I strained to hear a reply, but none came. I heard the door open and close, and peeled back a corner of the blanket over my window, expecting at any moment to see a smaller version of Darla waddle around the side of the house.

Katrina was thin. She was going to be tall, like her mother, but her figure was vastly different. Their hair was the same, long and dark, but that didn't set them apart from any other Indians I'd seen. Darla's steps were small and her daughter's were long. Katrina was wearing shorts, and I doubted her mother ever wore anything other than sweats. I watched her move, picking her feet up with purpose, her hands behind her back as though she was slightly bored, then dropped the blanket when she turned toward me. I waited five or ten seconds before looking again. I could see her face, but she didn't know I was watching. The first thing I noticed was the color of her lipstick. It was bright. As bright as Flo's. It might even have been the same shade. It made her lips look larger than they really were, giving them a puffy appearance similar to some of the high school girls' I'd seen back home. Her eyes looked large, too. Her lashes were long, coated heavily with mascara as black as her hair. All the make-up made her face look pale. Too pale. She wore a plain white T-shirt long enough to cover most of her shorts. It was patternless, and when she turned to the side I could see the shoulder straps of her bra through it. Her mother called out the door, and she disappeared. I was still standing at the window when my grandfather knocked on my door.

"Ready to eat, Kyle?" He lowered his voice. "You give it a shot and if you don't like it, well, we'll go to the stock auction up to Butte and get you a bum ewe. Now come on."

I dragged my feet to the kitchen, stood in the doorway a second, then took the plunge inside.

"Kyle, you've met Darla." My grandfather spared no time in making introductions. "This is her daughter, Katrina."

I looked at her just long enough to see her eyes, waved, looked away, then sat down, sensing everyone at the table was looking at me.

"They look alike don't they?" I heard Darla ask her daughter.

"We look alike, think alike, act alike . . . shit, ain't hardly any differences between us," my grandfather said. "Yes, cut from the same cloth, huh, Kyle?"

I didn't look up.

The brook trout and elk were good. I would have eaten a second helping, but Darla beat me to it. When we finished, my grandfather got out a bottle of whiskey. Yukon Jack.

"Shall we head north this evening, Darla?" he said as he poured her a glass. "Cool off a bit from our last voyage to Mexico. Care to join us, Kyle? Be hunting caribou soon."

I shook my head.

"Eastern teetotaler. We'll correct that before it's all said and done. Katrina, are you going to refuse me, too?"

"Not her," Darla said.

"My grandfather poured a little more than a swallow into a glass for her and she tipped it back. He looked at me as if to be sure I wouldn't have any, and I looked away. Katrina might have been fifteen, but I didn't think she was sixteen. I was beginning to wonder if drinking was a prerequisite to being an Indian. Neither of my parents drank, and I had grown up in a household where offering a teenager a shot of whiskey would have been unthinkable. I stood up, and three quick steps took me to the door.

Outside, I sat on the skidder tire and watched the sun set. It didn't go down for a long time, but when it did, twilight rapidly faded to night. The heat of the day evaporated, and soon I was cold. I didn't hear Katrina walk outside, and when she sat down beside me it startled me.

"They're drunk," she said pointing over her shoulder to the house. "Cole's singing."

It was true. I could hear him belting out his own adaptation of a sailor's song.

"What do you do with a drunken logger? What do you do with a drunken logger?" His voice was too strong to be held in by four walls. I flipped a pebble off the toe of my left boot.

"What, don't you think it's funny?" There was an echo of her mother in Katrina's voice.

I didn't think it was funny, but I nodded anyway.

"So, you're from New York?" Katrina's breath smelled as though her first drink might not have been her last.

"Yeah."

"What's it like?"

"Different." It was the shortest answer I could think of, and at the same time was probably the most accurate. "It's different."

"In what way?"

"I don't know, just different."

"How?"

"Everything."

"The mountains?"

"Aren't any. Not like these."

"Really? What is it, all flat?"

"Not all of it."

"Lots of cities?"

"Yeah."

"I've never been to a big city. Like to go sometime. Mom says there's lots to do. You live near any cities?"

"Syracuse."

"Is it big?"

"I guess."

"You been to Dillon?"

"No. I just got here."

"That's where I go to school. It's okay. Better than Butte." She stood up quickly, stretched, and reached for my hand. "You want to go for a walk?"

For a fraction of an instant, I did, but I got up without her help. "I don't know, I'm kind of tired. I'll probably go to bed."

"I think we're staying here tonight."

"Yeah. You can sleep in my room. My grandfather left a sleeping bag for me on the couch."

Nothing was further from the truth, but the sleeping bag he'd covered me up with my first night at his house was still wadded up on the couch. When Katrina and I walked inside, Darla and my grandfather had gone to bed. I could hear them in his room, their voices low, slurred from the whiskey, interrupted by kissing noises.

I had trouble falling asleep. Close to an hour passed. I hadn't heard anything from my grandfather's room for ten minutes and figured they must have done whatever they were going to. Then my grandfather punched something. The wall, the headboard, I wasn't sure what. The whole house shook from the blow, and his words were clear.

"Christ all fucking mighty!" I heard his feet hit the floor. "By god, this is an indignation if ever there was one."

Darla laughed and his door opened. I closed my eyes tight and pretended to by asleep. My grandfather walked into the kitchen and I heard water run in the sink. He stayed in there a while then came and sat down on the floor in front of the couch. He spoke quietly, but I'm not convinced he believed I was asleep.

"Here you are, Kyle, and I can't say I'm surprised. But that's all right. Just got a few too many morals in you is all. And here I am, too. You . . . you too many morals, and me . . . too old and too much whiskey. An unfortunate pair we are." He stifled a cough, stood up, and patted my back. "Don't ever get old, Kyle. It's pure hell on a man."

I watched him walk back to his room in his underwear, then closed my eyes. Without his clothes, he looked older. The veins in his legs and loose skin around the sides of his stomach gave him away. For no good reason, I felt frightened. The darkness seemed to hold something in it that would get

59

me as surely as it would my grandfather. Something dreadfully patient, willing to wait forever if need be. I knew it could wait, and I knew it wouldn't have to. I pulled the sleeping bag up over my head, but it was down in there as well. It was everywhere, and even as I slept it watched. It watched my grandfather more closely, but it had its eye on me as well, and there wasn't a damn thing I could do about it.

CHAPTER 6

C ALVIN BULLTAIL was the biggest man I had ever seen. Easily. He was six feet eight inches tall and my grandfather said he weighed three hundred and fifty pounds. His fingers were longer than my whole hand, and his biceps were the size of my thighs. He wore his hair in dreadlocks, tied off at their bases with brightly colored beads that clacked together like castanets when he walked. He'd played football for the Nebraska Cornhuskers for a year. Then he beat a man to death in an Ogalala bar and went to prison. My grandfather said during the ten years Calvin was locked up he found religion. Wouldn't hurt a flea now, he said. I was skeptical. Standing in front of the Six Point, dwarfing the motorcycle he'd ridden in from the Crow reservation in Hardin, his painted, sleeveless leather jacket zipped tightly around his massive chest, Calvin was not only the biggest man I had ever seen, he was scariest. His jeans were dirty, caked with grease and mud, and his Wellington-style cowboy boots were scarred like the tires on my grandfather's skidder.

"Calvin Bulltail, you big son of a bitch!" My grandfather shook his hand. "Damn glad you decided to make it. Lord's work you're doing, Calvin. Only I expect your presence will be equally . . . no, more effective than the Savior's himself." He stepped to the side to introduce me. "This is my grandson, Kyle. Kyle, say hello to the biggest, meanest, Sunday school teacher who's ever peeked at the Bible."

I eased forward and extended my hand. Calvin wrapped his around it and shook it gently. His voice was soft and calm, but somehow that added to his menacing appearance. He could squash me with one blow and he knew it.

"Nice to meet you, Kyle." He turned to my grandfather and I stepped back. "Actually, it's the biggest, meanest, English teacher now." He smiled a broad smile, and his teeth, unlike Badger's, were straight and white. "Got my certificate a couple of years ago. Teaching on the res full time now."

"By Christ, good for you." My grandfather reached up and slapped him between the shoulders. "Dealing with hellions like yourself. That's all right. Any of them beat up the cops?"

Calvin blushed.

"See, Kyle, Mr. Bulltail wasn't exactly the model student. Used to spend the school year here in Mistake. Lived with an uncle just outside town. When he was in the eighth grade he came to school drunk one day. Wouldn't leave. Had to call for the sheriff. Calvin man-handled the deputy they sent. Threw the poor bastard out the door by his nuts. He worked for me piling lumber on the weekends, so I got called to town to settle him down. He was a handful!"

Calvin looked embarrassed. "That was a long time ago. A long, long time ago." He straddled his bike. "What time you want me to meet you tomorrow?"

"Aren't you going to have a drink?" My grandfather stepped past him up onto the porch.

"No, not today. What time tomorrow?"

"Auction's at ten, so why don't we plan on getting there about nine. Give us some time to get things set up. Gonna be quite a party."

"Okay, nine." He rolled his tongue along the outside of his lips, looking down at the gas tank between his legs. I didn't think anything would make a man of his stature nervous, but he didn't look comfortable. "Won't be too wild, will it? I tend to think that you're the one who needs settling down now, Cole."

"Don't worry about a thing. I've got this all under control, and that's the way it's going to stay. All under control. We'll meet at the convention center about nine."

Calvin nodded, and with an effortless push of his right leg started the motorcycle.

"Wear the same coat and jeans tomorrow, too," my grandfather hollered after him as he pulled into the highway.

Calvin waved.

My grandfather said he wanted to finish skidding the logs we'd cut the other day. He said it wouldn't take too long, but by the time he'd taken Darla and Katrina home and met Calvin, it was after eleven. We ate lunch in the clearing where we parked the truck, swatting at horse flies between bites.

"Is that true?" I asked my grandfather, hoping I could engage him in a conversation that would prolong lunch. "Is Calvin really an English teacher?"

"You bet. Damn good one I imagine."

"And he killed someone?"

"Uh-huh." My grandfather wiped a piece of bread from the corner of his beard. "Big man like Calvin, he's a target in a bar. Every two-bit drunk wants to try him. Thinks if he can whip him it'll impress someone. Yeah, the way I understand it Calvin wasn't doing anything. Sitting there having a drink and some guy comes up to him and bets him a hundred bucks he can kick his ass. Before Calvin even answered him, the son of a bitch hit him with a pool stick. Knocked him out cold and gave him a concussion. Couple of his football buddies took him to the hospital, then to the police station. Supposedly the cops wouldn't do anything about it. I figure it's more likely that Calvin didn't give them time to do anything. It was late when he got back to the bar. Most everyone had gone home, but not the cock-sucker who clubbed him. He was going to brag as long as there were people who'd listen. Calvin hit him one time. Shoved his nose bones into his brain, I guess. Guy never quivered. Stone dead. Got ten years for it. Now, we ready to go to work?"

It didn't take long. I helped hook the trees to the skidder, and my grandfather pulled them down to the truck. He said a log truck would pick them up the next day. He drove the skidder hard, slamming it over brush piles, crashing down into ruts, and charging straight over stumps. In less than three hours, all that remained in the clear cut was a handful of broken tops.

"Okay, Kyle, you drive her out of here this time." My grandfather pushed himself back in the seat so I could sit between his legs. "I'll shift for you, but you work the gas and steering."

I sat on the foam cushion in front of him and turned the wheel. I expected to have to use all my strength, but the hydraulics moved the wheels easily. The accelerator went down hard, and I didn't give it much gas.

"Throttle her up, Kyle. She's a diesel. Got to run her like you hate her."

I stepped on the gas and the engine roared. My grandfather worked the clutch, and I drove around everything he'd driven over. By the time we reached the truck, I was having fun. It felt good to control such a powerful machine.

"There," my grandfather said when he shut it off. "Tell your folks about that. Just wait till your mom hears how you drove the skidder. She'll be so proud of you."

We both laughed until he began coughing. He hacked long enough to take his breath and had to sit down before getting into the truck. He knew I was worried.

"Fucking horse flies! Bad enough that they've got to put the chew on a man, but by Jesus when they cruise down your throat I say enough is enough."

I knew he hadn't swallowed a horse fly, and I think he knew it. He spit out his window and put on a good show of shuddering, but didn't look at me until we reached the highway. "Want to stop and scope it out?" he asked.

"What?"

"The rapids. The gorge. Take a closer look. Get right down by the river."

"Sure."

We pulled over to the side of the road, tight enough to the cliff on my side so I had to get out his door. With the engine off, the full rumble of the river filled my ears. We walked across the highway, stepped over the guard cables, and stood on a narrow strip of bank less than a foot above the water.

The river's movement was mesmerizing. There was a car-sized boulder peeking up a few feet off shore, bathed in foam, glossy and smooth from years of standing in the path of snowmelt. I watched the water collide with it, exploding into numerous droplets which disappeared into the raging current on the downstream side. All up and down the rive were similar boulders, some rounded or flat, others jagged like giant, prehistoric sharks' teeth. Medicine man or not, no one had ever successfully run this gauntlet. I was sure of it.

"Have to keep her smack against the far bank up there," my grandfather said as he pointed upstream. "Get past that white rock on the outside, then cut hard for the middle of the flow. Keep her from going sideways. That would be the key. Down through here we'd be like clowns in a rodeo. Only we'd be dodging boulders instead of Brahmas. Not much different though, really. Have to wait long enough so we knew which way we were being yanked before we tried to avoid them. Once we cleared the bend," I followed his eyes downstream to where the river turned, slamming into a rock wall in a churning expanse of whitecaps, "we'd be home free. What do you say, shall we take a crack at it?"

"You and me?"

"Goddamned right. Nobody else fool enough to do it."

I frowned. I wanted to believe he was kidding. It would have been funny then. But I knew better. He'd "take a crack at it" and if it killed us so be it.

"Kyle." He was getting worked up, the bright glimmer in his eyes like a train's light at the far end of a tunnel. "Kyle, every once in a while a man's got to prove to himself that he's still got a set of them. Otherwise he might as well go to Tibet, tear his balls off, and work as a eunuch. Know what I mean?"

I stepped back onto the road. Next, my grandfather would suggest swimming the gorge.

"We can do this, my man. Shit, it's in our blood to do it. Been too long since a Richards shot the gorge. We can do this." He crossed the cables and stood beside me, breathing heavily, his eyes still fixed on the river. He adjusted his cowboy hat, clapped his hands together, and skipped across the road to the truck.

I looked at the water once more, the roiling torrent that would bury us, then climbed in ahead of my grandfather.

"Cole, what'd you mean when you said it's been too long since a Richards shot the gorge?"

"What's that? Speak up." We were flying down the highway, a gear lower than we should have been.

"Back there by the river. What'd you mean when you said a Richards floated it?"

"That what I said?"

"Yeah."

"Must have been talking crazy. Maybe I said it as a metaphor. You know, just used it as an example. Meant it's been too long since we took a chance."

My grandfather meant what he said. If there was one thing I'd learned about him, that was it. Back at his house, I was still thinking about it, looking out of the corner of my eye at his canoe. The paint was worn from the bottom, and the sides were dented. It wouldn't fare any better in the gorge than a dry twig.

"Grab a set of your fancy clothes, Kyle." My grandfather's instructions snapped me out of my trance. "You and I want to look sharp for this."

I picked a pair of pressed slacks out of my suitcase and a matching button-down shirt. I emptied my duffel bag onto my bed and put the clothes inside.

My grandfather's phone began ringing from the kitchen. He was in his room, presumably gathering proper attire for the auction, and didn't seem concerned about the call.

"Want me to get it?" I called to him.

"No. Let it ring. We need to get out of here."

It kept ringing, stopped, then began again.

"Jesus Christ!" A dress shoe sailed out of his room, bounced off the couch, and slid in under the wood stove. He stomped into the kitchen, and I heard him pick up the receiver. "What do you want?"

I stepped silently into the living room to her the conversation.

"Kyle? Yes, he's here." My grandfather had his back to me, but from the tone of his voice it wasn't anyone he cared to talk to. "Well, I'm not sure. He's in bed. Yes, in bed. No, he's not sick. Christ almighty, woman, he's in bed because he's recovering. Made a man of him last night. Had a pretty little girl over for him and he took right to her. Told me this morning they did it three times. Now goddamn it, that's why he's in bed. In bed, flat on his back, in the only position you ever looked good in."

He slammed the receiver down hard enough so the phone protested with a feeble ring. And then it rang again.

"Now, by the love of god, woman, this is intolerable!" He was shouting. "Fine, you want to talk to him, fine. Kyle." He turned around, covering the phone. "Kyle, it's Boston. Do you wish to speak with her?"

"Who?"

"Boston. You know, that haughty bitch holed up with that fat banker. Your grandmother, Kyle. Do you have anything to say to her?"

I took the phone from him and waited until he went back into his room to speak. "Grandma?"

"Oh, Kyle, I'm so sorry." She sounded much closer than Gloucester, Massachusetts. "I'll tell your parents at once. We'll get you right back home."

"It's okay, Grandma. He's just upset."

"You don't need to bear the brunt of that man's anger, Kyle. Wait until your mother hears about this."

"Grandma, I said it's okay. Really. Thanks for my birthday present. I really like it."

"Oh, sweetie, you're welcome. Now put your grandfather back on please."

I glanced into his room. He was looking for the shoe he threw, kicking things around, swearing loudly.

"He's outside, grandma. Want me to tell him something?"

"No, that's all right. You hang in there, okay?"

"I will. I love you, Grandma."

"I love you, too. You call me anytime you want."

As soon as I hung up, my grandfather began grilling me about what she'd wanted.

"Wanted to get you back east I bet, huh?"

I nodded.

"Well, you want to go?"

"No." I meant it, too. Three days ago I would have jumped at the chance, but not now.

"Good. We'll tell Boston to use her ass for something other than her banker's humping pillow and get out here to see you. Where the fuck is my shoe?" He kicked the wall and every window in the house shook. I fished it out from under the couch and handed it to him. "Thank you. All right, we ready?"

"We're leaving tonight?"

"Yes. We'll get up there at a good hour, get us each a nice steak, and then go to the titty bar. Get you nipples to nipples with one of their dancers. That sound good?" He didn't wait for my answer. He had his clothes in a garbage bag, including the shoes, and wedged them behind the seat of his truck.

"Do you ever see much of your grandmother, Kyle?"

My grandfather's question caught me off guard. We'd been driving along Interstate 15 between Divide and Butte, talking about fishing and hunting, looking for antelope. If he hadn't asked, I wouldn't have dared mention her name in his presence.

"Grandma?"

"Yeah, Boston. You know, the woman who called."

"Not very often. Sometimes at Christmas or in the summer if we go to the ocean."

"And she's still with that banker, huh?"

"Something like that."

"Bitch." He tightened his grip on the steering wheel. "You know why she left, don't you?"

Other than the fact that, as my parents put it, "they didn't get along," I wasn't sure why. They'd separated before I was born so it never seemed strange to me.

"Well, I'll tell you why. And it ain't going to take long." My grandfather slowed only slightly at the junction of Interstate 90, smiling as the tries squealed and I leaned his way. "I met your grandmother when I was twenty-three years old. Her folks, rich, southern folks, had her out here on vacation. Had taken her down to the park to see Old Faithful and the rest of that bullshit. I working in the mines at the time, cutting talc, busting my ass all day, drinking all night. Living it right up. Rodeoing, to. That's where I met her. Big rodeo up to Butte. You see the buckles in my room?"

"Yeah."

"If it had hair, Kyle, I could ride it. Wouldn't let go for nothing, and there weren't many that could throw me. Shit, if it was as big as it is today, probably could have made some money. Anyway, she saw me ride and win, and decided she'd have herself a cowboy. Glamorous notion. Course she wound up pregnant with your dad over the affair. Insisted a marry her, too. Jesus, did it ever piss her folks off. Well, we did the proper thing and tied the knot, but we were just too different, Kyle. I reckon that's it in a nutshell. We were two worlds brought together by lust and it's a pity we couldn't have parted company without further . . . obligations."

A snake darted across the road and we served toward it.

"I get the fucker?" my grandfather asked, looking over his shoulder.

"I don't know." I was just glad we didn't end up in the ditch.

"Hope so. Looked like a rattler." He tapped the snake-skin band on his hat. "Right here's the only place I can stomach those sons of bitches." He shook like a wet dog and cleared his throat. "Well, where was I? Oh yeah, we were different. Real different. No other way of looking at it. Didn't take long to realize it wouldn't last. She felt she had to stick around until your dad was out of college. Don't really know whether to cuss her or admire her for that. But that's what she did. When your dad moved east, she did, too. And I can forgive her for everything. Everything except your mother. It's no secret that there's no blood loss between us, so I don't feel bad telling you this. Your dad wasn't maybe the whore-keeper I was in my day, but he got around a little. Used to bring a university woman home every now and then.

Brought your mother home. I knew that was trouble right away. Had the same look in her eye that your grandmother did when she saw me. Infatuation. Weren't no more than a piece of ass to your dad at first."

I shifted in my seat as the conversation grew too graphic and too close to home.

"I said at first." My grandfather lifted the carpet and looked at me. "No, can't say it was anything else in the beginning. But your grandmother took to this gal right away. They were a lot alike. She always made her feel right at home . . . not that I didn't, but she made her feel like she was home. Gave her the impression your dad came from somewhere he didn't. Your parents spent more and more time together, and there comes a point when love's inevitable. Your mom couldn't live in the west, and I knew it. So did your grandmother. And that was how she got even with me for being the man I was. For not lying at her feet. For not thinking about how we could make more money. For not giving a good goddamn about her fine southern up-bringing. Oh, she made sure your parents fell head over heels for each other. Maybe they would have anyway. Who knows? Guess it worked out for them, but I lost my son in it. I remember sitting in the living room right after he graduated when they were talking about looking for work. Your mom did the talking, and there wasn't a mention of staying in Montana. That was it. Over, done with, kaput. And how your grandmother smiled. Like she'd saved them. Yeah, I can forgive everything else that lady might have done or been, but I cannot and will not forgive her for that. And that, Kyle Richards, is the beginning and end of it."

On a green road sign, I saw we were one hundred miles from Missoula. It was a long way to ride without saying anything, but I didn't. My grandfather had two bad spells of coughing, pulling over for the second, but apart from that it was quiet. Even the exhaust seemed subdued. I stared at a beer bottle on the floor, trying to focus on something easier to grasp than what I'd heard. Each time I glanced over at my grandfather, the image of him in his underwear the night before, looking old and worn down, came back to me.

Despite the silence, the ride to Missoula didn't seem to take very long. We were coming into the city, being passed by a steady stream of vehicles, squinting against the sun, now low in the sky ahead of us, when my grandfather yanked the pickup over onto the shoulder and turned the key.

"I'll be fucked, Kyle, look at that." He pointed to a hill, devoid of trees, dotted with sage, that rose sharply from the interstate. Near the top was an oversized billboard with a sky-blue peace symbol painted on it. "That abomination should be cut down. Wish to hell I'd brought a saw. Do you see it?"

"Yeah. What is it?"

"A symbol."

"For peace, right?"

"It masquerades as such. Truth is, it's a symbol of Missoula's deterioration. Gone from a mill town of hard-luckers to a bastion of modern hippies. No more fist fights in these bars. No sir, now a man's got to wait for the folks at the counter to turn around before he knows who to hit on. Long hair don't separate the sexes in this city. Hairy armpits don't, either. Man's got to be careful around here. End up taking a faggot home. Or might get his balls cut off by some man-hating feminist. Kyle, the world's going to hell all around us." My grandfather spit forcefully and started the truck. "We're caught in a one-way shit slide, and it's all downhill."

We ate at a little diner on the west side of the city, not far off the interstate. My grandfather ordered us a pair of T-bones, extra rare, and got himself a pitcher of beer. The steaks arrived shortly, draping off the large, sliver platters they came on, dripping bright red juice onto our table. I liked my meat well done, but my grandfather had made a production out of ordering them rare. It meant something to him for us to eat the same meal. By the time we finished, the sun had set.

"Figure we'd better go get us a little tits and ass," he said loudly so the well-dressed couple near the door was sure to hear. The woman lowered her eyes and her date pretended he didn't notice. "Yeah, go out on the town and pick us up a mother/daughter combo. What do you think, boy, shall we try for a repeat of Reno?"

I ducked out of the diner as soon as the door opened wide enough to let me through. My grandfather tipped his hat to the couple and laughed all the way to the truck.

"Come on, Kyle, ease up on me. Just did it to get a rise out of them. Didn't like the way they were looking at me when they first came in. Think they said something about my hat. Come on, no harm done. Hey, you ever been to a strip joint?"

I didn't answer. The night was cool and I was tired. I would have been just as happy to find a motel.

"No, huh?" He pointed to the gearshift, and I pulled it down into second as we headed up the street. "Well, I know how manfully you resist the carnal impulses, so I won't lie and tell you it'll be fun. But I reckon you can soldier through it all right. Then again, this goddamned town may have gotten rid of the place all together."

It hadn't, and I knew as soon as I saw it, rough-log siding illuminated by the blue neon dress of a lewd-looking woman bending seductively over a table on the billboard above the parking lot, that it wasn't the type of place I'd enjoy visiting.

We entered, me a step or two behind, through a set of swinging doors covered with black padding. A big man, more fat than muscular, stopped us in a narrow hallway where the lights in the ceiling were dim and we could only partially see the dance floor. The silhouettes of naked women moved like shadows ahead of us.

"Hold it." The man put a beefy hand on my grandfather's chest. "How old's the boy?"

"Just turned fourteen." My grandfather took the man's hand and gently pushed it aside.

"Fourteen? You gotta be kidding me. Eighteen, maybe. Twenty, no problem." The man raised his hand again. "But fourteen, no way. Now get the hell out of here."

"Nothing he ain't seen before. Come on, we won't be any trouble." My grandfather sounded pleasant.

"Hey, what's the matter with you? I said no. Now get the fuck out of here, old man, and take the kid with you. Ain't gonna happen."

"Very well then." My grandfather stepped to the side as though we were going to walk around the bouncer. He couldn't quite squeeze by, and as he lowered his shoulder the man slapped him square on the cheek. My grandfather backed up, closed his fists, and the bouncer lifted his hands, bobbing his head back and forth like an overweight prize fighter.

"Kyle, the man fancies himself a pugilist. Well, I've got something for him." He stepped back, shoved me out through the doors, and headed for the truck.

"I don't care what you've got, you old bastard. If you try to come back in here I'll bust you up." The man stood in the doorway, sticking his chest out, shouting after us.

My grandfather kept his leather gloves tucked between the sun visor and roof on his side of the pickup. They were tight-fitting and stained from the fingertips to the wrist straps, which he snugged down on his way back to the bar, taking one step to every three of mine. The bouncer had just gone in, and a rusty hinge on one of the doors was still squeaking. We came in fast, and my grandfather caught him before he'd reached the end of the hallway. The fat man turned, looked surprised, then reeled backward as my grandfather drove his left fist into his face. He caught himself before he fell, stood long enough to receive an uppercut and a hook, then went down and didn't move.

"You tell your doorman to think about this the next time he raises a hand against someone. I won't be slapped. Not by him or anyone," my grandfather told the two men who'd come over from the dance floor when the bouncer hit the carpet. "He can be grateful I'm not ten years younger and in the mood to haul his ass outside and stomp him the way I ought to. Okay, Kyle," he looked over his shoulder at me without turning his back on the men in front of him, "we'll go now. I reckon we've worn out our welcome."

Safely on the road again, I breathed easier. The fight had been exciting, and it had happened so fast I didn't have time to worry, but I couldn't help thinking my grandfather would wade into a confrontation regardless of his chances of success, and that concerned me. I didn't want to see him end up in the position of the bouncer, or worse yet, "stomped."

"There are certain things a man cannot tolerate and still call himself a man, Kyle." We were stopped at a red light, and my grandfather wadded the loose carpet up against the roof so he could see me. "There are way worse things than an ass kicking in my book. Know what I mean?"

I couldn't think of many things I'd rather avoid.

"The bruises and cuts, they'll heal up. Quick, too. Quick compared to your mind. Soon as man lets himself be bullied, soon as he tucks his tail and turns his head, soon as he gets walked on when he shouldn't, he's ruined. Done for. If I'd let that overgrown tub of shit back there manhandle me without a fight, I couldn't sleep for a month. It'd hurt me more than if he'd busted every rib in my chest."

"How'd you know he wouldn't?" The light turned green but there was no one behind us, and we remained at the intersection.

"Didn't. Don't ever know for sure. You can see a lot in a man's eyes. Generally enough to know whether you can whip him or not. Most of the time those bullies don't have the look to back up their bluff, but you can't always tell. Anyway, that don't matter. Every man's got to have a line no one can cross without knocking him down. Then he's got to be prepared to get and stand his ground even if he knows he'll get knocked down again. You let someone walk on that little part of you that really cares, the closest thing you've got to a living soul, and you might as well cash in your chips. Game's over and you've lost everything that counts. A man can have all the morals of the pope, but if he don't stand up for them when push comes to shove, he ain't nothing more than a hypocrite. Nobody will say that about me. Even those who hate me.

The light changed again, and we pulled through. Driving through downtown Missoula, I was quiet. I was scared. Not afraid of my grandfather getting into more fights, but afraid because I couldn't think of anything I felt strongly enough about to take a beating for. And I knew my grandfather meant every word he said. It wasn't talk. If that bouncer had beaten him half to death and slapped him again a week later, he'd have fought him with everything he had, and wouldn't have waited a split second. The more I thought about it, the more frightened I became, and by the time we stopped at our motel I was ready to fight the world over anything just to prove to myself I'd do it.

Our room at the Economy Stop Motel, a single-story building sitting just above the flood plain of the Clark Fork River, smelled like urine. My grandfather complained at the office, then laughed when the man working the desk asked him what he expected for twelve and a half bucks.

"Fair enough," my grandfather said. "Good point."

So when I drifted off to sleep later that night, I did so with the strong ammonia-like odor of urine in my nostrils, and I didn't sleep well. I dreamed about floating through the gorge, only this time my canoe was tossed like an aspen leaf in a high wind. I smashed into a boulder, capsized, and water filled my lungs. I should have been able to wake up, but I couldn't. Everything around me turned red, my vision blurred, and then I was floating, not in the river, but high above it, and the air I breathed was icy cold. I figured I was dead, so when my grandfather woke me up in the morning, I looked at him suspiciously, trying to figure out if it had really been a dream.

My grandfather didn't like the looks of the convention center. He said the giant round building, ringed by ornate pillars, should be blown up. The judgement seemed rather harsh to me, but the modern building went against everything I connected with Montana, so as long as my grandfather didn't have any dynamite, I was willing to agree with him.

We were there early. The only other vehicles in the parking lot, which was the size of several football fields, were light brown trucks with the circular insignia of the state grizzly bear on their sides. Fish and Wildlife trucks. One of them was hitched to an enclosed trailer, and my grandfather said it was where they kept the animals that were going to be auctioned. We waited by it, hoping to catch a peek of the specimens as they were unloaded, but that had been done before we got there. A little before nine people began filing in, not just from Montana, but from all over the west. There were license plates from Idaho, Washington, Wyoming, and several from California. The drivers were wearing suits for the most part, though not so fancy that we felt out of place in our good clothes. My grandfather left his felt hat in the truck, and had combed his hair straight back away from his face. In his sport coat, he looked dignified. He stood by the entrance, nodding politely as the bidders walked by him as though he was with the Fish and Wildlife. Several men asked him questions regarding what was up for sale, and he made up answers without hesitation.

The Indians arrived together in a convoy of ten vehicles, led by big Calvin Bulltail on his motorcycle. He took them around the parking lot like the marshal of the Fourth of July parade in New York City, sitting a long way back on his seat, revving his engine, his long hair drifting out behind him. My grandfather met them at the door, shaking hands with most, whispering a short set of directions in their ears, bowing to Sarah, accompanied by her grandson, Allen. From his shirt pocket, my grandfather pulled out a crisp, new, one dollar bill and gave it to the boy. He was younger than me, but almost as tall, and as skinny a boy as I'd ever seen. He took the dollar, held it flat in his hands, and smiled.

Inside, folding metal chairs stretched across a tile floor, twenty rows deep and as many wide. They faced a podium behind which lay confiscated game, some bagged, all tagged, and as varied as Montana's wildlife. There was a wolverine pelt, vacuum packed in a thick bag, salted bear and lion hides, whitetail and mule deer antlers, and more than a dozen elk heads. Allen's was easily the best of the bunch. The long tines, black at their bases, white near their tips, were uniform and heavy, and the main beams looked like small tree trunks.

"Take this, Kyle." My grandfather handed me a pocket-sized notebook and pen. "You just come around with me. Stay back a little so they can't see what you're up to. Be writing in this, okay?"

"What do yo want me to write?"

"Anything. Doesn't matter. Just don't let anyone see. Just a little something I cooked up to make it look official. Ready? Looks like the boys are in place."

The Indians had spread out around the chairs, standing straight, their expressionless eyes trained on the elk heads. They were quite a sight. Any with tattoos were wearing muscle shirts, their arms folded in front of them so their hands pushed their biceps into full view. Other had long, black leather jackets buttoned all the way up as though there might be something underneath, and they all looked like they meant business. Calvin stood in the middle, a few feet behind the last row of chairs, and I noticed he'd stuck a long feather, maybe from an eagle, into one of his dreadlocks. He let it hang over his chest where it twisted in an undetectable breeze as though it still possessed some of the bird's ability to fly.

There were more than three hundred people prepared to bid, so most of the chairs were occupied. My grandfather started in the front, and went seat to seat, asking each person what they'd come to bid on, and where they were from. He told those who asked that he was doing a survey for the Fish and Wildlife. He had some trouble making eye contact because without exception everyone was looking at the Indians. There were five uniformed game wardens milling around behind the podium, and they too looked nervous. My grandfather told anyone who'd come to bid on the elk not to try for Allen's. He told them the circumstances behind its confiscation, and hinted that the Indians were not about to stand idly by and see it go to anyone other than the boy. Some men looked disappointed, but only one argued.

I was following my grandfather, scribbling in the notebook, keeping it tipped toward me so no one could see what I was writing, and we had made it through nearly the whole crowd. A man in a suit and tie, who I heard say was from New Mexico, had his heart set on Allen's elk.

"No, that's the one I want," he told my grandfather. I stopped writing. "Gonna look good in my restaurant. If the boy wants it, he'll have to bid against me. I don't know what else to tell you."

My grandfather bent over the man's chair and lowered his voice. "Don't you think the kid ought to keep it? Jesus Christ, he's just a boy. What's your problem?"

"I don't have a problem. Not unless you insist on trying to prevent me from bidding on anything here I want to. And then you'll have the problem.

Maybe I should go up and tell those wardens. I tend to think they'd take my side. The kid broke the law, right?"

"Why can't you buy another head?" My grandfather was prepared to reason with him. For how long, I wasn't sure, but he wasn't going to lose his cool right away.

"I'm going to bid on two of the others, but I want the big one, too. Hey, I've got a right to anything I can afford. Now why don't you go sit down before you find yourself in hot water. Okay?" The man dusted off the lapels of his coat and settled into his seat.

"Hot water?" My grandfather didn't raise his voice, but there was a new harshness in it. A cold edge that sounded intimidating. "Hot water? Listen to me you mean-spirited, self-righteous son-of-a-bitch." He was spitting on the man, whose face had lost all color when my grandfather's tone changed. "You see that man behind you? Go ahead goddamn it, take a look." He turned slightly in his seat and Calvin scowled at him. "That big bastard's their chief. Came all the way from the Wyoming line, and he ain't been smoking the peace pipe if you know what I mean. No, he's real concerned, and I don't just mean for the boy. His people have begun to talk . . . say he's leaning too far away from their culture. Pushing for more education in white schools and what not. No, he's come here with a different agenda. He's come to crack some skulls. Show he's not afraid to stand up to the white man. Mister, he's just itching to scalp someone. He owes me a favor from a long time ago, and it's all I can do to hold him back. Wanted to come in and just get with it. So you go ahead and get the wardens. They'll have me removed, and maybe him, too, if he doesn't kill them all first. Then you can buy whatever the hell pleases you, but someday you'll hear a heavy footstep in your restaurant. Sure as shit he'll come even the score, and I'll tell you what." My grandfather bent even closer to him so their faces almost touched and I had to inch forward to hear what he said. "When that day comes you won't have gotten up in the morning wishing you'd never been born, but that's exactly how you'll feel when the sun sets. And the biggest fucking elk head in the world won't make the slightest bit of difference."

The auctioneer announced the first item up for bids, and my grandfather straightened up, pointed to the wardens, and shrugged. The man didn't blink for a long time, then got up holding his stomach, and walked out the door. We didn't see him again.

I was surprised at how high some of the animals went for. Two men bid off against each other for a large tom lion pelt that eventually sold for six hundred and eighty dollars. The deer, especially the mulies, all went for around three hundred, and one cinnamon-colored black bear brought more than a thousand. The whole time none of the Indians moved. They stood without so much as twitching an eyebrow, eyes still fixed on Allen's bull. The wardens, in between marking the sold hides and horns, conversed in a tight group, each man looking up from the huddle frequently as though he was afraid one of the Indians would get him from behind. This gave my grandfather great pleasure, and if he told me once that the wardens were "up the Little Bighorn without a paddle," I heard it ten times.

The auctioneer began the bidding on Allen's elk at five hundred dollars.

"Who'll give me five hundred?" His voice echoed through the crowd and not a single hand went up. "Come on, five hundred. Scored three forty. Got the cape and everything. Make a fine mount. Let's hear it, five hundred dollars."

No one moved.

"Okay, four." The auctioneer wasn't talking as fast. "Get it cheap, get it fast, get it now. A steal for four hundred dollars. Big six point. Come on, somebody get us underway."

Allen's voice was high and clear, and even from where my grandfather and I sat in the back we cold hear him. His hand went up above the heads in front of us, waved confidently, and he made his offer.

"One dollar."

The auctioneer stepped back away from the podium.

"One dollar," Allen said again.

"Okay, we'll start at the bottom." The auctioneer tried to laugh, but it didn't sound sincere. "We've got one, now one, and one, and who'll give one hundred? One hundred dollars for the big boy."

Allen had dropped his hand when the auctioneer recognized his bid. When the man paused, dumbfounded that no one would offer it for such a fine trophy, he lifted it again. I could see the bill my grandfather had him sticking out from each side of his closed fist.

"One dollar. I bid one dollar."

The auctioneer turned away from his microphone and joined the wardens in their huddle. At exactly the same instant, every Indian took one step forward, their feet sounding like a single, heavy step. The wardens looked up, and equally on cue, took one step back. The auctioneer returned to his post, wiped his brow, and did his best to speak without his voice cracking.

"We've got a bid of one dollar." He stared straight down at the microphone. "That's going once. Twice." He looked up and paused, then quickly said, "Three times and sold. Sold to the boy in front. One dollar."

Calvin began the war whoop, so loud and close that I stood up without realizing it. The other men joined in, and soon their screaming filling the convention center. They sounded like demonic coyotes loosed from the depths of hell, eager to began tearing flesh off the bone. And then they stopped, leaving their echo to slowly fade until I wasn't sure if I could still hear it or if my ears were ringing. Then, in a single-file line, they marched out of the building, and my grandfather and I followed.

In the parking lot, Calvin and my grandfather began laughing so hard they hung onto each other, Calvin crying, my grandfather coughing. They laughed until they had to sit down on the pavement, tears streaming down their faces, unable to catch their breaths. Each time one of them began to gain his composure, the other would start up again, and for ten minutes they could do no more than laugh. Finally, my grandfather stood up, thanked each man personally, and gave Badger a check so they could buy "refreshments" for the trip home. I shook hands with Calvin, not quite as intimidated as I had been before, and they left. It was over.

I slept most of the way back to Mistake. The adrenaline that had built up in me during the auction had left all at once, leaving me tired, and the sun coming through the windshield of the pickup, diffused into a hundred separate rays by the cracks, made me sleepy.

I woke when my grandfather jammed on the brakes at the mouth of his driveway. A large white sign supported by a pair of varnished cedar posts, had been erected a short distance into the sage on the side facing the woods. As the dust thrown up from the skidding tires settled, the particles catching the sun like diamonds in a ring, we read the gold words at the same time. "Future site of the Tipton Buffalo Ranch."

CHAPTER 7

BUFFALO. They were as connected to the west in my mind as the Rocky Mountains or the elk. Reading the sign, it was impossible for me to think of anything other than early railroad days when trains stopped to allow the massive herds across the tracks and hunters sent tons of their tongues back to sell in Chicago. I liked the thought of having these shaggy, hump-backed bovines for neighbors and hoped the ranch would open before I headed back to New York. Then I looked over at my grandfather. His mouth was open, and his eyes moved back and forth as he read the sign over and over.

"Buffalo." He mouthed the word silently.

"Cole?" I said his name loudly, but he didn't respond. Instead, his eyes drifted from the sign down the driveway. Two men were doing something to the fence on the same side as the sign. They were close to the house, little more than specks among the heat waves rising in the late afternoon sun. They brought my grandfather out of his trance.

The tires spun a full ten seconds, sending the rear of the truck fish-tailing back and forth, before they grabbed and shot us ahead full speed. By the time we reached the men, we were in fifth gear doing more than sixty miles an hour, and we slid one hundred and eighty degrees, shooting past them backwards, when my grandfather mashed the brakes. I clung to the dash, digging my fingers into the sun-baked plastic, feeling cracks spread away from my hands, my eyes jammed shut in fearful anticipation of a crash.

"Get my shotgun, Kyle." My grandfather punched me in the arm, and I opened my eyes. "I want my side-by-side. It's in the gun cabinet right up front. Key's on top, under the box of ought-six shells. Hurry up."

He wasn't looking at me. He was staring straight ahead at the men by the fence. I recognized one as the man who'd made the comment to me about hair on my testicles my first night in Mistake. The other, a year or two older perhaps, with a western-style mustache that fell more than an inch off each side of his chin, had a can of neon-orange spray paint in his hand. The tops of the posts from where he was standing all the way up the driveway to the sign were freshly painted. Freshly posted.

"My goddamned shotgun, Kyle! I won't ask you again." It was the first time he'd raised his voice to me, and it stirred me to action even though I had no idea what I was doing. "There are two shells, light green, in the bottom right-hand corner of the cabinet. Load 'em in the gun and be quick about it. Move for Christ's sake. Get the lead out of your ass and run!"

I found myself running before he finished. Running much further it seemed than the hundred yards to the house. My lungs couldn't get enough air, my head pounded, and my calves seized up forcing me to support myself by clinging to the door. I stumbled into the kitchen, focused on the stove, then nearly vomited as it, and everything else around me, began spinning. I knocked the rifle cartridges off the gun cabinet in my search for the key. They hit the floor and one slid from the pack, spinning like top on its side. I watched it, unable to move my eyes, until it stopped, the copper-plated bullet facing me.

The shotgun was a twelve gauge. An old, nicely-engraved L. C. Smith with double hammers, a straight stock, and Damascus barrels. The shells were where my grandfather said they would be, close to each other, their faded cardboard casings as smooth as the stock of the gun. They slid into the chambers easily, and I closed the gun hard. It felt like it weighed a ton. So much that my arms hurt before I had carried it out of the kitchen. And I was crying. Tears ran down my face in a steady stream, and as I covered the distance between me and my grandfather, growing closer to something I knew would be terrible with every step, I was vaguely aware of the taste of salt on my tongue.

"Well done, Kyle." My grandfather reached for the shotgun with his right hand, opened it to be sure it was loaded, and almost as quickly closed it with a snap of his wrist. I sat down, shaking, the ground and sky rushing toward each other so there was little space between earth and clouds.

Neither of the men had moved. The older one still held the paint can, exactly as he had when I'd last seen him, and the other still stared at the pickup.

"You two are finished." My grandfather's voice came more steadily than

I thought possible considering he was pointing a gun at someone. He held it at his hips and in one liquid motion pulled both hammers back with the palm of his left hand. "Go on now. Get outta here. I'll take this up with your boss." He gestured up the driveway.

For a second, neither man moved. Then the younger one smiled.

"You ain't gonna shoot us, Cole. Shit, go on inside and let us finish. Ain't got many more posts. Bruce'll be rip shit with you if you send us home."

"Yeah, put the fucking gun away," the older man piped up. "Ought to have you arrested and locked up."

"Pete and Ed Lewis." My grandfather lowered his voice. "I got six silver dimes in each one of these barrels, and I'm close to spending the buck twenty of my life, even if neither of you are worth it. I'm not asking you, I'm telling you. Leave now. There will be no buffalo on this land. Not as long as I'm alive."

"Well, that's an idea, ain't it?" Pete, the man from the bar, stepped forward.

My grandfather never raised the gun, never took his eyes off Pete, just swivelled the barrels slightly and touched one of the triggers. The shotgun went off with a roar, ringing like someone had blown up a cash register. The closest orange post exploded, showering the ground behind it with slivers of wood and paint.

"I didn't miss cause I can't shoot." My grandfather sounded calm. He'd made a simple statement of fact. "One more step, Pete, and I'll bury you."

Ed moved first, backstepping slowly up the driveway, visibly shaken, his paint can twitching in his hand. My grandfather encouraged Pete to follow by bringing the gun to his shoulder and looking down the long barrels at the man's head. He didn't lower it until they were fifty yards away and had turned their backs on him, picking up their pace toward the highway. Then he sat down, broke open his weapon, and looked up at the sky.

"Beautiful day, isn't, Kyle?"

I couldn't speak. Most of my tears had dried up, but a lump in my throat was choking me.

"Least we didn't need to kill a man." He lay down and stretched his arms above his head. "Have to get ready for the sheriff I suspect. Just want to lay here and enjoy this for a little bit first. You did real good, Kyle. Didn't mean to holler at you the way I did." My grandfather rolled over to face me. "I wasn't completely myself. Understand?"

I nodded, wiping my eyes as I did. "You don't like buffalo, huh?" It seemed a foolish question. Moments earlier he'd been prepared to shoot someone over them, so the answer was clear. But I couldn't figure out why.

"Buffalo, buffalo, buffalo." He was stretching again, working his hands open and closed like a cat knitting its paws in the sun. "Course I like buffalo. What man don't? Can't hardly live in the west and not like buffalo. But goddamn it," he sat up fast as though something stung him. "There ain't been a buffalo in Montana in more than one hundred years."

This puzzled me more. It occurred to me that perhaps he had finally crossed the narrow gap into legitimate madness. My picture book had several shots of buffalo, grazing in the winter in Yellowstone, and there were even a few farmers in New York who raised them. I started to ask him what he meant, and he cut me off.

"I mean exactly that. There hasn't been a buffalo in Montana ... hell, not anywhere for that matter, for a damn long time."

"I thought ... "

"No, what you've seen are not buffalo. The may look like buffalo, but I assure you they are not. Ain't no different than Holsteins or Angus. Big cows is what they are. Domesticated versions of an animal that went extinct years ago. We killed them for their hides and tongues and to wipe out the Indians."

Here was more reasoning I didn't understand. Not only was my grandfather mistaken about the buffalo's extinction, I didn't see what shooting them had to do with wiping out the Indians.

"Come on. We'd better go on in. Get this shotgun put away and straighten out our stories. The law will be here soon enough."

He helped himself up with the gun and walked by me toward the house. I caught up with him at the door, and held it open. I wanted to ask him more about buffalo. Wanted to hear a rational explanation to what he'd told me so I could convince myself he wasn't crazy.

"Okay." He'd tucked the shotgun in the back of his cabinet, picked up the rifle shells, and was pouring a glass of whiskey. "Old Mr. Wilson ... that's the sheriff ... he and I get along pretty good. Be he's up for reelection this fall and Bruce Tipton is a powerful man. Might feel he's got to do something." He drained his glass and poured it full again. "Yeah, might feel he can't afford offending his more influential constituents. So in order for me to avoid spending a night or two in the clink, you and I had better figure the best thing to tell him. Course I'll do most of the talking, but it wouldn't hurt for you to help out. You know, add in something about being from New York and liking it out here. Sheriff won't want to haul me away and leave you here alone. He's basically a good man. He ain't always walked the straight and narrow himself. I'll use that angle as a last resort."

The whiskey bottle sat in front of me on the table, and I replaced it in the cupboard above the stove before my grandfather finished his second glass.

"That ain't exactly the kind of help I was thinking about." He swirled what was left in his glass around the bottom. "But I can see your point. So, what do you think?"

"I don't know." And I didn't. I had no idea how to sugar over threatening a man's life with a shotgun. The best way to stay out of jail was out of my realm of expertise.

"Okay, I can see how this type of thing is new to you. I figure I've got to make Wilson see where I'm coming from enough to sympathize with me. Only I can't really do that."

"Why not?"

"Well, if I told him the real reason I'm so ornery about having these buffalo here it might work, but I just can't do that. Ain't nobody's business but mine. Yours, too, but not right now."

"What is the reason?"

"Like I said, now ain't the time for that. You'll find out eventually, but for now you'll have to trust me that I have my reasons and they're good ones. Can you live with that?"

"I guess." None of it made any sense to me, but I'd learned quickly that it was best to agree with my grandfather. He might be right, or he might be wrong, but he wouldn't change course for anything.

A car pulled up at the house and we heard a door close. My grandfather stood up, looked out the door, and nodded.

Sheriff Wilson was older than I had pictured. He wore a mustache, and it was graying. He gave a firm knock on the door, any my grandfather waved him in cordially.

"Come on in, Jack. How are you?"

The sheriff stepped inside, let the door close behind him, and stood with his back against it. He looked tired. The bags under his eyes were due more to a lack of sleep than his age.

"Fair to middlin', Cole. Yourself?" He spoke slowly, biting his lip when he finished.

"I couldn't be no better. Got my grandson out here with me this summer. Came out from New York to see the wild west."

"And you haven't disappointed him, have you, Cole?" Wilson frowned.

"I reckon not. Ain't been here too long, but I figure he's realized it ain't the east."

"Yeah, I bet he has. What do you think of Montana?" he asked me.

"Oh, I really like it." I sounded as enthusiastic as I could.

"Uh-huh." The sheriff blinked. "Your grandfather had you out fishing yet?"

"Yeah, we got some brook trout the other day."

"Bet you did. You mind if your grandfather and I talk alone for a few minutes?"

I looked away from him, down at the table.

"Don't worry, I'm not going to haul him off to jail."

"Kyle can stay, Jack. He'll hear anything I will." My grandfather sat straight in his chair, as expressionless as the Indians at the auction.

"Okay. You know why I'm here, Cole. And you probably know I'd rather not be. What the hell's all this about? You know that's Tipton's land. If he wants buffalo on it, why do you care?"

"Don't like 'em."

"Who, Tipton?"

"Well, don't like that son of a bitch, either, but I meant the buffalo."

Sheriff Wilson sighed. "I'm not going to ask why not. Doesn't matter to me. I expect I wouldn't understand anyway. What does matter to me, Cole, is you blasting off your guns at the Lewis boys."

"Didn't exactly blast off at them. You ought to know that. Either of them full of holes?"

"That's not my point. My point is that as sheriff I can't allow it. You know I'd rather have ten thousand of you to one Pete Lewis, but in this case, you're the one who's in the wrong. Christ, Cole, it's the twentieth century."

"Yes, and the country's gone to hell in a hand-basket."

"I won't comment on that. Fact is, like it or not, Helena has laws on the books now about threatening people. Especially with guns. I. . . ."

"Point taken, Jack. Won't happen again."

"Can I have your word on it?"

My grandfather shifted in his chair.

"You give my your word there'll be no more gun play, and I'm satisfied that this is over. I'll tell Tipton you're sorry and that will be that."

"You can have my word, Jack. But I ain't sorry. Don't you tell him that, either."

"Please, Cole. Work with me a little on this. You've got no choice."

"Always got a choice. But you're right. Go ahead and tell him I'm sorry. But you know that I'll fight tooth and nail."

"You go ahead and do that. But do it legal. I mean it. If I come out here again, I want to do it when I'm off duty and have got a few hours to cast a fly. That fair?"

"You bet. Sounds good."

My grandfather and the sheriff stood up, shook hands, and walked to the door.

"One more thing, Cole." Jack paused before stepping outside.

"Shoot."

"Tipton says someone killed an elk on his place down by Divide a few nights ago. He's pretty worked up about it, too."

"Don't know anything about that, Jack."

"No, I didn't say you did. Just figured I'd mention it."

"Well, I appreciate you coming out here and handling this the way you did. Could have worked out different."

"Yeah, well, that wouldn't have accomplished anything more I don't guess. And as long as I have your word I'm happy. I know what it's worth."

"Okay, Jack. Give me a call when the river drops and we'll catch a few trout. You still using nothing but flies?"

"Fraid so."

"Well, I'll make a convert of you yet. Take care, okay?"

The sheriff tipped his hat and I heard him drive away a minute later.

"Good man, Kyle. Jack's a good son of a bitch." My grandfather was still holding the door open. "Won't use anything but flies when he fishes, but he's still a good man."

"You're friends?"

"Friends? Yeah, you could say that. Shit, he ain't ten years younger than me. Lived here all his life, too. Enjoys his job, and more importantly, he knows what his job is. That's the big difference between Jack and most lawmen. I don't mean just sheriffs. I'm talking about all of them. From the game wardens to the highway patrolmen. Most people in that line of work got into it because they like the authority that comes with wearing a badge. Like bullying people. Would rather write a ticket than give a drunk a ride home. Jack's just the opposite."

My grandfather started to open the cupboard I'd put his whisky in, then slid his empty glass across the counter toward the sink and sat back down at the table.

"Cole?" I had to know how he could believe buffalo were extinct. "How come you said there aren't any more buffalo?"

"I said it cause it's true. As true as can be." He leaned back in his chair and folded his arms across his chest. "The real buffalo are long gone. Won't ever be any again, either."

"What do they have in Yellowstone? They're wild buffalo, aren't they?"

"No, not really. They've got boundaries. Even if you can't see a barb wire fence or a cattle guard, they've got boundaries they have to stay in. Each winter it snows hard, they try to migrate out of Yellowstone into some of the gentler grassland country. Soon as they cross out of the park they get shot. Oh yeah, they can be buffalo as long as they stay in Yellowstone, but once they cross that line they get gunned down like cattle in a slaughter pen. You see what I mean?"

"Kind of."

"Well, let me say it a different way. What do you think makes something what it is. I mean an animal. Or a person. Or anything that's living?"

"I don't know. You mean what makes it different from everything else?"

"No, not exactly. Let's just talk about buffalo. What makes them buffalo?"

"The way they look, I guess."

"That's what most people would say. But they're wrong. I'll tell you now how come there are no more buffalo. Kyle, the species has been stripped of its dignity. And once something has lost its dignity it ceases to exist. Oh, sure, in the most literal sense there are still buffalo around. They ain't like the dinosaurs. But the real buffalo ... the ones that lived on the prairie, their hooves sounding like thunder and shaking the ground when they stampeded, their wallows sending mountains of dust into the sky like smoke from a forest fire, those buffalo are gone. And they were the ones who could hold their heads high and be proud, even if they didn't know it, of what they were. It's cruel to keep them around now. Ought to have killed off every last one if that's what we were going to do. Shouldn't keep them as spectacles so some tourist can sit down and eat a buffalo burger. We started killing buffalo 150 years ago. Shot them until our rifle barrels were too hot to touch and the Plains Indians began to starve cause they couldn't find no more to eat. Kyle, what we did was disgraceful, but by god it was the path we chose and we should have kept right at it until every last one of them was dead and gone. No sir, letting something live without its dignity ain't doing it a favor. You kill an animal outright, and maybe it's wrong, but at least it leaves this world the same as it came into it. You change a wild animal . . . make it live to suit us instead of itself, and unless you can make a real compelling argument for its complete domestication than what you've done is way worse than wrong."

I was quiet. My grandfather was passionate enough in his beliefs so I didn't want to say something that might upset him. We looked at each other for a long time, then he stood up.

"I'm gonna take a walk. Cool myself off a bit. Go ahead and flip through the channels on the TV if you want. Start thinking about what we'll tell Bruce Tipton when we go to see him tomorrow. If anybody calls, just let it ring. I'm not in the mood for talking right now. I'll be back later." He stepped outside, and I watched him move away into the sage toward the woods, shaking his head as though he was arguing with himself and not winning.

I called my parents. I hadn't talked to them since I left Syracuse, and I needed to hear their voices. Needed some reassurance that my closer relatives were more accessible, at least in terms of how they thought and acted, than my grandfather. I dialed the numbers slowly, turning the metal dial on my grandfather's old phone one number at a time, a biting sense of trepidation somewhere near the back of my brain making me wonder if my father would answer and begin raving about buffalo or swearing because I let the phone ring too long.

"Dad?" It was good to hear his voice.

"Kyle. How are you? How's Montana? Let me get your mom on the other line."

I waited until I heard her pick up the upstairs phone. "Hi."

"How's my western boy?" she asked.

"Good."

"I'll bet you are." My father was excited. "Dad had you out fishing yet?"

"Yeah. We caught a bunch of brookies in Cow Creek."

"Cow Creek, huh? He tell you about me fishing there?" I could tell my father remembered everything about it.

"Yeah."

"He hasn't put you to work in the woods has he?" my mother asked, knowing full well what the answer was. I knew from the tone of her voice I shouldn't mention driving the skidder.

"Oh yeah. First day I was here. Just piling brush though. We went to Missoula last night. Grandpa got in a fight. Beat up a man at a bar."

"Sounds like dad." My father laughed, but my mother was quiet. "Bet he didn't think anything of it, either. Probably acted as though nothing had happened."

"Pretty much."

"Well, you're getting an education I bet. Learned more than you have in school probably. Tell me, do you like it? I mean really. I know you had some pretty high hopes for Montana. Has it measured up?"

"Yeah, I guess. It's different than what I imagined. But I like it."

"Is your grandfather staying in line?" My mother sounded as though she knew the answer to that question as well. "Hasn't gotten you in any trouble, has he?"

"Oh, no. He's ... dad, has he always ..."

"You bet. He's the same man now as he was when he was eighteen. He's a one of a kind, Kyle. The last of a kind. Probably by the end of the summer I won't be able to say that. Bet you'll never want to come back."

I knew I would, but I hadn't heard my father sound this worked up in a long time. I could tell how much he missed the west, and how much he loved my grandfather.

"Dad, there's a man out here who wants to put buffalo by grandpa's house."

"Buffalo? What's he got to say about that?"

"Doesn't like it."

"No, I'm sure he doesn't." My father's voice had changed. He knew this was serious. "Well, you keep us posted. Anything you need?"

"Don't think so."

"Okay. It's good to hear from you. Call again soon." I heard him hang up. My mother was still on the line.

"Kyle, you sure everything's all right? I know your grandfather can be hard to take."

"Yeah, I'm fine."

"Well, you hang in there. Remember you can come home anytime you want to. We miss you."

"I miss you, too. Bye, mom." I hung up before she did. I didn't want her to suspect anything more.

I stood by the phone for five minutes. My parents had sounded so close I thought I should be able to walk into the living room and find them sitting there. And then I remembered my grandfather's walk. I opened the door and scanned the sage. I didn't think he had time to get to the woods, but I didn't see him. Yellow pollen was drifting off the pines, blowing out into the flats, gathering in clouds above the treetops. Over the Pintlers, thunder heads were forming. Great, slate-grey columns of clouds were rising above the mountains, piercing the blue sky like dull spears, shoving it away to the east. A dry wind was blowing, hard out of the west, hotter than the air, rattling the windowpanes in my grandfather's house. I paced back and forth between my room and the kitchen, looking expectantly toward the woods.

In half an hour, the clouds completed their conquest of the sky and had turned black. The final rays of the sun, shining down from high above them, penetrating unseen, illuminated everything with a synthetic-like orange glow. The first raindrops spattered against the house, nickel-sized and driven at an angle sufficient to bring them toward me as I stood at the kitchen window like the errant throw of a little league pitcher. I flipped on the bulb over the table, but the room did not grow appreciably brighter. Shadows in the living room, defined during the day, ran together into dark, shapeless masses. And then it was quiet. The wind let up, the rain stopped, and the clouds slowed to a more moderate speed. I thought the storm had given the land a reprieve.

I walked outside and sat down on the skidder tire. The air was still. Too still. It was as if Nature was gathering herself for a lethal blow that took all her strength and necessitated her momentarily abandoning her lesser activities. There was no sound, no rain, no breeze. Then the lightning came. Fast and forked, the jagged bolts crashed into the woods less than a mile away. The thunder from one bolt came as another struck home, the flashes and explosions like a fireworks finale. I ran for the house, just beating the hail. I stood in the doorway and watched it, sheet after sheet sailing across the sage, pounding all that was under it with marble-sized chunks of ice. It bounced off my grandfather's pickup, zipped along the ground ahead of gale-force winds, and collected along the steps of the house where rain ran off the roof. The lightning kept coming, closer all the time, the wicked bolts breaking into disfigured hands with many fingers. One hammered down near the canoe, the thunder clap shaking the house, sending me inside to my room where I flung myself down on my bed.

I pushed my face into the sleeping bag, scared of a storm for the first time since I was very young, afraid more for my grandfather than myself. I heard the hail change to rain, its drum-roll patter on the roof increasing as the wind let up. Unlike the thunderstorms in New York, welcome breaks to the summer's humidity that roll through in a matter of minutes, this combination of rain and lightning showed no signs of abating. In an hour, it was dark, the world lit only from the bolts of light so bright they blinded me and so rapid I couldn't look outside. If someone had told me that Armageddon was at hand, I would not have argued, and half of me would have prayed it would all come to an end quickly. I lay on my bed paralyzed, as if I'd had a debilitating nightmare that left me speechless, unable to move more than my eyes. Sleep, not as a result of fatigue, but in response to my fear, a built-in circuit breaker that was thrown to prevent stress, rescued me before my imagination totally ran away with me.

I don't know what woke me up. I wasn't dreaming, and the storm had blown through, so it couldn't have been lightning, but I was sure as soon as I opened my eyes that something had stirred me out of sleep. The house was cool, and the wind was still blowing, but not as hard as it had during the storm. My light wouldn't come on, and the clock in the kitchen had stopped a little after midnight. The door to my grandfather's room was closed, and I couldn't remember if it had been before I went to sleep. I assumed he must have come home, but I had to check. I turned the handle slowly, holding the door tightly in its frame until I heard the metal latch disengage. I opened it a crack, enough to see his bed, then let it swing into the room away from me. He wasn't there.

I was certain something horrible had happened to him. He'd been hit by lightning, caught in the open and battered by hail, or had fallen on the wet ground and broken his leg. Something awful was wrong, and I had gone to sleep. I barely made it to the bathroom before I threw up. I held myself over the toilet, dry heaves sending spasms of pain from my stomach all the way up through my throat. I panicked when I couldn't catch my breath, struggled to stand up, and cracked the back of my head on the underside of the sink. I ran a hand through my hair, didn't feel any blood, but the pain was tremendous. Not sharp like a headache, but dull and heavy. Hard to pinpoint. My eyes hurt, too. Pressure was building behind them, and I knew at any moment they would pop out of their sockets. I cupped my hands under the cold water spout of the sink, let them fill, then drank.

Back in the kitchen, I could see the moon working its way out from behind fair-weather clouds. Far away to the east, an occasional rumble of thunder sounded, distant and faint.

I knew I should go look for my grandfather, but there was a vast difference between knowing what I should do and finding sufficient courage to carry it out. I told myself I didn't know which direction he'd gone, wasn't sure if I could come up with a flashlight, and tried to convince myself he was all right. Anything to rationalize my inability to enter the night in search of him. I sat at the table, wondering what time it was, watching the still hands of the clock, wondering if perhaps the storm had extinguished the sun and it was really morning. Through the glass panes in the door, I could see the woods, blacker than the sky, waiting to swallow me if I stepped outside, and at the same time calling to me. That was where my grandfather was. There was no doubt in my mind. I knew it, and eventually I could longer stand the silence of the kitchen. It made my head pound worse, driving itself deep into my body. I was ready to hear anything, and my own footsteps sounded good.

Sage leaves held the rain water better than hardwoods. Each time I brushed against a bush, my pant leg dampened, and by the time I'd walked fifty yards, my legs were soaked from the knees down, and I was itching. I could see enough to realize I was drawing closer to the woods, but couldn't pick out individual trees until I was almost upon them. I stopped beside an irrigation ditch, muddy water cruising down the channel pick-axed out of the rocky ground. I looked at the woods before jumping across, noticed something standing there just as I leapt into the air, kicked my feet wildly, desperately searching for solid ground so I could turn and run, and didn't quite make the far bank. I cut my hands digging into the steep side of the ditch, and felt the sting of rock shards embedding themselves in my palms. I slid into the water, slipped in the current, and went under. I came up gasping for air, flailing my arms toward one bank, then the other. I couldn't find my footing, went under again, bounced off a submerged stone, pushed myself to the surface for one breath, then sank. My lungs were exploding, prying their way out of my chest. I spun a full circle, clawing for anything to catch myself on, tried to breath, and blacked out. I was unconscious, but I knew I wasn't dead. I was aware of the current surrounding me, pushing me downstream, mercilessly driving me onward. I felt a bump, then something grabbed me. I assumed it was Death, come to take me wherever dead people went, and I couldn't fight it. My body, submissively limp, was being taken away, somewhere where the air was very cold, and it felt good to breathe, even if I couldn't see where I was going.

CHAPTER 8

I REALIZED I wasn't dead when I moved my left hand and felt it scrape against the rough cloth of the living room couch. I knew exactly where I was. The faint aroma of aftershave, and the stronger odor of pine pitch, the smells I connected with my grandfather, left no doubt I was in his house, lying just as I had the first night there. It was light outside, and everything in the room, including my grandfather sitting on the floor next to me, came into focus when I opened my eyes. His knees were pulled up to his chest, and he'd wrapped his arms over them for support. He was still wearing the dress clothes he'd put on in Missoula the day before, and his head bobbed as though he was fighting sleep. His hat lay next to him, a drying ring of water around the brim, needles and bits of sage stuck to the black felt. My head didn't hurt until I tried to sit up, and then everything from it to the small of my back ached. I exhaled loudly and lay back down. My grandfather opened his eyes.

"Back among the living, I see." He patted my legs then leaned against the couch. "Christ, Kyle, it's my fault. Don't know what I was thinking leaving you here all that time by yourself. Brave thing you did coming out looking for me, but all the same I'm thankful we timed it like we did. Tell you what, you rest up a bit, and then I'll let you take me out back and kick the shit out of me. I reckon I earned it." His eyes were bloodshot and his forehead looked pale. I doubt he fell asleep until just before I woke up.

"Grandpa?" It hurt to speak. Like I hadn't had a drink in days. "Grandpa?"

"What?" He didn't insist that I call him Cole, but I felt foolish for forgetting anyway.

"Cole, thank you."

"No, sir, don't thank me. Be good and mad at me. Throw a fit if you want, but don't thank me. Go ahead, Kyle, call me a son of a bitch. Make you feel better. I guarantee it."

I tried to laugh.

"Kyle, your grandfather's a bastard." His expression brightened when he saw me smile. "Yes, a verifiable cock-sucker. An old stumble-bum. An ugly old hog who couldn't get laid in a women's prison with a fistful of pardons."

I couldn't help laughing. My stomach contracted, painfully working in and out, but I couldn't keep a straight face.

"Goddamn it, Kyle, I was worried about you. Worried sick. Can you forgive me?"

I reached over, draped my arms around him, and nodded.

"Very well." He stood up and clapped his hands. "You go ahead and rest. Take it easy for a bit. Looks like you took quite a bump on your head. Probably enough punishment to kill the common man. You're a tough young man, Kyle. I mean it."

He disappeared into the kitchen and I felt better. I looked up at the ceiling, smiled, then glanced at my grandfather's hat. He hadn't bothered to turn it upside down when he took it off, so I picked it up, brushed what I could from it, and set it down on its crown. Water had dripped from it during the night, staining the wooden floor. And there was something else, darker and thicker on the wood closer to where my grandfather had been sitting. A red blotch of blood as big around as a coffee can, congealing, but still similar in color to the blood that had spilled into the elk's tracks after it took a bullet in the lungs. I was staring at it ten minutes later when my grandfather returned with bacon, eggs, and a cup of coffee.

"Cole." I pointed to the stain.

"Holy shit, must have cut myself and not realized it." He began inspecting his arms, checking his pants for a tear, and looking over his shoulder trying to see his back. "Didn't come from you, did it?"

My hands were cut, but not nearly deep enough to bleed that much.

"Huh." he wiped at it with a napkin, leaving small bits of tissue on the floor. "I'll be damned. A mystery. How's that bacon taste? Supposed to be smoked. Any good?"

"Yeah."

"And those eggs? They tolerable?"

"Good. Thanks."

"You bet. We'll get you doctored up a little . . . think Katrina would like that job." I stopped chewing and he laughed. "Just kidding. A man don't want to get it out of sympathy his first time. Me, I'm past the point of pride. I'll get it however I can. I'll beg like a dog now, but you're too young to rely on anything but your manliness. No, I'm just kidding. I figure a good break-fast and a couple of aspirin . . . maybe a few band aids for those hands, and you'll be ready to rock and roll. I'll send you in to Tipton's rancid den and let you haul him out by the scruff of his neck. Got no doubt you could do it."

"We're going to see him, huh?" It was the first time that day I thought about the buffalo.

"You bet. Gonna drop in on him right out of the blue. Like a meteorite. Catch him off guard. Try to figure out what in the hell he's up to. Maybe reason . . . no, I doubt it."

"You're not going to beat him up are you?" I remembered what the sheriff had said.

"Beat him up? Well, that's an idea . . . glad to see you thinking along those lines, but today I'll just talk. Save the blows for later on if he don't crawfish away from this buffalo kick. Go ahead and finish eating. I'm gonna shower up and get out of these clothes."

The meal, especially the coffee, made me feel better. I was able to sit up straight without wincing, and my head, while it still hurt, had stopped throbbing. I heard the water running in the bathroom, and over it my grandfather singing. I looked into the kitchen and out the door toward the woods. I could just see the raised dirt along the irrigation ditch, trailing along the edge of the sage like thin, brown snake. I wondered what lay beyond it that had drawn my grandfather out in the storm, keeping him away half the night. I wondered, but I wasn't going to ask him. If there was something he wanted me to know, he'd tell me.

By the time he got out of the shower and turned the bathroom over to me, I had less than five minutes of hot water. The showerhead started blowing air, and then the heat that had felt so good on my back was gone and icy water pelted my body. I came out shivering.

"Ready to ride out and meet the enemy?" My grandfather no longer looked tired. He had his work clothes on and was switching bands on his hat to another snake-skin an inch wide, checkered with yellow and brown diamonds.

"Rattlesnake?" I asked.

"No, was a bullsnake. Mistook him for a rattler and gave him what-for with a shovel. Right out front here. Came out from under the canoe one day last summer. Scared me half to death, but I should have known it weren't no rattler. They don't come this high up the river very often." He worked one end of the band through a small, gold buckle, slapped the top of his hat, and put it on. "What do you think?"

"I like it."

"Good. Figure we'll stop in Twin Bridges on our way back from Tipton's and pick you up one. Can't live in Montana without a good felt. Get you a good Stetson or Resistol. Something sharp. Women won't be able to keep their hands off you then. Got the Fourth of July dance coming up here pretty quick. Man who can't pick up something there is hardly a man at all. Wait and see, Kyle, I'll send you back to New York a significantly less chaste individual than when you came."

I liked the idea of getting a cowboy hat, but wasn't excited about my grandfather's continued endeavors to, as he put it, "make a man" of me. There was no doubt it meant far more to him than it did to me. Why, I wasn't sure, and he wasn't always serious, but it consumed enough of his thoughts to keep me nervous.

"Kyle?" He paused in the doorway to button a denim jacket he had on. "Why don't you grab my .220? It's got the big scope on it. Think it's in the back of the cabinet. I'll pick up a box of shells at the Mercantile and maybe we'll blast a song dog on the way home. I'll take my coyote call and you can blast one if you want."

I didn't move. With my grandfather's hair-trigger temper, I didn't think taking a gun to Tipton's was a good idea, but I knew that if I didn't get it, he would. I kept it between me and my door when I got it the truck, and he smiled.

"Precautions, huh? Loosen up, Kyle. If we were going to shoot old Bruce, I'd tell you up front. Wouldn't want something like that to come as a surprise. No, ain't in the cards today. Now put that rifle over here in the middle where I can get at it."

I did as I was told, and I believed my grandfather. If he planned on killing

Bruce Tipton, he would have told me, probably only in passing, and I doubted he'd think anything of it. He bought his shells in Mistake, waved to Badger on the porch of the Six Point, and slowed down over Cow Creek.

"Water appears to be falling." He looked out my window, slouching low in his seat to see the tops of the Pioneers. "Can't be there's much snow left up there to come down. Another couple of weeks and river will be fishable. You'll like that. Nothing like the way a Big Hole rainbow comes out of the water." He brought his right hand abruptly off the stock of the rifle where it had been resting, twisting it back and forth toward the roof of the truck, letting it fall palm up onto the seat. "Your father must have told you about the fly fishing, huh?"

"Yeah. And I saved the pictures you sent."

"Well, we'll take some of you soon enough."

Instead of turning north toward Butte when we hit the Interstate in Divide, we swung south along the Big Hole, traveling through rolling prairie country where the largest shrubs weren't waist high. My grandfather pointed out a rocky hill where he said big horn sheep wintered, and I looked, but didn't see any. In Melrose, slightly larger than Mistake and equally close to the river, a dirt road took us east through more prairie, flatter and drier looking than anything I'd seen west of Wyoming. Small bands of antelope ran away from our approach, their white rumps catching the sun like blowing cotton balls. One good buck stopped a hundred yards off the road to stare defiantly in our direction, and I noticed my grandfather tighten his grip on the rifle, but we kept going.

Twin Bridges was pretty. From a knoll ten miles west of the town, my grandfather pointed out the three rivers which converged there to form the Jefferson. Heavy swaths of cottonwoods marked the paths of the Ruby, the Big Hole, and the Beaverhead, joining forces to cut through the valley between the rugged-looking Tobacco Root Mountains on the east and the Highlands on the west. All along the river were square, green hayfields, some dotted with cows, others striped with irrigation ditches. Along the foothills of the Tobacco Roots, the green gave way to brown above the irrigation line, then to the black of forests rising to the gray cliffs still holding snow. The variation in color, from the blue of the river to the white snow, was remarkable.

"Rattler!" my grandfather yelled as he jumped on the brakes. "Right on that rock. Big son of a bitch. Jesus Christ, they make me crawl."

There was a table-sized boulder growing from the prairie on my side of the road, and a thick snake was coiled up on top of it. Its head rested on its coils, and three inches of rattles hung off the stone opposite it. It was sleeping in the sun, enjoying the reflected heat of the rock.

"I'll back up and get you even with him, then you bust him with the Swift." My grandfather pulled on the gearshift, but it didn't want to go. "Goddamn it!" He pulled harder, releasing the clutch and jamming it to the floor. "Worthless fucking bastard!" He put both hands on the shift, leaned back as hard as he could, snapping the handle half way between the floor and where he held it. "Very well." He shut the truck off, got out holding the broken gear shift by its skinny shaft, and walked straight up to the snake. It rattled fiercely, its tail moving faster than I could follow, slithered for the back of the stone, stopped when my grandfather cut off its retreat, and lifted its head.

The black knob on the end of the gearshift zipped down, pulverizing the snake's head before it could strike. It writhed on the boulder like a night crawler on a hook, still rattling, moving in more directions at once than any animal, save one of its own, could. My grandfather hit it once more then tossed it and his club into the back of the truck.

"Make you a good hat band," he said as he got in. "See if you can't find something to wrap onto this." He tapped the substantially shortened shift. "I'll stick a screwdriver or something into it when we get back. Don't want to cut myself in the meantime. Might get mad. Here, use this rag." He handed me a pair of dusty underwear, women's underwear too small for Darla. I wound the cloth onto the metal and he looked pleased. "There, good as new."

I could still hear the rattle of the snake, dissipating only slightly when we grandfather started the truck, buzzing behind me like a hive of bees.

We drove south through the center of Twin Bridges, past a flashing light and sign for Dillon, and turned a mile out of town toward the Ruby River.

"You see all the orange?" My grandfather removed both hands from the wheel and gestured at the fence posts on either side of us. "It's Tipton's. Every inch of it. Owns more than five miles of river bottom. Ties up the best whitetail habitat in southwest Montana. Shit, there are bucks in here that'd make a man drool like a baby. Won't let anyone hunt of course. Just him and a few ranch hands. Not even any of the locals. Yeah, he's way different than his old man. Kind of insulates himself with his money."

We came to an open gate and cattle guard between three monstrous fir posts that formed an arch over the road. The crosspiece sported ornate carving at each end, and in the middle, "Confluence Ranch" had been burned into the wood.

"Here we are," my grandfather said. "Confluence Ranch. Pretentious bastard. Confluence Ranch. Where the hell did he come up with that? Let's see, you have a watch on, Kyle?"

I didn't. The bank clock in Twin Bridges said a little after one. "I think it's about quarter past one."

"Good. Probably catch him at home. Don't think he ever works more than half a day. Too hot for him in the afternoons. Probably he's in trying to satisfy his wife. No small task, either. He married some prissy bitch half his age who everyone figures is trying to fuck him to death. If that's the case, she's in for a rude awakening though. Someone like Bruce . . . someone who thrives on meanness . . . he'll live forever just to spite the world."

We stopped in front of a group of buildings; two barns on either side of a mansion. The house was a three story, white with black shutters and a large brick carriage port canopied by a pointed, shingled roof held up by marble pillars. The lawn must have had a sprinkler system built into it because the grass was lush and as uniformly cut as a golf course. Directly in front of the house was a fountain. A plump, naked woman made of greening copper stood in the middle, the water dripping from one of her out-stretched hands.

"Boston would think she'd died and gone to heaven if she saw this, wouldn't she?" My grandfather spit out his window onto the tarred drive-way. "Maybe this fits in around Atlanta someplace, but it sure don't belong in Twin. I say blow it to kingdom come."

Our footsteps echoed off the house when we walked on the bricks. I felt like I was entering a library or art museum: some place I'd have to be quiet and careful not to touch anything. The double oak doors were trimmed with brass, as shiny as the elk-head knocker, and their hinges weren't ex-posed.

"Take hold of those horns, Kyle, and give a good rap. Knock loud and get his attention." My grandfather lifted the knocker a few inches and I put my hand on it. The brass was cold, even in the heat of the day. I raised it to its limit and let it fall. I waited a second, then did it again. From somewhere be-hind the heavy doors, I heard footsteps, fast and close together, then the sound of a well-oiled lock disengaging. And then I got my first look at Bruce Tipton.

He was short. Less than five and a half feet tall, and even the clean, silver-belly Stetson he had on didn't add to his height. I had expected him to be disfigured by the evil my grandfather assured me he possessed, a dead ringer for the hunchback of Notre Dame, but he wasn't. He was clean-shaven, his dark hair cut short along the sides of his head where it stuck out from beneath his hat, and he didn't wear a mustache. I was surprised to see him in jeans and boots instead of an Armani suit, and even if his pants had never seen a streak of dirt or his full-quill ostrich footwear cost him over a thousand dollars, they were better than silk and polyester. His arms were chubby, as was his stomach, but he wasn't fat.

"What can I do for you?" he asked. He sounded as though he would be happy to help us as long as it wouldn't take more than a minute or two.

"I want to talk to you about the buffalo you plan on bringing up by my place in Mistake." My grandfather stepped in front of me, close to Bruce. He towered over him, tipping his head down to maintain eye contact. "I saw the sign yesterday and had a little run-in with the Lewis boy, too."

"Yup." Bruce didn't back up. "You saw the sign, you said. Not much more to it."

"Not much more than the sign, or not much more than what it said?" The same raspiness I'd heard at the auction was back in my grandfather's voice. If Bruce was frightened, however, he didn't let it show.

"Not much more than what it said, Cole. I've been kicking around the idea of having a few buff for the past couple of years. Found a man in Wyoming who's selling out, and it's the right time for me to buy."

"Why Mistake? Why the hell do they have to be in my backyard?"

"Best place for them really."

"In my yard?"

"Well, on that piece of land. Flat, not great value for anything else, and out of the way enough so I don't expect everyone will be screaming about the threat of brucellosis."

"What do you mean out of the way? I could open my front door and piss on them."

"Yes, well, out of the way of most people. I don't know why you care anyway."

"You ain't the one who's going to be smelling their stink day in and day out. Listening to the infernal bellowing and choking on the dust they'll drive up out of their wallows."

"So move." Bruce stepped back to look my grandfather in the eye without looking up. It was the first really cold thing I'd heard him say, but it was enough to convince me everything I'd heard about him was true. "You don't like it, Cole, move. It's a free country."

"Move? My father built that house a long time before any of you rich ... before your father ever thought about moving to Montana. I ain't got much in this world, but what I've got is mine and I've worked for it. I won't be driven off. Not by all the buffalo that ever set hoof to earth."

A woman, tall and pale, with long black hair and high heels emerged from behind Bruce and put her hands on his shoulders. My grandfather removed his hat and nodded to her.

"Charlotte," he said.

"Hello." She had a faint French accent.

"It's all right, dear. We'll step outside." Bruce ducked by my grandfather and closed the door behind him. He looked at me and extended his hand, but my grandfather brushed it away.

"This is my grandson, Kyle. He's staying with me this summer." He stood between Bruce and me, straight and tense as though he was protecting me from a mean dog. "What about an easement through that piece to the forest?" he asked, letting some of the hard edge go from his voice. "Means a lot to me up there, and I'm getting to the point where I can't get around as well as I used to. Any chance we could work something out? Put up a drive from my place to the forest?"

"Possibly." Bruce enjoyed bargaining when he had the upper hand. I could see it in his expression. His eyes gleamed and he smacked his lips. "Have to look it all over, but I won't rule it out."

A swallow sailed under the carriage port and landed on the roof above us. It was trying to build a nest. Bits of mud clung to the white wood where it had begun its masonry.

"Persistent little fellows." Bruce smiled. "Every day or two I get out the hose and wash it down. They won't win, but they don't know it." He bit at a fingernail. "I lost an elk a few nights ago from my Canyon Ranch." He looked at my grandfather carefully, waiting to see if he'd flinch. "Poachers."

"Not a lion, huh?" My grandfather held a perfect poker face.

"Not unless it lugged off everything but the head and hooves."

"Well, least they had sense to make use of it all. It's the sons of bitches that shoot something and just leave it there that really get under my skin."

Bruce nodded. "They all get under my skin," he said. "Got no business stealing. With all the welfare people like myself pay for, nobody has to be killing my elk. Probably the damn Indians, wouldn't you think?"

"Never can tell."

"No, never can tell. How are your lungs, Cole? Heard you weren't feeling so well."

"Never better."

"Uh-huh." Bruce had a malevolent smirk on his face. A smugness I suddenly wished my grandfather would wipe away with a haymaker. "Well, I've been meaning to ask you about doing a little work up there in your neck of the woods. Up on the Canyon Ranch. Putting in some subdivisions up there and the trees are too thick. Need them cut. It's pretty good fir, too. Bet you could use the work."

"A logger never turns it down."

"Didn't figure."

"What type of thinning are we talking? Those big trees skid pretty hard when you've got to leave too many."

"Oh, not looking to leave too many. Enough for aesthetics is all. The deal isn't quite set yet, and there's a chance the buyer ... some developer out of Bozeman will change his mind and want more trees left, so you'd have to stop cutting on short notice if it came to that."

"Could I skid those I already had down?"

"How many people are you using now?"

"Just me and Kyle."

"Yeah, you could skid what you'd dropped."

"And you figure it'd be worth my time to move my skidder in there?"

"It's work, right?"

"And you'd let me know yourself if I had to stop. Let it come straight from the horse's mouth?"

"Yeah, I'd tell you as soon as I heard."

"Well, sounds like a possibility. Why don't you show me the piece and maybe we'll look for the best spot to put a road through the buffalo at the same time."

Bruce shook his head. "My schedule is stacked full right now. Have to get one of the boys to show you. I'll have someone give you a call in the next day or two."

"Okay. And be thinking about that easement. It'd mean something to me."

"And you keep your ears open about that poacher. It'd mean something to me."

I knew by the way my grandfather slammed his truck door he was mad.

I couldn't believe he had been able to hide it as well as he had. The big vein in his forehead hadn't even stuck out. It was now, however, sprouting roots and limbs, its offshoots stretching from his eyebrows to his hairline.

"Napoleonic little son of a bitch!" He brought his fist down onto the dash, shattering a softball-sized area of plastic. "By Christ, I'd have liked to hit him just once. That's all I'd want. Take my fist and ram it right down his throat. So help me god, Kyle, with one blow I could do for that man."

"But you agreed to work for him?" I had expected my grandfather to spit at Bruce's feet when he mentioned the logging.

"Yes, well, that's a different matter." His breathing slowed and he settled back into his seat. "A logger can never cut off his nose to spite his face. I work for myself and I've got to eat. And, if it will get me what I want . . . that goddamn easement . . . well, I'm willing to trade a little. Make some money and reach a compromise. He'd better not fuck me on this, though. I've got something for those buffalo that I doubt he'd approve of."

"Easement?" It wasn't a term I was familiar with.

"Yeah. A right-of-way. Put a road through the buffalo pasture so I can get from my place to the national forest. All that land is public once you hit the timber. One man's got no right to block it. Every citizen in the United States has a right to access that land. Bruce might own all of Montana, but he sure as shit don't own all of America."

Until we stopped in front of Three Rivers Westernwear, on Main Street in Twin Bridges, I'd forgotten about my hat.

"Go ahead in and see if you can't find yourself a good felt. Price ain't an issue. I owe you for that load of logs we got out, and besides, this is something I've wanted to do for a long time. Take your time and look at as many as you want. I'll ease down the street and see if I can't find a watering hole. Get a little sour mash in me and relax." My grandfather headed down the sidewalk, and I saw him duck into a bar a short distance away.

I crossed the street, still wondering why he felt so strongly about getting an easement. The westernwear store bordered an alley that ran back between it and a laundromat with a high false front and a two-story apartment complex. There was a small yard bounded by a picket fence, and inside it was a rusty swing set, leaning slightly, and rocking as a young girl sailed back and forth. I stopped to watch her appear above the fence on her way up and again going backwards. She was five or six, and either she hadn't completely outgrown her baby fat, or she'd already begun to acquire the appearance of one of her parents. She had short blonde hair, pulled up on top of her head in a pink barrette, and a light blue dress on. She was young enough so she didn't care that it flew up above her thighs, and I was old enough to recognize how lucky she was in some ways. Her summers were swinging in her back yard and making mud pies, much as mine had been stalking through cornfields with homemade bows and chasing water snakes around culverts. I jumped when my grandfather put a hand on my shoulder.

"I might be a minute or two down there so I figured I'd give the cashier a check. She'll make it out when you find one you like, and you just bring me the receipt. Don't go getting some cheap piece of shit, either. You want something that will last."

We walked in together, and my grandfather gave a woman at the counter his check. There were no shortage of hats. The entire back wall was covered with them, hanging at angles from wooden pegs. There were straws, silver-belly felts like the one Bruce Tipton had on, smoke-gray hats with wide brims, and lots of black ones similar to my grandfather's. I wanted one of those and began trying them on. I looked at each one in a mirror the cashier wheeled out of a corner, but none of them was quite right. The crowns were too tall, the brims too wide, or not wide enough, or they just didn't feel good. In half an hour, I found myself trying the first one on again, and gave up. I headed for the door and noticed a row of hats above the counter I hadn't seen when I walked in. A piece of typing paper hung in front of them and read, "Do Not Touch." When I pointed to the one of the end, the woman smiled.

"Got good taste," she said as she handed it to me. I put it on and she nodded. "Looks good on you, too."

It did. It fit perfectly. I took it off and looked inside for the make. There was no writing on the glossy, satin lining.

"What kind is it?" I asked.

"It's a custom. Made right here in town. Twin Bridges Hat Company. 10-x beaver. You like it?"

"Yeah. How much is it?"

The woman hesitated. "Well . . . good question. Let me call Lois. She's the one who made it. We don't sell too many of them, and I can't remember what she gets. Hold on just a minute."

She picked up a phone next to the cash register, thought for a second, then punched the number. She talked longer than I thought necessary, and

I stopped paying attention. I looked at a saddle for sale in the middle of the floor. It was made from dark leather, trimmed with German silver. The original price of $1,400 had been crossed out, but I didn't see the new price. I heard the woman hang up and turned around.

"Lois said she'll stop by in a minute. Works just up the street. She said she'll bring you one other to try on before you make up your mind."

My mind was already made up, but I didn't want to offend her. I kept looking at the saddle.

"Pretty, isn't it?" The cashier set my hat back up above her.

"Beautiful."

"Yeah, some little heart-breaking barrel racer will snatch it up I expect."

The door opened, and an older woman carrying a hat walked in. "This the cowboy?" she asked pointing at me.

"This is the one. His grandfather's getting him a hat."

"Go ahead and try this one, dear. See what you think."

I put it on and couldn't tell the difference between it and the other one. "It's the same, isn't it?"

"Well, almost. Same make, just a little different on the inside." Lois reached for it, and flipped it upside down in her hands. "See this?" There was a small, tan stain on the satin lining. "Hands aren't as steady as they used to be. Must have spilled a little something on it just before it was done. Never show from the outside, but I've got to call it a defect. But that's all that's wrong with it."

"How much is it?"

Lois pointed to the one above the register. "Four hundred and twenty," then tapped the one she was holding. "How about eighty? That sound about right?"

"I'll take it. Thanks."

"You bet."

The cashier made out the check and gave me a receipt. She offered me a box for the hat, but it went directly onto my head. I paused at the door and stared at my reflection, then stepped outside feeling more a part of Montana than I had before I went in.

The girl on the swing set was crying. I turned the corner and looked down the alley. She was sitting on the ground, and I couldn't see her over the fence. The swing was moving crazily, twisting back and forth as it rose and fell. I figured she'd fallen. Her sobs echoed off the buildings, coming freely, loud and sincere. A door opened in the apartment building and a stocky man in a T-shirt and underwear came out. He set a bottle down, beer it looked like, and headed for the girl who began crying harder, her sobs turning into shrieks. I took a few steps down the alley.

"Goddamn it, you fuck around on this thing long enough and you're going to get hurt. I'm sick of telling you that." The man put a shoulder against one leg of the swing set and began pushing up and over. The girl stopped crying, ran to him, threw her arms around his legs and pulled in the opposite direction. I kept walking.

"Daddy, daddy, daddy. Please!" she entreated. "I'm sorry."

The leg broke free of the ground, carrying a crown of matted grass around its base into the air. The man grunted, and with a final heave tipped the swing set over. It hadn't bent enough to suit him, so he began working one of the legs, now leaning up above his head, back and forth, the soft metal giving way under his weight. The little girl let go of him, stepped back, wide-eyed with shock, then began screaming again. Loud, piercing screams that were as horrible a noise as I'd ever heard.

Her father was out of breath. His large stomach moved in and out rapidly, and he was red in the face. "Get over here," he said, extending a fleshy paw toward her. She didn't move. "Something wrong with your hearing? I said get your ass over here. Let me see what you've done to your dress."

She turned her back to him and started for the door he'd left open. I was almost to the fence, but neither of them had seen me. She couldn't run very well. Her thighs rubbed together, and her steps were small. The back of her dress was stained by the grass she'd landed on, the blue cloth now a light shade of yellow. Her father couldn't run much faster, but he caught her just before she got inside, jerked her into the lawn by one arm, spun her around to examine the dress, then began swearing.

"Fucking Christ! You've ruined it. How's that make you feel? You stop that bullshit crying and answer me. Son of a bitch! Now you'll want another one, too. You think money grows on fucking trees?"

She was struggling hard to get away, slapping at his arms, digging her feet into the ground, her white shoes staining as easily as her dress. I stepped over the fence.

The man let go of his daughter with one hand, drew it back across his body, and backhanded her. He struck her a little above the nose, his hand covering her entire forehead, and she tumbled away from him. She covered her head with her hands, balling up the way a man might protect himself from a bear. He snatched her up by a leg, cuffed her again, harder this time. She lay still when she hit the ground, either unconscious or no longer able to fight.

I was only a couple of steps away, even with the overturned swing set, picking up speed, coming up behind the man. He still hadn't noticed me. I closed my right fist, clenching my thumb tight to my fingers, feeling my nails bit into my palm. When I put my left hand on his shoulder, I felt him twitch. He turned my way, as wide-eyed as his daughter had been a few moments earlier, and I let loose with my right hand.

I'd never punched anyone before, and I didn't expect it to hurt as much as it did. Not in my knuckles, they'd been cushioned by his oversized nose, but deep inside my shoulder. It felt like my whole upper arm was connected to my funny bone. The man's head snapped back, but he didn't fall down, and I knew I'd better swing again. He pulled back a little this time, and my fist bounced off his chin, turning me sideways, taking my balance. I extended my arms like a tightrope walker, desperately trying to get my feet back under me. Then he caught hold of my shirt collar.

Holding me at arm's length, the hairy back of his hand rubbing hard against my chin, he ran his other hand across his nose and started in disbelief at the blood.

"What the . . . you little fuck, you want to hit me? You think you're some kind of tough man?"

He drew me toward him, into his oncoming fist. I was able to duck enough so he missed my face, but he nailed me on top of my head. It was still sore from the night before, and now there was a new pain. Sharp and clear. There was a flash like a camera in a dark room somewhere close to the center of my brain, and ozone, them smell of a transistor struck by lightning, filled my nostrils.

"You like that? How fun is fucking with me now?"

I wasn't seeing double, but my vision was blurred. He hit me again, closer to my left eye this time, then threw me onto the ground where I was vaguely aware of him drawing back his right foot, preparing to drive his boot into my stomach, almost grateful he wasn't going to punch me. I tried to curl away from his leg, but my muscles didn't respond in time. He caught me square in the middle of my gut, driving the wind out of me. I couldn't breathe. I couldn't get a bit more air than I'd been able to underwater in the irrigation ditch. He was going to kill me.

My hat had fallen off, and he stomped on it, crushing it into the ground, working it into a shapeless clump of felt, giving me enough time to catch my breath. I sat up, reeling from the pain, a voice inside my head screaming at me to get away. I crawled toward the fence, and he stopped destroying the hat. He held me by the back of the head, gathered himself for another blow, his breath coming in short chops like snorts from a bull.

I was facing the alley, and saw my grandfather before the man did. He was half way down it, unbuttoning his denim coat, his eyes beady and unblinking, his steps long and even, his mouth twitching. He stepped over the fence without missing a stride, pulling a heavy pistol from his belt as he did. He must have been afraid to let me see it earlier for fear I'd worry he was going to shoot Bruce. I heard the double click of the hammer drawn into the cocked position, and my grandfather stuck the muzzle into the man's face just before he hit me.

"Your fist . . . your fist falls and so does this hammer," my grandfather screamed. I'd seen him mad plenty of times, but never like this. It was a primitive anger. Pure and natural. An animal-like rage, untainted and unchecked. The man let go of me, and I rolled away. "What's this all about, Kyle?" my grandfather asked without moving the pistol.

I tried to answer, but hadn't sufficiently regained my breath.

"Kyle, what's going on here?"

I pointed to the girl, sitting up now, facing the action. "He was beating. . ."

"Why?"

"Grass on her dress." It was all I could say.

My grandfather put his thumb on the hammer, and lowered it, nodding. The man exhaled loudly, believing my answer had spared his life. Believing my grandfather saw it his way. He lifted his head and shrugged, then didn't have time to change his expression before my grandfather twirled the pistol in his hand, caught it by the barrel, and drove the hardwood stock into the bridge of his left eye. It connected with a solid smack, splitting the skin instantly, sending a mist of blood onto my grandfather's coat, sending the man to his knees.

"You hurt, Kyle?" My grandfather looked at me for the first time, still holding the pistol by the barrel. I held my stomach and tried to shake my head. "That your hat?" He pointed to the ruined cloth, and I nodded. "Fucking son of a bitch!" He let the pistol slide back in his hand, gripped it by the cylinder, and brought it forcefully into the man's cheek. I heard a bone break. In an instant, my grandfather had it by the barrel again, swinging it like an ax, down through the man's uplifted hands to the point of his jaw. Another bone shattered. "I'll kill you. I'll fucking kill you." Again the pistol struck home, the man's lips bursting between his teeth and the steel.

"Stop it! Jesus Christ, stop it!" It was a woman, standing in the doorway, screaming as loudly as her daughter had. My grandfather looked up. "You're killing him."

"That's the idea, ma'am. Now get back inside."

As soon as my grandfather said it, I knew he wasn't going to do it. The wild look in his eyes had lapsed into common anger, and he holstered the pistol. The woman didn't move.

"Ought not to be with a bastard like this," my grandfather said to her. "Whipped your little girl and beat my grandson with everything he had. He's worth nothing. Waste of fucking air!" He pushed the man over onto his back, where he groaned, gingerly tracing the outline of his bloody face with a finger. It would never look the same again. "If you've got the least bit of self-respect, you'll get yourself and your daughter away from him. Up to me, and I'd kill the motherfucker right here. That's what he needs. Plain and simple, no ifs, ands, or buts. World would be a better place for it, too."

With a final kick to the man's ribs, one which elicited a long, drawn out moan, my grandfather turned his back on him. He helped me over the fence, let me lean on him down the alley, and opened my door for me when we reached his truck. He took off his coat, removed his pistol, which he'd wedged back into his waistband, and pulled up to a set of gas pumps at a ominimart on the edge of town. I waited for him to get out, then tipped the rearview mirror toward me to inspect my face. I'd have a black eye before nightfall, and my nose, though probably not broken, was swollen.

While my grandfather filled the truck, I hastily sorted through the rack of cheap sunglasses inside. I found a pair that would hide my wounds and paid for them before he came in. I didn't put them on until we were back on the road, and when my grandfather noticed them he slowed down.

"No need for those, Kyle." He reached over and gently lifted them off. "Got nothing to be ashamed of. Much the opposite. It's like I told you, if more people were willing to wear a black eye for what's right, there'd be a lot less wrong with the world. Too many people turn their backs. Figure it ain't their business, but they're wrong. Something like that overgrown son of a bitch beating on a little girl ... that's everybody's business. She can't defend herself, and she sure as shit shouldn't have to take it. But if nobody does something, that's like saying it's all right. World's overrun with hypocrites." He looked over his shoulder as though he'd forgotten something, then swung the truck around. I feared he was going back to make doubly sure justice had been served. "I don't know, Kyle. I may have been born a century too late. Maybe more. I guess some of my views are outdated, but by god my sense of right and wrong shouldn't be. But I'll be lucky if I don't get sued over this deal. It's all right for him to whip his daughter and give you the boots, but when I do something about it I'm sticking my nose where it don't belong and become liable. That's the way it works now. Too many fucking close-your-door, cover-your-eyes, live-for-yourself pussies. Not one man in a hundred would have the guts to do what you did. And I say any man who wouldn't," we stopped across from the westernwear store again, "he ain't got no business calling himself a man. He's a mouse. A mouse or something worse. I couldn't be any prouder of you, Kyle." He got out and motioned for me to follow. "I only wish you were a few years older. Course then we'd likely have to go on the lam. A tub like him . . . well, you'd have killed him I reckon."

It only took a few seconds to walk across the street, but it was enough time for me to think about what had happened, and until then, I hadn't. It had happened too fast. I was acting, not thinking. Perhaps in my subconscious I was still worried about not having something I'd fight for, but I knew before we reached the yellow lines in the middle of the road that I did. I'd do the same thing again, and I took pride in knowing I would.

"Keep your head high," my grandfather said just before we reached the store. "Anybody tells you to do different, and they'll answer to me. And I suspect you have an idea how well it would go over."

The cashier and Lois came out from a room in the back when we walked in. I hadn't noticed it earlier, and my grandfather and I both saw the window they'd doubtlessly witnessed the fight from. I tugged at his coat sleeve, ready to leave before the cops showed up, but he smiled at them and spoke confidently.

"Good afternoon, again, ladies." He tipped his hat. "My grandson needs a new felt."

They looked at each other, then Lois stepped behind the counter and removed the hat I'd tried on first. "It looked good on you," she said as she handed it to me. "What's your name?"

"Kyle. Kyle Richards."

"How old are you, Kyle?"

I was afraid she was going to lecture me, and I knew my grandfather didn't have four hundred dollars. "I'm fourteen."

"And this is your grandfather?"

"Yes." He shook her hand. "Cole."

"Do you rodeo, Kyle?"

"No, I'm just visiting."

"He's here for the summer," my grandfather said. "Came west to give an old man some company. What do I owe you for the hat?"

"It's four hundred and twenty dollars," the cashier said.

"The other was only eighty," I said to my grandfather. He took out his checkbook and Lois lowered her voice.

"I think we can call it a replacement. If I don't have more than a five minute warranty on my products, that doesn't say much for me, does it?"

"Four hundred, you said?" My grandfather spoke to the cashier, ignoring Lois, still writing in his checkbook. "He's worth way more than that."

"That's my point, Mr. Richards." Lois put a hand on the checkbook. "Not many young men are, either."

My grandfather stopped writing. "No, that's the truth. Not many men are worth it anymore, and not many people recognize the ones who are."

"Mom?" Until the cashier said it, I hadn't noticed how much they looked alike. "What about . . ."

"Be quiet," Lois snapped.

"Well, my pride won't allow me to take the hat for nothing." My grandfather slid the checkbook out from under Lois's hand.

"And mine won't allow me to let you pay for it," she said.

"Well, we're at something of an impasse then, aren't we?"

"I suppose we are. I also suppose it's not in your best interest to hang around here all day and argue with me. What if you pay the eighty I charged for the first hat? Would that suit your pride? Anything more and I'll just rip up the check as soon as you leave."

"I guess I'm not left with much of a choice, am I?"

"No."

"Very well. Eighty dollars." He finished writing the check.

"And Kyle," I was headed for the door, and stopped when I heard my name. "Kyle, you think about staying out here, okay?"

I nodded and stepped out, again seeing my reflection in the door, thinking seriously about what Lois said.

"That woman restores some of my faith in humanity, Kyle," my grandfather said as we turned onto the dirt road back toward Melrose. "If she hadn't had a wedding ring on . . . well, I might just be spending more time in Twin."

I was growing tired, and my eye was swelling. The sun hurt my head. "I'm glad you came when you did, Cole." The bumpy road was rocking me to sleep.

"Yeah, good timing again, huh? Well, you look tired. Go ahead and sleep if you can. We'll get you back and maybe rethink what I said about getting some out of sympathy."

Just before I fell I asleep, I felt him touch my knee.

"Couldn't be prouder of you, Kyle."

And then I was dreaming of the gorge and the Indians, the water pulling me faster than the truck was going, faster than I could resist, sweeping me into the river. It sucked me downstream, its omnipotent current tossing me, turning me, rolling me onto my back to look up at the sky. The huge, blue sky that went on forever.

CHAPTER 9

OVER THE NEXT two weeks, as my black eye healed, and the knots on my head disappeared, I helped my grandfather prepare to log off fifty acres on Tipton's Canyon Ranch. A nervous-looking Pete Lewis showed us the land one evening and didn't mention the poached elk. In fact, when we drove up the draw, riding an uncomfortable three in the pickup, he purposely didn't look over onto the hill where it had fallen. If he noticed I'd been in a fight, he didn't bring it up, nor did anyone else. Darla had begun to tease me about it one afternoon when she and Katrina stopped by to see my grandfather about a going away party for Little Elk, but he shot her such a cold stare that she broke off in mid sentence. After a few days, I stopped worrying that my grandfather would be hauled off for felony assault. The state police hadn't showed up, and as he said, "It happened in Montana, and this ain't New York."

The trees we were going to cut, Doug fir more than two hundred years old, were far larger than the lodgepole we'd cut on national forest. Some of them were well over hundred and twenty feet tall, four and a half feet through at the base, and their rippled bark was six inches thick. My grandfather said the Goliathan timber would bring him enough money, even after Tipton's thirty percent, to live comfortably on for the next few years. Walking through the trees, years of cones crunching under my feet, rarely out of the shade, the massive trunks like great pillars that served to hold up the sky, I didn't see how the money Bruce stood to gain from the development could outweigh leaving them on his ranch. To my way of thinking, whatever replaced them would only mar the landscape. But I knew my grandfather needed the money, as well as the easement, and I also knew he shared some of my regret.

Moving the skidder was no small job. My grandfather borrowed a flatbed trailer from Sheriff Wilson and a dual-wheeled Dodge pickup from a ranch on the upper Big Hole near where we'd seen the moose. We spent the better part of a morning jockeying the awkward John Deere onto the trailer. I stood on the roof of the truck and guided my grandfather, and after a good deal of swearing and backing up we managed to drive it on enough so that only half of each wheel hung over the sides. We secured it with eight-foot lengths of log chain and crept all the way down the highway with it to the Canyon Ranch. There weren't many places for cars to pass us, and by the time we got there, some two hours after we'd started, there was a line of vehicles half a mile long behind us. With the operation completed successfully, which to my grandfather's way of thinking meant that no one got killed, he wanted to celebrate.

"You like parties, Kyle?" he asked, showing his teeth in the wide grin which I'd come to learn meant I wasn't getting the full story. "Got a humdinger of one to go to tonight. Think you heard Darla mention it."

"For Little Elk, right?"

"That's the one." When my grandfather got excited, his eyes seemed to narrow and shine from within. Their dark pupils zipped back and forth when he spoke, never focusing in one direction for more than a second or two. He had a raptor-like quality about him. "It's his going away party. You up for it?"

"Where's he going?" My lack of enthusiasm was apparent.

"Won himself a stay in the Big House." My grandfather rubbed his hands together. "You won't want to miss this one, Kyle. Going to have the old Six Point hopping this evening."

The only thing I liked about the Six Point was the elk antler. If everything else washed into the Big Hole — and as close to the river as the bar was I thought there was a good chance that someday it would — I wouldn't have lost any sleep. Whatever contest Little Elk had won must have been connected to the Rainier beer he drank. Probably he'd twisted off a lucky bottle cap, in which case it was fitting that he celebrate in the low-ceilinged, cigarette smoke-filled bar, but I didn't want to go.

"Ah, keep a stiff upper, Kyle." My grandfather tried not to laugh. "Your little honey'll be there, and if you don't want to stay, take her out by the river. Prime her up a bit for the dance on the Fourth. I hear through the grapevine she'd like to go with you."

There was no getting around it, and when we got home, the truck and trailer returned, I called my parents. My grandfather was in the shower when I talked to them, but I wasn't fully convinced he didn't know what we talked about. Even if he couldn't hear, I suspected he always knew what I was thinking.

My father wanted to know if I'd been fly fishing yet, and my mother wanted to know how much my grandfather was drinking. When she hung up, my father asked me about the buffalo.

"I guess he's trying to get an easement through them to the forest," I said.

"Be good if he could. You say he went to visit Mr. Tipton?"

"Yeah. I went with him. He bought me a nice hat in Twin Bridges."

My father lowered his voice to something just louder than a whisper. "How's your shiner?"

"What?" I couldn't believe I'd heard him correctly.

"Your eye? Dad said it swelled up pretty good."

I didn't say anything.

"Dad says you clocked that son of a bitch real good. It's all right, your mom doesn't know a thing about it. Dad had to tell me, though. Had to brag you up a little. He's proud of you, Kyle. Me, too."

I had never heard my father swear before, and I never pictured him as the type who would be proud of me for getting into a fist fight. It made me wonder how different he was when he lived in Montana.

"You still there, Kyle?"

"Yeah, and I'm fine. My eye, I mean. You won't tell mom, will you?"

"No, I won't. But she'd be proud, too. What have you got going on now?"

"Getting ready to log for Bruce. Got a party to go to tonight."

"A party?"

"Yeah, some Indian's going away party. Down at the Six Point."

"Uh-oh. Be a long night tonight, won't it?"

"Yeah."

"Well, keep track of dad. Don't let him get too far out of line. Hell, he'll probably try to fix you up with every woman under thirty. Is that about right?"

"Yeah, pretty much."

"I knew it. That's dad. Well, enjoy yourself. I'll talk to you soon."

"Dad?" I didn't want him to hang up yet. "Dad, do you know why grandpa wants that easement so much?"

"Doesn't like the idea of being boxed in I would say. Hates the thought of any man interfering the least little bit in his life."

"That's all?"

"That's my guess. Can't ever tell with dad. Why?"

I almost told him about my grandfather spending half the night in the woods, but I didn't. "Just wondering. Will you call me soon?"

"You bet."

"Okay. Bye, dad."

I was sitting at the kitchen table when my grandfather came out of the shower. "Cole, why didn't you tell me you talked to my dad?" He stopped toweling off his hair and sat down next to me.

"Didn't figure it was important. Why?"

"You told him about the fight."

"Of course I did."

I shook my head and he lifted my chin to look me in the eye.

"Kyle, I expect there's a lot about your father you don't know. Nothing major . . . there aren't any big secrets, but like I said, he and your mother are very different in some respects. Same as you and he are different."

"Cole?" He'd stood up and headed for his room. "How long before the party?"

"We'll leave in an hour and half or so."

"I'm gonna go for a walk, okay?"

"Sure. You want to take that .220? Might see something to shoot."

"No, thanks." I knew I could very happily spend the rest of my time in Montana without pulling a trigger. Breaking a brook trout's neck was one thing. Following a blood trail was another. I wasn't a hunter, and it was as simple as that.

The days were getting hotter. It cooled off enough at night, quickly each evening after the sun went down, so the hottest time of the following day didn't come until four or five in the afternoon, but when it did, the air was still and everything except the yellow and red locusts was quiet. Walking through the sage, retracing my steps from the night of the storm, I kicked up dust each time I lowered my feet. There wasn't a cloud in the sky, but the parched ground needed rain. Everything that wasn't irrigated had turned brown. It reminded me of the way New York looks after the first thaw in

January, when the snow temporarily disappears but no signs of spring can be found.

I stopped at the edge of the irrigation ditch. There wasn't much water in it. I looked downstream to where my grandfather had pulled me from the current. The banks dropped off sharply, leaving more than eight feet between level ground and the water. The rain must have quadrupled the natural flow.

The woods looked hot and dry. Heat waves rose from between the pines, and flies circled in the oven-like air, but in the shade it was at least ten degrees cooler and felt good. I headed away from the sage, moving in a straight line, in the general direction of the mountains I could see from the house and knew were ahead of me. Horseflies hovered over me, but as long as I kept moving and ran my hand along the back of my neck periodically, they didn't bite. I walked for twenty minutes, or maybe a little more, than sat down on a fallen fir. I had been climbing, gradually at first, but must have reached the foothills. The ground was growing steadily steeper and rockier, and the size of the pines had dwindled to little more than saplings, growing tight together, blocking much of the sun. I still hadn't fully adjusted to the altitude and was breathing hard.

A stick snapped somewhere behind me, and I sat up. I'd been lying on the log, enjoying the independent feeling that comes with being alone in the woods, and hadn't realized how close to sleep I was. I turned toward the noise, but the trees were too thick to see anything. Then another branch broke. No closer than the first, but no further away. Something was in the trees, and the sensation I was being watched pressed down upon me, rooting my legs to the ground, beading sweat on my forehead. I strained to see through the gray trunks of the little pines, blinking frequently to prevent my vision from blurring. Out of the corner of my eye, I caught movement. Too fast to identify, and far enough to the side so I sensed it as much as saw it. Like the shadow of an airplane that flicks over the ground and is gone in an instant, something was there, but I couldn't see what. The feeling of being watched departed with whatever had been there, and an eagle screamed high above me to break the silence that had been so complete.

"Have a good hike?" my grandfather asked as I entered the kitchen, out of breath from jogging back across the flat. "Anything of note in the woods today?" He looked at me as if he knew the answer. He always looked like he knew.

"Not much," I said between heavy breaths. "Maybe an elk or something. Didn't see it."

"Up there where the trees get thick and those big chunks of granite stick up like bleached bones?"

"Yeah." He was looking at me as though he'd been there and had played a trick on me, fighting back a smile, trying to decide if he should tell me.

"Probably an elk. They bed in that dense timber during the day. Try to lay still and get away from the heat." He dabbed cologne from a dark green bottle onto his neck, headed for his room, then turned around. "Quick, aren't they?"

I pretended I didn't hear him, and by the time we drove out of the driveway, at least one of us prepared for a night of reveling, I'd forgotten about it. I looked out my window, over the tops of the orange fence posts to the woods, blending into the twilight, the distance between the first row of trees and the mountains seeming to shrink as it grew dark, and I didn't think about what I'd seen, or where my grandfather had gone, or the buffalo, or the easement. I looked at the fading sunset, and it was beautiful.

The Six Point was packed. It wasn't any later than nine-thirty when we got there, and already half its occupants were well on their way to being drunk. Little Elk was holding court from behind a table against the back wall, a circle of Indians around him, and judging by the number of empty shot glasses in front of him, he'd been hard at it for quite some time. His face, big enough to begin with, was swollen from the alcohol, and his large, round eyes were glassy.

Darla and Dell were sitting side by side at the bar, and my grandfather had all he could do to wedge himself between them. Pete and Ed Lewis, sitting a few seats, glanced up when we came in, then quickly went back to their beers.

"Laurie!" my grandfather called at the top of his lungs to the bartender. "Laurie, give us three swallows of bourbon, please. Three shots, and see that they're good full ounces, too." He slapped a twenty on the bar, downed the whiskey, kissed each of the women on the cheek, and squeezed back onto the floor. A half-dressed white woman I hadn't seen before was dancing by herself, turning and pirouetting with no regard to where she was or who might be in her way. She bumped into my grandfather, gave him a nasty look, and spun away.

I stood near the door, under the elk horn, half-heartedly watching the crowd. I didn't see one person closer than fifteen years to my age. Badger got up from where he'd been sitting with his brother, headed to the bar, spotted me, and grinned.

"Take my seat, Kyle," he said as he put his arm around me. "We're getting Little Elk drunk, and he's telling stories. Funny as shit!"

I picked my way through the sea of people between the door and Badger's seat, getting there in time to hear Little Elk, enjoying his audience, say, "Of course it wasn't the first time I got arrested." Someone had bought him a pitcher of beer, and he was drinking from the side of it, sloshing great mouthfuls down, ignoring the rivulets that ran from his lips onto the Camel Cigarettes shirt he had on.

"Tell about the car up to Butte, Little Elk," Badger said as he leaned over me with another pitcher of beer. His brother pushed his stomach off the table, stretched his arms over his head, and belched.

"You mean the Camaro?"

"No, the big Oldsmobile. The one that ran out of gas on the interstate."

Little Elk drained more beer, from the new pitcher this time, and rubbed his eyes. "Oh yeah. Okay." He rocked back and forth in his chair, lifted his left leg and farted, much to the delight of his friends. "I was up to Butte, you see," he began, wiping all expression from his face, trying to remember every detail. "I was up to Butte, and I was looking for something to fix my toilet. Kept running all the time. Couldn't sleep or nothing. Kept making that water noise. You know, the one that makes you have to piss when you hear it?" He paused until enough people nodded so he was sure everyone understood. He looked dead serious, as though it was an important part of the story. "Yeah, so I was up to Butte, looking around in the hardware stores. They got fifty of them. Must be a lot that don't work up there and is always needing fixing or something."

My attention wasn't riveted to the story the way everyone else's seemed to be. I was more interested in the painting above Little Elk. It was a canvas, framed in rough wood, beginning to fade, acquiring the look of a valuable piece of art, more because it was old than particularly well done. In the foreground was an Indian, maybe a chief, seated on a speckled pony, wearing a high headdress, and holding some sort of ceremonial spear covered with feathers and multi-colored runes. He faced west, where the sun had just set, toward a herd of buffalo running across the prairie. The animals closest to him were clear, but the ones further away, diminishing in size to add depth to the picture, were fuzzy. Their silhouettes showed up, brushed in dark black, but they looked empty. As though they might be ghosts. Beyond the buffalo, on the horizon, was a steam locomotive billowing smoke. The white column rose up, cutting the orange sunset in half, and along with a single eagle feather, tipped with the same white as the smoke, falling from the Indian's headdress, it was the sharpest image. On the base of the frame, was a tarnished silver nameplate, which, in capital letters read "MISSING."

A loud outburst of laughter turned my attention back to Little Elk. His original pitcher of beer was empty.

"So I figure I'll have a few drinks. No need to hurry home," he said. "Yeah, so I went in a couple of bars. Of course I had to get loose. Jesus Christ, I was sick of explaining to everyone what I needed for my toilet. Couldn't none of them help me. Pretty soon it's dark outside and I didn't have no more money. I got out in the street for some air, and here's this big car parked against the sidewalk with the keys in it. I think maybe someone left it there for me, so I get in, and Jesus Christ, must have been a midget driving it. Seat's all shoved up by the dash. Look like an old lady sitting in it. But that's all right, don't want to fuck it up for the next person, so I leave it where it is. Got one fuck of a good radio in her. Could get the country station all the way from Bozeman. Lots of speakers, and real loud."

"He's telling about the Oldsmobile," Badger said in a hushed voice to Darla and Dell. They were fighting for position near my grandfather, and Little Elk shot them a disapproving glance. They were detracting from his story.

"Keep going," my grandfather said, pushing the beer in Little Elk's direction. He nodded, poured a river of foamy liquid down his throat, and smacked his lips. His eyes were beginning to close.

"Yeah, this radio is a good one. Can't even hear the engine start over it. Didn't even know I started it until I'm all the way down to Front Street and headed for the interstate. Oh, there was a nice big engine in that son of a bitch. Big V-eight I think. Got her on the highway and gave her hell. Swerving all over the road, about hitting the guard rails, just giving it to her."

He was swaying in his seat, either to imitate the motion of the car, or more likely because he could no longer keep his great weight in one position.

"Got her headed out toward Feeley and she quit. Ran dry. Didn't realize it until she'd stopped, either, and I weren't off to the side. Cars were going out around me, honking their horns, some drivers giving me the finger, but I didn't pay no attention. Radio still worked good. Didn't need no gas for that, and there was a good song on. Patty Loveless." He worked his hips up and down. "So here comes the patrol. Puts forty fucking lights on, and parks right behind me. Big fucker, too. Don't like Indians, neither. Comes up and says something, don't know what cause the music's so loud. He gets red in the face, reaches in and shuts it off, and I say, 'Hey.' Well, he puts a hand on his gun and tells me to get out. Can't hardly do it, either, cause I got my feet all jammed in around those pedals. Takes me a long time. Traffic is all backed up. Good scene."

He finished the beer, and Badger bounced to the bar for another pitcher.

"Cop says to me ... he says, 'You know this car was reported stolen?' I look right at him, all serious like, and say, 'No, sir, I just took the goddamn thing. Don't know nothing about what happened after that. Ran out of gas here, though.' Oh, Christ, he came undone. Roughed me up a little. Not too bad." Little Elk sighed. "Sure would love to have a radio like that." He swiped a row of shot glasses off the table, sending them skittering across the floor, and put his head in his hands.

"Little Elk?" Badger poked him in the side. "Are you passed out, Little Elk?" There was no answer.

"A round on me," my grandfather said, getting to his feet. "Come on, Laurie, fill 'em up quick."

A steady procession of Indians left Little Elk's table for the bar. The juke box, half way through Garth Brooks's "I've Got Friends In Low Places," began to skip, Pete and Ed Lewis waltzed two giggling women out the door, and Little Elk began snoring. I stared at the painting, wishing I was back at my grandfather's.

"Come on, Kyle." He called to me from his seat at the bar, pushing Darla and Dell aside.

"Yeah, you can sit on my lap," Dell said, splaying her mammoth legs. I didn't move.

Badger brought me a glass of Coke. "Come on, Kyle. Go see my sisters. They want to fix you up with Katrina for the dance on the Fourth. Be a good time." He put his arm around me and eased me from my seat. "Who knows, might work out real good. Maybe you and I can be related sometime."

"Now," Darla wrapped a hand around the back of my neck, pulling me toward her chest, smothering me with the scent of whiskey and cheap perfume. "Now, what about the dance? You got someone to go with?" She loosened her grip and I slid two steps back. "Well, do you?"

I shrugged. "I don't know."

"Of course he doesn't," my grandfather answered for me. "What are we going to do about that?" He stroked Dell's hand where it rested on his thigh, placing Darla's on his other leg.

"You gonna ask her out, or what?" Dell's voice was deeper than her sisters. "We'll call her up right now and get her down here for you."

"Ask who?" I tried to sound perplexed.

"You know who," Darla said. "She'd go with you."

"Does she want to?" I didn't know if I wanted to go under any circumstances, especially if Katrina felt as forced as I did.

"You bet. So ask her, huh?" Darla removed her sister's hand from my grandfather, tossing it off him, leaning over onto him, covering most of his body. The best Dell could do was pry one of her legs under his. The women looked as if they were performing some sort of contortion: seeing who could fit more of themselves on my grandfather. I left him in their clutches, making a break for the door while he lifted his glass, knowing he would drink long enough to allow me to escape.

Outside, the Lewis boys had successfully danced their girls to their truck and were pulling out of the parking lot. I watched their tail lights fade down Main Street, losing sight of them as they dropped over a knoll near Cow Creek. Since the storm, the nights had been clear, and above the few lights of Mistake, the stars were shining. I leaned my head over the porch railing, looking up at them, thinking to myself that in all that was up there, even if the universe was infinite, there couldn't be another place like the one I was in. Not even if there were planets so far away we'd never know about them was there another Cole Richards. I could hear his laugh behind me, penetrating the walls of the Six Point as easily as sunlight does an open window, and for an instant I was scared. A sense of dread, anticipation of something awful drawing closer every second, combined with unexplainable sadness, the same feeling I felt when my grandfather talked to me in his underwear as I lay on his couch, swept over me.

Something tipped over inside the bar. Glass broke, and the heavy thud of wood on wood resounded over the still-skipping jukebox. The cacophony of voices fell silent, everyone's attention turned to the disturbance, and Little Elk spoke.

"To chief Little Elk Fishtrapper."

I opened the door enough to see in, planting a foot in the crack to hold it. Little Elk was up, his table overturned in front of him, balancing himself against the wall, looking at the painting, raising a shot glass to the Indian on the horse.

"To chief Little Elk Fishtrapper," he said again. "Chief of the Big House." He dumped the whiskey toward his mouth, catching some of it, spilling the rest onto his neck, then reached for the frame. He tucked the painting under his arm, tripped on his way out the door, and fell on his face. He got up slowly, kicked at the jukebox, and I stepped back to let him outside. Something had punctured the canvas when he fell, tearing a thin strip from the painting that hung free, twisting in the wind created when he opened the door. He stepped past without making eye contract, down the steps, into the street, pausing under a flourescent light to examine the extent of the damage done to the painting. It had torn near the Indian, separating the falling feather from the rest of the scene. As Little Elk stood there, holding it above him, it looked for all the world as if the feather had actually slipped from the headdress, and, like a falling leaf, would land at his feet. He lumbered away, taking steps no larger than a child's, the dull slap of his rubber soles on the tar gradually lost into the melody of a new song on the jukebox.

"Oh, it'll go by quick," Badger said. He'd come out while I was watching his brother. "Six months is nothing. Not for Little Elk."

"Six months?" It seemed like a long time to me, no matter how luxurious the Big House was.

"Yeah, he spent two years before. Robbed a store in Dillon that time. Got caught the next day in Great Falls trying to cash a bunch of checks he'd stolen. Not so bad this time. They might let him out early. Why don't you come back in, Kyle? Chilly out here."

Badger held the door a second, shrugged, then let it close. I didn't want to go in. The participants in Little Elk's going away party, which I now understood was held in celebration of his journey off to prison, a trip he'd no doubt earned rather then won, could continue their drinking without me, while I tried to make sense of a place where outlaws were honored with parties and getting drunk was as commonplace as eating supper.

The more I thought about it, the more convinced I became that this liquor-driven culture was nothing I cared to be a part of. If my grandfather wanted to spend his money on Darla, Dell, and beer, there wasn't anything I or the rest of the world could do about it. But if he expected me to act in the same manner, to be pawed at by drunk women, to laugh and cheer because a man was going to jail, and to be a pawn in his match-making schemes, he'd be disappointed. Katrina could find someone else, someone who didn't mind her mother's beer breath or her uncle's incarceration, to take her to the dance.

I stayed outside until I heard Laurie give the last call. It was almost two, and even the Indians had consumed enough alcohol. Darla and Dell were having a heated argument over who would go home with my grandfather. They stood toe to toe, red-faced and puffy-eyed, yelling at each other with no regard for who might hear.

"You had him last time," Dell said.

"Bullshit!" Darla stuck a thick finger into her sister's chest. "I would have had him last time, but that goddamn whiskey took it all out of him."

"Ladies, ladies, ladies." My grandfather stepped between them, elbowing his way into the middle of what appeared would break into a full blown brawl at any second. "Why don't you both follow me home?"

They stared at each other over my grandfather, scowling out of their bloodshot eyes.

"Okay, but I go first," Darla said, folding her arms across her bosom.

"Fuck you do," Dell retorted.

"Fuck I won't. Tell her I didn't get none last time, Cole." Darla grabbed my grandfather, and I headed for the door again. It was more than I could stand. I sat in the truck until they came out ten minutes later.

"Rushing our departure, don't you think, Kyle?" My grandfather was trying to fit the key into the ignition. "What's wrong? How come you didn't want Katrina to come down here? Bet she'd give you a little."

I rolled my window down part way and faced away from him.

"Hey." He lifted his hand from the screwdriver stick shift and pulled at my shirt collar. "Hey, what do you think about that?" He pointed to Darla and Dell, jammed into the front seat of a Ford Pinto, ready to follow us home. "Think I've still got it in me?"

I pushed his hand away. "I don't care, Grandpa. Cole."

"No, I expect you don't. Must be hell not to be able to drink. Have to watch everyone make asses of themselves. Well, hey, what about the dance? You gonna ask her?" We pulled into the road and headed up the street toward the Wise River bridge. It was amazing how he could drive a straight line without looking where he was going. "That'd be fun, wouldn't it?"

"No."

"What do you mean, no? She's a good looking girl, right?"

"I don't care." I still wasn't looking at him.

"Don't you think it'd be fun?"

"Fun? What, to have her get drunk? To have her family get drunk? That's all they do, Cole. I didn't know Little Elk was going away to prison." My grandfather slowed down and pulled into the parking spot beside the river where I spent my first night in Montana. "Jail, Kyle. Not prison. He just broke into the school. Didn't even take anything."

"Jail, prison, whatever." Darla honked her horn behind us. "Everybody's happy about it. Everybody's getting drunk and celebrating. Having a good time listening to how he stole a car. Everybody's having fun except me. You think I like coming down here and being around a bunch of drunk Indians? That's all they do, and it sucks! I'm not going to the dance with one of them. I hate them!" I pulled the brim of my hat down even with my eyes, breathing hard, ready to stand my ground no matter what my grandfather said. He didn't say anything for a minute, then he got out, walked back to Darla to Dell, and they drove away. When he climbed back in, he looked stone cold sober, and he gripped the wheel tightly. A couple of times on the ride home he started to say something, only to stop and shake his head before the first word came out. He didn't speak to me until we turned into his driveway.

"You really mean that, Kyle?"

"Yeah." I didn't know if I did completely, but I'd said it, and wasn't going to take it back.

"They do drink a lot, don't they?"

"All the time."

"Why do you think that is?" We stopped between the skidder tire and the canoe, and neither one of us reached for the door.

"I don't know."

"But you don't like it, huh?"

"No."

"Think you're better than they are?"

"I don't know. I don't get drunk all the time. Don't brag about getting in trouble."

"True. But does that make you better?"

I was ready to go inside. I rolled the window up, and he stopped me. "Sit right there," he said, raising his voice. I instantly dropped my hand to my lap. "You don't have a goddamned clue, do you?"

I was getting scared. I hadn't meant to hurt my grandfather's feelings, just make him see that our ideas of entertainment weren't alike.

"You'll sit here and judge people by what they do, even if it doesn't affect you, huh? Condemn them for the way they live after they've all been as nice to you as can be. I guess it don't matter that Darla's trying to show you a friend, or Badger gives you his seat, or Sarah invites you into her house and gives you something to drink when she ain't got hardly a dime to her name. I guess all that don't matter, does it? No, they drink, and so to hell with them all, right? Fuck!" He kicked his door open, but didn't get out. "How long have there been Indians in this country, Kyle? Do you know?"

I shook my head.

"A long fucking time. And do you know how long they've had to adjust to us? To stop hunting buffalo, get used to the idea of owning land, pay taxes, and speak English? Do you know?"

I slid as far away from him as the seat would allow.

"About one hundred and fifty years. Not very goddamned long. You'd think they'd be a bit more bitter about that, wouldn't you? You tell me when an Indian's been rude to you out here. Well, don't just sit there, tell me."

"They haven't," I squeaked.

"Really? But you hate them. Go figure. A man like Bruce Tipton who owns all the fucking land in the world wouldn't let Allen shoot one elk, and Sarah, who don't own a thing, would offer you a drink. And you hate them. You know why I don't? Do you?"

"No." I wished I could have taken back everything I said.

"It ain't cause I feel that I owe them anything. I don't. What happened a century ago was beyond my control, and I don't feel guilty about something I had nothing to do with. No, I enjoy their company because they treat me, and each other, like human beings. And that's pretty fucking rare nowadays." He stepped out of the truck, slammed the door, and began coughing, leaning over the hood, holding his chest, his head jerking up and down as he fought for air. It took him a couple of minutes to catch his breath, and he couldn't hide the blood on his lips. It showed up in the moonlight, darker than his beard, wetter than the dew on the sage. He wiped it away roughly with the back of his hand, and said, "I've got something . . . I've got something for you inside."

I let him get all the way to the house before I got out, and then I walked slowly. He was in his room, standing on his bed, fiddling with the trapdoor in the ceiling.

"Come in here, Kyle."

I hesitated in the living room.

"I shouldn't get so mad at you," he said without taking his eyes off the ceiling. "It ain't all your fault, but like I said, you don't have a clue. Come here and hand me that light off the floor."

I gave him the flashlight, wanted to tell him I was sorry, but couldn't. He slid the door into the attic and pulled himself up after it. I heard his footsteps above me, walking out over the kitchen, shuffling along the floor. A cloud of dust drifted down into his room when he returned, leaving a fine layer of gray film on his bed. He lowered himself through the hole and replaced the door.

"Very well then. You took your ass chewing like a man, and I've said all I'm going to about this. It's up to you whether you go to the dance with Katrina, but before you make up your mind, you need to be fully informed of all the facts." He took a small, leather-bound book out of his pocket and set it in my hands. "I'm going back into town. Take care of some business with the ladies if I can. You stay here and read this. You read this, and see if you don't learn something. And Kyle, you keep this between you and me. It don't need to go no further. No matter what you find out, it stays between us. Maybe I shouldn't have showed it to you, or maybe I should have before now. Anyway, I have the feeling that it's going to be rather enlightening."

The book was heavy for its size, tied closed with a piece of string. The initials W. H. R. were carved into the cover, and I stared at them, having no idea what they meant or what could be inside. I heard my grandfather's pickup start, drive away, then back up.

"One more thing," he hollered to me. "In case you're wondering, that belonged to William Henry Richards. He was your great, great grandfather, and besides me you're the first person to see it in one hundred and thirty years. You take your time with it, Kyle. It's who you are."

CHAPTER 10

I N 1862, William Henry Richards, twenty-five years old at the time, did not follow his father off to war. Instead, he left Kansas City, Missouri, with sixty-eight dollars his grandmother gave him, for the Montana Territory. As my eyes moved across the pages of his journal, I tried to imagine how he must have felt. He was young, and scared, but very determined, and with the addition of a little more than a century, I could have been the one writing, describing my emotions as I boarded the Greyhound in Syracuse. I read slowly, letting the words soak into me, forgetting how late it was.

Like so many men I know, I too am leaving home. But my rifle is not the cap and ball army-issue I've seen carried of by my father, uncle, both cousins, and countless others who are bent upon proving their point with a bullet. Neither is my uniform gray, my leader an officer, or my destination in the east. Every man must make his own decisions and live with the consequences, and my decision to travel west is not a popular one. My father quietly disapproves while my cousins mock me and my friends turn their heads. And so along with the weight of my pack, what little money I take, my buffalo gun and horse, I bear the heavier burden of knowing I depart unwanted and have a dreadful feeling that should I return, regardless of the outcome of the war, that judgment will not have changed. But I am convinced that my destiny does not lie on a battlefield amid thundering cannons and dying men, and this conviction, this will I have to see the west, serves to spur me on and ease my soul: a soul torn between leaving my home and everything that is familiar for the wilds of the Montana Territory, and staying to fight for something I do not believe in. I have made my choice, and even as I write can look over my shoulder and not see my home. I expect with every additional step I take that the gap between myself and it is growing forever wider, and I terrified.

I read on, trembling with excitement, the burning desire to find out what would happen next, the desire that is created by all good stories, gluing me to the pages, transporting me back in time, so that I followed a half step behind my great, great grandfather, experiencing all that he did. We were in Nebraska, wondering about Indians, suffering from brutal heat and lack of water, leading a horse that had become too lame to ride when I fell asleep. The writing was so vivid, and I was so enthralled with the story, that when my grandfather awakened me, I was disoriented. I expected to lift my head off a tall-grass prairie instead of the kitchen table.

"Good morning, Kyle. Hell of a beauty it is, too." I reached for the journal, but it was gone. "Your grandfather can still lay some pipe when he has to." He twirled to the stove and set a pan over the flame with a flourish. "Yes sir, I'll bet there are men in their prime who couldn't have done as well. By god, I feel twenty-five again. Ponce De Leon," he said, raising his hands above him, "you were looking in the wrong place, my friend. Kyle, I think I shall live forever."

I yawned, rubbed my eyes, and looked around the room for the book.

"Don't worry, I've got it," my grandfather said as he dropped half a package of bacon into the pan. "I'll hang onto it for safekeeping. Let you read it at night. Good, isn't it?" He started singing, ignoring the grease that spattered onto him.

I was tired. The sun hadn't come up yet, and I could have used another few hours of sleep.

"Start the logging, today, huh? Knock down a few of those big fir. Got to earn some money if I'm to keep up this nightlife. What do you say?" He flipped the bacon onto a plate and dug a carton of orange juice out of the refrigerator. "Sound good?"

I nodded.

"Wake up, Kyle! It's a beautiful day in a beautiful place. "

An eighteen-wheeler turned into the driveway, its Jake brake whooshing as it neared the house.

"What's this?" my grandfather bellowed, slinging the door open, pretending he was madder than he was. "Is my bliss to be so rudely interrupted?"

The truck came to a stop in the yard, and the diesel engine quit thumping. It was a new rig, as shiny as the milk trucks in New York, painted recently with large red letters. "Western Fencing" sprawled down the length of the trailer, and a mural of a neatly-fenced pasture full of cows had been done on the cab.

"Hey!" my grandfather called to the driver. He was a little man, short and stocky, and he wore a straw hat. "Hey, what's the meaning of this?"

The driver, busy opening the sliding door on the back of the trailer looked toward the house. "Buffalo fence," he shouted. "Did I wake you?"

"No."

"Got two more loads to drop off. This gonna be outta your way enough?"

"No, but I reckon it'll do. You gonna start putting it up right away?"

The driver shrugged. "Probably. I'm just delivering. You ain't seen a couple of men around here waiting to help me unload, have you?"

"No. And if their names are Pete and Ed Lewis, I wouldn't count on finding them." My grandfather closed the door and sat down at the table, unable to express the anger he ordinarily would. "We'll get that easement, Kyle. I can feel it. Won't be that bad then. Hell, might even stick a buff in the freezer from time to time. That'd be all right with you, wouldn't it?" He didn't wait for an answer. "I'll pack us a lunch and we'll hit the road. Got trees to cut, money to earn, and work to be done. Gotta work if we're gonna play." He slugged down his juice, stood up fast, and yanked a loaf of bread out of a cupboard. He tossed it into the air, caught it behind his back, and grinned. "I really do feel wonderful."

There wasn't much for me to do in the woods. The trees were so big that I couldn't move the limbs my grandfather cut off, and it took him more than forty minutes to fall, limb, and cut each fir to length. We couldn't skid more than two thirty-foot sections at a time, and about all I did was ride on the skidder, fill the chainsaw with gas and oil, and make damn sure I was out of the way when a tree came down. They fell harder than the pines, crushing anything in their path, sending shock waves along the ground for hundreds of feet.

I spent twenty minutes before lunch counting the growth rings on one stump. The tree was three-hundred and fourteen years old. It had already lived half its life when my great, great grandfather set out for the west, and I wondered what it would be able to tell me if it could.

We stopped to eat at noon, and sitting side by side in the shade, looked over our morning's work. There were six fewer trees standing than when we began.

"Fourteen sections to a truckload, four to a tree..." My grandfather worked the math out loud. "I figure about eleven hundred a load, minus three for that asshole and another two and a half for the driver ... leaves us with what, about six and a half hundred? Not too shabby, Kyle. Not too shabby." He brushed the dull orange dust off his pants, and leaned back against his cooler. "There's plenty of work here for me until the snow flies, and then I won't need to lift a finger all winter. I figure I can drink, sleep, and fuck right through to next April. That's living pretty high off the hog, ain't it? You bet, pretty high off the hog," he said to himself. "If you want to take a hike this afternoon, go ahead. I'll drop a few more trees and we can skid them in the morning. No point sitting around here with a finger up your ass waiting for an old man to do his job."

I pointed to the hillside above where we'd poached the elk. "What's over the top?"

"More of the same. Gets pretty steep. Might bump into some elk up there. There ain't as scared of the noise as you might think. You walk careful and you'll find 'em. So, what do you think of William?"

"William Richards?"

"Yeah. Quite a fellow, wasn't he?"

"It's exciting."

"You bet it is." He lay down and pushed his hat over his eyes, shielding his face from the sun. "Gonna get better, too. Wait and see."

"Dad doesn't know about it? I mean the journal?"

"No, Kyle, he doesn't. Go ahead and get out of here now. Let me catch a wink of sleep."

"How come you never showed him?" I didn't want to leave yet, but my grandfather was finished talking, and I knew I'd have a better chance of pulling his teeth than I would continuing the conversation. I flicked a

130

horsefly off his chest and stood up. Before I reached the top of the ridge, I heard his saw start again, the pitch rising and falling like a distant plane's propeller, as it chewed into another tree.

On top, I had a good view of Mistake. I could see the cupola on the school, the large, dirt parking lot of the Six Point, the bright tin roof of Pioneer Mercantile, and behind it to the Big Hole, reflecting the sky like a blue ribbon. West of the village, beyond where the Wise River crossed the highway, I picked out the turn to my grandfather's house, and could see the sage flat between it and the woods. On the north side of the river, the Pintlers held snow, and my grandfather said they might all year. The Bitterroot Mountains, steep and jagged, formed the horizon to the west, dividing Montana from Idaho. I turned east toward the Highlands, then south to face the Pioneers rising up in front of me. I could see more country from one spot than ever before, and apart from Mistake, there was scarcely a trace of civilization. This was the Montana I had imagined.

I spent the afternoon exploring and found a brittle, well-weathered mule deer shed, part of a coyote skull, and a leg bone from a cow, and the whole time all I could think about was getting back to William's journal.

The ride home was painfully slow, and I was greatly relieved when we passed the Six Point without stopping. I wolfed down a plate of deer steak, finishing before my grandfather was half done.

"I expect you're ready for some reading, aren't you?" He stopped chewing and motioned toward his room with his fork. "It's in on my nightstand."

The words were no more than out of his mouth before I was gone, and when he came into my room an hour later to let me know he was headed into town for the evening, William and I were on the plains, still searching for Indians, half wanting to see some, half grateful we hadn't.

With each day that passes, I grow more anxious for contact with the Indians. I have seen evidence of their presence: the unshod horse tracks, the feathered arrow I found embedded in the bank of a rare stream, and last night I spotted a fire a mile or two from where I camped. It could have been a wagon party, but I tend to think not. I rode hard most of the day today and surely would have overtaken anyone traveling along this route, and as best as I can determine, the most recent wagon tracks are a week old. Perhaps I should be thank-

ful for my solitude. I have been well-warned about the native inhabi-
tants of these prairies, but still cannot shake the desire to see them
for myself. And I want to see them while they are still in their own
element. I am quite convinced that the time is coming when this will
be impossible. A country that divides itself as sharply as ours has recently is in need of more space, and it will only find that to the west.
I have heard the stories of massacres, of the scalps of young girls worn
round the necks of their murderers, of the barbarous nature of these
tribes, and how a man has a better chance of walking unscathed
through the entirety of hell than through Indian territory when they
are on the war path. I have heard the stories, too many to totally dis-
count, and doubtless I would have a different opinion if my relatives
had fallen to a barrage of arrows and been left to rot without their
hair on this ground, but that is not the case, and my view of the Indians is carved only from what I have found for myself, which, up until
now, is very little. Even if all I have heard is true, I cannot place full
blame on them, and I am keeping an open mind. My father may be
lying in a Union prison or scattered over a battlefield, and not because he is fighting to preserve his home as the Indians are. I do not
understand how a country can kill off its own citizens for no great
gain, and condemn another race for defending what has been theirs
since the dawn of time.

I came to the end of a page and stopped. Reading the journal, it didn't seem
possible that more than a century had passed since my great, great grandfather wrote by the light of a small fire somewhere on the Nebraska prairie. I
could picture him clearly, looking out over the sea of grass, wondering if he
was alone, and it was only when I thought about Little Elk, Badger, and last
night's gathering at the Six Point that the writing seemed out-dated. And the
more I thought about it, the more I realized what my grandfather meant
when he said one hundred and fifty years wasn't very long. The changes that
had taken place between the time William Richards wondered if his scalp
would adorn the spear of an Indian brave, and Cole Richards wondered if
Little Elk could finish his car theft story before passing out, were irreversible
and complete.

I'd wanted to apologize to my grandfather for my disparaging comments about his friends since before he gave me the journal, and had he been there as I read, I could have done so sincerely.

I wet my fingers on my tongue to turn the stiff paper, holding the page by a corner, pressing the book flat against my covers. What I found in the next paragraph, even though I knew such occurrences weren't unheard of back then, shocked me.

I killed a man last night. A small, red-bearded man who crept into my camp to steal my horse. I have no idea who he was, or where he came from. He looked as if he had been living underground, some-where where the soil is dark and moist. His clothes, or what was left of them, were tattered and so stained that I could not make out their original colors, but the few buttons left on his shirt were brass. He may have been a soldier, and I can only imagine what disturbing turn of events led him to the desperate act of thievery. Had my horse not whinnied, I should never have awakened, and this morning, writing less than ten feet away from a freshly-dug grave, half of me wishes I hadn't. I have grown accustomed to sleeping with my rifle, and reaching for it was automatic. In the night, outside my small tent, my eyes not yet adjusted to the starlight, when he turned to-ward me, crouched on the ground, close enough to land on me if he sprung, I believed I saw a knife flash. I do not remember shooting, although my wrist is swollen and sore this morning so I believe I did so from the hip. All I remember is seeing the little man thrown back-ward from the impact of the big bullet, his back opening like a cup-board door, one hand reaching forward to me, slowly falling as life slipped away. I tried most of the night to close his eyes, but they re-mained open, and this morning, when I buried him, I laid a clean handkerchief over them as the only humane gesture I could offer. He couldn't have weighed much over one hundred pounds, and his concave cheeks looked hollowed from starvation. I cannot shake the image of those eyes, for they were blue, even in the night, and as wide as any I've seen. He was unarmed.

This seemed an appropriate place to stop reading. I didn't blame William for what had happened, and it was clear it wasn't his fault. Even so, it was a sobering image, and as I tried to sleep, I too could see the eyes of the dead man, blue against a dirty face and stringy, red hair. I saw him in my dreams as well, lying face up on the prairie, small clumps of yellow grass rocking in the night wind around his sides, a neat hole in the middle of his chest. It was a horrifying dream, so real that I believed I could hear the whinny of a horse and smell its pungent animal odor when I woke up.

It was gray outside. Mist had settled over the sage flat during the night, and it had not yet begun to rise. The journal was lying as it had been when I fell asleep, tied shut on the floor beside my bed, but my door, left open, was closed. I opened it quietly and walked barefoot to the kitchen. It was only four-thirty, but I'd had enough sleep.

My work boots rubbed against my heels, and the soles felt harder without socks. I didn't want to walk back into the living room and wake my grandfather, so I took his denim coat from the hook next to the door, and slipped outside wearing it and a pair of shorts. The mist was damp. I could feel it washing over me like airy waves of water, drifting along the ground, perfectly tracing the shape of anything it came to, swallowing everything less than four feet high. Standing in the sage, I looked back at the house, which seemed to float without a foundation, hanging motionless above the ground as currents of fog flowed all around it.

The air underneath the pines, across the irrigation ditch, was clear and ten degrees colder. Most of the dew had attached itself in glossy beads to the needles of the trees, leaving the ground as dry as it had been during the hottest hour of the previous day. Tiny twigs, buried under a thin blanket of needles, snapped each time I put my feet down. The crisp report of broken wood was amplified several times by the silence of the dawn. I walked uphill, trending toward the dog-hair lodgepole and massive granite monoliths where my grandfather said the elk bedded. Through breaks in the trees I could see the mountains, and behind them stars unwilling to give way to the new day. They looked like pinholes in the sky: bright punctures in the silver dome above the treeless mountaintops.

I ducked into the group of small trees where I'd heard something the last time I'd walked in the woods, parting their lower branches ahead of me, leaning to see under them. They grew so close together that I had to walk sideways, constantly shifting my feet around their limber trunks, keeping my open hands in front of my eyes to block the clumps of needles that poked at my face. The ground was steep, and as I ascended, the granite boulders grew in size, until, as I neared the top of a rise, they looked like prehistoric temples from a lost civilization, covered with centuries of moss, protected from discovery by an impenetrable forest. One in particular caught my attention. Its smooth sides sloped gently up to a flat top twenty feet above the young pines, and by jumping up a row of stones, each one slightly larger than the one in front of it, a natural set of stairs, I was able to reach its peak. Eons of rain had pitted the rock, giving it a sandpaper-like texture, slowly but surely transforming it into soil.

Behind me, the mist began lifting, sucked into the sky in strips, shrouding the entire Big Hole valley, thicker along the river, whiter near the trees. From the boulder, I had a good view of the Pintlers. The stars were gone, and the sky was turning blue. There was more foothill country in front of me than I would have guessed, and the lodgepole thinned out as the land rose and fell, rippling in swells toward the point at which it shot nearly straight up.

The bull elk appeared in the middle of a near-dry stream bed forty yards ahead of me, standing still, steam coming from his nose to prove he was alive, the water changing course at his feet to prove he was there. His velvet-covered antlers blended with the tan ground behind him, and his dark mane matched the trees he'd emerged from. He looked in my direction, our eyes meeting with only one of us aware of it, then took one step forward. A cow came behind him, a calf at her feet, and then the woods were full of elk, walking toward me, slipping through the forest as quietly as the mist in the valley met the sky. A calf, new to the art of walking in the woods, blundered into a fallen pine and received a reproachful stare from its mother. It trotted to her side, nudged her face with its nose, and together they disappeared into the trees behind me.

The bull walked slowly. He'd take fifteen or twenty seconds between steps, look over his shoulder, and lift his head, nostrils flaring for any scent that didn't belong. It took him ten minutes to cover the ground between the creek and my boulder, and twice he stopped to stare at me. He drew even with the rock, stiffened, and turned around. There was something behind him. Something I couldn't see, but it scared him. He let out a guttural whistle, threw his head back so his antlers lay flat against his body, and crashed into the tight timber. For a few seconds, the woods echoed the chaotic stampede of the elk. The snapping and cracking of low, dead limbs drowned out the babble of the creek. Then they were gone; melted back into the forest, absorbed by the country from which materialized.

I hadn't taken my eyes off the woods on the far side of the stream, and as I stared, fighting not to blink, shadows were transformed into alien creatures, and tree trunks were animated, all able to see me. The wilderness watched me the way a hawk does a mouse, waiting for the exact moment to swoop, giving my imagination time to anticipate its talons sinking into me. It took all my strength to turn my head, and I stared at the rock between my bare legs, I didn't want to look up, but not looking made it worse. While I turned away, it advanced, stealthily drawing nearer, approaching with dreadful accuracy, coming from every direction at once, immobilizing me with terror.

When I looked up, he was standing in the creek, exactly as the bull had, equally silent, equally still. His eyes were just as watchful, and when he moved he appeared to float, smoothly traversing the uneven ground like the fog. He turned before he reached the boulder, stepped behind a clump of head-high stones, and then my grandfather was gone.

The first rays of the sun lit up the mountaintops in front of me, driving away all fear, bringing a brilliance to the woods that comes only on clear days in thin air, cutting through the last wisps of mist, instantly heating the back of my neck.

I ran as hard as I could out of the woods, desperately trying to beat my grandfather home, imagining the whole time him floating along behind me, covering the ground effortlessly, moving through the trees like the elk. I cleared the irrigation ditch easily, more aware of the sound of my running feet than of how out of breath I was. I charged into the house, tore off the coat, and headed for my room.

"Good morning, Kyle." My grandfather was sitting on my bed holding the journal. "Been for a walk? I love to watch the sun rise. Watch the mist evaporate, and the trees come into sharp focus. Watch the elk move to their bedding ground . . . walk right underneath me." He stood up, set the book on my covers, and said, "Sometime I'll take you up into the woods. I know a great spot up there. A big rock you can sit on. Good place to see a bull."

I lay down on the bed, shaking from my run, wondering if there was anything my grandfather didn't know. I wanted to ask him, but didn't have the courage. I still didn't see how he beat me home, and if he'd told me hadn't been in the woods, as he probably would have, I would have gotten mad. As it was, I was shaken up badly enough. I had a hard time getting my spoon to my mouth without spilling my breakfast cereal, and couldn't keep my stomach from growling all the way to where we were logging. It rumbled and churned, twisted over on itself, trying to tie me in knots.

"What's eating you Kyle?" my grandfather finally asked. "You look like you saw a ghost. Where'd you go this morning?"

"You don't know?" I wasn't in the mood to fool around.

"I could guess. Probably up there in the forest where you went the other day."

I nodded. "Cole, what's up there?"

"What do mean?"

"In the woods. What's up there?"

"Well, lots of stuff I imagine." He began laughing. "Why?"

"I saw you there this morning." I said it fast, as though I'd been trying to get it out for some time.

"Yes, and?"

He didn't sound surprised. "Did you know I was there?"

"No, not exactly. I suspected I wasn't alone, but I didn't know for sure. Where'd you see me?"

"In the little creek."

"See the elk?"

"Yeah."

"Was there a bull?"

"Yeah."

"I knew it!" He slapped the dash. "Good one?"

"I guess. Where were you?"

"Just walking. Same as you I reckon. I love the woods before the sun comes up."

"You didn't go anywhere special?"

"Sure. That whole piece of country is special to me. Now, ready to go to work?"

I wasn't. He was taking everything too much in stride. "How'd you get home before me? I ran the whole way right after I saw you."

"I don't know." He got out and stretched. "Must be something last night added a little bounce to my step. Wonder what that could have been?"

He couldn't take anything seriously for too long, and when I asked him again, he started his saw, revving it each time I opened my mouth.

By noon, we had a high pile of logs on the deck, pushed on top of each other with the skidder, in need of a truck after less than two days. It arrived early in the afternoon, and I watched it load. It amazed me how easily the clam lifted the fir, and how skillfully the driver positioned the logs. He took twelve sections and said he'd be back for another load before dark. Whether or not my grandfather's actions from the night before added a bounce to his step, the prospect of the truck returning, bringing a check, certainly did. He hopped between the trees he cut, singing loudly each time he paused to let me fill his saw, scampering up the fallen trunks to limb them as easily and sure-footed as a chipmunk.

"Rolling in it, Kyle," he said when we'd parked the skidder for the day and collected our check from the log truck driver. "We'll be rolling in it like pigs in shit." He held the check to his lips. "Nothing sweeter. Not that I ever gave a good goddamn about money, but nor have I ever been too quick to pass it up. Besides, we've earned it. Can't feel guilty about pocketing green-backs that come as hard as they do in this line of work. Desk-bound, suit-wearing, five-hour-a-day working sons of bitches are the ones who should feel guilty, not us. Why don't you come into town with me tonight? Beer's cheap, ass is free, and a good time's guaranteed."

My grandfather was determined to get me into the Six Point again. I could see him thinking about stopping there on our way home. He shifted the truck into neutral, started to slow down, then kept going. "Too hungry. Getting too old to go at it with an empty stomach. What do you say, Kyle, you gonna come with me after dinner?"

I'd sworn a personal oath to never set foot in that bar again, but for some reason I didn't understand why it seemed to mean so much to my grand-father for me to accompany him. "How late will you stay?"

"Hell, who knows? Why, you got someplace you gotta be?"

"No, I'm just tired."

"Well, we don't have to stay too late if you don't want. Just keep in mind that the women all look prettier at closing time."

I looked at him suspiciously, staring all the way down the driveway, wait-ing for his face to break into the wide smile the way it would if I wasn't get-ting the complete truth, but he'd switched gears to buffalo. The fence, five strands of high-tensile wire was half up. It had already cordoned off the sage closest to the house and all along the driveway. Four men were still working on it, moving the barrier down toward where the irrigation ditch cut under the main highway near the Big Hole, winching the wire tight, driving the posts with sledges, encircling the pasture, cutting off access to the forest.

"Wonder where they'll put the gate to let me through," my grandfather mused. "Should have left room for it right here in front. Huh." He pulled at his beard, then reached for the check he'd slipped under his sun visor with his leather gloves. "What the hell. I got a good feeling about it anyway. He ain't gonna box me in that much. Oh give me a home," he began singing. "Where the buffalo roam . . . and I can piss on their heads from my porch. Where a man shall not starve, with buff in his yard . . . they'll fall down at the rifle's report."

My grandfather put three slices of deer steak and most of a stick of butter into a pan, set it on the stove, and headed for the shower. When the kitchen began filling with smoke and jets of orange flame leapt up in the skillet, I hollered to him. He came out with a towel wrapped around his waist and reached for the pan without noticing the fire that was lapping at its underside. He had the flame on high, and the old stove had plenty of pressure.

"You goddamn motherless bitch!" He jerked his towel off to use as a potholder. The door flew open when he kicked it and the pan sailed over his truck, the charred steak remaining in it. It landed across the driveway, skipped along the ground for fifteen feet and came to rest just the other side of the fence. "By god, I've got something for you," he bellowed.

He stomped into the living room, I heard the gun cabinet door open, and then he was back in the kitchen, naked, his thirty-ought-six at his shoulder. When it went off, I threw myself under the table, covering my ringing ears. My grandfather jacked another shell into the chamber, leaned against the doorway, and fired three more times, the blasts followed instantly by the slap of lead on iron.

"There." He was out of breath, his wind sapped by anger. "Sufficient retribution has been exacted. We'll eat out tonight, Kyle." He laid the gun on the table above me, gave the stove a forceful boot, and began coughing. It sounded as though there was something lodged in his chest. Something too large to cough up.

My hat was lying in on my dresser. I picked it up gently, careful not to let the snake-skin slide up the crown.

"Hurry up, Kyle. Your grandfather isn't going to let a little fir dust in his lungs keep him off the town for a night. Don't make a horny . . . I mean hungry man wait," he screamed from the kitchen.

I didn't know the Six Point served meals. I'd seen the long, silver grill behind the bar, but figured it was only there for show. When we arrived, only the die-hard drunks, an Indian wearing a cowboy hat that years of sweat and dirt had turned from black to gray, and the woman who I'd seen dancing alone at Little Elk's party, were in the building. Laurie looked relieved when my grandfather asked her for a menu instead of a drink.

"Still think you might want to give her a try, Kyle," he said without looking up from his menu as though he was suggesting the house special. "Yeah, I gotta believe she'd be a good one."

I went with a cheeseburger and fries instead, so embarrassed I couldn't look at Laurie when she took the order. The beef was good. Better than in New York. My grandfather said it was because it came from a local ranch instead of a meat packing plant. He said a lot of it was knowing how to cut it, too. He said in Montana the butchers have more pride than to "throw everything that won't make steak into burger."

By the time we'd finished, the bar was filling up. Badger and Sarah came in and took a table near the jukebox, and as soon as they sat down my grandfather sent a pair of drinks in their direction. Darla and Dell came in together, each fighting to be the first through the door, and Katrina followed a few steps behind. She waved when she saw me, and I pretended not to notice. Three men I'd never seen before, big men dressed in leather with lots of flashy metal on their coats, came in and looked around as though they were new. One of them noticed Katrina and gave a catcall, then they sat down against the wall under the antler and ordered two pitchers of beer. Their hands were blue with tattoos and two of them had earrings in both ears.

"A handsome lot for sure," my grandfather said to Laurie when she returned from dropping off their drinks. "Native Montanans, don't you think?"

Darla had somehow managed to work herself in between my stool and my grandfather, and in the process had all but shoved me onto the floor. Her broad back pressed into my shoulder, and I had to hang onto the bar to keep from falling. After a minute my arms began to ache, and I got down. The sun was setting, and I walked outside to watch it.

The Big Hole didn't look as formidable as it had a few weeks ago. Its slaty color was easing into a clearer blue, and the roar of the current was diminishing. Even so, there was still plenty of water, and where it turned in against the far bank it looked too swift to hold a trout. On the surface, tiny insects dimpled the eddies where boulders broke the river's flow, dotting the water like rain. Swallows dipped back forth between the banks, turning sharply over my head, feasting on flies.

As I watched, the sun fell behind the Bitterroots, and instantly the temperature dropped. Mist began forming over the river, the thin layers building on each other, imperceptibly accumulating, working gradually toward the point at which it would shield the land from night and remain until the sun rose.

"Hi, Kyle." It was Katrina. "Whatchya doing? Don't you want to come in?"

I didn't answer and she walked quickly to my side, saw I was staring upstream and stepped between me and the river.

"Come on," she said, giving me a playful push toward the bar. "You're gonna freeze."

"I like it out here," I said. "Too smoky in there." She shrugged, turned her back to me, and started away, her feet vanishing in the fog. She paused at the corner of the Six Point, then came running back.

"What are you doing on the Fourth?" She was wearing makeup, meticulously applied to make her dark eyes stand out against her cheeks, and when she asked, I almost said I'd go to the dance with her.

"I don't know."

"Don't you?"

"No, not yet. I'm not sure what my grandfather's doing."

"I know what he's doing," she said as if everyone did. "He'll be with mom. Maybe Aunt Dell, too." Her smile was much smaller than her mother's, and I caught only a glimpse of her teeth behind her lips. "I was wondering if you'd like to come to the dance with me?"

Now there was no getting away without answering. I scuffed a toe along a well-worn fisherman's path and stared at the line in the dirt.

"Well?" She was smiling wider, tilting her head to catch my eyes, still glued to the ground.

"Maybe." I said it softly, wondering why I couldn't say yes, half wishing I had.

"Maybe, huh? Is that maybe yes, or maybe no?"

"I just don't know what I'm doing."

"Okay." She didn't sound disappointed. "Well, if you want to go, give me a call or tell Cole. Only if you want."

She walked away, everything below her waist now enveloped by the mist, her footsteps fading into the thump of bass from the jukebox. I stood next to the river, watching the water slide past me as night set in, until the rapids and backwaters ran together into one dark shape, moving in unison below its blanket of fog.

Inside, loud voices, angry and fast, caught my attention. I headed for the door, hearing my grandfather clearly before I reached the porch.

"By Christ, I've listened to enough."

I cracked the door and saw him, off his stool, standing close to the table where the three rough-looking men were sitting, now surrounding half a dozen empty beer pitchers. I slipped in, and instantly a very excited Badger had his arm around me.

"They been making fun of my sisters. Said something to Katrina when she came back in, too." He was running his words together but the action was temporarily counteracting the effects of his alcohol, sending the glaze in his eyes far back, nearly out of view. "Cole ain't gonna take it no more." He squeezed my neck hard enough to choke me. "Ought to be one get going if they don't quit."

One of the men stood up, slamming his glass on the table.

"Sit down!" my grandfather roared. "This ain't gotta go any further, but I'm telling you now I'm not prepared to listen to any more. Not a single word. I'm willing to ask you once to stop, but once is all I'm asking." He stared at the men individually, training a hard eye on each of them for more than ten seconds, then turned back to his seat.

"Old man's scared," one of them sneered.

My grandfather was back at the bar when he heard the comment, and he swivelled in his stool slowly.

"Scared?" The jukebox finished its song, and the bar was quiet. "Let me tell you something. You ain't gonna listen, but I'm going to tell you anyway." My grandfather sounded calm, the way he did when he meant business. "I've seen the walls of mines fall in around me three times, been charged by moose, run over by bear, stomped by bulls, gone for six days without food or heat in the middle of winter, damn near drowned two or three times, and been given the boots so hard that snot rolled out of my nose and blood poured from ears. Mister, I've been called a lot of things, and I'm guilty of most of them. But if you think even for one split second that I'm scared of you ... of any of you, then you don't know me and you ain't done much living."

"Well, pardon me." One of them said. "Just go back to your fat bitches and we'll leave you alone. If I was you I'd be scared of them."

My grandfather came off his stool as though he'd grabbed a powerful electric line. "On your feet." He pointed to the man closest to him, a huge, barrel-chested Mexican-looking individual. All three of them stood up, and for more than a minute no one spoke. The Six Point was as silent as it was an hour after closing. "I know what you're thinking," my grandfather said in that dreadfully relaxed tone. "There's three of you and one of me and there's only two steps between us. Why don't you take 'em and find out what happens?"

The Mexican came first, but he hesitated too long. My grandfather hit him twice with a pair of short punches that drove him back into the table. Then his friends came, together from opposite sides. One of them hit my grandfather high on the head, knocking him off his feet, while the other drove a boot into his side as soon as he hit the floor. The Mexican jumped back in, kicking wildly, while my grandfather tried to cover his head. I was transfixed with terror.

"They're killing him!" Darla screamed. "Call the sheriff."

Badger was suffocating me now, wincing each time my grandfather absorbed a blow. Behind me, the door opened. A shadow moved across the floor as the person entered, then Calvin Bulltail, even bigger, it seemed, than the last time I'd seen him, arms bulging from a tight T-shirt, his dreadlocks swinging loosely around his shoulders, stepped into the Six Point. He picked Badger up out of his way, breaking the stranglehold on me, and closed his fists. The veins in his forearms looked like heavy yarn under tightly-wrapped cellophane.

It was over quickly. The three men lay broken and bleeding on the floor. It sounded like stout boards breaking when Calvin hit them, and I was afraid they were all dead. My grandfather wouldn't let Calvin help him to his feet. He was cut above his right eye, bleeding from the nose, and his lips were split, but the beating hadn't dampened his spirits.

"A round on me, Laurie," he said as he wiped his face on his sleeve, looked at the blood and laughed. "A round on me, and give Calvin a double shot of whatever he wants." He put his arms around Darla and Dell. "Sorry about the interruption, ladies, shall we continue?" He kissed them quickly, slammed down a shot of whiskey, and ordered another round.

CHAPTER 11

T o celebrate his beating, my grandfather got up extra early the following morning and was especially cheerful. I could hear him singing in the kitchen well before the sun came up, whistling country songs in their entirety, moving quickly between the stove and table. Shortly after the smell of brewing coffee penetrated my room, he stuck his head inside my door.

"Morning, Kyle. One hell of beauty, too. Shame a man's got to work on so nice a day." He skipped to the bed and pounded the mattress near my feet. "Got bacon, juice, muffins, and I've even sliced a few choice potatoes. Wake up and eat!"

I rubbed my eyes.

"Tired, huh?" My grandfather headed out into the living room then spun around. "Ain't been sliding a little ass in here without me knowing, have you?" He was back at my bedside hammering the mattress again. "Ain't been pouring the coals to some little cutey? Slipping her in through the window when I'm asleep maybe? That a boy, Kyle. That a boy." He bounced out of the room and began singing once more, belting out the words with unabashed gusto. "I'm a man of means . . . by no means . . . king of the road."

During breakfast, while the world outside slowly brightened and I gradually woke up, tractor trailers began chugging down the driveway. Unlike the one from Western Fencing, these looked rough. Their iron-slat sides were rusted and stained, and their cabs were a dull, off-white.

"Buffalo shit!" my grandfather hollered. "Can you smell it, Kyle? Can you?" he ran to the door and threw it open. "Christ, here they come.

Haven't been here ten seconds and already I despise them. Goddamn exotics!"

The trucks loomed up from the mist like giant ships, their high tops drifting in and out of focus, seemingly much further away than they were. And I could smell the buffalo. A heavy cattle odor crept into the house, able to cut its way through the fog, thoroughly saturating my nose. Over the engine noise, I heard loud braying and occasionally the thud of a hoof on metal.

"Listen to that infernal racket." My grandfather bit his nails and paced back and forth just inside the door. "Jesus, Jesus, Jesus. Worse than I thought. Intolerable. Just listen. Listen to that awful noise they're making. And that's nothing. Wait till the cows come into heat. Probably got a dozen bulls out there and all they'll do is bellow. Bellow from dawn to dusk. Bellow all night. Fuck!" He punched the door frame, then it looked as if his breathing slowed. "Okay, gotta make the best of it. Gotta get my easement. I've got something for them if it comes to it anyway. No use having a heart attack."

I watched the trucks unload their hoofed cargo while my grandfather dressed for work. Through the fog, the animals looked strikingly like the buffalo in the painting Little Elk had stumbled out of the Six Point with. They came out single file, and were herded into their new pasture through a break in the fence that I hoped would also allow my grandfather access to the woods. I couldn't tell how many animals were delivered. The trucks kept coming, some holding mostly cows and their light-brown calves, others hauling massive bulls whose shaggy, winter coats still hung about their thick shoulders and whose horns looked devilishly pointed. One bull, noticeably larger than the others, complete with horns which splintered into jagged tridents more than eighteen inches from his skull, hadn't enjoyed the ride and was ready to vent his wrath on the first thing he came in contact with outside the trailer. He charged down the loading ramp and careened into another truck, tossing his head madly against the grill, shearing off twisted hunks of metal, bellowing in rage and agony when he pierced the radiator and was drenched with steaming antifreeze.

My grandfather was right: the buffalo didn't fit in. Not simply as neighbors, but as a species. Watching the big bull bury his snout in the ground trying to ease the burn, I had no doubt that he wasn't cut out to be penned in, and I knew there was no longer any country where he belonged.

"Is the transplant complete?" my grandfather inquired from his room.

"Or have they begun unloading aliens as well? That'll be next. Step right up, ladies and gentlemen. Come and see the buffalo. See the buffalo and take a peek at the Martians, too. Buff from the past century, deep-space creepies from Roswell. Yes, indeed, right in Cole Richard's front yard. Just as natural as can be. Fuck!" A shoe whistled by my head and crashed through the window above the sink. "You want to go outside and pick that up, please, Kyle? Don't cut yourself on the glass, though. If it's too bad, just leave the goddamned thing. Hell with it."

I found the shoe several yards from the house, shook a few crystalline chunks of glass out of it, and brought it back in. I set it beside the door rather than give it to my grandfather, who I didn't figure needed any more ammo. I heard his bed squeak when he stood up after tying his boots, and then the whole house shook from a blow to the living room wall.

"You mark my words, Kyle. . ." he paused to cough. "I'm telling you straight that if this don't work out . . . if this don't go to my liking, that Mr. Bruce Tipton won't fear going to hell when he dies. He'll have been there and beyond long before his time's up, and will gladly embrace the devil himself as a kinder and gentler soul than Cole T. Richards. You can write that down on paper."

The door cracked against the siding, blasted open by a right hand from my grandfather on his way out. A breeze was blowing off the river now, billowing the fog, mercifully obscuring the buffalo. We drove up the driveway fast, pausing only once when a truck driver we nearly ran over gave us a dirty look, but as soon as my grandfather determined there was no chance for a fight, we were off again, going like a bat out of hell.

"Was all that stuff really true?" I hoped engaging him in a conversation would give us better odds of getting to work alive.

"What stuff?" He didn't take his foot off the gas, and when we crossed the Wise River we were going almost seventy five.

"What you said about everything that's happened to you and you not being scared. Before the fight last night."

"Every word. Never said I wasn't scared, though."

"I thought . . ."

"No, I said I wasn't scared of those men. Didn't say nothing scared me. Couple of those cave-ins about made me shit myself."

My tactic was slowly working. As we passed the Six Point, our speed decreased. "When you were mining, huh?"

"Yeah. They were a bad deal." He shook his head, and I could see him switching gears. "Nobody works a whole lot underground anymore. Too many fucking regulations. Too many people trying to take all the risk out of something that is inherently risky. No, not many gophers around now. Shit, used to be any two-bit company with a claim could go underground. Weren't no shortage of workers, either. It was profit, profit, profit. No EPA, no MSHA, no Board of Health. You didn't like something . . . felt it weren't safe enough, then you quit. Simple as that. Christ, nothing was safe. Like I said, I saw the walls come in three times. The first time it weren't real bad. Lost a couple of men and a few days of down time. The other two . . . they were big ones. Sounds like a roll of thunder way back in the mountain some-place. Low grumbles at first that take every bit of strength from your legs and lock you tight wherever you're standing. By the time most men are able to move, it's too late. Everything gives way, and I ain't seen the man yet who can hold up the earth. Even the dust is heavy. Thick . . . like trying to breathe sand. When it's all said and done, the men who weren't buried, they stand around looking at each other wondering why they lived and everyone else died, and if their time is coming next. Course I was scared. Scared to death."

"And when you said you went without food and heat in the winter? When was that?"

"I was twenty six or seven."

We stopped at the gate at the base of the draw below where we were cutting. It had never been repaired. Staring at the few pieces of fence post left, it seemed like years earlier that I had cowered in my seat awaiting a hail of bullets from the range riders.

"Hey, you still with me?" My grandfather punched me in the arm, and I blinked. "Good. Like I said, I was in my mid twenties. Spent a winter trapping the upper Big Hole. Some of that country around Jackson and Wisdom. Lived in the woods pretty near all winter long. I was running a long line about thirty miles. Had a few camps set up along the way where I'd stashed dry wood, spare rifle shells, and other odds and ends. Got stuck in one of those little fuckers for damn near a week. Blizzard howled all around me, putting down foot after foot of snow, cutting visibility to zero. Hadn't counted on that and didn't have enough food. Stupid mistake on my part. If she'd turned warm after that and all the snow had gone soft, I'd have been in a real pickle. Weren't no fun as it was." We started up the dray in low range. "Now, you ready to kill some trees?"

I nodded. "How's your head?" The cut above his eye had scabbed over during the night, leaving a dark gash in the skin.

"My head?"

"Yeah." I touched my eye.

"Oh, that's nothing. Don't bother a bit."

"Really?"

"Hell no. Ass whippins only hurt for a little. It's like I told you. The bruises heal a lot quicker than your pride if you tuck your tail and back down when you know you hadn't ought to. Can't ever be bullied, Kyle. If you never let anyone walk on you, then you won't ever lose. Hell, this old face has been through way worse than that." He slapped his cheek. "This ain't nothing. But all the same, I wasn't sorry to see Calvin show up. Lordy, can that man ever throw a punch."

I was going to ask him about being "stomped" by a bull, or his brushes with drowning, but decided to save the questions for a more strategic time, when they might prevent a bad wreck.

We began cutting a stand of a dozen fir considerably larger than the other trees. They had sprouted on a south-facing slope long before any white man had the slightest notion of what Montana looked like, perhaps even before his concept of the world reached west of Europe. I usually didn't stick around when my grandfather began cutting, but I wanted to see these trees come down. I wanted to watch several hundred years of history end.

The first one was hollow. Its center had rotted long ago, leaving a shell of healthy wood to hold up its prodigious weight. My grandfather and I peered into the cavity once the tree was lying prostrate, looking into the dark chasm, the inner cancer eating away at the wood.

"I'll be damned," my grandfather said. "Hollow." He removed his hat and brushed the orange dust from it. "Probably leave these others, huh?" I think he knew I wanted to anyway.

"I guess. Are they all hollow?"

"Probably. It's time's way of catching up with them. Letting them know they aren't immortal."

Time had a way of catching up with everything. No matter how great it was, what it had been through, or how long it had lived, nothing could escape the cycle of life and death. A cycle about which, at the age of fourteen, I had only been vaguely aware until I'd come to Montana. In the few short weeks I'd spent with my grandfather, however, it seemed time was catching up with everything I saw. Everything from the way the Indians were living, to Tipton's buffalo, even to my grandfather. And although he'd never admit it, as he sat on the ground next to the fir, sweat running down over the purple bruises on his face, his hands cracked between their wrinkles, coughing quietly into his shirt collar, he was showing the inescapable signs of time. He was aging, probably faster than ever before, but he wasn't catching up with the world around him. As I thought about him wading into the fight last night, threatening Pete and Ed Lewis with his shotgun, and a dozen other things he'd done as naturally as getting up in the morning, it hit home that he and the twentieth century were on divergent paths. Suddenly, I wanted to hug him, but before I had a chance to move he stood up.

"Happens to the best of us," he said, giving the cavity in the fir a half-hearted boot. "Now, we can leave the others, or try one more. Lot of wood in it if it's solid."

I pointed to a slightly smaller tree that was straight and relatively free of limbs. "How about that one?"

My grandfather scanned it, and nodded, and even before his saw was a third of the way through it, he knew it was hollow. The dust billowing out around as he worked the blade deeper into the wood was too fine to be coming from solid lumber.

The tree began leaning sooner than expected. Its crown, one hundred and thirty feet above us, shifted violently, and my grandfather yanked his saw free and stepped back just as the fir uprooted, pulling ten yards of dirt from the hillside, exposing a circle of dry earth that hadn't seen the light of day for three hundred years.

Something protruded from the soil, too white to be a rock, and my grandfather and I saw it at the same time.

"Pick it up, Kyle." He gestured toward the object with his saw. "Some sort of bone, I think."

I tugged at a corner, bending close to the ground, pulling for all I was worth, falling over backwards when it broke free. I sat up, looked at my grandfather, and he smiled. At my feet, was the better part of a buffalo skull.

"Now that's a buffalo. A real one," he said.

I had hoped for something more exotic. "I thought it was a dinosaur bone."

"It is," my grandfather said under his breath as he headed for another patch of trees. "Buffalo Extinctosaurus."

I stuck close to my grandfather all afternoon, afraid to let him out of my sight. I couldn't stop thinking about the hollow trees, still standing yet connected much more closely to the punky remains of their ancestors, lying in various stages of decay below them, than ever before. They were waiting now. Waiting for a gust of wind during a summer storm, a night of heavy snow in December, or a week of rain in May. No longer could they expect to shuck off nature's barrage of weather as they had one hundred years earlier. They had reached the point in their lives when a single extreme event would prove too much for them. As I picked clumps of dry earth from the cavities in the buffalo skull, I wondered if it was this way with everything. If it was, I wondered where my grandfather was at in his life, and what might have happened if Calvin hadn't arrived at the Six Point when he did?

A cloud drifted in front of the sun, momentarily shielding me from its searing heat, and in the short time I sat in its shade, no more than a few seconds, I realized what all young boys do at some point: that they will become men, and as surely as the sun rises and sets men grow old and die like everything else.

"Kyle Richards, you're not earning your keep sitting up there playing with that fossil!" My grandfather waved me to him. "Get over here and give me a hand."

I walked to him slowly on legs as unsteady as if they'd never taken a step. Twice I slipped, the second time cutting my hand on a coarse chunk of granite. The pain returned me to full mobility, and by the time I reached my grandfather I was no longer concerned with aging.

"Scraped yourself I see," he said pointing to my hand. "Goddamn sharp stones. Should have flung the son of a bitch down the hill. You want a band aid?"

I looked at my palm. It wasn't cut badly, and I didn't feel like going to the truck.

"Tough it out," my grandfather said proudly. "That's my man."

I looked around him, wondering what it was he needed help with. He'd finished limbing a pair of trees he'd dropped side by side, their tops almost touching.

"Decision time, Kyle. Time to choose." My grandfather worked a fir needle between his teeth like a toothpick. "The way I see it, we could either spend the rest of the afternoon here and get maybe another load of logs dealt with, or we could go home and get ready to head up to Firewater Lake in the morning. How do you weigh the options?"

In my mind, the choice was clear, and I'd been around my grandfather long enough to know he appreciated me saying exactly what I felt. "Let's go camping."

"Very well, my sentiments precisely. All my life I've worked to live, not the other way around. If you keep that in mind, there are a lot worse things you could do." He slung his saw over his shoulder and without another word headed down the hill to the pickup. I came along behind with the buffalo skull, disregarding my grandfather's suggestion to lay it in the back. I kept a tight grip on it as we bounced our way toward the pavement, pressing the chalky bone into my lap, thinking it had moved far further in the past ten minutes than it had since becoming entombed under the fir three centuries earlier.

Tall strands of pink fireweed were coming up in the ditches along the highway where the road crews had burned the dead grass in the spring. Their delicate flowers were just beginning to show, and mixed around their stems were hundreds of blue lupines. Along the Big Hole, the cottonwoods had, overnight it seemed, lost their golden spring hues and their leaves blew bright summer-green in the afternoon breeze.

My grandfather shut the truck off at the head of his driveway and stared at the buffalo. They were milling around near the fence, cropping the grass that grew under the sage, talking to each other in low bellows.

"You hear that, Kyle?" He thrust his head our his window and shuddered. "Like souls in hell. Let us out, let us out." He held my buffalo skull to the windshield and said, "This is what you become, ain't it?"

One animal left the herd, the massive bull with the broken horns, and trotted toward us.

"And what do you have to say about this, my beady-eyed gentleman?" My grandfather set the skull down on the seat and opened his door. The bull stopped even with the pickup and tossed his head side to side. "Have you come to pick a fight? If that's what you're thinking, I suggest reconsidering. One hundred and twenty years ago I'd have left your bones to bleach right where you're standing, and you underestimate me if you think I wouldn't do the same today." My grandfather let the truck roll forward, turned the key, and said over his shoulder, "I don't get my easement and you and I will have ourselves a little understanding."

The bull followed us all the way to the house, hooking his horns under the fence in several places, staring at my grandfather as though he'd understood every word. He did not appear dissuaded.

I was anxious to get back to the journal. My grandfather said he would pack the camping gear if I wanted to read before dinner, and I jumped at the chance. Lying on my bed, I untied the diary, opened its pages carefully so I wouldn't skip past where I'd left off and see something that would give away what was coming. Before I'd finished the first paragraph, I was more concerned with what William did after shooting the would-be horse thief than my buffalo neighbors, my grandfather's easement, and even the prospect of camping at Firewater Lake, something I looked forward to very much, had faded to a dim sense of anticipation.

I rode hard today, putting distance between myself and the mound of disturbed dirt I left without a marker. Doubtless it is but one of many mounds on this trail, but the others, and what they cover, are not mine. I will never know who he was, only that from now until eternity he will call this Nebraska prairie home.

I have still not seen an Indian, and although I came across another set of unshod tracks this afternoon, they looked old. I am beginning to wonder how many Indians there are. Living as they do, much at the mercy of nature, I expect they run no danger of overpopulating.

My horse is tired, and I do not think I'll get off to an early start tomorrow. He's earned his rest, and being the only company I have, I want to ensure his well-being.

I have always kept to myself, but this is the first time I have spent my days so totally alone. It affords me a great deal of time to think, and invariably by thoughts turn to my destination. It is hard for me to imagine exactly what it will be like, and perhaps all I really know is that it will be different. I suppose that is why I am going. I want to be part of something new. To make a home for myself that can be mine alone, and see part of this country that can, with good conscience, make the claim that it is wild. I dream about the territory often. The mountains that hold snow in summer, the vast herds of buffalo, and clear streams as cold as winter air where gold glitters under the surface and beaver are plentiful enough so even a novice trapper like myself can catch them. And then I dream of a river. A huge, powerful river that thunders through canyons, sprays its misty breath high onto its banks, and dashes to pieces anyone foolhardy enough to enter it. This dream is always the same, so real that I have trouble believing the river does not exist. It flows through more than my mind, and I am convinced it holds something for me.

I stopped reading. Was this the Big Hole? Did my great, great grandfather ever have the dream about the Indians the way I did? Probably not, but I felt a strong connection to him that seemed to tie me closer than four generations. I read on with interest, holding my breath when he described an encounter with rattlesnakes, sharing his anxiety over the constant possibility of a disastrous meeting with Indians, wondering just as he did if he would ever reach the Montana Territory. I could smell his campfires, picture the soldiers he met at outpost forts, and understand, at least to some extent, how he felt being alone so much of the time. As he crossed into the Dakota Territory, it became apparent just how dangerous a journey he was making.

Buzzards. High soaring proclaimers of death. Dozens of them drifting on the horizon, rising and falling without a quiver from their ragged wings, soaring above the baked earth and rotting flesh.

That is how my day began: leading a lame horse toward death. From four hundred yards, I could make out the charred wagon. The black smudge among thousands of serpent-like heat waves, and the smaller objects lying around it, were the only things visible in the ankle-high grass for half a mile in all directions. For a long time I debated skirting the scene, and now wish I had.

I understand the line between life and death narrows in this new country. It's easily crossed, usually when least expected, almost always with horrific, irreversible rapidity. To go from the living to the dead is as easy as stepping on a snake, miscalculating a river's flow, allowing the tiniest cut to become infected, or building too big a fire to cook on. That's what this family had done.

The blackened circle on the prairie, the overturned kettle of soup, the potatoes shriveling like skin held too long under water, told the story all too well. An evening dinner had turned into a massacre in which four people had lost their lives. The bodies had been left as they fell, so a reconstruction of the killing was possible, and even though my stomach was churning and my head pounding, I was unable to continue until I had examined the scene long enough to get a vivid picture of what had happened.

The mother, a woman in her early thirties, was cooking supper and had been the first to die. A roll in the land scarcely large enough to conceal a badger had provided the attackers with sufficient cover. Attracted by the column of smoke, they'd crept in unnoticed, and she'd been killed before she could turn around. She probably stepped from life to death without realizing she'd done so.

I expect her husband died when she fell into the fire, knocking over the kettle. He'd taken two arrows in the chest, but had managed a few steps toward the wagon where his daughters were likely resting. Dark trails of blood from his wounds painted the grass around him for several feet. He might have screamed, possibly a last-breath warning to the girls.

The older of his daughters lay twenty feet from the wagon, shot in the back as she ran for her dead mother. Her sister, as young as six or seven, never made it out of the wagon.

It was the most shocking thing I have ever seen. So terrible that nothing could have prepared me for it, grisly beyond belief, and it drove home how barbarous humans can be. A bear or lion that kills to eat fits far better into the scheme of nature than predators who kill for the sake of killing and leave their victims naked, scalped, and sporting the arrows upon which their life blood ran out.

Everything of use had been taken from the wagon before it was set on fire, and so little of it remained that it had only partially cremated the girl. She lay drooped over a side rail, her body black and peeling, save her left hand which was still white, soft-looking, and so very childlike that I am not ashamed to say I wept.

It is one thing when men willingly go off to battle, no matter how trivial a cause they fight for, and are killed. It is quite another when defenseless women and children are slaughtered, and I cannot believe that the sanctity of the family differs so greatly between our culture and the Indians' as to permit this type of wanton killing. I prefer to

believe these murderers are radicals. It is the only way I can begin
to rationalize what I saw. To believe there are people on earth who
would not be appalled by this, and who still possess any morals, goes
against my basic instincts. If we have driven the Indians to this point,
stripped them of all values, making them desperate enough to strike
out at every aspect of our society, than it is regrettable, but better to
continue our campaign to wipe them out entirely than allow a war
against our women and children to continue. My sympathy extends
only so far, and should I have the opportunity to avenge the people I
saw today, I would take it without hesitation.

Tonight, my fire is small and my senses are sharp. I doubt I shall
easily be overtaken by sleep, and perhaps that is just as well. I dread
to think how my unconscious mind might pervert what I saw today,
and even as it is I imagine buzzards overhead, circling patiently, waiting to feast on me exactly as they do everything that dies on these
plains. They do not discriminate between a deer and a woman, and
for them death means sustenance. As horrible as it sounds, this is a
comforting thought. One which provides a tiny shred of purpose to
what appears so senseless.

I will be glad to get where I'm going.

I ate my supper of deer steak outside, sitting on the overturned canoe alone.
My grandfather must have sensed I didn't want to talk, and probably knew
where I was in the journal. Between bites I watched the buffalo, wondering
if my great, great grandfather had seen any yet. The more I read from his
diary, the more I understood how much things had changed in the past century. Like cutting down a tree that took three hundred years to grow, the entire west had become something as different now as day from night. I had
trouble imagining, partly because I didn't want to, the murdered family, and
it was odd to feel so strong a connection to William and not be able to picture everything he saw. I had no trouble seeing the prairie, some of the people he met, and sharing his desire to reach Montana, but my head refused to
create images of the naked bodies lying around the burned wagon. It was
too foreign for me. Too impossible to happen now. I did understand what
he said about a narrow line between life and death, and clearly saw how it

had widened over time. Even my grandfather, who prided himself on being impulsive to the point of reckless, wasn't in much danger of dying unexpectedly due to a missed step or a minor cut. And the idea of Badger and Calvin ambushing him, sticking him full of arrows, was absurd.

Darkness descended over the Big Hole valley slowly. The sun made a final curtain call, sending a beam of light onto the mountains east of Mistake, a good-night kiss that faded quickly, leaving the world dim and the shadows growing. The buffalo lay down, content to chew their cud, and behind them in the forest an owl called. I sat outside until I could no longer see beyond the fence, listening to the owl's persistent hooting, then ran for the light in the kitchen window.

CHAPTER 12

T HERE WASN'T as much water in Cow Creek as when my grandfather and I had first fished it. Moss-covered boulders that lay completely submerged earlier in spring were jutting up from the current, their green heads exposed to air for the first time since snow began melting in May. I followed my grandfather up the stream on an elk trail that ran twenty yards from the water, watching his pack with our tent and sleeping bags in it shift each time he took a step. I carried a much smaller load: our frying pan, sandwich bags of flour, salt and butter, a few packs of matches, and a bottle of mosquito repellant. I also had our rods, and this time we were using flies. Tucked into the light jacket I wore, I could feel the rough corners of William's journal against my ribs.

We stopped to rest where a tree had come down across the path, and my grandfather slipped his pack off.

"What do you think, Kyle? This beat logging?"

The sun was beginning to poke through the limbs above us, evaporating what little dew had fallen the night before, stirring to life a swarm of mosquitoes that whined around my head, constantly trying to land on my ears. They didn't seem as bent upon biting my grandfather, and I wondered if sometime during the many years he'd spent in the woods he'd reached a truce with them.

"Well?"

"Yeah, I guess."

"Yes, indeed. All work and no play makes Kyle a dull boy. Now, speaking

of play. . . ." He eased closer to me, and I cringed, knowing full well what was coming. "What about the Fourth? Are we double dating? Having ourselves a little mother/daughter combo?"

I looked away and tossed a dry pine cone toward the creek.

"How 'bout it? You can at least go to the dance, can't you?"

"Just the dance?" I wasn't really sure if I wanted to go, but if it would keep him off the subject for the rest of the trip, I was prepared to give in.

"Yes, just the dance."

I studied my grandfather carefully, looking for any signs or deviltry in his eyes. As I nodded, part of a dream from the night before came to me. I was sitting next to the Big Hole with Katrina, watching the night close in, listening to peeper frogs, which was odd because since coming to Montana I hadn't heard any. I strained to remember more, but I might as well have tried to hold the ocean at high tide or the sun from rising, and as we began walking again I wasn't sure if I'd dreamed anything at all.

The elk trail began to side-hill away from the creek where the ground rose more sharply, and we left it in favor of a more direct route through smaller trees and larger boulders. Half a dozen magpies flapped up from behind one stone, their black and white wings beating furiously, their long tails dragging behind them.

"Come here, Kyle, this is good." My grandfather had gone to investigate what the magpies had been feeding on. "What do you make of this?"

And elk calf lay partially buried under needles recently heaped onto it. Its stomach had been torn open, and most of the meat from its midsection was gone. My first thought was a grizzly bear, and I looked around nervously.

"That's right, they're close," my grandfather whispered. "Could be watching us right now."

I lifted the pack from my shoulders and back away. "Bears?"

"Lions. Look here." He pointed to the tracks. "Here's mama." He traced the outline of her foot in the loose dirt thrown up around the elk. "And here's her kittens. Two of them."

I cautiously moved close enough to see the tiny pads, then backed away again. My grandfather stood up, and as he did something moved through the trees fifty yards uphill. "There!" he hollered. "Did you see it?"

As far as I was concerned, it could have been a shadow. It was there, and then it was gone. Like the dream I'd had.

"Not everyone gets to see a mountain lion in the wild. Damn few in fact. That's a good sign. Gives me the kick in the ass I needed to keep going. What'd I tell you about keeping your eyes open while you're out here? Never know what you'll see."

I'd seen something, and if my grandfather said it was a lion then that's what it was. All the same, I would have been just as happy to see it from the confines of his pickup.

My mid-morning, the hot sun had sweat all fear of lions out of me, and I simply wanted to reach the lake. We were climbing a series of steps in the mountain, and I fully expected to see shimmering water at the top of each one. Instead, I found more granite and pine.

"Take that damn coat off if you want, Kyle," my grandfather said without turning around. "You can put the journal in my pack."

I stopped walking. He knew everything.

"We don't have much farther to go. See, listen."

Something that sounded like thunder came to me, rumbling deep in my chest, fading slowly. "What is it?"

"The lake."

"What?" I was out of breath in the thin air and needed an excuse to rest.

"The lake. You'll see."

Twenty minutes later I could see it, a small oval of blue lying in a bowl rimmed on three sides by cliffs holding chimneys of snow and great opaque patches of ice. As I stared, a rock slide started below one chimney, gaining speed and size as it pounded toward the lake, sending a jet of water thirty feet into the air and a two-foot wave across the surface.

"Yes, and hello to you, too, my dear," my grandfather said as he tipped his hat to the lake. "Been a long time."

The ground was spongy along the shoreline, and each step we took drove several dozen mosquitoes into the air. They followed us in clouds, deterred very little by the greasy repellant I doused myself with. Near a circle of stones, an old fire ring now sheltering a clump of lupines, my grandfather dropped his pack.

"This will work right here I believe." He sat down, lay back to stretch, than sat up fast when a horsefly bit him on the neck. "That's a fine how do you do," he said crushing the insect. "Hey, why don't you take a hike while I set up camp? Fishing won't be worth a damn until this evening, and if you keep walking the mosquitoes are somewhat less apt to carry you away."

I set the rods and my pack down beside him and looked up at the cliffs.

"Be careful if you go up there. Don't get too near the edge, okay? Those goddamned things will stand just fine for ten thousand years, but the minute a man steps on them they're liable to let loose. Look for mountain goats. Ought to be a bunch of them around someplace."

A spear of stunted lodgepole shot up along the rim of bare rock separating forest from cliff, and I worked my way through these trees toward what appeared to be the top of the world, until above me there was only sky, stretching away so far in all directions that looking at it made me dizzy. I could see south over three mountain ranges well into Idaho, north to a fuzzy horizon of light blue, the combination of earth and sky, east all the way to the edge of Yellowstone, and west over the Bitterroots to more mountains, their snowy peaks standing like white pyramids. Closer, I could trace the Big Hole's path from the wide hay meadows near Jackson, green smudges between the blue Pioneers and Pintlers, all the way through the canyon to Mistake.

Soft clumps of winter goat hair clung to the rocks all around me, and in less than three minutes I'd filled my pockets. I found a reasonably flat rock to sit on, close enough to the edge of the cliff so I could see my grandfather, working like an ant below me, far enough from its face so I wouldn't tumble off. I turned into a gentle breeze, welcome relief from the heat and mosquitoes, and opened William's journal. I read about his first encounter with buffalo and Indians, and unlike the macabre scene he'd described earlier, I took in all of it as though I were there.

More buzzards. Too many to feed on another party of humans, they fill the sky like winged ants come to feed on a slice of honey-drenched bread left behind after a picnic. They keep coming, from everywhere it seems, and each time the wind shifts into my face I smell the sickly-sweet aroma of souring flesh.

My horse is better, and I have been riding most of the morning, making good time, but the closer I get to whatever has died in such mass quantities to foul the air more than a mile away, the more inclined I am to walk. I expect it is my, and all humans' reverence of life that makes me wary. Whatever lies ahead is dead. There is no mistaking that, and however rudimentary a life form it is, it was recently alive. That common bond between all creatures, the fact that we all live and die, already ties me, if only remotely, to what I'll discover. I am hesitant.

Nighttime. Five miles upwind of death's perfume, I cannot rid my nostrils of the smell. It hangs there like heavy fog over the Mississippi, the river that seems a million miles away. Much farther than the one in my dreams, and far more unfamiliar. My home and family are equally distant. The weeks since I left feel as if they've stretched into years. A premonition of how long it will be before I return? Perhaps. Perhaps I have been traveling with a half-buried notion that I could quickly retrace my steps any time I wished. Turn around and be home in time for supper no more fatigued than if I'd spent the day catching catfish three miles from my house. Perhaps what I saw today, combined with the lingering visions of the dead family, finally pounded into me the magnitude of what I'm doing.

I saw my first buffalo and Indians. The buffalo were dead, and the Indians were ghosts.

The first thing to strike me about buffalo is how enormous they are. Lying hideless on the short-grass prairie, they looked like giant, pink boulders. There were a hundred or so of them, all dead, save one calf that refused to leave its mother. It kept nudging her open stomach, unable to see it would be as apt to get milk from a stone.

Thousands of pounds of meat were rotting, and where the skinning knives had inadvertently opened the paunch, horrible odors spilled into the air, calling buzzards like a dinner bell. Three sets of deep wagon tracks led away to the south. Somewhere beyond the horizon, the hunters, laden with hides and tongues, their mules straining against their heavy loads, were headed toward civilization. They left behind a winter's worth of meat for a small village, toting only what would bring them immediate profit.

I have heard there are so many buffalo that the earth shakes when the great herds stampede, and one can see more than ten thousand animals at a time. Their numbers have been likened to the stars, and I hope it is true. If not, there is little chance they can survive. It is clear they have limited fear of people and no concept of what a rifle is capable. Spent casings, fifty caliber cartridges, like the ones for my gun, littered the ground. Backed by a liberal charge of cordite, their destructive power was clear. Gaping red wounds, bloodshot and punky, stood out like whiskey-crazed eyes on the animals. Some bullets had passed clean through, leaving a trail of pulverized flesh and powdered bone six feet beyond where the buffalo fell.

I stared at the lone calf, the sole survivor, destined to starve, or, if it was lucky, go down to wolves. It had been born into a harsh country, more so since our arrival, and through its pitiful bleating seemed to be asking me why this had happened. A buzzard, its head gleaming with blood, landed on the mother buffalo and thrust its beak into the soft meat along the backbone. It stared with contempt at the calf, a look it carried to its grave when the big bullet from my rifle turned it into a cloud of feathers, drifting down around the frightened young animal like snow. The calf jumped at the shot, then went back to nuzzling its mother. The was nothing to echo the blast off, and the flat country swallowed it quickly. Until I shot, I hadn't noticed the Indians. They'd seen me coming and had taken refuge behind the carcasses. When they first stood up, materializing from the plain fifty yards in front of me, I was scared. This fear vanished quickly, however, when I saw the expression on their faces. And expression of hunger and suffering that transcended the language barrier between us.

There were nineteen of them. Women and weather-worn old men, their wrinkly skin as tough looking as leather, their eyes receding faster than their long, gray hair, their cheekbones as sharp as the hips of the buffalo. They had been cutting the meat, salvaging what they could, and my first impression was how wrong the artists who depict them as fierce-looking warriors are. These Indians, dressed in rags, working with crude knives and leaking cloth bags, had long ago forfeited whatever dignity they had for survival. They were starving. Willing to consume putrid meat in order to face another day. A day sure to bring only more suffering.

One woman laid a bundle of rags beside the buffalo she been butchering before they moved away, shuffling like tired children, carrying little sacks of meat no more fit for consumption than the buzzard I'd shot.

I wanted to call to them. To tell them it was all right, that I wasn't there to harm them. But it wasn't all right, and I said nothing. As they disappeared, dropping below one of the countless knolls in the prairie that only appear when one reaches them, I wondered how long it would be before they vanished for good, and for the first time I saw why the family in the wagon had been killed. I agree with it no more than I did, but I no longer believe it impossible to turn sane humans into ruthless murderers. I knew where the boys and men, so noticeably absent from this group were, and I am reasonably sure of their fate. I've heard it said more than once on my trip that the long range rifles kill "injuns" as well as they do buffalo. Better in fact.

I led my horse to the bull the woman had been working on to see what she'd left behind, and covered by the dirty blanket she was carrying, found her dead child. It was a girl, as delicate as the one I'd seen in the wagon, and every bit as dead. And even though it was not pierced by arrows, its sunken, emaciated face left no doubt we were as responsible for its death as the men who killed the settlers were for theirs. Her mother had left her without looking back, an act she could not have committed unless she has been through far worse or it has become a common occurrence.

I have thought ever since I left, and even before, that I want to become part of the settling of the west. But from what I have seen, settling is a euphemism for conquering. I am sure that in the eyes of the Indians I saw today, my personal views mattered little. I was on the opposite side, and it was as simple as that.

I didn't want to read any more. Far from the grand image I had of the old west, one of cowboys and bank robbers, this was depressing. I closed my eyes and tried to think about home, but, like William, found it remote and unfamiliar.

Across the basin, on the other side of the lake, another slide rumbled. I stared at the cliffs, wondering how long they would last. As impressive as they were, formidable barriers to this lovely place, time was eating away at them just as it was the hollow fir trees. In light of their destiny, their existence seemed somehow pointless. I worked a rock roughly the size of a basketball to the edge of the precipice and shoved it out into space with my feet. I heard it connect fifty feet below me, dislodging more rock, beginning an avalanche of stone which shook the ground I sat on for more than a minute, ending in a tumultuous roar as it reached the lake. As soon as the noise subsided, I wished I hadn't done it.

My grandfather was lying in the tent when I returned, picking through his assortment of flies.

"Something small, Kyle. That's the ticket with Firewater." He sucked on his upper lip and narrowed his eyes, something I'd seen my father do a hundred times, and watching him made me homesick. "Here we are. Parachute Adams, size 14." He held the tiny, white-winged fly up for my approval. "Got a three-pound cutthroat written all over it. What do you think?"

It was smaller than any fly I'd ever used. I didn't see how its minuscule hook would hold such a large fish, or why a big trout would bother eating something so little.

"Quite a slide we had a bit ago, wasn't it?" My grandfather knew I was responsible. He couldn't hide the gleam in his eyes. "Half figured I'd see you come tumbling down with it." He looked at me, waiting for a response, but I gave him none. "Your dad got one going up here about like it when he was your age."

"Dad?" My grandfather hadn't said much about their time together.

"You bet. Heaved a big old boulder down that would have liked to take everything with it. Scared him in good shape, too, I think."

"You took him camping here?"

"Twice. Once when he was about your age, and then again just before he graduated from college. They were both good trips, but one was a beginning, and one was an end."

"A beginning and end?"

"Yes. The first time we came marked the start of something good we had together in the outdoors. He was old enough so we fished and hunted more as friends than father and son for a long time afterwards."

"And the next time?"

My grandfather shook his head. "I like beginnings better. Get in here and stop letting the bugs chew on you."

Sitting in the tent, everything tinted blue by the sun coming through the fabric around us, I was reminded of camping trips with my father in the Adirondacks.

"Did dad catch any fish when he was here?"

"He did indeed. The first time he caught a beauty about four pounds right out there where that rock sticks up." He pointed to a triangular boulder twenty yards offshore. "Kind of funny . . . I haven't thought about that fish in a long time, but I can see it plain as day now. Jumped five or six times. You know something, that was the first really big trout your dad caught, and the whole time he played it, must have been five minutes, he looked like he couldn't believe he'd hooked it."

"And the next time you were here?"

"We didn't fish much then." My grandfather stretched out on his sleeping bag and pretended to sleep. It was his way of saying he didn't want to talk about it, and soon he was snoring in earnest. I lay down next to him, not intending to fall asleep, but found I could not keep my eyes open. I held on to consciousness as long as I could, then suddenly found myself on the Big Hole, going down through the gorge above Mistake, alone this time, at the river's mercy, unable to pull myself from the current, unable to wake up.

It was evening when my grandfather woke me, the time of day immediately after the sun goes down when the earth retains an afterglow of light high in the sky and rocks radiate heat stored for the past ten hours. Firewater was glassy, the reflection of the cliffs on its surface so perfect that it was hard to determine where water ended and rock began. The mosquitoes had not let up in their battle against us, but the horseflies had retired to wherever it was they went at night. In the eastern sky, a bright planet appeared perched on top of the stone wall I'd climbed in the morning.

"Mountain goats, Kyle." My grandfather pointed across the water to five animals making their way down to the lake. They came single file, two adults, a kid, then two more adults, picking their way off the cliffs. "Surefooted beasts, aren't they?"

I watched them descend, reaching the lake just as mist began rising from its surface, its white waves absorbing them, completely hiding them from view. Somewhere between us a trout jumped, the heavy plop of his body returning to the water amplified in the still air.

My grandfather ran for his rod, leaning against a pine a few yards away. "There by Christ is a good one. Hurry up, Kyle, I think he's out by the boulder." I headed for my rod, but my grandfather cut me off with his. "Go ahead and take this one. It's all rigged up." He herded me to the edge of the lake and pointed to the boulder, its outline drifting in and out of view as the mist passed over it. "Right tight to the stone. Get it out there as close as you can."

I peeled line from the reel, false casting over my shoulder the way I'd done hundreds of times before, waiting to feel the tug of the line behind me before bringing the rod forward, hearing it cut through the air above my head, gauging the distance to the boulder, the smooth cork handle becoming part of my hand. I watched the leader disappear into the fog when I cast, heard the fish sip the fly, lifted the tip of the rod, and instead of an inanimate piece of graphite suddenly found myself gripping a living creature, an extension of the fish, and extension of myself.

The trout ran out and deep, ticking line from the reel, bending the rod into a gentle arc the way a big fish will, pulling more than thrashing, electrifying my arm, my body, my entire soul. As I played him, objects around me began to fade, not simply from view but from existence, until, as his struggling subsided and he came toward me near the surface on his side, all that remained was the trout, the rod, and myself, and a faint, almost subliminal understanding that this was Montana.

The cutthroat turned a tight circle at my feet, then lay still when I reached for him with my left hand, holding the rod high with my right. My fingers touched his side, slid forward to his gills, then into his mouth where the tiny fly was lodged in his upper jaw. With a quick twist, the fly was free and the trout was gone, swallowed by the dark water, which in turn was vanishing into night. I stood at the edge of the lake for a long time, afraid that the feel of the fish would leave me, but it did not. When I turned around, my grandfather was gone and a small fire was crackling in front of the tent, not in the circle of stones I'd seen when we arrived, but in a new ring gathered especially for it.

As I walked to the fire, I realized that unlike my father, I hadn't been surprised to catch my fish. In fact, I'd known I would through a sense of déjà vu so powerful that I believed I'd caught him before in some other lifetime. I sat down across the fire from my grandfather, watching him through the flames, wondering if perhaps time was not as destructive as it was cyclic; the same stage and roles, different players.

"Kyle Richards." My grandfather's strong voice brought me out of the trance I was in. "Kyle Richards, I'm going to make you a trade. It's a good deal for you, so listen up." Our eyes met, tongues of orange light dancing in my grandfather's. "I'm going to trade you that rod of mine for a promise. You get that custom Winston, and I get the satisfaction ... the peace of mind of knowing that I have your word on something. Deal?"

I was still holding the rod when I agreed.

"Good. Time was when I wanted to live forever. Wasn't that long ago, either. But I don't anymore."

I looked away. Why did my grandfather want to ruin so perfect an evening?

"Look at me, Kyle." He was smiling, and our eyes locked again. "No sir, I doubt I would be much in favor of the changes I'd see if I stuck around a lot longer. So when my time comes to get out of here, you've got to make me a promise."

Chills were coming for me out of the night, out of the darkness that no longer seemed merely a blanket.

"You promise me that on that day you'll take that rod and use it. I don't care where, but you take it and go fishing. That's how to remember me. Not by going to some frigging funeral or singing any hymns." He spit into the fire then pointed to the lake. "What I just saw was as close to perfection as we can get. Apart from the fact that you didn't whack that big son of a bitch on the head, it was beautiful. Call me a softie, but that's how I want you to remember me." He poked another stick into the fire, then looked up quickly. "And you gave me your word, so I know that you will. Now come here and give your grandfather a hug. Rod has a nice action, doesn't it?"

I held him as tightly as I could, fearing that if I let go he would slip away, my eyes jammed shut so no tears could escape. I didn't say much as we ate the pan of brook trout my grandfather had caught in the lake's outlet while I slept, and when he retired to the tent I heaped all the wood that remained from the pile he'd gathered onto the fire, enough to hold the night at bay several yards in all directions, and read from William's journal by the same light he wrote it by. I read about the brutal side of nature and what a man who's dying of thirst thinks about. The handwriting was shaky.

This damned Dakota Territory has no end. It is as continuous as my hunger, which twists my stomach with the fervor of a crazed baker kneading his bread dough. I haven't eaten in four days, nor have I seen a deer, buffalo, or any other game. No coyotes call at night, I've not heard a wolf for a week, and even the birds are absent. During the day, it is so hot that the reins by which I lead my horse become brittle and my skin blisters wherever the sun touches it. I am suffering from sun fever, and that has made for some very unpleasant nights shivering under my blanket, shaking uncontrollably, caught between retching and fainting.

Worse than the hunger and sun is my thirst. It has been two days since I foolishly emptied my canteen, and I am in desperate need of a drink. My voice, when I talk to my horse, or speak simply to hear words, has been reduced to a cracking whisper that burns like a branding iron from the base of my throat to my coarse lips. The inside of my mouth could not be drier if I began eating sand. Along with tremendous headaches comes an overpowering urge to urinate: a task which, without sufficient fluids in my body, is not possible.

My horse is faring no better. He plods along behind me on unsteady legs, no longer bothering to swish flies off his flanks with his tail. Burdened by his coat, he must need water more than I, and I fear he may keel over at any moment. I refuse to entertain the notion that the same fate may befall me. But there is no comfort in this landscape of barren red rock, blowing sand, and countless maze-like furrows in the earth. Rock pillars, grotesquely shaped like the gravestones of some lost civilization of giants, rise all over, some to a height of more than one hundred feet. In the heat of day, mirages form on their sides: hideous, twisting demons, so vivid I freeze with horror and wonder if I have slipped into the realm of the devil.

The wind, when it blows hard, and it does so often, carries so much sand that it is impossible to breathe without the aid of a handkerchief, and to open my eyes, exposing them to the hail of gravel that assaults my face would be suicidal.

I was warned about these lands. "Bad lands" they are aptly named. Country where outlaws rule and Indians lie in wait for them and anyone else unfortunate enough to pass by. I was cautioned to take plenty of water, and should have heeded this advice. Chasing a disk of red sun westward, I have not the slightest idea where I will encounter that precious liquid again. Much of what I see appears never to have felt a single drop of rain.

In the evening, the sky clouds over with ominous black thunderheads, but they are dry clouds. Violent lightning and deafening thunder tear across the land, and hot breezes follow to usher in more storms, but there is no rain.

My legs move without being told, refusing to let me sit. When I do, at the end of the day, often within sight of where I began before sunup, they cramp painfully and become so rigid that I must pound feeling and motion back into them in the morning. The gritty soil wears on my boots, thinning the soles, lapping eagerly at my tender feet.

Then there are my eyes. Swollen and burned, rather than move them, I find myself shifting my entire head to change my view. They throb as though my heart has relocated directly behind them, and with each beat I wince.

Even sleep is small relief. Fever dreams consume me, leaving me as tired and pained when I awake as when I fell asleep. I no longer dream of the Montana Territory. I see huge, disfigured buzzards, eyeless lizards that slither like will o' the wisps, and a caricature of me, gaunt and quivering, walking a road through hell that grows only longer.

My horse's breathing has become labored. I feel spastic twitching under my hand when I place it on his chest, and watch his head jerk as quickly as it would at the end of a noose. As I write this, I see that his tongue has lolled from his mouth and he has died.

The blood from his neck, seeping out around the edge of my knife, is hot and salty, sure to raise havoc with my stomach, but my throat needs moisture, and any sort will do.

There was a short break in the writing. The dry pine on my fire had burned down to a deep bed of pulsing coals, still throwing enough light to read by, but the night had crept closer. Strange shadows danced on the tent, twirling like the mirages William described. A single rock rolled down to the lake, its regular bouncing like approaching footsteps, and I returned my head to the journal.

The human spirit is a remarkable thing. Stronger than the body, it refuses to succumb, pushing me along, if only at a snail's pace, when it would be so easy to give up. It provides me with hope: the cruel unshakable sensation that tomorrow will be better than today. And

when it is not, when it brings me one day closer to death, I find myself looking to the next day.

I have begun traveling at night, seeking shelter from the sun during the day. Often I wake in the middle of the morning to find my
shade gone and my body sweltering. I no longer sweat, and my lips
have become as cracked as the ground I walk on. I find myself chewing them in search of blood to help me wash down the strips of meat
I peeled from my horse. My rifle seems to have increased ten fold in
weight, and I find myself constantly fighting the urge to leave it behind.

So far I have been able to ward off the panic spells. I get them
more and more, however, and my irrational mind comes closes to
defeating my ability to reason. It's telling me to run. To keep moving. That I am lost and the only way to find the right path is to go
quickly. It screams at me to shed my clothes, forget my rifle, and
change course. It is amazing how practical these notions seem, and
it is with the greatest difficulty that I decline the destructive urges
that plague me. I am unsure what is holding my senses together, but
I fear its grip is weakening, and despite the optimism I attempt to
maintain, I know I am reaching my physical limits. Death, instead
of the grim and greedy monster that he is, masks himself as a friend:
a release from my torment.

Here there was another break in the diary, and it appeared a page had been
torn out. Where the writing began again, it was steadier.

Like a ship's crew that encounters a shore bird after many weeks at
sea, my joy when I spotted a gull this morning was unbounded. I
danced without care of who might see my foolish twirling, and if my
vocal chords had been more than the withered organs they were
would have shouted aloud. The bird came over high and alone,
moving toward the west, and I watched it as spellbound as I would
have a sphinx or Pegasus. On the horizon, it dipped, and I was sure

enough it landed to press on through the day, fighting a war between my mind, screaming at me to continue, and my muscles, alternating between cramping and going limp. In the late afternoon, I was reduced to pulling myself along with my hands, dragging my body prostrate through the sand, but all hardship seems a million miles away now.

I never imagined something as common as a slow-moving river could elicit so much joy. I stumbled off its banks and let myself sink to the bottom, rolling like a stone in a set of rapids, paddling about on my scorched back, letting the water soothe my throat and fill my stomach. After ten minutes, I was able to give a hoarse whisper of thanks, and I believe my voice, as unlike me as it sounded, was the sweetest noise I've ever heard. I stayed in the river until all thoughts of death and despair had washed from me, down around the bend, gone I hope for a long time to come.

When I climbed out and dried off, sponging myself with my shirt, the sun was working its way toward the horizon, low wooded hills, and I lay down beneath a giant cottonwood where I slept a hard, dreamless sleep until just before dark when I was awakened by a hand on my back and a creaky voice asking me if I was alive.

"You livin?" it asked.

I rolled onto my back and looked up at a white beard and a pair of squinting eyes.

"Huh, guess so," the old man said. "Thought I might have found me a good rifle. Reckon not, aye?" He frowned and shook his head. "Looks of you though, I didn't miss by much, did I? Where's your ride?"

I pointed in the direction I'd come, and he smacked his lips.

"Who-wee! You done walk right through the devil's own living room, didn't you. Lucky you still got your hair."

I tired to sit up, then rolled onto my side to vomit. The man's face spun before me, and I clamped my eyes shut.

"You's in bad shape," I heard him say as if he was telling me something I didn't know. "Been prit-near roasted alive I'd say."

When I stopped spinning, I raised myself up on an elbow, and he handed me a canteen fashioned from a buffalo bladder.

"You sip on this. River ain't no good to drink down this far. Got beavers and muskrats and who knows what shittin in her. Make you good and sick."

I took a small swallow and managed a weak "thanks." I hadn't noticed his wooden leg, and when I saw the peg, he laughed.

"Arrow," he said. "Doctor said I was lucky." He spit a mouthful of brown tobacco onto the wood. "Lucky my ass. If I'd have woke up when he was hacken it off, I'd have kilt him. Hey, you ride a mule?"

I nodded, hoping I could. He had two of them tethered to the tree I lay under.

"You can come on to town with me. Got whiskey and whores there, and if you don't mind me sayin, looks like you could use a little of both. Say, where you from?"

"Missouri," I whispered.

"Souri? By Christ, mister, you's a long way from home. Where you gettin to?"

"Montana."

"What? Can't hear ya."

"Montana," I said again as loudly as I could.

"That's good," he said, parting his lips to show a single, dark tooth. "That's a stroke of luck for you."

I looked at him questioningly, and he laughed.

"Shit, mister, you's there."

William's reaching Montana inspired me enough to crawl into the tent. My fire had almost gone out, and a cool breeze was blowing out of the north. My grandfather mumbled in his sleep, and I burrowed deep into my sleeping bag where I heard only the soft sounds of my breathing.

CHAPTER 13

As the Big Hole continued to drop and the green of Montana's spring faded into duller shades of brown, I worked in the woods with my grandfather. The Canyon Ranch was high enough above the river, and we started working early enough in the morning, so most mornings I could look down on a strip of fog, following the Big Hole's course as perfectly as the water underneath it. That was my favorite time of day, my grandfather's, too, I think, before he started his saw, when the air was cool and the world was silent, and a few times he waited to begin cutting until the sun rose.

In the evenings, pleasantly tired after working all day outside, we would take long rides through the Pioneers or Pintlers, scattering elk before us, my grandfather pointing out the remains of trappers' cabins, stopping to let me explore around the mossy logs where I picked up pieces of window pane, square spikes, and a whiskey bottle tinted amethyst from spending more than one hundred years in the sun.

At night, I traveled back in time to join my great, great grandfather as he made his way through the Montana Territory, reading in awe from his journal. And when I slept our Montanas often merged, forming one country that spanned all of time.

On July third, one day before the dance, an event I had secretly begun to look forward to, going as far as to practice dancing in my room late at night with the door shut, my grandfather and I took the day off from the woods and drove to Butte where he bought two hundred dollars' worth of fireworks. I rummaged through the brightly-colored boxes on our way back to

Mistake, pulling out Roman candles, long strings of firecrackers, mortars wrapped in gaudy tissue paper, buzz bombs, lady fingers, bottle rockets, and a dozen other types of pyrotechnics straight from the Orient.

"Figure we'll have our own little display tonight," my grandfather said. "We'll see how the buffalo like it. Shall we invite the ladies?"

I wanted to, but I didn't want my grandfather to know it. I shrugged.

"That's my man. See, you're coming around. Wasn't any doubt in my mind that you would, either. Yes sir, you're beginning to figure out what it's all about. Now..." He pulled the truck to the shoulder of the interstate. "Now, what shall we drink?"

I didn't think he'd be in favor of Pepsi, but my knowledge of liquor was too limited to suggest anything else.

"That's rather disappointing," my grandfather said, wheeling the pick-up into the grassy median between the north and south bound lanes. "I'd hoped you were making better progress than that. Let's go find Mr. Daniels."

I wondered who Mr. Daniels was, and why we were going back to Butte to see him. I said nothing until we coasted to a stop in front of a liquor store ten minutes later.

"Mr. Daniels lives here?"

"He does indeed." My grandfather coughed when he stepped from the cab, disappeared into the store, and came out hugging a large paper bag. He set it down on the seat between us, and I peered inside.

"Mr. Jack Daniels, Kyle. A fine southern gentleman."

I watched for antelope along the interstate between Butte and Divide on our way home, carefully scanning the sage gulleys

"Odd beasts," my grandfather said when I spotted a small band of them walking toward a metal water trough. "Not really antelopes. Not like the antelopes in Africa anyway. They're pronghorns. Nothing else like them in the world. A family unto themselves."

"Where'd they come from?"

"Somewhere far away, I hope." My grandfather adjusted the screwdriver stick shift and geared down as we headed up to the top of the Continental Divide. It was a much less dramatic crossing than the one on Interstate 90 I'd seen from the bus. A big swell in the prairie and a green sign was all there was to it, but all the same it was exciting. "Back in the east again," he said. "But thank God not very far."

Darla lived in a single-wide trailer about half a mile out of Mistake. A long, rutted dirt driveway ran through a pasture of close-grazed grass to her home, light blue with white trim, in need of a paint job. Her station wagon sat in the yard, providing shade to a scruffy-looking red healer, which barked furiously as we approached. As if the dog had not sufficiently announced our arrival, my grandfather stepped on the clutch and revved the engine to its limit, grinning when he let off the gas and the pickup backfired. Yellow curtains in a small window parted slightly, and a few seconds later the door opened. I was expecting Darla, not Katrina.

"Christ have mercy," my grandfather said softly. "Ain't that a sight to see."

She was wearing tight white shorts and a hot pink tanktop cut off a few inches above her waist to show her belly button. She stood barefoot, one leg a little in front of the other, her toenails painted to match her shirt. The eye shadow she wore made her eyes appear large and glossy, and I could not look away.

My grandfather waved a hand in front of my face. "You want to go say hello, or are you just going to stare? You look too long and you'll burn your eyes. I look too long and I'll really start hating how goddamned old I am. Come on." He got out, knelt to wrestle with the dog, and I opened my door.

It was fourteen and a half steps to the trailer's front porch. I know because I was counting them, concentrating as hard as I could, hoping I would say something reasonably intelligent to the girl in the doorway. But I couldn't. I couldn't say anything at all. Not after she said, "hi," not after she smiled and tilted her head waiting for a response, not even after my grandfather shoved past me and went inside, leaving the two of us alone. My brain and my voice could not combine, and I stood there in uncomfortable silence until I heard my grandfather bellow something about Barnacle Bill the sailor arriving. I forced a weak laugh, and Katrina skipped by me to the dog, standing next to the truck.

"His name's Cougar," she said. "Call him."

I snapped my fingers and he approached slowly, his nose extended straight in front of him. He sniffed my pants, and closed his eyes when I scratched his ears.

"He likes you," Katrina said. "Want to see something cool?"

I nodded, not yet able to speak.

"Where's your ball, Cougar?" At the question, the dog tore off across the yard and came back holding a blue Nerf football in his mouth. "Good boy. Now give it here." He set the ball down at her feet, took one step back, staring fixedly at it until she picked it up. "Let's go," she said. Katrina ran down a well-worn path that led to the river two hundred yards behind the trailer, and flung the ball into the water. Cougar dove off the bank, angled into the current, his head sweeping back and forth as he looked for the football. He caught up with it in a small set of rapids, brought it back to shore a few feet downstream, shook himself hard, then dropped it in front of me and looked at the river.

"Go ahead and throw it for him," Katrina said.

I picked it up and tossed it into the water.

"Well, I hope you can throw further than that. Try again."

Cougar wagged his tail as I wound up, and jumped off the shore before I released the ball. I threw it as far as I could, and Katrina laughed.

"He'll like that." We watched him swim for it, this time coming to shore well downstream from us. "That's enough," Katrina said when he brought it back. "Go lay down."

I stared at the beads of water on Katrina's legs, shiny drops sprayed from the dog, and once more found I could not look away.

"So, you're going to the dance?" If Katrina noticed me staring, she didn't seem to mind. "We'll have fun."

I bit my lip, wanting to say something, not sure what it should be or even if I could. A raft drifted by with three fishermen in it, their fly rods sticking up, catching the sun like miniature masts.

"We bought some fireworks if you want to come tonight," I blurted, saying it quickly enough to lose my breath.

Katrina ran a finger along the brim of my hat below the rattlesnake band, then turned back up the path away from the river and stared running again. "Sure," she said over her shoulder. I followed at a fast trot, wondering if my feet were actually touching the ground, wondering why I felt the way I did.

In the dooryard, I stopped to show Katrina the assortment of fireworks, finding that as long as I didn't make eye contact, talking was manageable, and I didn't look up when I heard my grandfather come outside.

"Have you showed her your Roman candle?" he hollered.

I blushed instantly, something Katrina picked up on.

"You're red," she said, and then whispered, "but it's cute." She kissed me quickly on the cheek, her lips touching my skin for the briefest of moments, a fleeting sensation of warmth that I would have given anything to keep with me longer. And then she ran for the trailer and didn't look back.

"Well, well," my grandfather said as we headed up the driveway, "it appears I'm riding with Romeo."

I wasn't sure if I was riding in the truck or somewhere above it.

"Shall we stop in at the Six Point so you can steal Laurie's heart as well?"

I hardly heard him. I was reliving Katrina's kiss, over and over, wondering why so ephemeral an act remained so vivid in my mind, knowing that whatever the reason, I would remember it for the rest of my life.

"Snap out of it, Kyle." My grandfather pumped the brakes, bucking the truck. "Don't get mushy on me." I didn't realize I was touching my cheek until he pulled my hand away. "Oh my god." A strand of seriousness entered his voice. "Your first kiss."

My grandfather let it go at that. He kept both hands on the wheel the rest of the way home, and an expression of immense pride on his face that I hadn't seen since Allen bought his elk for one dollar.

The bull buffalo with the broken horns was standing near the fence, a few yards in back of the overturned canoe. When we stopped, he began pawing the earth, ripping jagged clumps of dusty soil from the ground, thick streams of mucus leaking from his nose, a guttural noise coming from his throat that made the hair on the back of my neck stand up. My grandfather looked at him curiously, as if he was seeing something for the first time, then walked to the fence.

"Splinter Horn, you drooling son of a bitch, look at yourself." The buffalo stopping pawing the ground, and returned my grandfather's stare in eerie likeness. "My good man, you and I may have quite a bit in common." The bull didn't seem to like that suggestion. He bounced forward and narrowed his eyes, drawing them up into slits. "I expect we're both men's men." My grandfather looked as if he was delivering a speech. "But, unfortunately for you, we're the type of creatures whose natures oppose each other. Perhaps because we see some of the other in ourselves, perhaps because we know there's only enough spotlight for one of us, or perhaps simply because that's the way it must be. We're Pat Garret and Billy the Kid." At this comparison, the buffalo drove his head into a post inches from my grandfather, cracking it up the middle, bowing the fence. "That's right," my grandfather said calmly, "you know which role you get to play." He turned his back on the bull, took two steps toward the house, then turned around again. "And I would shoot you in the back without hesitation. Do not test my resolve." They stared at each other a long time. Finally, the bull swung his great body around and trotted toward his herd, and my grandfather laughed. "Splinter Horn," he said, "my grandson's falling in love. And that's apt to spawn more problems than will ever come between you and me. Right, Kyle?"

I didn't answer. I had half a day to kill before I would see Katrina again, and I was convinced that the only way to do it, the only way to ensure that time would progress, was to read William's journal. I flopped down on my bed, opened the book, and began reading about his journey up the Yellowstone River, his harrowing encounters with outlaws, Indians, and a sow grizzly bear. When he began describing Butte and the surrounding mountains, I felt very close to him. He was working in a mine, and it didn't take long to convince me that Butte was just the place my grandfather could have found plenty of "men's men."

I arrived in Butte a week ago, ushered into the city by a host of men drawing a wooden cage containing a massive grizzly bear, shackled with heavy irons and muzzled with a steel band wrapped tightly enough around his head so it had worn away the hair. The scene, befitting of Caesar's Rome, immediately confirmed my hopes that the western frontier need not be termed civilized. I asked one of the men what they were doing with the creature and was told that the bear would fight a bull to the death and if I was thinking about betting on one of the combatants I should wager on the bull.

"Bear's got a busted foot," he told me when his companions had pulled the cage out of earshot. "Keep it to yourself, too," he warned. "Last time we brung in a crip the bull tuned him up so bad wouldn't nobody bet on the bear next time. I try telling them they can't be using so big a trap, but ain't a one of them gonna put the bracelets on a good griz. Reckon old Black Nelson would do it, but seems to me that he got himself kilt in a knife fight the other night. You take my advice and put your coin on the bull."

Normally, this sort of barbarous sport would not appeal to me, but I could not help feeling some desire to witness the event, if only to see what type of people would attend the fight.

In Butte, living conditions fall a distant second to the mining.

The strike has drawn men from all over, many of whom I understand have been living in tents for the past year. Whiskey, "Butte water," is a staple in everyone's diet, and there are as many places to drink it as there are to find a fight. I learned my first evening in town that both are exceedingly easy when a man with a heavy Irish accent introduced himself to me as Jerry O'Mally, shook my hand, and promptly delivered a blow to my midsection that knocked the wind out of me. He helped me to my feet, commented that I was "a bit soft," then bought me a shot of some strong, vile-tasting whiskey.

Across the street, a dusty, narrow drive littered with unspeakable forms of refuse, in a saloon called the Levi, I had a much more unpleasant experience. The place was full of unsavories: men with hands stained forever black with grime from the mines, Indians more dead than alive from living on booze, loose women wearing suggestive apparel who followed the winners from the poker tables around like dogs looking for hand-outs, and half a dozen rough-looking men all wearing badges. One of them, a tall, thin man with a scar over his left eye, was cleaning his Colt's, meticulously spit-polishing its ivory handle. His eyes moved erratically, working separately from his hands, and he tapped his boots continuously. An Indian at the bar, red-eyed and bruised along his jaw line, put his hand on a woman as she passed and slurred something to her. She slapped his hand down without paying much attention, but when he began to follow her, the Colt's went off not ten feet from where I stood and sent a bullet into the man's brain, cracking his head like a ripe melon, bursting a bottle of whiskey on the rack behind the bar as it sped out through the wall.

"Be a dollar for the bottle, Bill," the bartender said. "And damn it, haul him outta here before he leaks brain all over the place."

Bill did not haul him out right away. As he continued to polish the pistol, people walked over the dead man as if he were a sleeping dog.

"Needed killin," a man said when he saw me staring. "Gonna swing a few more of em tomorrow, too. You watchin?"

I wasn't planning to, but a morbid curiosity compelled me to stand outside the courthouse the following morning with the two or three hundred other people who had gathered for the hanging. At ten o'clock, six men were led from the building to a hastily erected gallows consisting of a platform fifteen feet high, above and slightly in front of which hung nooses fastened to a stout crossbeam. The men, five Indians and one white, were herded through the throng of greedy onlookers, taunted by children holding miniature gallows complete with tiny dolls suspended by string.

"What did they do?" I asked a well-dressed lady standing beside me.

"Three of the Indians are thieves, two of them are suspected of murder, and the white . . . I believe he got drunk and killed a boy firing off his pistol. I thought there was going to be a Chinaman, too, but I don't see him," she said disappointedly.

A hooded executioner helped the condemned up a rickety ladder and into the nooses. The crowd fell silent while he inquired if any of them had any last words. The Indians said nothing, but the white man, an Irishman, gave a short, sobering speech.

"Bein a slight man, I wonder if one of ya might tug on me feet a bit if I gets to kickin around? I just wanna go quick. Seen a man dangle fer five minutes t'other day, and I don't wanna go like that meself."

The executioner gave a nod, two men burst forward from the crowd, eager to aid in the man's last request, and platform was tipped forward. The thud-snaps of broken necks escorted the Indians from this world, but the Irishman was light, and he began flailing around at the end of his rope, trying in vain to lift his bound hands to his neck, opening and closing his mouth like a fish out of water. The two men who had volunteered to "tug" on his feet couldn't reach them. They jumped several times, once brushing the bottom of the man's boots, then gave up, leaving him to choke to death. I turned away before he was dead, knowing I'd seen my last hanging. The value of life has degraded here to the point where a man dies for stealing a pair of boots, and the law is only slightly less ready to hang a man than the people are to watch.

With my money being nearly gone, in the afternoon I was forced to seek temporary employment, which I quickly found with one of the major parties that has staked a claim on the hill upon which the city sits.

As I understand it, several groups are in direct competition with each other, working feverishly day and night, each sure it will be the one that hits a main vein of gold. This expectation drives the men, who work on an incentive basis, receiving more pay for moving

more rock. I'm told the first whites to mine near Butte used sharp-
ened elk antlers and froze to death their first winter because, in their
zealous pursuit of riches, they did not build proper shelter. Even
now, I believe there are many who would as soon be rich for a day
and then die, as they would live a long life on a more moderate in-
come. But the men with the real money do not have dirty hands, and
that is no different from anywhere else. I expect, too, that more than
one enterprising lady has put away a fair share of gold working on
her back, as prostitutes are in as high demand as whiskey.

I have signed on as a gopher. A man who works underground.
Together with two others, a man near my age from further east in the
territory, and an older, foul-mouthed drunk from Kentucky, I work
hauling a metal cart full of rock to the surface, where its contents are
sorted in search of gold. The tunnels are narrow and full of men.
Dozens, perhaps hundreds of us pack into these small passageways,
where the quarters are so close and the hours so long that fights are
inevitable. One young man bumped into our partner from Kentucky
and did not apologize fast enough for his liking. The result was a
sharp stone to the man's temple which got the blood gushing and
knocked the poor fellow unconscious. There were a handful of wit-
nesses, and none of them spoke so much as a word.

On Sunday, my day off, I watched the bear and bull fight, and am
sure from the reaction of the crowd that feeding people to lions would
be an even greater success. Nearly everyone in Butte appeared to be
there, as well as many mountain men who came carrying rifles and
long, unsheathed knives.

An outdoor arena, built especially for such contests, complete
with a balcony for the city's dignitaries, was the site of the contest,
which, just as I had been advised, the bull won, though only after
being mauled so severely I'm told he died shortly after the fight.

More brutal than the battle between the beasts was one I witnessed between two women. I don't know what they were fighting
over, but they were passionate enough about it to nearly kill each
other. It had been going for quite some time before I realized what
was happening. A crowd of men had drawn away from the log fence
and were huddled in a tight circle around what I assumed was someone taking bets. Suddenly, a ball of two women rolled out from their
midst. I was pushed from behind toward the fray by a score of men

more eager to see human blood than that from a bear or bull. I unwillingly became part of those in the front row, and my ears began to ring from the cheers going up all around me.

The women were Indians, probably not much older than twenty. They'd torn each other's clothes off and were going at one another viciously, biting, gouging, kicking, digging with their fingernails, oblivious to the crowd around them. A big man with a huge felt hat and drooping mustache got them separated, and was successful at keeping them apart until he was struck in the face by a whiskey bottle hurled by someone who had not yet seen his fill of the war. As soon as the cowboy dropped, the women pitched onto each other, refreshed after their short rest. So intense was the fight that neither of them spoke, the only sounds coming from the spectators and the concussion of flesh and flesh. One girl had the other by the hair and was bouncing her head off the ground, driving her knees into her opponent's kidneys. Then, without warning, the girl on the ground bucked upward, snatched the bottle the felled the cowboy, and, holding it by its slender neck, back-handed it into the other Indian's mouth, sending a shower of broken glass and teeth in all directions. At this point, a sheriff stepped in and finally put a halt to it. Pleased by what they'd seen, there was no shortage of men offering their shirts to the women to cover themselves with, but neither accepted. They limped off in opposite directions, and instantly everyone returned to the less-dramatic fight inside the fence.

With the bear dead, trampled to a bloody pulp, and the bull bleeding uncontrollably from gaping wounds in its side, the crowd broke up, and I am told that many went directly to church services.

I spent the afternoon talking to a store owner who supplies trappers for the winter fur season. He informed me that beaver, bobcat, coyote, lynx, pine martin, wolverine, and fox all live within a mile of Butte, but that if I was serious about making money and wasn't superstitious I should look into the upper Big Hole River country fifty miles southwest of town.

"Timber country," he said. "And wild, too. No place for a tenderfoot. Ain't much in there that won't kill a man if given the chance, and don't none of it need much of a chance. They's injuns, bears, and bad weather. Lots of it. That's what gets most of them. Snowed in and freeze or maybe starve. Me, I don't want no critter come nibblin on me or get shot full of arrows. Ain't nothing worth that. Besides, that country's haunted. Big Ed Parker went in there for a week last winter, and you won't find no tougher a man than him. He come our right quick, babblin like an idiot, his hair gone all snowy white and his left arm so frost bit it turnt black and had to get hacked off. Alls you could understand of him was somethin about a wolf, or a man that looked like wolf, or somethin like that. Went plumb crazy. Started carrying his rotten arm around with him and sleeping outside. Finally froze to death one night. Understand they found him stark naked in the street lookin mighty blue."

I ran the story by a clerk working in a trading post specializing in rifles, and heard a similar tale there.

"Big Hole?" the clerk asked. "Yeah, got fur in there. Good fur, too. But it ain't no place for you. Not unless you care to meet the devil. That's his country."

I prodded him to elaborate, and nervously he told me about a hunting expedition he'd outfitted the year before.

"Five of 'em. Rangers bored with Apaches and tired of Mexican bandits. Supposed to have been a group of real rough customers. Wanted to see some wilderness. Well, they seen it all right. Four of ems still out there someplace."

"Four?" I asked.

"Yup. They swung the fifth. He come back tellin some crazy tale about how somethin hunted them for three days. Picked them off one by one. Judge figured he killed his buddies, so they showed him the rope for it. But I believed the fella. And I'll tell you something else, too. When they walked him to the gallows, why, he climbed right up. Weren't no foolin around. Almost as if he wanted to get dead quick as he could. Some said it was cause he had a guilty conscience, but not me. He weren't guilty. I figure whatever he seen in the woods scared him bad enough so he just as soon be outta its way for good."

These frightful stories do not give me much pause. In fact, they are exactly the type of legends I would expect to find on the frontier, and they whet my appetite to get out of Butte. From what I've seen, the fur country of the Big Hole can only be safer.

The money is slow in coming from working in the mine. There are so many men that reasonable wages need not be paid, but traps and gunpowder are cheap, and as soon as I've saved enough for adequate supplies I'll leave for the woods.

At night, I gaze south into the unbroken line of mountains and wonder what lies out there for me. I am sure there is something. I feel it drawing me, strengthening its pull, tugging at me every waking moment. And I am dreaming again. Dreaming of the river, the Big Hole for all I know, and it is difficult to remain in bed upon waking. The desire to see new country is so strong I cannot concentrate on my work, and fear if I don't leave soon I'll end up hurt through my own inattention.

As I write, the stars are out. Millions of them. More than I thought could exist. Where they meet the southern horizon, shining over mountains still clad in snow, they form a narrow, silver band of soft light into which the peaks jut to hold up the roof of the world.

Darla's car made almost as much noise coming down the driveway as my grandfather's pickup. I heard a broken strut protesting with loud clanks each time it hit a bump, a loose belt shrieked, and it sounded as if the exhaust pipe was broken at the manifold. I stayed in my room with the door closed until the racket ceased, then slid into the living room where I could peak out a window. My grandfather was over by the canoe squirting lighter fluid on a bed of charcoal, hosing the briquettes liberally. He struck a match on his belt buckle, tossed it toward the barbecue and leaned away from a pillar of fire that soared ten feet into the air.

"Kyle!" he yelled.

I moved away from the window.

"Kyle, get out here."

I stayed where I was.

"What kind of gentleman won't open a door for his girlfriend? Kyle Richards, quit playing the peeping Tom and come outside."

Darla and Katrina hadn't gotten out of the car. They were watching the fire, visible, I imagined, from Mistake. I stepped out the kitchen door, quietly enough so my grandfather shouldn't have heard, but he did.

"That's better," he said. "Now, go help your lady friend."

I opened the car door without looking inside, keeping my eyes fixed on the ground while my grandfather wrestled Darla out the driver's side. The first thing I noticed about Katrina was her jeans, faded and torn at the knees, running tightly up her legs, drawing my eyes to her waist, then to her face, and then I looked away. She stepped past me quickly, close enough so her hair brushed my cheek, leaving me with the faint scent of shampoo and something more, a clean smell similar to clothes that have hung all day on an outside line.

"Darla, my dear, there's something brewing in the air tonight," my grandfather said. I looked at him and winced, praying he wouldn't start. "Not that, Kyle," he said. "Well, yes, that too, but I was talking about the storm." He pointed to the western horizon where a thin line of lead-colored clouds was creeping over the Bitterroots. "I can feel it in my bones. Gonna be a doozy. Good night to stay in and snuggle." He pulled Darla to him and began mauling her with his lips, making great slurping noises.

"Gross," Katrina whispered in my ear.

I turned toward her, then away, suddenly embarrassed that I wasn't quite as tall.

"Can we go inside?" she asked.

"By all means," my grandfather said. "We all can. Mr. Daniels awaits us."

I'd forgotten about Mr. Daniels, and now wished more than ever that he wasn't joining us. I was the last one inside, walking slowly, my feet growing heavier as I approached the kitchen table where four glasses had been positioned.

"A toast," my grandfather announced, filling Darla's glass then his own. "There's pop in the fridge, Kyle, hurry up."

He didn't need to ask me twice. I poured Katrina's first, leaving no room for any whiskey, leaving little more than a swallow of Pepsi for myself.

"Want me to top that off?" My grandfather spun the cap on the whiskey bottle and thrust it in my direction. I cupped my hand over my glass, and he frowned. "Didn't figure. Very well, what do you say, Darla, the bull?"

She raised her glass. "The bull."

"Splendid. Pay attention, Kyle, you may want to recite this for Boston at some point." My grandfather cleared his throat. "Here's to the bull." He pointed to Darla.

"And to the bee that got the bull to bucking."

"And here's to Adam and to Eve."

"That got the world to fucking." They finished in unison, drained their uplifted glasses, and reached for the bottle at the same time. I ducked into the living room and sat on the couch, greatly relieved when Katrina joined me.

"He's . . ." I didn't know what to say.

"He's Cole," she laughed.

"Yeah." That summed it up. "You want to go look at the buffalo?"

"Sure."

They were gathered in the middle of the pasture between the house and woods, all lying down except for Splinter Horn who faced the west as if he was readying himself for battle with the storm. I thought to myself that mother nature would have to put on quite a performance to beat him.

"He's huge," Katrina said. "Where'd he come from?"

"The last century." That's what my grandfather had said.

"What?"

"I don't know. Bruce Tipton brought them here."

The first flicker of lightning brightened the clouds over the Bitterroots, too distant to see exactly where it struck. The sky turned from gray to yellow, then back to gray. I waited for the thunder roll, but it didn't come. Katrina was still looking at the buffalo, and for an instant, no longer than the bolt of lightning lasted, it seemed we'd looked at them before, sometime so long ago that the memory had faded to the dimmest sense of recognition.

"It'll be dark soon," I said. The sun had fallen behind the clouds, and the eastern sky was losing light fast.

"Good. Then we can have the fireworks." Katrina moved closer to me, and I stood on the balls of my feet so our shoulders met. It was an uncomfortable position, but I didn't want to move. I had the sense that something bad was coming, something more than the storm, and any touch from Katrina was comforting.

Inside, my grandfather was singing, blasting out the words from a ballad about a ship going down at sea. He was giving it all he was worth, but his voice sounded muted, as if the air was thickening or he was moving away.

A hot breeze spun tiny cyclones of dust into the sky from the wallows in the pasture, and Splinter Horn began pacing. He extended his neck, tipped his head up, and bellowed, but even that awful sound seemed distant, far away and slow to reach me.

"Do you have a girlfriend back home?" Katrina asked it quickly, putting more weight on my shoulder as she did.

"I guess not right now."

"No?"

I shook my head. "Why?"

"Just wondering." She shoved me sideways, and it took three or four steps for me to catch my balance. When I did, she was almost to the kitchen door, running fast, and though I couldn't see her face, I was sure she was smiling.

The storm clouds had obliterated the mountains by the time we finished dinner, and, hungry to consume more than the Bitterroots, they were descending upon the Big Hole valley. I could see individual bolts of lightning, coming in rapid succession, and the continuous rumble of thunder came like hundreds of fir trees dropped at once. Overhead, a handful of stars winked on and off, quivering it appeared, anticipating what was coming.

"We'd better light 'em up if we're gonna, Kyle." My grandfather pushed outside with the fireworks, followed by Darla and the half-empty whiskey bottle. "How 'bout it, buff, you ready for the show?" He held a bottle rocket loosely in his hand and touched a lighter to its fuse. It whined away over the pasture and blew up a few feet above the herd. They were on their feet instantly, charging wildly for the woods. "You don't like it, you can move," my grandfather screamed, breaking into sustained laughter. Only Splinter Horn remained where he was, a great black bulk against a great black sky.

I moved up onto the doorstep and sat down beside Katrina, convinced more than ever that the night would not end without some sort of catastrophe. A Roman candle flared near the fence, its shower of pink and lavender sparks blowing toward the house in a stiff wind. My grandfather touched off some sort of whirling rocket that spun crazily toward Splinter Horn, and behind him I heard stampeding hooves.

"Run, run, as fast as you can," my grandfather called after them. A battery of bottle rockets lifted off and sang away into the night, their reports mixed with approaching thunder.

I began to shiver. The warm presence of Katrina next to me did not sufficiently block my dread until she took my hand. When she did, gripping it firmly, drawing it into her lap, heat ran through my entire body, filling me so completely that I believed my toes tingled because it was searching for a way out.

"Grenade!" A white flash and deafening boom followed my grandfather's cry. A string of firecrackers blew up, and a mortar exploded high over the pasture, dripping green sparks toward the earth. Buzz bombs twisted into the sky, leaving red afterglows to mark their paths. Something took off with a whoosh like gasoline ignited in a confined space, and a second later I could see running buffalo, lit up but a giant blue sheet of light near the woods. My grandfather was dancing, throwing ladyfingers at his feet where their tiny explosions produced a strobe effect, making his motions appear disjointed and jerky.

The hot breeze that had been blowing suddenly turned cold, and I pushed closer to Katrina.

"You know something?" she whispered.

I looked at her, the reflection of white sparks from another Roman candle dancing in her eyes. "What's that?"

"I'm glad you don't have a girlfriend." She squeezed my hand tighter, and I felt as if even the impending storm, if it concentrated all its fury on one point, could not break that hold.

A rocket spewing yellow fire roared away from my grandfather, leveled off ten feet over the pasture, then dipped into the sage. As its pastel flames burned out, a new fire appeared, a dull orange glow spreading outward from the crash site, white smoke curling into the air above it.

"There, by god, I've set the place on fire." My grandfather took a momentary break from the fireworks display to sing something about setting the woods on fire.

I watched the flames advance rapidly toward the house. Fanned by the wind, they raced along the ground like snakes from hell. I started to say something to Katrina but lost the words.

"Ladies and gentlemen," my grandfather said in his deep, calm voice, "I present you with the finale."

I watched him bend over and light something, run back a few steps to where Darla sat next to the canoe, and then the night came to life with fireworks, screaming away toward the woods, bending back at the house, spinning along the ground, exploding high and low. Lightning intensified in the background, its thunder loud and frightening, the grass fire crackled, the buffalo herd charged past, and in front of it all my grandfather was dancing again, stripping off his shirt, raising his arms to the sky, stamping his feet, calling for rain. There was something primitive about the scene. I leaned into Katrina and closed my eyes, pressing my head against her chest, breathing her perfume, my muscles frozen until a raindrop the size of a nickel struck the back of my neck. As it trickled around toward my throat, I looked up. Katrina had let go of my hand and was hugging me, and if the expression on her face had been a place I could have gone, it would have been the safest spot in the world.

Later that night, as I lay on the couch, the house shaking from a howling wind, the light outside the kitchen door flickering as power lines along the driveway swayed, I thought of Katrina lying asleep in my bed and wondered if her expression was the same. I imagined it was, and under my sleeping bag could picture it clearly.

Like a raging beast, the storm whipped through the valley, humbling everything in its path. Storms in the east had never frightened me, and I had seen my share of them in Montana, but this time I was scared. More than a weather disturbance, this storm seemed a living, breathing, furious creature that had shape-shifted to assume a more powerful form. Rain and hail pounded the house, waiting for me to step outside, daring me to brave its violence for so much as a second. I lay as still as I could, focusing on Katrina's face, an image that finally pulled me into sleep.

CHAPTER 14

I DON'T KNOW how long I slept. When I woke up the storm had passed, though not before blowing the kitchen door open. The house was cold and damp; like everything else in the valley it had been beaten into submission. I splashed through a puddle on my way to shut the door, picking my feet up quickly, recoiling from the water.

Something outside had the buffalo stirred up. I could hear the cows calling to each other, and occasionally a bull would bellow. I looked through the open door toward where the animals were bunched together in a single black spot, their heads toward the woods. They shifted position, pawed at the ground, and began edging toward the house, sliding across the prairie like a giant spider. As they retreated, one remained defiantly behind, snorting loudly enough to echo his baritone voice off the walls of the kitchen. A dark bump against the sage, I had no doubt which buffalo chose to face whatever lurked in the woods, and if anything short of another storm or some sort of monster had emerged to challenge him, I would have bet on Splinter Horn.

I reached outside for the doorhandle, began to pull it shut, then stopped. I listened, breathing with my mouth open, to a long, low, lugubrious howl that floated without resistance from the woods, through the clean night air, so clear that I wondered at what point it diminished in volume, and thought perhaps that it did not. It sounded as if it might have carried forever, sailing into space somewhere beyond the blue Madison range I could see from the Canyon Ranch. It wasn't as threatening as powerful sounding. Awe inspiring. Not angry like the snarl of a bobcat or growl of a bear, but mighty. Like a single gust of winter wind that drives pellets of snow as fast as birdshot into a picture window and sings through chimneys like trapped demons. It triggered an instinctive reaction of fear, but at the same time it called me. Telling me to come closer. Asking me to follow. I peeked into my grandfather's room to make sure he was there, saw two lumps under his covers, then stepped into the night, barely aware I was moving.

The buffalo were stampeding again, whirling around the pasture in a cyclone of pounding hooves and flailing legs. Even Splinter Horn was running, leading the way, plowing through the sage, thundering along at top speed, and I didn't need to see his eyes to know what they looked like. Wild with terror, to look at them would have been as paralyzing as to stare at a gorgon. But I couldn't help crawling under the lowest strand of wire and walking steadily, like a front-line soldier who has a sixth sense that the bullets aren't meant for him, toward the woods. The herd tore past me near the irrigation ditch, so close that I could feel the ground shake and see saliva dripping from mouths opened wide to expose black tongues. It crashed away like a freight train without brakes, and I jumped the ditch, wiggled under the fence again, and stepped into the forest.

Rain enhances the scent of everything in the woods, cleaning away the dust of dry weather, imparting a renewed aura to the plants and trees, leaving the forest fresh and spring-like. I could smell the pungent odor of fir, musty fungi growing on fallen trees, and the rich aroma of decaying needles. I could also smell the forest as a whole: the wild smell that comes from places devoid of people.

Beneath a three-quarter moon, I could see well. Branches stood out sharply from tree trunks, and the boulders' textured surfaces were plainly visible. I walked, or more appropriately was drawn, up the rocky knob to the same monstrous stone from which I'd seen the elk and my grandfather appear from the trees across the little creek, now entirely dry despite the storm.

When it came again, the howl was close. So close I expected to feel the animal's breath against my face. It wailed like siren, rising and falling in pitch, trailing off into the universe, echoing inside my head. And suddenly, its luring power, its enormous drawing force that had led me into the woods in the middle of the night, was gone. My bare feet, which moments before had been oblivious to the ground I walked on, stung from countless needles

I'd stepped on, and I began to shiver. My tongue thickened with fear. Fear so strong I could taste its electric, bitter flavor. Throat-closing, eye-watering fear that robbed me of my ability to do more than close my eyes. I shut them, pressing my fingers into their lids, but it was if I was holding my breath. In thirty seconds, the pressure behind my temples was unbearably strong, pulsing against my skull, and to prevent my head from splitting, I had to open my eyes. When I did, a fraction of an inch at a time, my vision did not return immediately. Gradually, the silver spots I saw were replaced by trees, blurry at first, then crystal clear.

Something was in the creek bed. Something that hadn't been there before, and I didn't see how, with everything else in such terror-sharpened focus I couldn't make out what it was. When it moved, it appeared that everything behind it moved, too. It was coming closer, no doubt about it, but the forest was camouflaging it: wrapping around it to keep its features hidden. Rocks, fallen limbs, and the few tiny pines between my boulder and the creek, objects which could hardly have sheltered a rabbit, shrouded this creature perfectly. I sensed more than saw it advancing, and I was as powerless to move as the stone I sat on.

It was right in front of me. I knew it, but I couldn't see it. It was watching me, gauging the distance between us, preparing to spring. I imagined its fangs burying themselves in my throat, and this thought, the first thought of my own death, broke the spell I was under, returning my muscles completely to my control. Just as I turned to run, my legs as tense as a sprinter's on the starting blocks, I saw it. It stood motionless before me, staring, not with the blood-lust I had imagined, but with an omnipotent eye that I believed looked into my soul and beyond it, through the woods, all the way over the mountains I was sure its call had drifted to.

The black wolf looked like the ones in my picture book. No bigger, no more menacing, than the ones on page fifty-eight that trotted toward the photographer through six inches of fresh snow in the heart of Yellowstone Park where they'd been released. Only its eyes were different. Close-set and dark, blacker than his coat, blacker than the night, they sucked me in like a black hole. Obsidian, pupilless eyes that took me in at a glance, absorbing everything about me as they watched, and then, just when I thought they might physically yank me from the boulder, the wolf turned and trotted back toward the creek, fading to smoke gray as it crossed patches of moonlight, drifting away to become part of the forest. Part of forest and probably much more.

My grandfather was sitting at the kitchen table when I walked through the door half an hour later, all visible signs of drunkenness gone from him. He sat in the dark, his hands folded in his lap, staring blankly at the sink.

"Good way to get yourself gored, Kyle. Best to avoid those buffalo."

I didn't want to know how he knew where I'd been. "Cole?" I sat down across from him, feeling the cold from the chair even through my pants. "Cole, what's out there?"

"What do you mean?"

"I mean in the woods. Up there by the creek where I saw you that morning."

"All kinds of things, I suppose."

He was beginning to enjoy the conversation, and I could tell that he was fighting down a smile. I was tired, and if I wasn't going to get straight answers, I wasn't going to ask questions.

"What'd you see, Kyle?"

"A wolf," I whispered.

"Black?"

"Yeah. And, Cole, he saw me, too. Looked right at me."

"Good."

"Good?"

"Certainly. I'm glad he's still around."

"You've seen him before?"

"I expect. He hasn't showed up for a while, but I'll bet he's the same one."

"Where do you think he's from?"

My grandfather tipped his chair back and set the front legs down hard. "Canada. Probably came down the Bitterroots from British Columbia." He stood up and pointed in at the couch. "You'd better get some sleep."

He was almost to his room when I caught him, and I could tell he didn't want to turn around, but I braced my feet and pulled hard on the back of his shirt.

"Jesus, Kyle, you'll rip the goddamn thing."

Before I went to sleep, there was something I needed to know. "Cole, is the wolf why you like those woods?"

"No, Kyle, it is not. Now good night."

"Well then . . ." My grandfather put a finger to my lips.

"Good night."

That was the end of it. In the morning, when I woke up to a sun so bright it was hard to believe it had ever rained, I seriously wondered if I had dreamed the whole thing. Katrina stayed in my room a long time, and when she came out she looked exactly as she had the night before.

"By god, Kyle, there's woman for you," my grandfather said when she joined us for breakfast. "Yes, sir, I believe she gets lovelier every day. And look at you." He heaped a forkful of bacon onto my plate. "Look worse than this pig. You get any sleep at all? By the looks of her, you weren't keeping her up. Although she is smiling. What do you say, Darla?" Darla was trying to eat a slice of toast whole. "Have the kids been doing some mattress thrashing? Let's have the truth now, Kyle. Out with it. Give us all the details. Katrina, feel free to add anything he omits. Don't be shy."

Katrina sat down next to me, close enough so I could feel her heat, a warmth I believed she carried wherever she went. And even after breakfast, after she and her mother had gone home, if I concentrated, I could still feel her near me. It was a feeling of contentment, as if I'd unexpectedly found something I hadn't realized I was looking for. I closed my eyes and pictured the upcoming dance, imagining how I would hold her, the things I would say, the way she looked at night when the sky and her hair were the same color, and how much I hoped she would kiss me again. They were thoughts I could not drive from my head, and they came swarming to the front of my brain, holding the hands of the clock at a standstill, imparting an unbearable sense of anticipation. Nightfall seemed an eternity away, something that would never happen, and until my grandfather began coughing in his room I wondered if everything in the world had stopped.

He coughed for more than a minute, and after he stopped, through his closed door, I could hear him sucking great breaths of air as if he'd been holding his breath for a long time.

"Come here, Kyle." He sounded tired, and on my way through the living room to his bedroom, the sensation of dread I'd felt the night before returned as suddenly as if I'd walked through a ghost, an evil spirit that chilled my soul and caused my body to tremble. All thoughts of Katrina were gone, and I waited to open his door until he called me again.

"How are you coming with the journal?"

The journal. I'd almost forgotten.

"I've got some work outside to do this morning, if you want to check in on William."

It seemed as good a way to occupy my mind as any, but I was worried about my grandfather.

"Cole, are you okay?"

He looked at me carefully, a stare he used to judge how much I knew, then grinned. "Right as rain, my man. Right as rain." He swung his legs over the side of the bed where he was sitting, and before I could move he'd grabbed me around the waist and slung me over his shoulder. He trotted into my room, flipped me onto my bed, and punched the mattress. "Why ain't she broken in yet is what I want to know? What's this business of lounging around on the couch while Sleeping Beauty rests in here? Wouldn't hurt you to spend less time in the woods and more in the bush."

As soon as my grandfather left me, the room grew cold and I felt lonely. I was frightened when I began reading from William's journal, not certain why, but I was afraid. I read about him working in Butte, spending an entire year there, then homesteading in the Big Hole valley, and when I found I could not put the book down, my fear increased exponentially, and, like a nightmare I was powerless to awake from, all I could do was keep reading.

September, 1864

Snow descends from the high country, creeping down toward the Big Hole like an unstoppable regiment of troops. Each morning the frost on my windows is thicker, and it takes the sun longer to warm the earth. In the woods, it is always cool. The animals — the deer, elk, bear, and moose I see on a daily basis — are bracing themselves for winter by increasing their coats and feeding heavily. I watched a large grizzly graze in a meadow most of the day yesterday like a cow. He kept his head low, chewing steadily, consuming summer's last green grass, preparing for his long sleep. I could have shot him with my Sharps any number of times, but this time of year I feel some-thing of a kinship with the animals. I can sense, just as they can, that tougher days are ahead, and as they eat and I fortify my woodpile, we both look to the white mountaintops with leery anticipation.

There are still plenty of good days when the air is hot and butter-flies flit over patches of tall, pink wildflowers that fill every fire-formed clearing in the forest, but strangely enough it is on these fine days that I find myself thinking about winter with the most dread. When the sky turns gray and the mountains are lost in snow flurries it is easier to accept what is coming, but when summer bolsters her doomed battle with good weather I realize all too well what soon will be gone and find myself thinking over and over about the stern warnings I received in Butte concerning the brutal winters here.

My cabin in tiny. Three rooms scarcely large enough to turn around in. At night, when the temperature drops, the pine logs pop and creak, and I am forever filling new openings in my walls. I have shoveled sod up even the first three tiers, no small task in this rocky land, and they remain free of frost while logs higher up are often coated richly.

During the days I explore the country, and it seems that even if I lived three lifetimes I could never see it all. It is as endless as the sky, and from its rocky peaks to swampy beaver meadows and wide sage flats, it is as diverse a land as I imagine exists anywhere. And it is full of game. The elk are breeding, herding together while the bulls lock antlers in impressive shows of force and their haunting calls quicken my heart. They sound like spirits born of the wind, and the airy challenges they send back and forth are the wildest sounds I've ever heard.

Along the river, in the prairie land between the mountain ranges, buffalo tramp paths through the grass and it grows harder to distinguish the calves from their mothers. I have laid in a good supply of meat, drying it on racks and storing it in a double-log shelter that so far has kept out all but a few mice.

Often at night, especially if I've had a disconcerting experience during the day — seen an Indian's footprint or heard a pack of wolves on the hunt — I think about home. This wild country I have come to is hard to call home. I feel so insignificant here that I wonder if I shall ever come to think of it as such, and hardly believe I will. Confronted with so much wilderness, so much raw power, I feel out of place. I think about the smell of my mother's hotcakes, the way fresh catfish fell apart in my mouth, and how good one slice of apple pie would taste. I miss summer gatherings when my hands dripped with melon juice and outdoor evening fires drew friends together and there was no talk of war. I have heard it is going badly for the south. I cannot block out reports that list the dead in the thousands nor can I put enough distance between myself and fighting to cease fearing for my father. This fear is the one thing distance hasn't numbed. Everything else seems like a pleasant dream I only half remember hours after I've been awake. And even my dreams of home are not vivid. Most of the time it appears more as emotions than a tangible place: recollections of my childhood melted into an area I've never seen. Sometimes when I am out in the woods with no one but myself for company, I have urges to head east that are almost as strong as the ones which led me west. My decision to come here has an irreversible finality about it that scares me. While I am drawn to these big woods, there is no comfort in them. It is true that I take some satisfaction in knowing that I am one of the very first whites to chip out a living for myself here, but at times, perhaps more in the fall of the year when my spirits become naturally dampened, I wonder if people are supposed to be here at all. I haven't encountered the hostile Indians or supernatural forces that I was assured would quickly do away with me, but I sense something ominous is lurking nearby. In places, the forest is full of unseen eyes that look at me with little kindness. I feel the trees themselves are watching. Watching and waiting. But all these fears, all the misgivings I have about being here, are quickly dispersed when the morning sun lights up the mountains all around me, so lovely that mere words cannot describe it, or I see something as simple and yet so perfect as a young moose snuggled next to its mother beside a stream that flows as pure as the air I breathe. I remind myself that these are reasons I came, and so far it has been enough to keep me going.

My traps are ready for the fur season. They hang in rows on the north wall of my cabin, sheltered from the weather by a crude overhang on the roof. I have over one hundred, and as many different sizes as kinds of animals I hope to catch. I have practiced a little with coyotes and beaver and have had enough success to prevent me from becoming prematurely discouraged.

I very rarely see another human being. From time to time, I wander down the Big Hole to Mistake, the tiny settlement named after two prospectors struck a rich deposit of fool's gold, and, believing the were wealthy beyond their wildest dreams, laid claim to most of the surrounding country. The town, such as it is, is a rough enclave of trappers, mountain men, and a handful of Indians who are drawn to the saloon like moths to a flame. It has less than sixty residents, and can, after the sun goes down and the saloon's patrons have gone home, be more desolate than the woods. There is nothing more empty than a main street without anyone on it, when it appears twice as wide and much longer than it really is. I have stood alone in the street there under these conditions several times, with the gurgle of the river nearby and a ring of mountains closing me off from the rest of the world, and thought it a more lonely place than my small cabin which is far more removed from people.

November, 1864

Winter's icy breath has blown away the last traces of fall and transformed the Big Hole valley into a world of quiet whiteness where the only sounds are wind in the trees and snow falling on snow. The deer, elk, and buffalo have trended their way downstream, leaving the thin sliver of river that remains open to a few long-legged moose and hares. In the woods, where the trees bend from the weight of the snow and the weak sun no longer penetrates, winter's blanket is broken only by the tracks of fur-bearers and my own blundering footsteps pursuing them. And it is cold. Colder than I knew it could get. At night, the air stings my lungs and directs my stare to my woodpile. The dry logs lie buried beneath the snow, and on more than one occasion I have felt a pang of panic when I looked out and could not see them.

Trapping is exhausting. As soon as I manage to pack a trail between my sets, it snows hard again. I find myself leaving well before the sun rises and returning long after it has set. Walking in these dark woods is both more peaceful and more trying than anything I have ever done. The utter solitude that surrounds me, the empty forest, the snow-packed meadows, and the frozen streams, stretch on forever, a never-ending mosaic of wild, white country, but at the same time, I sense it is only empty on the surface. I am caught between losing myself in the vast spaces here and feeling that at every moment I am being watched. I've seen no evidence in support of this sensation, but it is too strong for me to ignore. At night, on my way back to my cabin, the soft shadows of the snow take on sinister shapes, and I constantly think I see movement just far enough ahead so that I cannot make out what it is. Invariably, when I arrive at the spot there is nothing there. No tracks in the snow, no creature waiting among the pines, and no trace that anything has set foot there since the beginning of time. I wonder how much this land has changed since time began, and doubt it has much at all. It is easy to see in the expressions of the animals held fast in my traps who the newcomer to this country is. The uneasiness I feel here must be a very old instinct, left from a time when my stooped ancestors had far more to fear than I do today. And whatever it is that produces this uneasiness is very old, too. For all I know, it has been here since there first were trees and rock, and whether it is more than the humbling power of uninhabited places, its effects, my long strides after dark, my urges to stay inside, and the way I look over my shoulder, are quite tangible.

Bruce Tipton's metallic-green Chevy pickup was so quiet that I didn't realize anyone had pulled into the yard until I heard his door close. I shut the journal, more than ready for a break, fearing that without some outside distraction I would be sucked into its pages. My forehead was beaded with sweat and my hands burned. The more I read, the more acute my feeling of dread grew, as if the words were leading me toward something terrible beyond my imagination. I slid the book under my bed, further than I could comfortably reach, half expecting to see the covers above it begin glowing or beating in time with a great, invisible heart.

Outside, the sun did not seem as bright as it had earlier in the morning. My grandfather and Bruce were leaning against opposite sides of the truck, talking quietly.

"Kyle." My grandfather opened the passenger door. "Mr. Tipton has something he'd like us to see."

I climbed into the middle, closer to my grandfather than Bruce, and we started slowly up the driveway.

My grandfather played with a button on his door, raising and lowering his window like a bored child. "What's the big surprise, Bruce?"

Bruce didn't answer. His jaw was set firmly and he stared straight ahead through the tinted windshield. At the end of the driveway, he turned the truck west and eased it off the road to parallel the upper boundary of the fence. A hundred yards in front of us, lying in a twisted heap, tangled in a ball of wire, its neck outstretched and its tongue sticking stiff from the side of its mouth, was a dead cow buffalo. Bruce stopped a few feet in front of the animal. Behind it, the ground was pocked with running tracks, divots of sod turned up everywhere.

"That's two thousand dollars, Cole." Bruce didn't turn his head or part his teeth when he spoke.

"Well, not no more it ain't." My grandfather stared past me at Bruce.

"No, it isn't. And that's the goddamned point of it."

My grandfather made a clucking noise and pushed his hat back. "Good man like you hadn't ought to take the name of the lord in vain, Bruce."

"Stampeded into the fence." Bruce acted as if he hadn't heard my grand-father. "Looks like they were all running. Something had them worked up. What do you think that was, Cole?" He turned to face my grandfather now, looking at him from behind his dark sunglasses, his eyes appearing gray.

"Lightning. Had a strike right in pasture that started a little grass fire. Maybe you saw where it burned."

"Lightning." Bruce reversed the truck and backed up fast. He drove down the driveway in second gear, braked hard, and got out more fluidly than I expected he could. The sodden remains of fireworks lay strewn about on the ground, colored tissue paper like fallen flower petals. Bruce picked up the spent case of a mortar and set it on the hood. "Lightning."

"That's right, would you like me to spell it for you?" My grandfather swung himself out of the cab and started around the hood toward Bruce.

"No, but I want you to be careful. Be careful what you say to me, and be careful where you let the boy shoot off fireworks."

My grandfather picked a dead bumble bee out of the grill and flicked it away over his shoulder. "Careful. That's an interesting word. Sounds a bit like a threat. So while we're on that subject, let me tell you something. Bruce, I don't know what the hell scared your buffalo, and it's too bad one of them got hung up. I mean that. Wouldn't say it if I didn't. But they aren't the smartest animals. Indians used to drive them right off cliffs for Christ's sake. No, I don't know what caused that. I do know, however, that if you speak to, or of, my grandson again, even if it's just in passing, your words had best be well chosen." He extended his right arm to Bruce, pointing at chest level.

"For I tell you true, mister, they will be the last you speak with a full set of teeth."

My grandfather turned toward the house, and I followed a half step behind. Inside, it didn't take him long to find what was left of the Jack Daniels. He poured a tall glass and took a long drink.

"Takes something stronger than this to wash the taste of that bastard out of my mouth. What the hell does he expect? He wants everything in the world accountable to him, even the buffalo. Well, they ain't. Neither are you and I." My grandfather slammed his empty glass down on the table. "And if he's stupid enough to whisper a word to you again he'll good and goddamn well wish he didn't. Son of a bitch!"

Splinter Horn bellowed from somewhere close to the woods, a drawn out moan followed by a short series of grunts. He sounded like an oversized bullfrog.

"Keep right at it," my grandfather said. "You can push me too far, too." He stomped into his room and slammed the door hard enough to rock his whiskey bottle off the table. It fell to the floor, did not break, and slid slowly with the slope of the house toward the living room.

In my own room, lying on my bed, I was suddenly overcome with fatigue. I watched a spider descend from the ceiling toward the window from a strand of web I couldn't see. He reached the blanket hanging from the curtain rod, scurried out of sight, and then I blinked and fell asleep. I slept a deep sleep of retreat from something I sensed coming and felt powerless to stop.

When I woke up, I felt better, rested, and once more thinking about the dance. From the kitchen window, I could see the upper end of the pasture, and above it the Pioneers. High in the sky, a lone bird circled, floating on its ragged wings. I looked away.

"Ready to get spruced up for the big night?" My grandfather sounded as though he was feeling better, too. He appeared from the bathroom, his face covered with shaving cream, a towel wrapped around his waist, the seam in front, not covering much. "Dust off your hat, douse yourself with cologne, cut yourself a good stout stick to keep the women at bay, and you'll be ready to go." He pranced into the kitchen, adjusted his towel when he saw me looking away, then positioned his face inches from mine and stared hard, a look that made me feel as if I'd done something I shouldn't have and he'd found out.

"We can't have this, Kyle. Come on." He steered me ahead of him to the bathroom, where the water was pouring down the little sink, and pointed in the cracked mirror above it. "Time to tame those chin hairs."

I didn't see any chin hairs, but my grandfather was quite convinced they were present. He wiped shaving cream from his cheeks, dabbed it onto my face, and handed my his razor, an old flip-open straight blade with a mother-of-pearl handle.

"Down to the chin, up from the neck." He took my hand in his and guided the razor around my face, pressing lightly enough so it never really touched my skin. After each stroke, he held it under the stream of water until it shone. "Christ, probably plug the drain with hair. Be working on it with a snake for sure." When he finished, he ran a finger over my lips to the tip of my chin. "Much better. And I'm sure Katrina will agree." He slapped me on the back, hard enough to make me cough, and as I walked out of the bathroom, the scent of his shaving cream, a smell I had connected only with him, came with me. Like the feel of Katrina's lips on my face the day before, I wished it would never go away.

The buzzard I'd seen earlier was tightening his circles above the dead buffalo, descending slowly, his naked head bent down toward the lifeless beast below him. My grandfather stopped on our way to the dance to watch him.

"Should have brought my shotgun, Kyle. I know they serve some sort of purpose, but I don't like them anyway. Death picked a good bird to clean up his handiwork."

They were my sentiments exactly. Since reading about them in William's journal, I would have been perfectly happy to see them wiped from the face of the earth. As we turned onto the tar, I looked over my shoulder at the woods on the other side of the pasture. The buffalo were grouped together as they had been the night before, staring out across the irrigation ditch, Splinter Horn tearing at the ground with his hooves.

"Will the wolf eat any of the buffalo?"

"No, they don't hunt alone. Not big animals anyway. That fellow you saw keeps his belly fed with mice."

"But they're afraid of him, aren't they?"

"Sure. That's one instinct we haven't driven out of them. They still know enough to be afraid."

"Is that why I was afraid of him, too?"

"No."

"Why was I?"

"Look at that." My grandfather pointed to the Wise River where it flowed under the highway. "Gone down in good shape. Big Hole should be perfect for flies. I think perhaps you and I will look into that soon."

"Cole?"

He waved off my question. "You'd better get your mind off wolves and onto the matter at hand. Unless of course you want to play Little Red Riding Hood with her." He grabbed his crotch. "And here comes the big bad wolf, baby! All the better to . . ." I wasn't laughing, and he let it go. "Really, Kyle, this is going to be great tonight. We'll acquit ourselves very well. Wait and see." We pulled into the parking lot at the Six Point. It was first time I'd seen it full of cars, and behind the bar, along the river, a band was setting up under a white canvas tent. I looked for Darla's station wagon but didn't see it.

"They'll be here soon enough. Be here with bells on, I suspect. And you know something, Kyle?" My grandfather had an uncanny way of becoming serious in an instant. So serious he sounded prophetic. I imagined him at a pulpit, arms outstretched, eyes closed, preaching solemnly. "I couldn't be prouder of you." He squeezed my shoulder, holding on several seconds, something he'd done before, but this time it felt like a good-bye. I watched him walk away from the truck, toward the throng of people beside the river, and until my lungs began to ache I didn't realize I was holding my breath.

The band began warming up, playing short numbers from various country songs, tuning their guitars, fiddling with the large box speakers and knob-covered amplifiers, their lead singer tapping his microphone, surveying the ground in front of him, turning in short dance steps. I walked down to the river, to the exact spot where Katrina had first asked me if I was going to the dance the night my grandfather had gotten into the fistfight. I thought that if things had worked out differently, I wouldn't have remembered much of our conversation. As it was, I remembered every word. Time had been powerless to take that away, and I felt a certain amount of comfort in believing it never could. A beaver cutting floated by, both ends of the willow chewed to a point, carried downstream from somewhere high above Mistake where the Big Hole twists slowly through swamps and moose wade back and forth across its deepest pools without getting their knees wet. It had traveled a long way, and I wondered where it was going. I watched it spin into a backwater, drift toward the bank, then bob back into the current and disappear in a riffle. The sun was shedding soft, evening light onto the water, signaling the time of day when shadows seem deep enough to become lost in, and the landscape appears two-dimensional, rich colors painted in many coats. Cliffs a mile downstream where the river bent in against the opposite bank were turning red, their blunt peaks sticking into the sky like giant molars worn smooth with age. An eagle flapped overhead, black wings rising and falling between splashes of white, and I heard Katrina call my name. Everything was perfect.

"Hi, Kyle."

Katrina's reflection appeared in front of me in the river, and I thought that if I didn't turn around it would be easier to look into her eyes, but it wasn't.

"Cole said you were down here." She moved closer to me and I smelled perfume. "Ready for the dance?"

"Yeah." I hoped it wasn't a lie. The muscles in my legs were beginning to ache, and the practicing I'd done in my room seemed far away and foolish.

"I'm gonna go talk to mom. Come get me when the music starts, okay?"

I nodded, then as Katrina's reflection turned, so did I. I watched her walk up the bank toward the crowd, step behind a man with a large straw hat, then vanish. As soon as she was out of sight, I wished I hadn't let her go. I kicked a round stone into the river, letting its ripples wash out my own reflection, and as the water calmed I did it again.

The Bitterroots did not permit much twilight, and shortly after the sun fell behind them darkness rushed in. The river turned from deep blue to gray, then suddenly to black, its rapids flowing like silver ink. The band began their first set with Southern Pacific's "Any Way The Wind Blows," the bass drum thumping in my chest, the colored lights under the tent sending thick beams into the sky.

My grandfather was easy to recognize. He had a plastic cup in one hand and Darla in the other. Dell danced in front of him, rubbing against his chest, her massive legs turned outward to allow her as close to him as possible. Badger spotted me from where he sat on a picnic table, and before I could get away he was at my side, thrusting a bottle of Rainier into my hand.

"Good man, Kyle. Good man." He took my free hand and pumped it vigorously. "Let's go get your girlfriend, hey?" Badger pulled me through the crowd to where Katrina stood talking to an Indian two or three years older than me. His hair was as long as Badger's, but he'd spent more time combing it. It hung untangled past his shoulders and was trimmed evenly. We stared at each other, and I had no trouble meeting his eyes.

"Your boyfriend was looking for you, Katrina." Badger pushed me toward her, and the boy she was talking to smirked. I hated him instantly. "Who's this?"

Katrina looked at Badger when she spoke. "Danny Twofeathers. He's down from Browning."

"What's the news from the res?" Badger let go of me and offered his bottle to Danny. He drained it without taking his eyes off me.

"Same shit as always."

I hated the way he talked — a bad impression of Jack Palance, hoarse but smooth.

Badger took his empty bottle and frowned. "Now I need another one. You want one, Kyle? How 'bout you, Danny?"

"You bet." Danny still hadn't looked away from me. The band began Garth Brooks's "Shameless," and he reached for Katrina's hand. They moved away into the crowd, leaving me alone. I watched for them through half the song, then turned my back and walked to the road. In the pull-off where I'd spent my first night in Montana, I found a rock and tried to throw it across the river. When I heard it splash short, I hurled another. It didn't make it either.

"Fuck it." I tried to make it sound natural, but it didn't, and I grew more angry. I picked up a third rock, concentrated on the far bank, then stopped. A duck drifted into view, and I switched targets, hurling the stone at it for all I was worth. I heard a solid smack, the bird tipped onto its side, one wing extended perpendicular to the river, and as quickly as it died my rage turned to sorrow. I followed the bird downstream until it floated to shore where I picked it up, wishing that the tears that fell on it would restore it to life. I held it in the pull-off until I could no longer feel warmth through its feathers, then laid it gently in the water and watched it float off into the night.

"Your grandfather said you'd probably be here."

Katrina's voice wasn't very comforting. Neither was the fact that my grandfather knew where I was.

"Are you gonna ask me to dance, or what?"

"Looked like you already were."

Katrina sat down next to me. "Danny's just a friend."

"Whatever. Besides, I can't dance." Fireworks were going off now, but I didn't look up from the ground.

"I bet you can."

I shrugged, and Katrina stood up fast.

"Here, get up."

I didn't move.

"Come on, do it." She pulled on my shirt, and I stood up. "Now listen." The fireworks stopped popping and I could faintly hear Blackhawk's "Goodbye Says It All." "Put your arms around me. Here, like this." She took my arms and placed them on her waist, pulling at my elbows to draw me closer. "Good."

I concentrated on the music, straining to hear the beat so I could stay with the song, but it was too far away, and soon we were moving to our own rhythm. As we turned slowly in tight circles, events of the day began to fade until everything, including the duck I'd killed and Danny Twofeathers, had moved to a fuzzy horizon of memories of home, my parents, and other things that seemed so far away. I listened to the river running a few yards behind us, and unlike my trip to Firewater when I'd been keenly aware that what I was doing I could only do in Montana, I understood that what I was doing now I would only do a few times, maybe even just once, in my life. Our feet slowed until we were rocking togther more than dancing, my hands met behind Katrina's back to pull her closer, heat from her body fully penetrating me, I looked into her eyes and kissed her quickly, though not as awkwardly as I'd feared, on the lips. She sighed then stepped away from me, and in the split second before she said something I felt as if I would explode, not knowing if I'd done the right thing.

"About time," she said. "Ready to go back to the dance?"

I was ready to do anything. I felt like swimming the Big Hole, climbing the highest peak in the Bitterroots, or racing the buffalo across their pasture. Walking back to Mistake, the earth seemed springy, pushing my legs into the air like the jumping balloons I'd played in at the New York State Fair when I was very young. And I had no more trouble looking at Katrina. In fact, it was difficult to keep my eyes off her. I was afraid that if I looked away too long she would disappear; gone the way objects from a dream too good to be true vanish upon waking. She stopped several times, started once to ask what I was looking at, then just smiled.

My grandfather was the first person we saw at the dance, standing in the Six Point parking lot, his back to the highway, Pete and Ed Lewis huddled in front of him.

"One goddamned dead buffalo is costing me my easement?" he roared. "That's what he said? One filthy, stinking, good-for-nothing buffalo? We'll see about that. Yes, we will." My grandfather started coughing and Pete and Ed saw it as a chance to escape. They ducked away toward the crowd, looking over their shoulders to be sure they weren't being pursued. "Kyle."

I didn't have as good luck slipping past.

"Kyle, it appears I'm not to have my easement. What do you think about that?"

My grandfather was drunk. Drunk and mad, and I knew that wasn't a good combination.

"Well, what's your take on it?" He steadied himself on the hood of a car, then dropped his hands to his sides. "Oh, Jesus. You've got the Chinaman's grin. Look like you've been hard at the opium pipe. You do this to my grandson?" he asked Katrina. "Well, good for you. Loosen the boy up a bit. Go ahead, go on. Sun don't rise and set in the crack of my ass. Don't let me spoil the night for you." He waved us away in the direction of the band, and I didn't see him again until just before the last song when he and Darla came walking arm in arm up from the river. "Mollified, Kyle," he whispered as he past.

The final song was Restless Heart's "The Bluest Eyes In Texas," and I held onto Katrina until the last note had faded into the conversation of couples leaving and the clank of beer cans being thrown away. I squeezed her once before I let go, and as we drew apart a bolt of panic shot through me. It had been the best night of my life, but now it was over, gone faster than any night I could remember.

CHAPTER 15

I NEVER ASKED my grandfather about the easement. We continued cutting on the Canyon Ranch, working through the hottest month of Montana's summer, working in air hazy from forest fires across the Bitterroots in Idaho that stained the sunsets crimson and left the entire Big Hole Valley smelling like smoke. We worked slowly, sometimes no more than half a day, and spent the rest of our time fly-fishing the river, barbecuing elk steaks, hiking to high mountain lakes in the Pintlers, and of course, drinking at the Six Point. I left William's journal under my bed, and if my grandfather knew I'd stopped reading it he didn't mention it. My present was full enough. Full of the things I had dreamed about ever since first hearing of Montana, and bit by bit the urge to learn of things that had happened more than a century before abated.

I was seeing Katrina on a regular basis, each time amazed that whatever had happened the night of the dance, whatever magic I'd felt, whatever it was that made it so difficult to take my eyes off her, hadn't disappeared. I took her fly fishing one evening early in August to a stretch of the Big Hole that had become my favorite, four pools below the buffalo pasture where the water ran in the shade of massive, leaning cottonwoods and trout rose close to shore where they were easy to reach. We kicked locusts up out of the grass on our way to the Big Hole, great yellow and red insects whose wings clacked together when they flew and carried them upwards of fifty yards.

Splinter Horn followed us on his side of the fence, something he did whenever I went to the river, and the murderous look in his eyes seemed doubly intent as he stared at two of us. There was no peace to be made with him, no way to tell him I had nothing against him, and I could not help worrying that someday the posts that stood between us might not be enough.

I had long since grown comfortable talking to Katrina, but as we walked to the river that night neither one of us said much. We crossed the highway, leaving Splinter Horn to toss his head and bellow until we returned. We made our way through the cottonwoods to the Big Hole, but instead of fishing we sat down on two smooth stones and stared at each other for a long time. Something was different. Not necessarily wrong, but different.

"Cole told my mom you're leaving soon."

"What?" That wasn't like my grandfather. I'd never known him to think further ahead than a day or two at the most, and I wasn't scheduled to leave for more than two weeks.

"That's what he said."

"Well, I don't want to talk about it."

"I know." Katrina smiled, but that looked different, too, and suddenly, I realized that like Splinter Horn, time would not permit a truce, either. It had been waging its patient war since I arrived two months earlier, and it had been winning the whole time. "Are you gonna help me catch a fish?" She tried to sound enthusiastic.

"I guess." I looked at my grandfather's rod in my hand, and realized the time would come when it was no longer his.

"You don't have to if you don't want."

I heard a trout rise twenty feet downstream. It seemed pointless — everything seemed pointless, but at this moment it was there to be caught, and I figured we'd better do it. Katrina had never fly fished before. I stood behind her, looking around her shoulder, holding my hands on hers, helping her cast the way my father had taught me.

"Don't whip the rod so much. Let the line come all the way back behind you. Wait till you feel it pulling before bringing it forward. Use your arm instead of your wrist. Okay, here we go." The fly, a small grasshopper, touched down near where the fish had come up. "Can you see it?" Katrina nodded, and I let go of her hands. "Just move it a little. Make it look like it's swimming. That's it, good." She twitched the fly across a riffle and the trout took it hard, setting the hook himself.

"Got him." Katrina's smile was back to normal. "Look, it's jumping!"

A rainbow eight or nine inches sailed into the air, made two short runs downstream, then came to the surface on its side.

"Reel him in now."

Katrina reeled the fish to me, and I removed the fly.

"Can I let him go?" she asked. I handed her the rainbow and she set him at her feet, waving as he zipped off. "Bye."

We fished until dark. Until the mist rising off the water was too thick to see where the fly was landing. I wanted Katrina to catch one on her own, but she didn't. Splinter Horn had grown bored waiting for us, and had rejoined the herd. They were staring at the woods, just as they'd done every night since the fireworks. Halfway to the house I thought I heard the wolf. I stopped and listened, asked Katrina if she'd heard it, but she hadn't. Later that night, after my grandfather had taken Katrina home, after I had watched her walk slowly into her trailer, watched her go without saying good-bye, I listened again out my bedroom window, but I heard nothing until I feel asleep. And then it came clearly, not from the woods, but from all around me, filling my dream, echoing all night, ringing in my head after I woke the following morning.

The wind blew out of the north on our way to work, a cool breeze which my grandfather said reminded him of fall.

"Won't be long now before the elk start bugling. No sound like that anywhere."

"You think I'll get to hear one?"

"Could be. There are a lot of bulls around. Wouldn't be surprised if some of them start squealing a little."

"Do you like fall?" It was my favorite time of year.

"No. I hate endings."

The way he said it made me afraid something more than summer was coming to a close, and I rode the rest of the way to the Canyon Ranch in silence. We had made good progress cutting, taking half the trees. My grandfather said that before the first real snow he would have it done.

"Gonna take her easy this winter, Kyle," he said. "For once in my life, I'll have enough money so I can behave the way a retired man should. Evenings at the Six Point . . . lounge around in bed until noon . . . watch the snow pile up outside and not give a shit. Sounds regal."

To me, it sounded like a dream; a man serving life in prison thinking about what it will be like when they let him out. It didn't suit my grandfather, and we both knew it.

Pete and Ed Lewis were waiting for us at the skidder, and when they saw us coming they edged close to their pickup.

"What do you suppose the rat terriers want this morning?" My grandfather stepped on the gas. "Come to tell me Bruce has changed his mind about the easement?"

I didn't say anything.

"No, I doubt it, too." We skidded to a stop less than a foot from their truck, and my grandfather got out fast, reached in the back for his chainsaw and winked at me. The Lewis brothers had their doors open. "What's going on with the two of you this morning? Up awful early, ain't you?"

"Cole." Pete looked as if he was going to take his hat off when he spoke. "Cole, we came to tell you ..."

"Came to tell me what, goddamnit?" My grandfather raised the saw.

"We're just doing our job."

"Ain't your job dealing with those infernal animals your boss has living in my dooryard?"

"We don't deal with the buffalo no more," Ed said. "Got new men just for them."

"Too bad, who's Bruce going to get when it comes time to artificially inseminate them? I was looking forward to watching that."

"Cole, have you talked to Bruce?" Pete took a tentative step toward my grandfather.

"Fuck no. Why should I?"

The brothers looked at each other and Pete backed up. "Cole, you gotta stop. Bruce says something's come up with that developer from Bozeman. Says the rest of the trees got to stay. I'm sorry, Cole, but that's what he says."

"Says to who?" The vein in my grandfather's forehead was throbbing. "Says to you, or says to me? Deal was he had to tell me himself. What's so damn important that he can't do his own dirty work? First the easement and now this? Snot-nosed little shit can't face me himself?"

"Like I said, Cole, we're just doing our job."

My grandfather hurled the saw across the hood of their truck. "That's my whole point, Pete," he screamed. "You're not doing your job, you're doing his job. And by Christ, until he does it, I refuse to stop. He think he can yank me around by the balls like this? Think he can get away with this? Deal-breaking bastard."

"That what you want us to tell him?"

"Fuck him! Tell him that. You tell him to come on up here and hear it straight from the horse's mouth, too. Fine and dandy for him to lay back and dictate what goes on. After all, he ain't the one counting on the money from this wood. He sure as shit doesn't need it, and heaven forbid a man who does gets it. His father was never this shabby."

Pete had eased into the truck and was fumbling with the key.

"Yeah, go on. Get out of here. And fuck you, too." My grandfather stepped fast to the chainsaw and slammed in into a boulder, laughing crazily as the kickback bar broke free of the block and the chain twisted loose. "Kyle?"

I was feeling nauseous.

"Kyle, a man who ain't worth his word ain't worth a shit. Tipton wants us to shut down, he can goddamn well come up here himself and tell us to stop. Who's he think he is?" He picked up his saw, looked at the chain, then tossed it into the bed of his truck. "Hell with it. Let's go. I can play hardball, too. I've got something for that son-of-a-bitch."

I couldn't help wondering as we bounced down off the ranch, faster than we had since my first night in Montana, what was in store for Tipton. Whenever my grandfather "had something" for someone it wasn't good, and in the back of my mind it occurred to me he might shoot Bruce. Go to his house and call him out the way they did in the old, black and white westerns. Blast him to smithereens and come back to the Six Point to brag.

"What can you do?" I had to ask.

"Plenty," he said as we bucked onto the highway.

"What?" I hated to press the issue, but I felt as if I might vomit.

"Never mind what," my grandfather snapped. "You'll find out soon enough, and that'll be soon enough for you. I'll tell you this much, however." He swerved across the center line, yanked the truck back into his own lane, and stifled a cough. "People will talk about this for a long time to come, and if Bruce Tipton lives to be one hundred and ten and forgets everything he ever knew, he'll remember that fucking with Cole T. Richards was a grave mistake!"

The explanation didn't quell my curiosity, but I was relieved to hear my grandfather say Bruce would have the opportunity to live a long life.

Splinter Horn ran to the fence as soon as we pulled into the driveway, and my grandfather smiled. "You fucking dinosaur, I've got proven medicine for you, too." He spun the tires away from him and left the engine running in front of the house. "Go ahead in, Kyle. I've got business in town. Take a look at the journal if you want. William would have known what to do with these buffalo. I'll be back this evening."

"You're not going to see Bruce, are you?"

"Not yet. Got other plans. You can come with me in the morning, but right now you're better off here. Call up your woman if you want. Tell her you want to see how good your bodies line up." He gave me a pat on the knee, his way of reassuring me he wasn't going to kill Tipton, then drove away without looking back.

I wanted to call my parents. Explain to my father that something terrible was going to happen. I dialed the number, let it ring for more than a minute, then hung up. Katrina wasn't home either. I sat on the couch, staring into my grandfather's room at the elk on his wall, then remembered the journal. Dust clung to its leather cover, and for an instant I thought about not opening it. When I did, returning to William in his cabin in the winter, I understood perfectly what he meant when he said he felt completely alone.

December, 1864

It is harder to tear myself away from my fire each day to wander this land of deep snow. I have not seen another person for over two months, and I find myself thinking only of the day to come, when I repeat the routine of checking my traps. A routine that I have become so accustomed to I could perform it in my sleep. Some days it is as if I am doing everything in a sleep-like state. The kiss of a warm sun on the back of my neck is a dream.

My cache of fur is growing. As it becomes harder for predators to find prey, they come more readily to my baits. I caught my first lynx today on a tributary to the Big Hole in a dense stand of small spruce. He came to a hare pelt I'd hung from a low limb and was held fast in my trap by one of his disproportionately large front feet. Unlike his smaller relatives the bobcats, he did not fly into a rage when I appeared but rather arched his back, snarled only once, and retreated to the limit of the trap's chain. With his yellow eyes set between ears tipped with long tufts of fur, I don't whether he more closely resembled an owl or a devil. He was surprisingly light for his length, most of his bulk being silver hair that I'm sure will bring a good price in the spring.

Spring. What an impossibly far off season that is. It is hard to believe that the earth will ever awaken to show more color than its somber shades of gray and white. I can hardly imagine that the streams I cross on bridges of snow more than five feet deep will rush down mountainsides covered with green grass and wildflowers. The notion that I will ever care to remove the heavy buffalo coat that has become a part of me is absurd.

I have killed a wolverine which for some days was bent upon getting into my supply of meat. Each morning I would see where he'd walked round and round the log storage, trying every kink with apparently unending patience. The night I waited for him, bundled in all the clothes I could wrap around myself, there was a full moon. Tiny ice crystals filled the air, falling I suspect as frozen dew, and with the exception of a lone wolf somewhere close to the river who spent half an hour lamenting summer's exile with long, sad howls, I heard only my breathing. Just when I believed I would freeze to the log I sat on, I caught sight of a dark shape on the snow, moving with practiced stealth toward the meat it smelled through the pine barrier. I waited until I had a good view of him, raised the Sharps slowly, and between shivers I put an end to his nightly visits. His pelt was rendered useless by the big bullet, but it felt good to shoot him. I suppose I saw it as one small victory over Nature at a time when more often than not I feel completely at her mercy.

The trepidation I felt earlier in the winter, the eyes all around me, the crawling sensation on my back, and night-time mirages, hangs with me, but I tend to think now it is little more than my unconscious mind's way of telling me to stay alert, reminding me that Death has a watchful eye and is always greedy for souls.

January, 1865

It will never stop snowing. It will fall until it covers the world entirely, obliterating all life. Drifts lap eagerly at the roof of my cabin, blocking out what little sun there is from ever entering my windows. I have already raised my stove pipe twice and must soon do so again. The high snow banks prevent my fire from obtaining sufficient draft, and my house fills as thick with smoke as it does with darkness.

My meat and dry wood supplies are dwindling. I am rationing

both at the expense of my comfort, if not my health. And trapping
has slowed to the occasional coyote or martin. It seems everything
capable of leaving this valley has done so. I attempted to walk to
Mistake two days ago and was turned back by chest-deep snow and
a north wind that howled about me, stinging my face with icy crystals it sucked from the ground, hurling them viciously at my eyes like
tiny spears. I am only able to continue checking my traps because
so many are in the timber, sheltered enough from the wind so that
if I exert all the energy I am capable of I can follow the frigid loop
through the trees. I walk it out of obligation to anything I've caught
and to break the monotony of sitting in a house where it is always
night. Even making the best effort I can to ensure that no creature
waits in a trap too long, many are frozen when I find them. Yesterday
I discovered a hare which had stepped in a coyote set, dead from its
shattered leg and the brutal night. It's eyes were open, reminding me
of the man I shot on my way west. They followed me as I walked
around the trap, staring at me with the terrified look they'd held
when the animal died. A little ways further a silver fox was too weak
to lift its head from its front paws, one of which was ringed with a
heavy band of trap, and tonight, as I write, I am debating pulling the
rest of my sets and calling it a season. The time is fast approaching
when, if I have no luck procuring fresh meat, I will be too gaunt to
check them. Plowing through snow is no easy task, and when my
stomach pains with hunger it becomes many times more difficult.

For several weeks I have not dreamed, but recently I toss and turn
at night while my mind takes me on fantastic journeys to places I
would never venture under my own power. I find myself spinning
down a mighty river, unable to avoid its jagged boulders, gasping for
air as my lungs fill with water. I dream of the forest and my traps and
of the hideous animals they hold. Odd crosses that nature never intended smile wickedly at me and lift their swollen feet shake the trap
in reproach. I dream of a creature that stalks me, always just out of
sight, never far away. I see its tracks in the snow and listen with terror to its devilish screams. And worst of all I dream of home and of
spring and am more afraid when I wake from these than from any of
the others.

JAKE MOSHER

February, 1865

Once more I find myself at Death's doorstep. This time I am freezing. Freezing and starving. My dry wood is gone and I have only
enough meat to last a very few more days. I have been scraping the
hides of the animals I trapped, collecting the frozen flakes of flesh in
my hands and eating it, the coyote, fox, bobcat and beaver, as if it
was Mississippi River catfish. It leaves me feeling sick as often as
not, but I have no choice other than to choke it down. I am constantly tired. Tired to the point where even the simplest acts seem
like impossible chores. On the days I go outside, I have no idea
when I rise what time it is. When I can, I force myself to go out in
search of dead wood, but the trees grow tall and straight and are
limbless to a height of forty or fifty feet. The few branches I collect,
an armload if I am lucky, are all I can carry, and by the time I stumble
through my door with them my arms are as numb as the sticks they
hold.

I am quite literally living in my buffalo coat. I cannot remember
when last I took it off, and the thought occurs to me that I never will.
The short-lived fires I build throw enough heat to take the stiffness
out of it, but before the last embers fade from red to gray it is as rigid
as stone.

My feeling that I have not been alone all this time in this country
has been substantiated. Every night a great wolf comes to prowl about
my cabin, leaving his massive tracks on the snow that has buried my
roof, pacing back and forth in front of my door, disappearing into
the forest before I wake up. Earlier, when I was stronger, I set traps
for him, but it took little time to realize he would not be caught. He
walked tight circles around each of the sets as if he knew exactly
where they were. And there is something else. Something that no
matter how hard I search for a rational explanation of I cannot find.
One morning after the beast spent most of the night wearing paths
around my cabin, I followed his trail where it led away into the timber. It was snowing, not hard, but steadily, falling into the tracks
ahead of me, slowly covering mine behind me. Fearing I would lose
the trail, I picked up my pace, pushing through a stand of young
pines. Where the little trees sheltered the track it was clear, its claws

216

plainly visible, the pads of its feet larger than the palms of my hands. The track appeared so fresh that I cocked the hammer of the Sharps, certain I was only moments behind. But where the trees gave way to more open forest the track vanished. I try to tell myself that it became snowed in or that it branched off somewhere and I missed it, but I know this isn't so. It was as gone as a falling star that shines bright then disappears without a trace.

I have seen other things in the woods that are hard to explain. I have found trees whose limbs have been torn from the trunks at odd angles, a boulder the size of a wagon in the hollow of a fir, and places where streams flow underground. But the disappearance of the wolf track is the first thing to completely baffle me. I can think of no explanation, save a few that make no sense and go against all reason. Wherever that animal went it is impossible for me to follow. Unlike myself, he does not appear confined to these woods or to the laws that govern transportation. I know not where he came from or why he insists on prowling about, but his presence is greatly troubling. I am afraid it is only a matter of time before he is no longer content to allow the walls of my cabin to stand between us. Along with starvation and freezing, I am beginning to fight madness. I lie awake for hours in my bed, fearing each noise I hear announces the arrival of the wolf inside my house. My rifle is loaded and close at all times, and I do not button the pocket of my coat that contains four extra cartridges. I find myself fondling the smooth casings, flicking frost off the hammer of the Sharps, waiting like a nervous soldier for his first glimpse of the enemy. Going at the current rate, I do not know whether it will be my mind or my body that gives out first. As they deteriorate, my muscles to thin, weak bands of flesh, my thoughts to insanity, I am becoming desperate to leave. I would trade the pelt of every animal I've trapped to awaken, even penniless, naked, and without food, in Butte. And I would trade far more to once again see the muddy Mississippi and hear the squabble of ducks, wrap my mouth around a piece of pumpkin pie, and listen to the familiar voice of a friend.

I let my grandfather's phone ring a long time before I answered it, and didn't say anything when I picked up the receiver. I listened to Katrina say "hello" twice before speaking, thinking how small my voice sounded when I did.

"Is something wrong?" she asked.

"No."

"You sound ... I don't know ... you sure you're all right?"

I wasn't sure. Not at all. I felt as if my body had split and was being drawn down two equally unpleasant paths, one half toward some sort of disaster with my grandfather, the other toward something even worse with William.

"What are you doing now?"

"I don't know." That was the truth. I wasn't sure how I fit into everything that was going on around me, but I was certain that somehow I did.

"Want to come over? My mom's gone to Butte."

I did. Badly. I wanted to leave my grandfather's house, but since I'd begun reading I'd felt as though that would be far more difficult than walking out the door. "My grandfather's not home," I said.

"You could walk."

"Yeah."

"I'll meet you halfway, okay? At the Wise River bridge."

"Okay."

It was even harder to hang up than it had been to answer the call. I knew that when I did I would have to start walking, and I was afraid my legs weren't going to move. I stood in the living room, listening to my own breathing, my heart pounding harder and harder, then ran for the door, convinced there was something behind me. I ran up the driveway without looking at the pasture, picked up speed when I hit the road, running until my lungs grew hot and my head ached.

I waited at the bridge for fifteen minutes before I saw Katrina, the whole time feeling as if something was pressing down upon me. Pressing with the great weight of the sky, toying with the idea of crushing me.

"Been waiting long?" Katrina stopped a few feet away from me, and I closed the distance between us without realizing I'd done so until I smelled the perfume she had on. "You sure there's nothing wrong?"

I tried to shake my head but it wouldn't move.

"What is it?"

"I don't know."

"You still want to come over?"

"Yeah."

"Good." She took my hand, then let it drop. "God, you're hot. You have a fever?"

"No."

It took twenty minutes to walk to Katrina's, and every time a car passed I jumped. Cougar snarled at me from a hole he'd dug himself under the steps, showed his teeth and growled.

"Hey, you remember him," Katrina scolded. "Be nice." Cougar snarled again. "That's weird. He never does that."

The inside of the trailer was small, but neater than I expected. I sat down on a couch that faced a large, wood-framed television, and Katrina sat down beside me, close enough so that our legs touched.

"There's nothing on TV," she said.

I didn't care. It felt good just to sit.

"Think you'll come back next summer?"

"Maybe."

"You want to?" She snuggled closer to me, leaning so her head rested on my shoulder.

"Yeah." What I really wanted was for everything to stay the same. I wanted to stop the changes I saw taking place both in and around me. Changes I felt could not be undone. Changes I feared would alter my Montana forever.

"I'd still like to see a city," Katrina said. "Maybe I could come visit you sometime."

"Maybe." I hadn't given any thought all summer to entering high school, but when Katrina suggested a visit, it hit me that soon I would be a freshman. Soon, even what I had grown accustomed to at home, what was familiar and safe, would change. I began to feel claustrophobic, pressure building on my chest and behind my eyes. I pulled slowly away from Katrina, toward the end of the couch, and she didn't follow.

"You'll probably find a girlfriend back home. Probably won't even remember me." She wasn't teasing. "You think?"

I didn't know what was going to happen when I returned home. I didn't know how much might take place before I did, either. But I did know I wasn't going to forget her, and I wanted to tell her. I tried, but the words did not come. They were stuck in a lump half way down my throat. A lump so large that it occurred to me it was my heart being pulled from my chest.

When she reached for my hand, I let her take it, and when she pulled me to her I did not resist. I wasn't entirely sure why I was crying, and I didn't care if she saw the tears in my eyes. In fact, I think a part of me wanted her to.

I was asleep with my head in Katrina's lap when my grandfather arrived early in the evening. I heard his voice filling the trailer before I opened my eyes.

"I may be the only man in the world who's disappointed to find his grandson fully clothed with a girl. You're going to give me gray hairs, Kyle. Have I got to print you up an instruction manual? Lord knows I'm qualified."

I sat up slowly, looked at Katrina, and knew she hadn't slept. Her eyes looked tired, her face was tense, and I was embarrassed.

"Come on, young man, if you aren't busy here, and it pains me to see that you're not, you can ride home with me."

I waited for my grandfather to walk out before hugging Katrina. I locked my hands behind her, squeezed gently, but she felt rigid. The wonderful warmth she had given off was gone, and all that remained was a faint hint of perfume.

On the way to his house, I asked my grandfather how he knew where I was. He always seemed to know.

"Well, Kyle, it didn't take much to figure it out. After all, you are a Richards. Just not quite Richards enough sometimes." He reached for my shoulder, and his grip was strong.

William's journal was still lying open on my bed when I walked into my room a few minutes later. I didn't really want to read any more of it, maybe not ever, but it was calling to me. I picked it up, stared at the black ink, and found my eyes moving from word to word, across the lines, down the pages. As I read, the cold from outside, the chill of the first day that summer allows autumn to preview what is coming, crept into the room. I crawled into bed, peeking out of the sleeping bag only enough to see the journal, turning the pages with the tips of my fingers, fully expecting I would soon see my breath. The sensation that I was being watched, the feeling that had driven me out of the house on a dead run in the afternoon, returned in full force, so acute that I believed the walls themselves had eyes and could imagine a long-clawed monster under my bed, waiting patiently for the sun to set when it would come for me in the dark.

March, 1865

In the morning, I will bid this godless country farewell. For the sake of my sanity, and very probably my life, I am attempting the walk to Mistake. I have killed a raven, the first bird I've seen in weeks, and have carefully removed its head, feathers, and feet, leaving its entrails inside. Tonight I shall consume one third of the meat, tomorrow morning one third, and the same tomorrow evening. After that, I shall be either in Mistake or a place where hunger and cold have no meaning.

There is far more light in the sky than a month ago, and even though the nights are as frigid as ever, the snow begrudgingly becomes damp and slowly melts during the day. The change in weather has combined with a few other events, much more unsettling, to give me the determination to leave. There will be no more waiting. The morning will see me off and with any luck I shall sleep in a warm bed within a day.

I have seen the wolf that has plagued me with his mysterious visits, looked into his black eyes, listened to his demonic howling until my head echoes the sound all day, and watched him float over the snow like an eagle on a breeze. He scratches at my door now as soon as the sun goes down and persists with this routine most of the night. And I cannot say I have not had the urge to let him in. There are times when I awake from a nightmare to the rasping sound of claws on wood and consider throwing the bolt, opening the door, and being done with it all. From my bed, I have fired the Sharps through the door on more than one occasion, only to hear the clawing increase. Another time, the morning I saw him, I had a better chance to dispatch him that ended in equally disappointing results. I met the beast while searching for wood. He materialized before me, studying me with eyes darker than the night yet brighter than the sun, and a black coat tipped with silver like a grizzly bear's. I lowered the rifle, sighted carefully, and fired. His eyes narrowed, I saw a flash of white fang between blood-red lips, and he trotted away unscathed, loping on long legs, fading into the wilderness or wherever it is he hails from. I am in hopes that after tonight we shall never meet again and that over time his memory will slip away exactly as he did.

I have moved all of the furs into the shelter where the meat was. They should be well protected until I return and have been scraped so clean of flesh that they should not attract the attention of anything more than a few rodents. With me, I am taking only my rifle, the raven, and this diary. I have reinforced its leather binding with the idea that if something happens to me at least some record of my experiences will survive.

I dare not venture a guess at the outcome of this trip, but the very thought of any journey has always given me energy. From the time I was a boy and would go on weekend excursions with my father into the hardwood delta country, my sense of adventure has been stirred by traveling. If nothing else, it feels good to have made a decision to do something.

Morning. A peachy sun rises in the east and looks like snow. There was no wolf last night, and I had no dreams. I slept later than I intended but the extra rest has fanned the flames of my desire to be on my way. The air coming in from my open door is damp but warmer than the past few days. I have checked and double checked my rifle to be certain everything is functioning as it should, and have filled my pockets with spare cartridges. I have two small flints and a bit of brown grass from the inside of the log storage which I have wrapped in wax-coated canvas and tucked inside my shirt. I will do the same with my diary and in a few moments shall be one step closer to civilization and one step further from this cabin that has come to seem more a cell than a home.

Afternoon. The Big Hole, through some ancient instinct that detects the slightest change in seasons, has begun to open. Gray water seeps over black ice that is pitted with bubbles and honeycombed with cracks. Along the banks, snow droops over the water in heavy arches and icicles hang long and silver from their undersides.

Overhead, the sky has taken on an orange tint and a wet breeze blows out of the east. A storm is on the way as surely as night. My hands swell and the rifle becomes awkward to carry. I have been glancing more and more at the last third of the raven, doing my utmost to postpone eating it until I have made sufficient progress for the day. The snow I walk in, up to four feet in many places, is soft. The consistency of quicksand, it slides away from my feet causing them to continually fight for purchase, and the wearing action of my heels slipping is vexing. I slide half a step back for each one I take forward. My wool pants, mended in five places, soak through soon after I leave, and while they serve to keep me warm, they chafe my legs, bringing a host of tiny blisters to the surface, tormenting me with the uncontrollable urge to itch.

Concentration comes with difficulty. Like a drunk whose eyes refuse to remain focused on one object, I cannot look, even at this paper, for more than a few seconds. My head involuntarily leans back on my shoulders to show me the sky. The orange clouds, as copper-colored as a carp's scales, stretch on forever, building into massive blocks that hang above me, lower I believe all the time.

Evening. Cold, wet, hungry and exhausted I sit before the small fire I kindled from cottonwood branches and the tinder I brought from the cabin. The little flames quail away from the sky above them, running in fingers close to the ground, giving off less heat than I believed a fire could. So erratically do they jump from the heap of wood I sit over that I must chase their crazy movements with my hands in order to warm feeling back into my wrists. I am able to write only by gripping the pen with my entire hand, moving it very slowly, pressing the thick ink onto the page with all my might.

The first snowflakes strike my face and my fire gives up the ghost. I have sheltered myself as best I can, digging away the snow from a felled cottonwood and using it to block at least one direction of weather. The wind comes ferociously and brings shivers and aches to my whole body. I can hear it in the forest behind me, rushing like the ocean's surf, bearing a sound still more frightful that I fear shall make sleep impossible. The howls seem to come regularly from all directions at once, converging upon me like a horde of arrows. I wince as they draw closer and stare with attentiveness at the darkening landscape and thickening snow. My senses, though distorted by fear and the intoxicating effects of going too long without food, are sharp, but my reactions are slow. I am in no condition to put up a fight and can only hope that whatever creature it is that screams from the woods does not intend me harm. Perhaps it is the wilderness, the pure unsettled land that has somehow taken the shape of a wolf to impress upon me the fact that I am unwanted here. If such a thing is possible and is the case, it has worked splendidly and I tell myself that should I survive I will never again set foot in this valley.

Morning. Night has passed, the wolf did not appear, but the snow falls harder than ever, limiting visibility to less than twenty feet. My legs have no feeling and I am incapable of standing. I have eaten the last of the raven but haven't the energy to move. My mind no longer prods at me to fight for my life, and my thoughts are of the home I shall never see again.

There is a cove on the Mississippi not far from where I grew up, where my grandfather used to take me to catch catfish. The spring nights I spent with him there, listening to a chorus of small frogs, smelling the rich mud and tangy odor of hickory smoke from our fire, watching our cane poles for the bouncing of a bite, stand out to me now as the happiest times of my life. When I close my eyes, I can see the way the river curled in against the bank, watch my grandfather bait my hook as if I was there, and hear the fire popping. The image is strikingly clear: so vivid that I wonder if I am soon to experience those times again in a place where time and distance weave together and I will have no recollection of this harsh land. I am ready for a change, and prefer to keep my eyes closed.

CHAPTER 16

T HERE WAS a smugness about my grandfather in the morning that I hadn't seen before. He had the look of a cat who had eaten the canary without leaving a trace.

"Kyle," he said at breakfast, not bothering to swallow the mouthful of hashbrowns he'd forked directly from the pan. "Kyle, every once in a while even an old logger has a stroke of genius. The blind hog and the acorn. The mouse who outsmarts the cat." He disappeared into his bedroom and came out dressed for work in the half the time he usually took. "Today Bruce Tipton shall learn that doing business with me isn't a one-way street. Got a little something cooked up that will bite him right in the ass."

"What are you going to do?" I asked hesitantly, not sure if I liked his new attitude. There was a little too much confidence in his voice, and as much as he hated Tipton, I knew only striking a serious blow to the land baron would justify his optimism.

"Not me, Kyle. It's we. It's what we're going to do."

"We?" My heart began to pound. I had a rapid, dream-like vision of approaching Tipton waving a white flag while my grandfather concealed himself nearby with his thirty-ought-six, waiting for the perfect shot. My apprehension was apparent.

"Remember the war party we took up to Missoula to get Allen's bull?"
I nodded.

"I've assembled a similar one." My grandfather began to dance around the kitchen, unable to contain his jubilation. "Fifteen, maybe twenty men.

Big strong men from two or three tribes. Men with one thing in common."
He paused and waited for my question.

"What's that?"

"They've all got saws." He clapped his hands together and picked his
feet high off the floor as he continued his jig. "Formed a little non-partisan
anti-asshole nation. Now, hurry up and get ready. We've got a long day
ahead of us."

As I changed, I looked at William's journal beside my bed. With the new
day, much of the terror I'd felt while reading had vanished. Then I remembered the way Katrina felt when I hugged her goodbye, stiff and unemotional, and in an instant I was scared again. Frightened of what I would
discover about my great, great grandfather, frightened of what my grandfather was going to do, and most of all, frightened because time had a way of
making everything I worried about happen much sooner than I wished. I
knew that my final two weeks in Montana would rush past faster than the
two days I spent on the bus in June.

"You ready, Kyle?" My grandfather was pacing in the living room. "Let's
go, let's go." His mind was set on a one-track course, and even Splinter
Horn, trotting even with the truck on the other side of fence on our way up
the driveway couldn't distract him.

Along with the gas can we took to work every other day, I noticed four
new ones in the bed of the truck, stacked tight to a full case of bar oil and an
oversized cooler. We chugged to a stop in front of Pioneer Mercantile,
where, after my grandfather swore savagely when he noticed the price of gas
had increased two cents a gallon, making a reference to "Jesus Moth-Eating
Christ," I filled the cans.

"Better grab a six of pop, too, Kyle," he said. "Gonna be a hot one. Make
up for yesterday I believe. Yes, sir, gonna be real hot today." He stared at the
sun, up less than half an hour and already burning hot, and grinned.

Dew had collected on the dusty, one-lane road at the mouth of the
Canyon Ranch, and from the number of dark tire tracks in it, we were a small
part of a steady stream of vehicles that had already headed up. We parked in
the landing, near the skidder, next to Calvin's motorcycle, Sarah's old Pontiac land yacht, and three pickups. Above us, on the hill, I could hear saws
running, and before I'd gotten out my door a tree slammed down. The explosion of limbs on rock was followed by what sounded like a less than sober
cry of "timber." I walked to the skidder, but my grandfather shook his head.

"Not today. No skidding today." He pointed to the gas cans. "You're in charge up there. Keep their saws full and oiled up. Just stay back a bit. Not too far . . . they won't like having to walk, but I don't want you to end up on the wrong side of one of those trees." Another fir came down, eliciting another roar from the sawyers. "Christ, they're hard at it, aren't they? Music to my ears, too."

As if he knew what I was about to ask, my grandfather said he'd left a standing offer of five dollars a tree at the Six Point yesterday. Five dollars a tree, and all the beer anyone could drink at the end of the day. He had no shortage of takers.

We met Badger on the way up, wielding a new Stihl, sweat leaking from a blue bandana he'd tied around his head.

"Hurry up, Cole!" There was a hint of irritation in his demand. "How do you expect me to work without gas?" He rolled his eyes, then smiled. "Got three trees so far. Fifteen dollars, right?"

"Absolutely, Badger." My grandfather looked at the Stihl and Badger's smiled widened into a full brown grin, exposing the irregular gaps between what teeth he had left.

"Worked for the Forest Service last summer," he said. "Pretty good job. Good benefits, too." He tipped the saw toward my grandfather and winked.

I let the blue-green gas spill over onto the bar of Badger's acquisition, where it foamed away the layer of red dust that had built up there. Like the pit crew for a professional stock car driver, we filled the oil, Badger spinning the cap off, twisting it tight before I'd finished pouring, starting the saw with one hard yank, and revving the engine as high as it would go.

Higher up the hill, with eight trees fallen around him like the pillars of an ancient temple, Calvin was chewing out the back cut on one over a hundred feet tall. He'd shed his shirt, impervious to the barrage of wood chips continuously striking his chest. His forearms flexed as he worked the throttle, and a spider web of muscles rippled across his back, drawing into knots as he leaned into the trunk to guide the fall. The tree glided off the stump and smashed down with a deafening boom. Calvin wiped his brow and turned to Sarah, seated regally on a cooler of her own, her legs crossed beneath a pink and white dress, an open notebook in her lap. She nodded and wrote something in her book.

"Sarah! Damn it, Sarah!" My grandfather bellowed over the running saws. "Don't be letting them into that booze you've got too early. Too many trees to cut today to have everyone liquored up by noon. Besides, good way for someone to get dead. Real quick like. These ain't exactly pecker poles we're laying down." As an afterthought, he turned to me. "You remember to stay back, Kyle. One of these comes down on a man and it saves the grave digging. Drive you a good solid six feet under. Okay?"

"Yeah. Can I sit by Sarah?"

He surveyed her position and told me I could. "Help her keep the lid on that goddamned cooler, too. Shit, I should have known this was coming." He took a small socket set and a couple of screwdrivers from a rusty tool box he'd hidden under a pile of limbs and stomped off to see what could be done about fixing his saw. It looked to me as if it had suffered a good deal of damage the day before, but my grandfather had it running in less than ten minutes.

I made two trips back down to the truck to haul up the rest of the gas and oil, and I arranged the jugs far enough in front of the cooler so Sarah couldn't relay beer directly to the cutters when they filled up.

Throughout the morning, as the heat became oppressive, my lungs incapable of drawing in enough air, my head and back cooking even in the shade of Sarah's cooler, more Indians straggled up the hill. Sarah knew most of them, but they weren't familiar to me. Word of my grandfather's offer had spread rapidly, and Rick and Jason Bighawk arrived from Divide with their cousins, four huge men from Dillon, in tow. There was a pair of older, chubby-looking men from Butte with noisy saws and more coolers, and just before noon five men rode up the hill, packed onto one four-wheeler, brandishing axes like tomahawks.

Sarah kept track in her notebook of how many trees each man cut, twice telling Badger the scrub junipers he cleared away from the bases of the fir didn't count.

"No!" she said sharply the second time he asked her to mark one down. "Now back to work." The stern matriarch, enthroned on her cooler, was enjoying her authority. "If he asks again, I'll take one away," she said to me, tapping the neat line of checks beneath her son's name.

By lunch time, Bruce Tipton had noticeably fewer trees than he had when the day began. The woods fell silent as the men ate, tearing into what food they had brought like a pack of starved wolves. With their sandwiches consumed, they began casting eager glances at the coolers, and in order to prevent what he called a "mutiny," my grandfather gave them each a beer.

There was a symphony of top popping, gurgling, and belching as they drank, and for most of them, the twelve ounces were tortuously little. Eyes still stared at the blue plastic oasis under Sarah, and my grandfather gave in to a second round.

"That's it," he announced when Sarah handed the last man his drink, slipping two out for herself when she thought no one was looking. "Any man who has a third draws his wages and walks. Got it?" There was a silent affirmation among the Indians. "Good. I promise I won't hold you back when we're done, but that's a ways off. Right now you'll have to get by on two."

Calvin started his saw, and like a cue from a conductor, the others followed suit.

My hands were covered with pitch and oil, gummed so thick around my fingers that they stuck together, but Sarah, feeling the compounded effects of the beer and heat, didn't mind taking them. She held them gingerly, pulling on one, then the other, to help her balance.

"How's Katrina?" She studied my face, searching closely for signs of blushing. "I hear you two are getting along good."

"I guess."

"Do you really like her?" Now she was searching for something else in my face, and I wasn't sure if she saw what she wanted.

"Yeah."

Sarah dropped my hands and sighed. "Cole doesn't make you nervous around her, does he?"

"Not really."

"What's he do, want you to take her to bed?"

The candidness of her question surprised me, and before I realized it, I'd nodded.

"I'll bet he does." Sarah wobbled on the cooler. "Now, tell me. Is it just Cole?"

My face started warming, growing hotter than the sun could make it.

"Maybe you two should just . . ." Sarah leaned back, toppled off her seat, laughed to herself, and passed out. I looked at her lying on the ground, hands straight over her head, and I wondered for a moment what it was I truly felt for her granddaughter.

Through the afternoon, I tried to keep my mind off the ever-rising temperature. Heat waves squirmed up from everything, including the fallen

trees. The sun prickled my skin, biting me like ants, and what little breeze
there was blew sporadically. Toward five o'clock, after I'd awakened Sarah
three times to move her closer to the front line, the saws began tapering off.
Badger was the first to throw in the towel. He made is mother tally his earn-
ings, nodded contentedly when she told him he was fifty-five dollars richer,
and began rummaging around in the cooler. He dumped a handful of ice
down his Black and Decker power tools T-shirt, and retreated to a small
patch of shade under a gnarly juniper with an open beer in each hand. Sarah
frowned at me when he began belching, a routine he carried on for the better part of ten minutes.

"Badger needs a wife," she said.

At six, the Bighawks and their cousins cashed it in, their bodies slick
with sweat, their pants covered with dust, their long hair dripping out from
beneath their ball caps like dark seaweed. An hour later, the crew with the
axes called it a day, and soon only two saws were running. Calvin's souped-
up Husky, and my grandfather's abused Jonsered. Some of the Indians
began to make bets on who would quit first. They began as jokes, but when
Rick Bighawk put fifty dollars on Calvin, Sarah created an additional column in her book. The betting was fast and furious, seconded only by the
beer drinking, and the more beer the men consumed, the more money they
bet. Before long, they all had their day's pay bet on one of the saws. The two
factions had polarized themselves at opposite ends of Sarah's cooler, which
was rapidly losing weight. Each time one of the chainsaws stopped, half the
men would cheer while the other half looked with great concern at Sarah's
ledger.

I kept waiting for it to cool down. It was eight-thirty and still as hot as a
sauna. On the edge of the horizon, far away to the north, a line of clouds was
forming, and at nine, a dry breeze began blowing from that direction.

The sunset was red. A deep crimson that spread well up into the sky. At
nine-thirty, with thunder booming up around Butte, the Indians stopped
arguing over conditions of the bet as Calvin and my grandfather slowly
made their way toward us together, their saws on their shoulders, their
heads drooping. Every man held his breath, waiting to see if one of them
would fuel up, but they were finished. There was heated squabbling over
who actually quit first, but rather than ask and risk being wrong, it was decided that it had been too close to call and all bets were nullified.

My grandfather announced he would pay at the Six Point, and since the coolers, including his, were empty, this proclamation met with a healthy round of applause. A river of headlights flowed out of Tipton's Canyon Ranch, leaving behind it a mountainside littered with close to three hundred fresh stumps. Not every tree had been cut, but as my grandfather said, Rome had not been built in a day. As we crossed Cow Creek, I thought to myself that if its emperors had known how to motivate their workers as well as my grandfather, it might have been.

My grandfather asked if I would rather go home than to the Six Point, and protested minimally when I said I would.

"Good young logger like yourself ought to go get his honey and show her what real timber is made of," he said. "Be happy to drop you off at Darla's. She'll be at the Six Point so you'd have the house to yourselves."

I didn't relish the thought of being home alone, but I chose it over going to Katrina's. I sensed there was something wrong between us, something that had to do with my leaving, and I didn't want my fears confirmed. By the time my grandfather's single taillight vanished into the night, leaving me standing in the kitchen door, watching the storm roll in, I wished I'd taken him up on his offer. Not knowing was worse than I thought it would be.

I tried to put off reading William's journal. I paced around the house, looked at my grandfather's belt buckles in his room, dusted the antlers of the elk on his wall, and washed a few dishes left over from breakfast. But the diary was calling me, and I found myself powerless to ignore it. It fell open to the page I'd left off on when I picked it up, and I brought it into the living room where there was more light.

April, 1865

Rescued from the clutches of death, I am resolved to never again be so complacent about accepting fate. As long as there is breath in me, I will appreciate the world, taking pleasure in everything from a sunrise to the way soft mud feels between my toes, and I will fight to the bitter end to continue being a part of this earth. After all, I am alive for but a short time and am dead forever.

I do not know how long I lay beside the Big Hole the morning of the storm, only that it was long enough so I resigned myself to entering an eternal rest. The events I imagine once I lost consciousness, when deep sleep came to deliver me from the cold, take me away from my frozen, bark-like clothes, blur together, and it is impossible for me to separate dream from reality. I believe it is safe to conclude that the visions of home, my family, and the places I spent my boyhood were images conjured up by memory and transposed on dreams. But the sensation of being carried must have been real. Whether I was borne along with dizzying speed as I believed, I am unsure. I distinctly remember opening my eyes at one point, but what I saw made no sense. The snow had stopped falling, and since I knew it had been snowing, I could not have been totally delirious. I was above the Big Hole looking down into a steep canyon where the water was too swift to freeze, even along the banks. There was a duck bobbing in the rapids, but the drake's head shone with the golden brilliance of the sun instead of the emerald green it should have. Aware that I was being carried, I looked at my companion, half assuming that I would see a winged angel. It took no long glance to realize that the creature holding me by a wizened hand was not of the realm of angels, nor were we, as I had assumed, on terra firma. I was being whisked along many feet above the ground by something between man and beast, more like beast above the belt, more like man below. I stared into a gray, expressionless face, and a chest as hairy as a bear's, sporting a silver wolf's coat that moved not an inch though we were traveling very rapidly. The hand that held me and the bare, motionless legs that dangled near my own, were withered with age but were as human as mine, wrinkled and scarred as anyone's who spent a lifetime in the woods would be.

Not caring to see any more, supposing I was either on my way to the netherworld or too crazed to reasonably survey my surroundings, I closed my eyes. I am unsure when consciousness returned, but have a feeling it was not for a long time. When I was once again in control of my senses, I found myself lying on a bed of buffalo hides, a round dirt floor spreading away from me, the haze of smoke from a heap of embers close by filling the air. Skins, pale and stitched tightly together rose up around me between high pine poles, and from the peak of my roof hung a painted buffalo skull decked with long feathers that slowly turned in the rising smoke like vultures drifting on a windless day. The fingers of my left hand throbbed, and when I looked at their tips and saw they were black and gray with frostbite I fainted.

I awoke some time later and was immediately aware of two things. It was dark outside and I was not alone. The sewn hides, the color of flesh when lit by daylight, were now a deep orange, reflecting the flames of a fire that burned less than two feet from my head. A sixth sense, one that lies dormant in people who do not spend long periods of time by themselves, told me there was someone behind me. I rolled onto my side, toward the fire, and sat bolt upright. It was the creature that had carried me above the Big Hole. I rubbed my eyes, staring in disbelief, powerless to look away. Seconds passed, perhaps minutes, before I composed myself sufficiently to look beyond what I saw and search for a rational explanation. When I did, I was greatly relieved to see that the man before me was not half wolf as I had first assumed but was wearing a wolf's pelt about his head. All the features of the wolf's face had been left on the skin and aligned themselves perfectly with their counterparts on the man. The muzzle came from the center of his face, showing a set of sharp, white teeth, the neck ruff blended into his chest, the tail hung down from the middle of his back, and the eyes, leathery slits in the fur, were positioned precisely where the man's should be. I could not see them through the mask but felt certain he was looking at me. On his legs, he wore buckskin chaps and he had fashioned a pair of moccasins from buffalo hide, leaving the hair on to insulate his feet. His arms were long and sinewy, muscular without being thick. In one hand, he held a short, smooth stick decorated at one end with what appeared to be the better part of an eagle, and in the other was a tin cup billowing steam from some hot liquid inside. He did not stand still but rather rocked back and forth, listing first one way then the other, nodding his head in rhythm. Behind him, obscured by his shadow, which in the dancing light from the fire looked like a separate entity, a wolf that moved fluidly along the floor, knelt someone else. I shifted my head for a better view of the second person, and the man side-stepped to block my sight. Suddenly, my head began to pound and the room to spin so violently that it appeared the feathers on his stick had taken flight. The skull above me was whirling, the fire seemed to increase, and I shut my eyes.

When I felt the warm tin cup against my lips I could not draw away, and though its contents were as foul as any I could wish to encounter, bitter and smelling of something long dead, I swallowed. As soon as I did, the dizziness passed and I opened my eyes in time to see the man leaving through a small opening in the far wall. His partner followed, pausing to look at me for an instant. Our eyes met, we stared, and I cannot shake the image from my head of the dark-haired girl I saw, close to my age, decidedly Indian but with a paler face than most. She was both beautiful and wild, each quality enhancing the other. Her skin appeared soft, unblemished and silky, and her legs were long and powerful, their muscles as plain as if they'd been sculpted by a master artist. But it was her eyes that captivated me. We looked at each other no longer than it takes to focus, but she drew me into her eyes, physically it seemed, into those bright, black eyes, and in an instant I felt she absorbed everything about me, knew exactly what I was thinking, then let me go without so much as changing her expression. As she stepped through the door, a night breeze rippled her hair, blowing it back over her shoulders, separating it into individual strands that undulated like cottonwood leaves. Then she was gone, leaving me with an overpowering urge to find out who she was: to learn as much about her as her eyes had gleaned from me. Whatever I drank soon escorted me into the world of dreams, and I found myself on the familiar river of my sleep, shooting over a falls in a canoe, staring at the back of the girl's head, wishing before we crashed into the foam far below us that she would turn around so that I might gaze upon her face.

It was several days before I had the strength to venture outside, and during that time I have no memory of eating or drinking more than whatever the old man brought me from his tin cup. He came every day, and though I looked expectantly behind him, he was alone. He would stalk around where I slept, wearing his wolf skin as religiously as I had my buffalo robe, and try as I might I could never see his eyes. Sometimes he would bring the stick, waving it over me while he chanted some sort of incantation, and once he laid a snake skin over my feet, watched it as though he expected it to slither away, then threw it into the fire where it flamed and hissed far longer than it should have taken to burn.

During this period of recovery, when I believe I slept as much as twenty hours a day, I had fitful dreams in which I died all manner of horrible deaths and from which I would wake drenched in sweat as I would with a high fever. While I was awake, the question of where I was ran circles in my head without answer. And then one day, just when I was beginning to believe I would never know, that I would lie on my buffalo hides forever with nothing more to look forward to than the old man's visits, the girl appeared in my doorway and motioned for me to get up and follow her.

My legs were steadier than I suspected, and the fresh air from outside felt good in my chest. The sun was shining brightly from directly overhead, and my eyes took some time to grow accustomed to its glare. As they did, a curious scene unfolded before me. A group of a dozen or more tepees, some made of stretched buffalo hides like mine, others of canvas, encircled a hut of heavy logs much like the one I had built for storage. At the peak of the roof, a sod chimney protruded a foot or two above the wood, and smoke, a great square column of it, ascended through its opening, washing out over the tepees like fog. Following the girl, I passed a woman who walked with her head down and a baby tight to her chest. She gave us a quick glance without letting her eyes focus for more than a second and kept moving. The door of a tepee fluttered and two boys, tall and gaunt, burst from it with miniature bows fashioned from willow twigs, to shot dozens of imaginary arrows at me. Playing along, I grasped my chest and reeled backwards much to their amusement. Their smiles drew one across my own lips, the first in several weeks, and I laughed out loud. The girl ahead of me found no humor in the charade and looked back at me with stern eyes, waving me along like a disobedient dog. We passed in front of the door to the hut, low to the ground, water dripping from its eaves, a giant grizzly skin attached between wooden pegs at the top of the frame and held against the ground with four large stones. The girl gestured to me to remove my shirt, which I did reluctantly there being snow all around and not caring to take a chill, but the sun was warm and I did not shiver. My boots came off next, as did my pants, and under her watchful eye and expressionless face I had soon stripped naked, removing my last article of clothing with my back to her. No at all embarrassed, she snatched my left arm, spinning me toward her forcefully, looking

235

only at my eyes, slid away two of the stones from the bear skin, and shoved me inside.

Steam stung my eyes and choked me, while intense heat caused me to sweat instantly. A hand, the girl's, gripped my wrist and pulled me to the ground where the smoke wasn't quite as thick and the heat was more bearable. Seated around a fire pit containing a handful of sharp-edged, porous-looking rocks, were seven men, three on each side of the one who wore the wolf pelt. He and the girl were the only ones who weren't naked. He rested his hands on his knees, rocking back and forth as was his wont, the wolf looking frighteningly alive through the haze of steam created by water that dripped onto the rocks from a tiny opening in the ceiling.

We sat in silence for upwards of five minutes, eyeing each other, the men going far longer between blinks than I was able to. Their looks were ones of slight displeasure combined with a touch of wonder, as if they were looking for the first time at something they didn't think much of. When the man in the center spoke, a slow monotone of harsh consonants with the intonation of a question at the end, I was surprised to see the wolf's muzzle remain motionless. It appeared so life-like that I believed it would move in time with his speech and be capable of uttering no more than a growl or howl. The girl at my side poked me sharply in the ribs and the question was repeated. Not knowing what else to do, I tapped my chest and introduced myself.

"William," I said.

Not a face changed expression. The girl put her mouth to my ear, and holding her head firmly between her hands said, "He wants to know what you were doing beside the river."

Hearing my own language, I was too shocked to respond. I tried to face her, but her strong hands would not allow my head to turn.

"Answer him," she commanded and from the tone of her voice I dared not delay further.

"Leaving," I said.

She relayed the response and the wolf spoke again, this time a statement that elicited nods from the other men.

"He says you are very foolish and he should have left you there to die. He wants to know why you came here at all."

"Tell him first I am grateful to him for rescuing me."

The girl said nothing.

"Tell him."

She frowned and spoke three words, all short and similar sounding. There was no answer.

"Tell him I came here because of a dream. Tell him I walked for many months to see this new country because when I slept it called to me."

She spoke longer this time, gesturing with her hands, and a few of the men smiled, seemingly amused. The wolf gave a short reply.

"He says there is no new country here. That it is all very old and a man who cannot interpret his dreams any better than you must be as stupid as a bird who doesn't know it can fly."

"Tell him then that I wish to leave and never return. If he will tell me where I am, I will be on my way."

"No." The girl jerked me to my feet and pushed me back outside where the sun blinded me and I fell headlong onto my face. Disgusted, she threw my clothes at me and walked away. I dressed hurriedly, not bothering with my belt or boot laces so that I might catch up with her. I did just as she passed my tepee and out of breath began asking her questions. Who was she? Where did she learn English? Was I free to leave? At this final question, she whirled about and snapped at me in her native tongue. Her eyes were ablaze, exactly as they had been when I first saw her, and to avoid their pulling power I looked away. I could feel them burning into the back of my head, and that night as I slept they appeared again, in the sky this time, two glossy holes in the heavens in which there were no stars and from which blue light radiated, bathing the world in a soft glow like evening sun on snow.

"Good morning, Kyle." My grandfather tugged on my right leg. "Ready to skid some trees?"

I rubbed my eyes and looked around the living room. The journal was nowhere in sight.

"Put it back on your bed," my grandfather said. "Be there for you when we get home tonight. Getting rather interesting, isn't it?"

I nodded sleepily, and thought about William all through breakfast. I was nearing the end of his diary, and the closer I drew to the final page the more convinced I was that there were no happy endings in store.

"What happens with William?" I asked my grandfather on our way to work.

"What?"

"With William? What happens to him?"

He grinned and winked. "Guess you'll just have to find out, won't you?"

"I want to know." I half wished he had never given me the book, and feared that soon I'd wish it with all my heart.

"Keep reading," he said. "Now, the business at hand." We turned into the mouth of the Canyon Ranch. It was only quarter of eight, but someone had driven in ahead of us. My grandfather slowed down. "Huh. Wonder who this is? Some Indian who got his days mixed up maybe. Thinks he was supposed to be here today."

Bruce Tipton was waiting for us in the landing, sitting inside his shiny pickup next to the skidder.

"Fine," my grandfather said when he saw him. "We'll settle this right now." He pulled along side the Chevy, revved the engine, and shut it off. I didn't want to get out, and I sensed my grandfather would have much rather found a misinformed Indian. The vibrance he'd exuded the day before, the natural high that had kept him cutting all day, was gone, and he looked tired. I knew he hadn't had much sleep, but it looked like something more. Like he was winding down.

Tipton got out first, slowly extending his python skin boots, one at a time, as though they still possessed some of the snake's attributes. His gold-rimmed Ray-Ban sunglasses caught the sun, their lenses darkening automatically to hide his eyes. The boots slithered up onto a stone, tested the footing, and became motionless. My grandfather pushed himself from the cab, and extended his right hand, then let it fall back to his side. Bruce wasn't in the shaking mood. His Stetson tipped forward to throw a shadow across his face, and his hands dug for the bottom of his pants' pockets.

"Good morning," he said dryly.

"Damn right it is," my grandfather answered. "How the hell are you? Couldn't be anything but capital on day like this, could you?"

His jovial approach didn't cut any ice with Tipton. Everything from his coal-black leather belt with the German silver buckle to his fancy Swedish wrist watch was screaming "money."

"You know why I'm here," he said.

"Of course." A gleam appeared in my grandfather's eyes, banishing the bloodshot lines to the far recesses of his retinas where they faded to pink stripes. He looked better. "Lewis boys were up here the other day. Said something about your deal with that fella in Bozeman changing a bit. Happens sometimes, huh?"

Tipton knew my grandfather too well to believe he'd take the news this well. He shifted back and forth on his rock, his tongue flicking in and out, trying to detect the source of my grandfather's pleasure. "Have to shut you down, Cole," he said without emotion. "Developer wants more trees around. Means more money for me, and I can use it."

"Of course you can. Can't we all?"

"Anyway, I need you to clear out of here as soon as you can. Gonna have prospective buyers coming up to look around, and we can't have . . . well, it's better if you're gone." A pale hand crept up from Tipton's pants and instinctively pushed the glasses tighter to his face. The boots twitched.

"You bet. Don't want any messy old logger hanging around and screwing it up, huh?" My grandfather stepped closer to Tipton's perch. "Need to make a good impression, don't you?"

Tipton didn't answer. He was becoming nervous, and his icy demeanor couldn't mask his concern. His other hand emerged, searched for its mate, and twitched in time with the boots, now bouncing up and down, stealing the man's balance. He stepped backward off the rock, trying to hide a near fall by breaking into a jog that put more distance between him and my grandfather.

"How long do you have, Cole? The boys said there weren't many trees on the ground." He kept his voice from cracking by consciously enunciating the words very clearly. He looked like a man on the gallows waiting for the trap door to fall open. Sweat leaked from around his glasses and again he pressed them to his nose.

"How long?" My grandfather tugged at his beard. "Well, got some skidding. Take some time I imagine."

Bruce was ready to bust. He was at the breaking point. "How much time?" he hissed from clenched teeth.

"Oh hell, hard telling. What do you think, Kyle? Come on out here."

I opened my door and put one foot on the ground. I was shaking. My hands were trembling and I didn't want my grandfather to notice. The sensation that something horrible was on the way, the feeling I had see-sawed with over the past few weeks, had blossomed into an awful premonition that I knew would come true. I would have bet as much on it as the sunset. Something dreadful was lurking nearby, and neither my grandfather's smile nor the August sun could keep it at bay much longer.

"Kyle, Bruce wants to know how much skidding we've got left. What do you figure?"

"I don't know," I whispered.

"Well, what do you think then? Should we all head up and survey the situation?" My grandfather led the way with Bruce coming along a few steps behind. I stayed back. My feet had begun shaking as hard as my hands, and to keep from falling I had to shorten my steps considerably. A severe case of heartburn had set it, filling my nose with the acidic stench of bile, burning my throat, sapping my wind. Each step was a chore. I was moving as fast as I could, and I wasn't getting anywhere.

As my grandfather and Bruce neared the crest of a rise, a knoll from which the complete devastation of the ranch would be visible, I wanted to call them back. Scream at them to stop. Think of any excuse to pull them off the ridge. But I couldn't, and in ten seconds it was too late.

Neither of the men had spoken when I reached them. My grandfather stood with one hand on his hip, the other extended before him, posing like an explorer at the North Pole or Victoria Falls. Before him, as far as I could see, anything short of an atomic bomb could not have done more damage than his cutting crew.

"By Christ, Kyle," he said proudly. "Looks like we got our work cut out for us, don't it?"

Bruce was quiet, but even through the haze of his sunglasses, I could see his expression had changed. He was no longer frightened. He was the condemned man who finds that the anticipation of death was worse than death itself.

"I figured no easement, no trees," my grandfather sang. "Won't be bending old Cole over for the greaseless treatment this time, will you? Reckon I can do business with the big boys, too." He craned his neck down to look into Tipton's face. "What? What's that? Something wrong, Bruce? Surprised to see a poor logger step up into your dog-eat-dog world? Thought you'd roll right over the top of me, didn't you? Well, no, sir. Not this time. Gotta suck it up like a man this time. Go home and lick your wounds. Cut your losses. Plan on a few less million this year." He cavorted about, basking in his glory, twisting the knife deeper and deeper. "'Bout time someone knocks you down a peg or two," he shouted at the stone-like figure in front of him. "Put you on the shit end of the stick and made you muckle right hold of it with both hands. Mr. I Own Montana . . . Mr. High and Mighty. Well, how's it feel? How's it feel to get sledge-hammered by a man like me?"

As my grandfather worked himself up toward some sort of climax, bellowing like a late-night preacher, Bruce took off his glasses. He folded them with a crisp click, tucked them into his shirt pocket, and looked through unveiled eyes at his fallen trees. His steely glance fell across the hillside, calculators whirred in his head, and then he smiled. Not the smile of a man who good-naturedly admits defeat, but the diabolical smirk of a card player who keeps an ace hidden up his sleeve.

With a forceful, "You son of a bitch," my grandfather folded his arms on his chest, gave a hard nod, and began breathing deeply, trying to catch his breath and slow his heart.

Bruce looked at him curiously. "Do you know who I am? I mean really? Do you have the slightest notion who you're dealing with?"

"Why, of course," my grandfather said between breaths. "You're Bruce Tipton. Mr. Bruce Tipton if you prefer. And I'm Cole T. Richards. The man with the name I reckon you won't soon forget."

"It's all a game to you, isn't it?" Tipton looked puzzled. "Well, never mind. It doesn't matter now. I'll turn this over to my attorney. In between dealing with our senator and a few others I'm sure he'll straighten this out for me. You're not worth much, Cole, but you're worth ruining. I make and break men much greater than you."

My grandfather hit him so fast I didn't realize what knocked him off his feet. "And I mostly break 'em," he snarled. "Your father should have done that a long time ago, but in a way I'm glad he saved me the pleasure. Now, pick your spoiled ass off the ground and hike it outta here. You can tell your lawyer I'll serve him the same, too."

Bruce was bleeding from the nose, but he wasn't really hurt. He headed back toward his truck, still wearing that amused look on his face as if he couldn't believe anyone could be so stupid.

"There!" My grandfather rubbed his hands together and brushed them off on his shirt. "I'd have smacked him harder, Kyle, but you know shit splatters. Fuck him and his attorney. In my book, a deal's a deal."

I'd stopped shaking, but the feeling of dread hadn't passed. I watched my grandfather work from a distance, thinking he wasn't moving as quickly as usual. I wondered if he was beginning to have second thoughts about what he'd done. If he was, he wouldn't let them show. The trees would never stand again, and he could never pull back the punch he'd thrown. He'd make the best of it, eventually convincing himself it was the right thing to do.

Sheriff Wilson showed up at noon. He looked even more worn down than when I'd seen him earlier in the summer. His mustache had gone from gray to silver, and there were a few more lines in his face. His cowboy hat was on crooked, and one of his boots was ready to come unlaced. He came walking up the hill, carrying several sheets of paper loosely enough so their corners wobbled. He was biting his lip, continuously working it between his teeth, and his eyes darted back and forth from his boots to the papers, looking everywhere except at my grandfather.

I sat down on a stump close enough to hear what he had to say.

"Afternoon, Cole." He sounded like an old man.

"Beauty, too, ain't she?" As my grandfather spoke, I knew he was scared. Like an over-the-hill prize fighter who suddenly finds himself up against the ropes with his legs ready to go out from underneath him, he was putting on a good front, standing behind his record, but for the first time since I'd met him he was visibly worried.

"Cole, this ain't nothing I enjoy. Don't always like this job."

"Why do it then, Jack?"

"What? Why do it? Well, gotta do something, Cole."

"Not something you don't like. I never did. Not once."

"Well. . ." The sheriff fumbled with the papers, took a deep breath, and extended them apologetically to my grandfather. He looked up from his belt at the hillside and shook his head. "By God, you sure did a piece of work, didn't you?"

"Reckon we did," my grandfather said softly. His smile was a general's gazing over a battle field of fallen men. "We done quite a piece of work." He closed his eyes, and when he opened them he'd braced himself for whatever was coming. Any regrets were gone for good. "What have we here?" The papers snapped rigid in his hands. "Looks like a bunch of legal jargon. Christ, why can't these bastards write in plain old English?"

Wilson said nothing. He was someplace else. Perhaps casting his flies on the Big Hole or home with his wife.

"Now comes the state of Montana," my grandfather began reading. "Giving due notice this day . . . that the falling, removal, and any other lesser acts affecting Douglas fir trees belonging to Bruce James Tipton on said Canyon Ranch located . . . shall cease immediately. That furthermore, all equipment belonging to Cole T. Richards currently in position on above-mentioned ranch shall be removed within forty-eight hours. . ." He paused, and Wilson frowned.

"Read the other pages, Cole. The injunction isn't all."

My grandfather began reading again, deepening his voice to an official-sounding octave.

"That being informed of property boundaries adjacent to his residence off Montana Highway 43, Cole T. Richards shall respect these boundaries, in particular the north/south running fence line . . . what the hell?" His reading slowed and he mouthed several lines to himself. "That failure to remain permanently off these and all other properties of Bruce J. Tipton shall constitute unlawful trespass, regardless of purpose of entry. Furthermore, Cole T. Richards is instructed under penalty to law to remain at least one hundred feet from the buffalo grazing on Bruce J. Tipton's property." He let the papers fall from his hands, and a stunned look, similar to the one Tipton had left with, appeared on his face.

Sheriff Wilson, rocking back and forth like a stage-frightened child in a spelling bee, took off his hat. "There's one more, Cole."

"What?" My grandfather looked punch-drunk.

"One more page, Cole. And it ain't getting no better." He picked up the papers, stacked them neatly on top of each other, looked once more at the fallen trees, and handed them over gently.

"In accordance with Montana civil code, section. . ." There was no more grandstanding, and I had to strain to hear. "Willful breach of contract . . . destruction of private property. . ." His eyes were moving too fast to follow the words. "Shall be held liable for the sum of four hundred . . . four hundred and . . . four hundred and forty-one thousand dollars payable in currency or assets amounting to the same. Having been served this notice, named defendant shall have ten working days to answer to the complaint, or will appear in Silver Bow County civil court. . ." Again the papers drifted down to the woodchip-strewn earth. This time a breeze scattered them away in different directions, rolling them over the ground like large, dry hardwood leaves in the fall.

"Wants blood from a stone, don't he?" my grandfather asked himself. "Blood from a stone."

I watched his stomach jump as he coughed more violently then ever before. His T-shirt rippled and his face darkened from pink to red to plum-purple. He dropped to his knees as he fought for air, angrily tossing Wilson's hand from his back, beating the ground in front of him with closed fists. He managed a couple of wheezing gasps, coughed for another thirty seconds, then fell onto his face. Wilson rolled him over and wiped the blood from his lips. Where it had trailed down his beard, it was darker than his face.

"Son of a bitch, Cole." Wilson dropped his hat and it began chasing the papers down the hill.

"Exactly," my grandfather murmured. He blew a light fountain of blood into the air, most of which spattered down on his neck and shirt. "May get blood from me after all," he said as he shoved an elbow under himself for support. "What do you say, Kyle, am I done for?"

I didn't look at him. I was watching Wilson's hat. It had hung up in some sage like a drift log in a beaver dam. The legal notices had blown out of sight.

"If I am, I ain't going quiet," I heard him say. "Besides, what the fuck can he really do? Ain't like I got nothin' he wants."

"Jesus, Cole," Wilson was firm this time. "This ain't about what you've got that he wants. He ain't doing this for gain. Shit, you think he needs anything of yours? Hell, he don't need anything from anyone. This is about revenge, Cole. You made a fool of him and he's mad. Shit, you get mad and you'll stroke someone and get it outta your system. Well, Bruce can't do that. But he'll damn sure take your skidder, box you in on that little piece of land you've got . . . hell, he'll probably come after your house."

"My skidder . . . my house? He'd take my living away from me?" My grandfather began coughing again. "Can't take that, can he?"

"Maybe not, but he'll try. He'd take it and give it away. Part it out. Jesus, didn't you know . . ."

My grandfather cut him off savagely. "By Christ, don't you pass judgement on me." Blood was running down his chin, but he didn't wipe it away. "For goddamn near seventy years I've lived exactly as I've wanted. Exactly as I've wanted and not one whit different. Ain't many men who can say that no more, either. Reckon I'll trade the lumps I get for who I am any day of the week. A man who wouldn't ain't much of a man in my book. Jesus, hundred years ago when there were more men around like myself, snakes like Tipton were pretty well weeded out of this country. It was called Montana justice, and it's a fucking shame more folks don't stick to it today. Time was that when a man needed killing that's just what he got. Where the hell did Montana go in the past century?"

Wilson shrugged as much to say he didn't know what to make out of my grandfather.

"Went straight to hell in a hand basket. That's where. Shit, where's all the hard-luck prospectors? The beaver trappers? The goddamn buffalo hunters?"

Wilson shrugged again and began scanning for his hat.

"All swallowed up in less time than it takes one of these trees to grow forty feet. Quicker than the river can make one good trout hole or an elk shed on this hill turns to dust." He started coughing again, not bleeding this time, but doubling over in pain, having serious difficulty breathing. When he continued his speech, he spoke calmly. "I don't guess I can stop time. If the world wants to turn to shit, it's gonna do it with or without my permission. But I tell you true, I ain't going with it. I can't change everything, but I can change some things. Tipton's gonna find out all about that. I've got something for him."

"You gonna kill him?" Wilson asked casually.

"Kill him? Well, I don't intend to invite him to no picnic. An asshole dies just the same as a great man. Trouble is, they don't ever die in as great quantities." He wiped his face, roughly removed his hat to push his bangs up under the brim, and stomped off.

"Where you headed, Cole?" Wilson's right hand was working toward his revolver.

"Right now I'm going to get drunk. And keep that six-shooter holstered. You ain't gonna shoot me, Jack, and a shot in the air won't do no more than disturb some elk. Bring Kyle out to my place if you will. Please."

I heard pickup tires bawling on the tar far below us less than three minutes later, and soon the loud exhaust faded into the complete silence that pressed down upon me. A silence that stemmed from the realization that for the first time in his life my grandfather had been forced to face some of the sharper edges of the modern world: a world, which, for the most part, he'd been able to conform to his liking or avoid altogether.

CHAPTER 17

MY GRANDFATHER'S TRUCK was at the Six Point when sheriff Wilson and I drove by. When I was sure Jack had seen it, I asked him if he would come back into town to talk to Cole.

"You bet. Gonna get outta this uniform first, though. Cole doesn't think much of me when I'm wearing it." He unclipped his badge and laid it on the seat between us. "I'll go talk to him. Probably end up drinking with him. Hell, probably get pie-eyed and gutter-bound together. I'll talk about fishing, and the elk, and how the world's gone to hell if he wants, but I won't mention Tipton. Won't say one word about him. It'd be best to leave that quiet, don't you think?"

I nodded. "You really think my grandfather hates everything about the world? Hates it as much as he says?"

Wilson looked surprised. "Kyle, Cole means everything he says. None of it's acting. And it doesn't matter what he says, he'll stand behind it with everything he's got right to the end."

"You think he'll kill Bruce?"

"Not if I can help it. I've known Cole a long time, and I don't want to see him end up that way. He's a smart man ... hides it pretty well sometimes, but I suspect once he cools down he'll keep himself in line."

Someone had tacked shiny, new No Trespassing signs to every fence post along my grandfather's driveway. Sheriff Wilson looked from them to the buffalo, started to say something, then shook his head. "You know, Kyle, your grandfather's often right about things. Especially when he talks about all the real men being gone. They are gone. Most of them anyway. He's one of the last." I opened my door and heard him say softly, "Goddamn though, hard believing there were ever any quite like him."

From the kitchen window, I stared at the woods and wondered if the wolf was sleeping. I was tired myself. Ever since I was young, in times of distress, my body would shut down, sending me off to sleep, where whatever bothered me would go away.

In the living room, I looked at the couch, heavily stained and losing stuffing from around the armrests. The coffee table in front of it was dotted with the outlines of plates and mugs set on its lacquer surface while they were still hot, and one of its legs had been fashioned from a two-by-four. When I thought about Sheriff Wilson telling my grandfather that Tipton would come after his house, it made me sick to my stomach. There was nothing here that a man like Bruce could use, and for a second, as I looked into the gun cabinet, I didn't care if my grandfather killed him or not. Tipton's trees had been cut, and whether that was right or wrong, he had plenty more of them. My grandfather had only one house. One house, one small piece of land, and one old skidder. It wasn't much, but it was his, and I knew he'd never give it up. I had to call my parents.

My father answered, and I told him what had happened before my mother got on the other line.

"Dad, Mr. Tipton's got a lawyer. I think he's suing him, and the sheriff says he'll try to take Grandpa's house."

"Kyle, you listen to me." It was good to hear my father's voice. "Your grandfather won't do anything to hurt you, so if you're worried about that, don't be. I know how he gets, and I know how you must feel. If you want to come home ... if you want to come home right now, you can. Whenever you want. Where's Dad now?"

"At the Six Point."

"Getting drunk?"

"I think so."

"Well, there's nothing you can do about that. In fact, when it comes right down to it, there's nobody your grandfather will listen to except himself. That's the way he's always been, and that's the way he'll always be. Does he have a gun with him?"

"I don't think so." The forty-four was lying in the bottom of the cabinet, and all the rifles looked as if they were there.

"Well, that's good anyway. This'll probably all blow over in time, and if he doesn't blow up first I'm sure it will work out. What about the buffalo? They get moved in?"

"Yeah, lots of them. One got tangled up in the fence and died, and Grandpa's being blamed for it. The sheriff brought him something that said he couldn't go near them."

"A restraining order against buffalo? That's a new one."

"And now there's a bunch of No Trespassing signs on the fence posts. All of them."

"Has Dad seen them yet?"

"Not yet."

"So he's not getting his easement?"

"No."

"Damn! He's bull-headed himself right into a jam. Well, just remember what I said about coming home. And remember that none of this is in any way your fault. You can't fix what you didn't screw up. He's got to sort this out for himself."

I had always been aware of the tension between my grandfather and mother, but this was the first time I sensed my father had some hard feelings of his own. I wondered if they were one reason it had been so long since he'd been to Montana, and if moving to New York really was completely my mother's decision. Cole Richards had been a good father. My father had said so many times, but I knew first-hand that he could be hard to live with, too. If my father had experienced twenty-one years of what I'd seen in less than six weeks, I understood how it could have worn thin.

"Dad, did Grandpa ever talk to you about our ancestors?" My grandfather had explicitly told me not to mention William's journal to anyone, and I wasn't going to, but I wondered just how much my father knew.

"Just about his father. Why?"

"Just wondering. What did he say about his dad?"

"Not much. He was gone before I was born. I never knew him. Only that he was a trapper and one tough individual. Like his son."

"How did he die?"

"I don't really know. All dad told me was that he left. He was a young man when it happened, and it bothered him. And I'm sure you know how much he hates to admit anything bothers him."

"What about his cough? It's getting worse."

"I expect it's from his mining." My father was quiet for few seconds. "Too much dust in his lungs. Think he'd see a doctor?"

"No."

"Then you know him pretty well. That's something else you can't change. Try not to worry about it. I know that's easier said than done, but it's best if you can do it. Be sure and let us know if you want to come back here early, okay?"

I said I would, then talked to my mother for a few minutes. To my surprise, and relief, she didn't grill me about my grandfather, and when she said she loved me and hung up I instantly became homesick. I picked up the receiver three times, dialing half the numbers to call her back, and if I had I would have asked to come home the next day.

Something kept me in Montana. Something more than affection for my grandfather, which, although it had grown strong, wasn't enough to make me stay if I believed I did so at great risk to myself. It was more than what I felt for Katrina, too. Part of my resolve to remain in Mistake was because I didn't want to admit defeat. I hated to admit I couldn't tough it out. And part of it was inherited stubbornness. If William Richards had been able to stick it out more than one hundred years ago, Kyle Richards should be able to last at least one summer.

I walked back to the kitchen and looked at the woods again, knowing they were partly why I wanted to stay, too. I wanted to see the buffalo situation through, despite my fear that it would end badly. I wanted to find out why the easement to the forest was so important to my grandfather, and now I was curious about my great, great grandfather and what had become of him. If any of these questions were going to be answered, I knew it wouldn't be right away. It would only be when my grandfather was good and ready to answer them, and that wouldn't be until he calmed down.

In the meantime, I couldn't leave William in the Indian village he'd been taken to. I opened his journal, carried it to the couch, and started reading.

June, 1865

Here on the upper Big Hole, where the river is little more than a
blue seam between two sets of rugged mountains, I have found some-

thing that has been absent from the day I left Missouri. In this land of pristine beauty, where only the deer and elk traverse the forests and time passes without notice, the days blending into each other like streams into a river, I have found a home, and an emptiness inside me has been filled. I believe I know now why I came west.

For the past weeks, I have lived with the small tribe of Indians, apart from them at first, but increasingly connected to those who rescued me from certain death during my bungled trek to Mistake in March. I have been accepted, more completely by some than others, and am beginning to feel a part of something I haven't since I last saw my parents.

There are just under fifty of us: a dozen men of my age, most with wives and children, and a group of elders, at the center of which is the man who wears the wolf skin. I understand that his function is chief and medicine man, but even among his own people much mystery surrounds him.

An ancient woman has taken it upon herself to teach me their language, which she does with unending patience for it does not come easily to me. Named Falling Elk, she seems to enjoy our lessons, laughing at my frequent mistakes, never growing discouraged with my slow progress. From her, I have learned a great deal about the tribe, loosely affiliated with the Nez Perce I believe, and it amazes me how closely their history and legend run together. She knows her ancestors back eight generations, and speaks of their accomplishments, often of Herculean proportions, as if they occurred very recently. She describes the world around her as very ordered, in which everything serves a purpose and destiny is a key force. She tells me everything is born with a specific reason but it is up to the individual to determine what that might be. When I asked her how one knows when he's found it, she laughed and told me that after six husbands, ninety winters, and as many descendants as trout in the river, she is still searching.

I cannot help but think, as she explains a life without the monetary constraints and material emphasis of the one I have known, that all who call these people uncivilized, who brand them savages and destroy them for no other reason than that they sit on land desirable for some sort of exploitation, are badly misinformed.

Falling Elk has a wealth of knowledge about the natural world, and although some of her explanations for the way it operates are tied to myth, she knows everything that goes on around her. I have asked her many times about the man who wears the wolf pelt, and her answer is always the same. He was sent by the spirits shortly after the first Indians were created as a guardian for his people. He is younger than the stars but older than the trees and knows everything that will come to pass. When I inquire as to his strange outfit, she replies that he has no eyes so views the world as a wolf. It is a bit frightening to see how convinced she is that everything she says is true, and she takes it all in stride as if it is as normal as a new day. The man's name, one to which the closest English translation I can make is Star Stepper or Walker, was given to him by the first generation of the tribe more than a thousand years ago because they believed he came from the sky. In fact, Falling Elk can point to the exact star he arrived from, a blue dot in the northern sky, and she always points to the same one. Her explanation of the girl who dances attendance on him is at least as bizarre.

Some years ago the old man realized he would be, as Falling Elk put it, transforming. She told me that the tribe does not see death as the final stage of living but more as means for the body to take a new form. Similar to reincarnation theories, she said one might come back as a buffalo, a bear, or a single drop of rain, but that one continued to exist. When Star Stepper realized his time of transformation was approaching, never having married, he was without child and longed for a daughter. Evidently, when the spirits created him they neglected to provide him with the proper anatomy for procreation. But he did not let this oversight hinder him. He walked for two days and nights without food or water to the river's source and there, high in the mountains, plucked an aspen sapling from the very spot the water issued forth from the earth. He sat with it on top of the highest mountain on either side of the valley for six more days, holding it to his chest as a mother would a newborn. On the seventh morning, it began to rain and as the water fell upon the tree it took root, but instead of limbs and leaves it sprouted arms and legs and soon the girl, fully mature, stood in front of him. The rain ended, and as the sun began to shine a beautiful rainbow appeared, one end descending on top of the girl, who, when it touched her, walked away from the mountain exactly as she is today. Appropriately enough, her name is Aspen.

I questioned Falling Elk as to how Aspen became acquainted with the English language, and her explanation was both simple and grisly. Soon after her arrival, a white trapper wandered up the river into their camp and without provocation shot one of the men. At this, Star Stepper fell upon him in full form of a wolf and devoured all but his tongue which he allowed Aspen to consume so that she might speak his language. Once she did, he touched her forehead with one of the wolf's claws in order for her to forget the experience.

All this Falling Elk relayed to me in her slow monotone as if she were giving the names of the forest animals or introducing me to members of the tribe, and there was a haunting truthfulness in her eyes that I see vividly each time I ponder other explanations of who Aspen is. Whatever her origins, she is of striking beauty, and I confess that I find myself looking at her with longing. The shroud of mystery that surrounds her only makes her more appealing, and my thoughts turn frequently to her. I hinted once to Falling Elk that I would enjoy the opportunity to court her, and although she did not respond, she gave me a look which leads me to believe it is not outside the realm of possibility. Her slight smile and lifting of her eyebrows was a look that is not confined to one culture. It was the look of a wise woman who knows and approves of the heart's desires, and it gives me hope.

August, 1865

As the river valley quietly assumed the rich shades of late summer, the grass turning chestnut brown, pines and firs donning less brilliant green coats, even the sky exchanging its light blue for a deep indigo, my days are spent in total contentment. I hunt buffalo and elk, catch trout and whitefish from the Big Hole, and explore the country all around, climbing to the top of bare-rock peaks, wading through beaver ponds, and walking carefree through meadows of sage where ground squirrels chirp at my passing and the shadows of hawks send them scampering for their holes. I think more and more, as memories of hard times fade faster than the red stripe on the trout

I often eat for supper, that this is how man was intended to live. The war in the east, if it is still going, seems as distant as those of the Roman Empire, and while thoughts of my family are still strong, they do not produce the constant worry they once did.

In the evenings, after the sun has set but the world has not yet relinquished all heat of the day, when the mountains around me gradually become inseparable from the gray horizon, I sit next to the river and talk to Falling Elk. We discuss the day past and the one to come, commenting on the weather, the growth of animal young, and any happenings on interest within the tribe. I have sat at two weddings, short ceremonies during which little but the obvious is said: two people share a love which has made them one and should be respected by all, allowed to grow like a river, carrying on through all time. After the second, when Three Ravens, a man not yet twenty, wed one of her great granddaughters, Falling Elk asked me when I would marry. She asked it as if I had been involved in a relationship that was inevitably leading in that direction, and when I laughed with surprise she scoffed at the reaction, telling me an eagle might try with more success to hide its white tail on a sunny day that I to keep my feelings from her. Apparently annoyed, she went on to call all men as simple as children when smitten with love and liken their actions to those of young deer who lie down and believe if they are very still they cannot be seen. She told me my subtle attempts to disguise my affection for Aspen work as well as a white swan who tries to blend in with the blue river it swims on. According to her, all the women in the tribe are talking about it, most sharing her opinion that I am a fool for being so slow in my advances and believing my intentions are known only to myself. When I asked her why the men I hunt, fish, and travel with have said nothing to me, she said that she might as well instruct me in shooting a bow as a man advise me on matters of the heart. I asked her then what I should do and she laughed and told me she'd just given me the answer. She walked away shaking her head, mumbling something to the effect that she hopes I'll have more sense as a husband than I do as a bachelor.

In truth, I have been careful to keep my hopes on the subject in check. Aspen is often difficult to read, and I cannot help wondering if our many differences, the most obvious being race, preclude us in her mind from sharing more than friendship. She permits me to hold her hand as we walk together, and we do so often, strolling along the river at sunrise, watching the trout rise for sluggish grasshoppers that have fallen from the banks and moose that plunge crazily away at our approach. It is a gesture she initiated, grasping my hand quite unexpectedly one day, looking at me as if to say I should have known to do it. When we are together we talk little, speaking only of things of importance. It is difficult to make her laugh, but her seriousness enhances her beauty. One of the few times she gave in to laughter was when I broached the subject of her past to her. I relayed what Falling Elk told me, trying not to make light of it, and when I finished she looked at me gravely and said it was true to the last word. Instinctively, believing either that she was not sound of mind or, worse yet, that it could all be accurate, I drew away, at which she began laughing and could not compose herself for some time. Finally, when she did, she said she had never heard that story but that she liked it and would not say otherwise. Seeing it disturbed me, she said she has very few memories of her childhood. She said sometimes she dreams of a square building with rows of desks and other children around her and a lady dressed always in the same long, pink dress who is speaking to them but she cannot hear what is being said. Other times she has strong feelings that she's doing something she's done before, and another dream that she is traveling with a different tribe of Indians, falls sick, and is left for dead.

It is hard to know what to make of all this, but in my attempts to reason it out I believe perhaps she was schooled with whites as a young girl, probably for several years, then for some reason returned to her native family, took sick with a brain fever, was left for dead and found by Star Stepper much as I was. It is a loosely constructed theory, but offers a far more settling explanation that Falling Elk's story.

The shred of sense I can make from her past is more than I can of my attraction to her. I know only that when I see her, morning or night, from near or afar, an uncontrollable smile spreads across my face and my legs lose all feeling, as though I have slept in a cramped position all night. There is nothing more gratifying than a love that is returned, and while I am unsure of the extent of Aspen's feelings for me, I sense a certain degree of similar interest from her that adds a spring to my step and joy to my soul wherever I go.

When Falling Elk tells me I am too slow to show my emotions, I think of the night Aspen and I spent alone on the river, staring into the flames of a fire with the soothing sound of water spilling over a bar of stones in the background, sitting side by side long after everyone else had retired. When she stood to leave, well after midnight, with the fire burned down to a bed of coals reflected like a dozen points of light in her eyes, I placed my hands behind her back, feeling the combination of the soft fabric of her shirt and firm muscles running from her waist to her shoulders, drew her close to me, and would have kissed her had a night breeze not blown her hair in front of her face. I brushed it away, more clumsily than I would have liked, but when I looked at her again I lost my nerve, letting her go with a gentle squeeze, standing and watching long after she and the night had become one.

September, 1865

Today, at the height of summer's encore performance, as yellow cottonwood leaves rattled against each other and flocks of geese drifted south through a deep blue sky, I became a married man. On the north bank of the Big Hole, amid a stand of giant cottonwoods whose limbs joined high above us as lovely as any cathedral's vaulted roof, in a ceremony completely free of the somber overtones surrounding the Catholic weddings I recall from my youth, I promised to love Aspen as long as I live. It is a promise I look forward to keeping and only wish everything would be as easy.

I do not know if every man feels as I do when he marries, but if he does than he knows what I speak of when I say my soul is completed. As I held Aspen in my arms when the final words of Star Stepper, words of the happiness two people in love can share forever, faded into the choppy, autumnal babble of the river, all around me ceased to exist and I found myself staring with utter contentment into the most beautiful face I have ever seen. I kissed her, the only tradition I cared to bring from my culture's ceremony, and as I did, feeling her warm lips against my own, for an instant I was overcome with sadness, believing I would never experience so perfect a moment again. But the feeling passed, more rapidly than the bobbing leaves in the river ascended from the crest of one wave to another, and as those around us, in particular the young men, began laughing and joking, good-naturedly offering to perform the more intimate marital rites for me, I found myself laughing as well, knowing that with Aspen I will always be happy.

It is evening now, and I am alone near the river, so full of thoughts that I could never write them all down. It is enough for me to let them fill my mind, inundating it with all that has happened in the past few months. They pass before my eyes, the images of my first look at Aspen, the way Falling Elk sits with her legs crossed, hunts with the men that blend together in a swirling vision of game we have killed, country we have seen, and nights spent together in the woods, and the morning I asked Aspen to marry me, recur in my head, standing out sharper then the others. And the last keeps coming to the forefront where it is as clear as the water flowing in front of me.

We had walked in the white mists of dawn some distance downstream to the head of a gorge where the river's flow is forced between two high cliffs and the water roars a frothy slate-blue around boulders the size of buffalo. We sat on a flat stone worn smooth from eons of flood water and rain, facing the sunrise, and as usual we said nothing. A thin line of clouds in the eastern sky caught fire from sunlight pouring onto them from somewhere beyond the massive, rounded mountain they hung above, and I called her by name, something I had never done. She turned to me, and as she did the sun burst over the mountain, silhouetting her against a flaming ball of yellow. A bull elk called from across the river, his hollow, throaty voice seeming to say I'd better get on with the asking if I was going to, and so with no pomp or grandeur, no presentation of a ring or poetic phrasing, I asked Aspen to marry me. For a fraction of a second, her eyes lost their hard look, becoming as soft and disarming as a doe's, she leaned forward to kiss me, pressing her hands against the back of my neck, and if ever a man has been happier than I at that moment, I would like to know who he was.

That happiness has stayed with me, trapped inside like the sun's heat in a rock that remains warm long after dark. Falling Elk has been to see me tonight and has just now told me that Aspen waits in my tepee and unless I am the most foolish man who has ever lived I will stop writing and go to her. I think it very good advice.

◇◇◇◇◇

The Big Hole, where I had fished it with Katrina, was lower than I had seen it. Slick mats of moss undulated under the surface like green hair, and even the deepest pools looked shallow. I watched a long, slow stretch for ten minutes, straining to see a rise, forcing myself to look for a trout rather than contemplate what I was reading in William's journal. When no fish surfaced, I skipped stones, bouncing them off the water toward the far bank, throwing them harder and harder. Upstream, the sky was dark gray with smoke from the forest fires in Idaho that had been burning out of control, lapping at the west sides of the Bitterroots, sending ash hundreds of feet into the air. I sat on a piece of driftwood, the better part of a cottonwood washed down in high water, and stared at my reflection close to shore until the dark eyes that looked back at me seemed capable of sight themselves, unblinking and judgmental.

Splinter Horn hadn't harassed me on my way to the river, but as I walked back to my grandfather's he followed along, snorting and hooking at the fence. I wondered what it was he feared in the woods behind him, hoping it was no more than the wolf. I was beginning to imagine much more frightening possibilities, and I found it hard to look at the trees without feeling they were full of eyes. Eyes that fixed on me and nothing else. Eyes that belonged to something as awful as any nightmare and as real as the ground I stepped on. Just before I reached the house, Splinter Horn turned away from me, toward the forest, and stiffened. Heat waves slithered up from along the irrigation ditch, intertwining, the pines behind them appearing to bend as if in a strong wind. I could smell smoke, and the Bitterroots were lost in its haze.

Through the late afternoon and into the evening, then on into the night, time passed for no other reason than because it could not be stopped. I found myself looking at the clock in the kitchen every five or ten minutes, fully expecting hours to have gone by. I fought down the urge to read any more of the journal. The unread pages were dwindling rapidly, and I had enough to chew on for the time being. Once, sitting at the table, I tried to picture William with Aspen, but it was an image that would not come. Instead, I thought of Katrina — the dance, the evening of fireworks when I'd held her hand, our fishing, the way she'd looked the first night I saw her when she and Darla had come for dinner, and finally, the tired, troubled look she wore the last time I saw her. I could not shake this last image and began to believe it was a sign that wonderful things are so because they don't last. I thought about my time in Montana winding down, the mountains above Firewater Lake eroding, the buffalo skull I'd found, and the colors of the brook trout I'd caught in Cow Creek fading to a single shade of pale yellow on the stick my grandfather had carried them on. And then I thought of my grandfather.

Until I woke up, my head in my hands on the table, I hadn't realized I'd been asleep. Blue and red flashing lights and a roar I immediately recognized as my grandfather's skidder came from behind me. I opened the door, blinking hard to adjust my eyes to the dark, and saw him coming down the driveway full throttle, escorted by a pair of highway patrol cars, the shattered remains of Tipton's buffalo sign dangling from the skidder's front blade. I could see the outline of my grandfather perched in the cab, both hands of the wheel, looking straight ahead, coming with all the engine could muster.

"Mr. Richards, you are to pull to the side of the road and shut off your machine," one of the patrolmen said over his loudspeaker. "This is your last warning."

Last warning before what I wondered? If they were planning to pit their Chevies against the John Deere, they'd get the worst of it. One car swerved alongside the skidder, and without slowing down my grandfather cut the wheels, forcing it off the driveway opposite the pasture. Twenty yards from the house, he grabbed a gear and I heard the engine respond as he floored the accelerator. The massive blade tore into the ground, peeling up earth, shoving a wave of dirt forward toward the kitchen, and I dove for the living room, landing hard on my side, feeling the pain all the way up through my head. Like a football player reaching for the endzone, I rolled toward the coffee table. Under it, I watched as a sea of dirt and rock smashed through the open door, crushing the frame, collapsing part of one wall, broken glass sliding across the floor, the cracking of timber as loud as a big fir coming down. Instinctively, I reached onto the couch for William's journal, clutched it to my chest, and closed my eyes. It sounded as if the whole house was breaking in half. A board popped under me, bucking like a disgruntled horse, I felt a hand on my back, and fearing it was death, drew away from it, pressing myself to the carpet.

"Stop cowering under there, Kyle," my grandfather commanded. "Now's the moment of truth for us." He flipped the coffee table onto its side, pulled me up into a crouch beside him, and belly-crawled to his gun cabinet. I heard the solid click of his 30.06 bolt closing on a shell in the chamber, and he crawled back to the barricade. "Hold it together now, Kyle, I'll be bullied no further."

Outside, the skidder stopped running, literally in the doorway. Lights zipped around the walls as the patrolmen pulled close to the house with their sirens wailing.

"Intolerable!" my grandfather screamed. He rested the rifle over the table, steadied himself behind the scope, sighted out through the kitchen, over more than two feet of debris, and cut loose. The volume of light cruising through the recently-widened kitchen door diminished by half. Tires threw gravel as the cars jammed into reverse, and my grandfather worked the bolt.

"Angle's no good," he said without picking his head up from the scope. "Could have smacked the other light if they weren't so chicken shit." He punched the table, then by way of acknowledging my presence said, "Good piece of work you did to get out of the way. I knew I could count on you to be on your toes." He pointed to the journal. "Got William and Aspen together yet?"

Not knowing what else to do, I nodded.

"Good. Keep right at it."

A treble-filled voice entered the house over one of the speakers.

"Cole Richards, this the Montana highway patrol. I order you to throw down your weapon and come out with your hands up."

My grandfather rolled onto his side to face me, and with a disgusted look on his face said, "Now, if that's as original as they can be, we might as well tell 'em they'll never take us alive. Do it up in grand old fashion. What do you think?"

He was so close that when he spoke a drop of saliva landed on my lips. It tasted like pure whiskey. I closed my eyes and shook my head.

"Come on, Kyle, chin up. I ain't ready for us to play Butch Cassidy and the Sundance Kid just yet. Got a few things to do before I'd contemplate an end like that." He peeked over the table, filled his lungs, and hollered, "You get Tipton out here and I'll talk. You tell him I got something for him."

"Cole?" It was another voice on the speaker. One I recognized. "Come on, Cole, let's go sober up." It was Jack Wilson, and I was damn glad to hear it.

"Christ, Jack, ain't you gonna leave me alone tonight?" My grandfather stifled a cough. "Persistent bastard," he said to me. "Did all he could to keep me at the Six Point."

"We'll let you sleep it off, Cole," Wilson entreated.

"Sleep my ass! Get all I need of it when I'm dead. You best clear outta here until you get Tipton. If his voice ain't the next one I hear, I'm telling you true that all merry hell's gonna break loose. You bring that bastard out here, Jack, and show him what he'll get if he wants my house. I'll drive that fucking skidder right straight through her. One pass will pretty well do for her. I ain't bargaining no more." He started coughing, dropped the rifle, and his head hit the floor. A pool of blood leaked from the corner of his mouth, and he didn't move.

I ran out through the jagged opening, tripping over stones and broken boards, heard Wilson scream not to shoot, dove into his car, and told him to call an ambulance. A young patrolman, white as a sheet, his hand wrapped around his pistol, inched toward the house, disappeared inside, and came out a minute later with my grandfather over his shoulder. His cowboy hat had fallen off, and his hair swayed in front of his face like the moss I'd seen in the river. He was bleeding heavily, and the blood showed no signs of stopping. It dripped from his lips, down the back of the patrolman, thicker and darker than the night. Wilson helped lay him on his side near the car, and we waited in silence for the ambulance. The twenty minutes it took to arrive were the longest of my life.

I kept staring at my grandfather, the blood running from him like a leaking faucet, wishing with all my heart I could turn back time, if only for a couple of days, thinking how vastly different things would be if I could.

The ambulance whisked my grandfather away with the patrol cars following, leaving me and the sheriff alone for the second time in less than a day. This time I spoke first.

"He'll go to jail, won't he?"

Wilson tugged at his hat. "Well, tonight he'll go to the hospital."

"And then?"

"Oh, I doubt they'll lock him up. Wouldn't gain much by it. Partly my fault for helping him get so liquored up I guess."

The buffalo had scattered when my grandfather came in with the skidder, but were gathering back up near the fence. And suddenly I wanted to kill every last one of them. Blast them straight back to where they belonged.

"You should come into town, Kyle."

I heard Wilson but couldn't respond. He said it again, and I shook my head. I hadn't taken my eyes off the buffalo.

"Can't very well stay here, can you? Who knows what might fall in during the night?"

If I stayed, I wouldn't spend any more time inside than it took to get my grandfather's rifle and every shell I could find for it. For the first time in my life, I was ready to kill something.

"Kyle?"

I looked past the buffalo to the woods. They were watching me again, glaring into me, waiting to pounce. But this time I wasn't scared. I took a step toward the fence, and Wilson cut me off.

"Ain't hurt are you, Kyle?"

I stepped around him, my anger building to the point where I began to shake. My upper lip twitched and the balls of my feet were hot with sweat. I stared into the woods until my eyes began to burn, standing with clenched fists, waiting for something. I didn't blink until the first howl came. The sad sound moved from the forest like a tidal wave, driving me back as it washed over me, trailing away into nothingness, leaving me feeling empty, as if it had sapped all my energy when it passed through me. I turned to Wilson.

"Ready, Kyle?"

"Did you hear ..." I mumbled, and it came again. Louder. Closer. A penetrating call accompanied by a cold wind I imagined was its breath. Wilson's face registered no emotion. I turned to the east and gazed at the horizon, wondering how long the howl took to carry that far. A bright star flickered, from the impact of the sound waves I figured, and then it was gone and so was the wolf. It was gone much further than it had time to run, too.

"We could go to the hospital if you want," Wilson pleaded. "I'd wait with you if you'd like."

I nodded and heard him exhale loudly.

"You sure you're all right?"

"Fine." My voice was dead: flat and weak.

"Good. Anything you need from here?"

I went inside for William's journal, found it lying open near the coffee table, gave one glace at the rifle beside it, then walked back out, picking my way around the smashed wall.

The No Trespassing signs flicked by my car window on our way up the driveway, their reflective paint catching the headlights, strobing into my brain like a subliminal message telling me to keep out. And behind them, further than the buffalo, further the edge of the woods, somewhere between me and the Bitterroots was something much stronger than the signs telling me to come along.

CHAPTER 18

ALL HOSPITALS smell the same. The chemical-clean odor of the one in Butte reminded me of the one in Syracuse I went to when I needed dental work. I walked up a long hallway next to the sheriff, following a large woman in a white outfit with heavy shoes that echoed off the walls each time she set them down. She paused in front of a plain, wooden door, gave her nurse's smile, and tromped off.

My first impression when I saw the man inside, lying asleep in an oxygen tent, was that I'd been escorted to the wrong room. The old man with the wrinkled face and thinning hair couldn't be my grandfather. His hands were bound to the sides of the bed with translucent rubber straps, which in the yellow light of the small room made his wrists appear cadaverously pale. Some sort of tube protruded from his mouth and ran out through the tent wall to a machine making regular sucking noises. Each time it slurped, a few drops of blood inched up the line, collecting after a journey of several feet in a plastic bag. It was almost full.

My grandfather's chest fluttered as he breathed, rising and falling in stages, quivering like a cold dog. His eyes were closed, but I could see them moving under their lids, darting from one side to the other, jumping as if they wanted to break free.

I sat down on a metal stool too high for my feet to reach the floor and studied a row of machines hitched to my grandfather at various points along his body. Most displayed red or green digital numbers that changed too rapidly to read. I reached forward and touched the tent, found it thicker than I had imagined, like calloused skin, and pulled my hand away. A young doctor entered the room, made several quick adjustments to the machines, checked his watch, and asked me if I knew how much my grandfather had had to drink, and when he'd begun coughing up blood.

"What's the matter with him?" Wilson asked.

The doctor fiddled with his stethoscope, looked at his watch again, and spoke in an expressionless, professional tone.

"Silicosis, I believe. Quite advanced." He put his hands into the front pocket of his coat and looked at me. "Your grandfather has lost over half his lung tissue. He's very sick."

I examined the doctor's face, searching for the answer to my question, couldn't find it, and had to ask.

"Is he going to die?"

"It's too early to say," the doctor said, and I believed him. "He's not very well off, and I'm afraid the prognosis is gloomy. I mean it will be impossible for him to ever make a full recovery. He should use oxygen … probably need it in high concentrations … frankly, it's amazing he's gone on as long as he has. We're doing everything we can for him, and he's comfortable."

Wilson and doctor talked for quite a while in the hallway, keeping their voices low and their backs to me. I didn't care. I knew what they were saying. I didn't need a medical degree to see what was going on. Time was no longer being patient with my grandfather. In a few short hours, he'd gone from a fire-filled logger ready to hold off the Montana National Guard to a sick old man who looked much more than his age. As I watched him, his eyes opened briefly. They were glassy. His pupils were barely visible behind the fog they fought to see through. His right hand jerked, he coughed an unbroken stream of blood into the tube, and his eyes closed. I'd seen enough. I absent-mindedly ran a hand over my snake-skin hatband and didn't look at my grandfather as I closed the door behind me. I was convinced I'd never see him again.

The sun was peeking up by the time we rolled back into Mistake, evaporating the mist above the Big Hole, shining brightly on the roof of the Six Point as if nothing had happened. Darla's station wagon wasn't in her driveway, so I had Wilson drop me off at Sarah's, the only other place I knew and made him promise we would go back to Butte later in the day.

"You're tired," was all Sarah said when I described my grandfather's recent turn for the worst. "You sleep here on the couch." She tried to take the journal from my hands, but I wouldn't let go. When she went off in search of a pillow, I slid it under the sofa, far enough so it was out of sight, close enough so I could reach it. I was asleep as soon as I lay down, and all that existed was an enveloping darkness to which I gave myself fully.

Badger woke me early in the afternoon.

"Come on, Kyle, the doctor says you should go see your grandfather. He called Sheriff Wilson."

I grabbed William's journal, barking my knuckles on the floor, and stood up fast enough to make the room spin around me. I stumbled forward and Badger caught me before I tripped.

"Easy," he said. "Cole ain't dying. Just not answering any questions or anything. Doctor thinks he might talk to you."

My worst fear was relieved, but I was still dreadfully concerned. I debated calling my parents and decided against it. The doctor had probably already done it, and he knew far better what was happening.

The ride to Butte in the back of Sarah's 1977 Pontiac was interminable. I fiddled with the journal's leather cover, pulling a piece the size of a dime loose, working it between my fingers until it fell apart.

"What'd he get thrown in for in the first place?" Badger asked when we finally reached the hospital's large parking lot. "In there I mean." He pointed to the yellow brick building. "His coughing?"

I nodded.

"Gettin bad, huh? I heard he was bleeding."

This was the most excitement Badger had seen for a long time. He breathed heavily, twisted around in his seat, and began running his words together in his eagerness to get them out.

"Probably all that mining. Or maybe an old rodeo wound. Hey, did he really drive the skidder through his house?"

"Badger!" Sarah snapped at him. He looked sheepishly into his lap, then shook off the reprimand.

"Wow! Must have been a party ... shootin' at the cops, too, huh?"

Sarah shot him a cold stare, and with a good deal of self-restraint, he closed his mouth.

My grandfather had been moved to a larger room. One with a bigger bed and double window that looked out over the city to the Highlands and the Continental Divide. He sat in front of it, his back to me, in a wheelchair with an oblong oxygen tank fastened to its back and a slender tube running from it over his head to his nose. An older doctor standing behind him made a small adjustment to a valve on the tank, and gave me a big smile.

"Are you Kyle?" he asked in an unnaturally pleasant tone as if I were a baby.

"Yes."

"Your grandfather," he put his hand on my grandfather's head, a gesture I could only think would have gotten him set squarely on his rear end two days earlier, "has gone into shock we think. He's not talking right now, but I think he can. It doesn't look as though he's had a stroke or anything to prevent him from it. I'm sure he'll know who you are, and I'll be down the hall if you need anything."

Sarah persuaded Badger to remain outside the room while I talked to my grandfather. He looked in bad shape. His left hand twitched, his thumb meeting his fingers like a crab's claw, and the listless look in his eyes from the night before hadn't improved. I swivelled the chair so I could sit on his bed to talk, then turned him back toward the window. He'd rather look at the Highlands.

"Hi, Grandpa." His face didn't change expression. "Hi, Cole."

He blinked, but for the time I stayed with him, over two hours, talking about anything that came to mind, that was the only reaction I got from him. His hand never stopped moving, and more than once I turned away to wipe at tears. Sarah and Badger came in to say hello, and the doctor helped him into bed.

"Rest is the best thing for him now," he said. "I've seen this a few times . . . this depression . . . if you will, and each time the patient's come out of it. I've spoken to your father in New York, and he'd like you to call him when you can."

I wanted to ask him when my grandfather could go home, but the room had a permanent look to it, and I didn't dare.

I knew what my father was going to say even before the call from the hospital's pay phone had gone through. I held the receiver more than three inches from my ear, staring blankly at the mauve wall in front of me, as he told me my bus would leave Butte in three days. He tried to take the sting out of it by telling me we'd spend a weekend in the Adirondacks when I got home, but the thought of it paled so much in comparison to spending a single day on the Big Hole with my grandfather that I already dreaded the trip. And all the way back to Sarah's, as we passed alongside Fleecer Mountain, the prairie country between Feeley and Divide, the Big Hole, and the Canyon Ranch, the hollow feeling inside my stomach was growing. By the time we hit Mistake, driving slowly by the Six Point, I felt as if I was looking at Montana for the last time. The Montana I so badly wanted to accept me, without fully knowing why, and the man I had loved as only a grandson can love his grandfather, were slipping away from me, leaving me not so much homesick as empty. The growing sensation that I was leaving too early and would never, not in my entire life, be back, had eaten out my insides and left an emptiness as great as the loss of a loved one. Over and over the image of my grandfather sitting in his wheelchair with his hand working like a wind-up toy and his eyes as bleak as a rainy day in March ran through my head, flashing before me in rapid succession until it was all I could see and I felt as though I might well fall into a similar state. I was keeping tears at bay for no other reason than to prove to myself I could take at least that much away from Montana: come away knowing I was stronger than before. But it was a losing battle. All my thoughts were of my grandfather, and everything, no matter how ordinary, reminded me of him. As I pulled myself up the stairs to Sarah's apartment, flooded by a host of memories that seemed dramatically distant, I could no longer hold myself together and began crying, sobbing at first, then letting the tears stream down from my eyes in a continuous river, crying as much for what my grandfather had lost as for what I was going to lose as soon as I boarded the bus bound for New York.

Mercifully, Sarah left me to myself, alone on her living room couch, where I cried until I had no more tears.

At first, William's journal was just one more reminder of all I'd soon be leaving, and I wanted nothing to do with it. But as the day wore on I found myself looking at it, staring without reading first, then allowing it to consume me, which it did thoroughly, whisking me away from my present troubles as efficiently as a dream. In a state close to a trance, I absorbed the words on the pages, learning more about my past, remembering what my grandfather told me when he gave it to me.

"It's who you are," I could hear him saying, and once again I found I could not put the book down.

November, 1865

It began as a buffalo hunt. Fifteen men riding across the prairie before light, their horses painted for the ritual gathering of winter meat, their bodies clad in ornate dress for the occasion, their spirits high as all men's on the hunt are. The night before had been one of celebration: ancient dances performed around a fire whose flames appeared to lap at the heavens and whose light rivaled the sun's. It was a night to honor the buffalo and the men who were to kill them, and before it was done there was not a member of the tribe who hadn't a full stomach or enough dancing. As the fir logs burned down and men retired with their wives, Star Stepper asked to speak with me in private. He had not done so since before the wedding, and as he led me to his tepee, smaller than the others, adorned with the skulls and skins of every animal imaginable, I had no idea what he wanted to say.

Inside, sitting across from each other, a circle of embers between us, he said nothing until he had taken a pull from a long, elk horn pipe and passed it to me. The smoke was harsh, like poor man's tobacco not properly cured, and it made my eyes water. I coughed, cleared my throat, and he began speaking. He apologized first for saying he should have left me to die beside the river in March. I had forgotten the comment, but it seemed important that I forgive him, which I did by saying neither of us should ever think of it again. He went on to tell me he was pleased to see that I was making a good husband for Aspen, but I sensed he was leading up to something more important. Rocking back and forth, looking from one side of the room to the other, the muzzle of the wolf tipped forward from years of being worn about his head, he looked as if he really might have been a thousand years old. His hands trembled and his chest barely rose as he breathed. And then he began speaking very slowly, just louder than a whisper, and for the first time since we met ceased all movement so that his voice seemed to be coming from some-where outside his body. He talked at first of the upcoming hunt and how the men were happy I would be joining them. Then, without pausing, he asked if I knew that a day would come when there would be no more buffalo to hunt and that the men who had hunted them would vanish like the first snowflakes that fall and melt on wet, brown leaves in October. He said that such would be the fate of the Indians. That they would follow the buffalo and that eventually the earth would follow them. He said the forests would be cleared, houses built in the valleys until their lights at night outnumbered the stars, and the animals of the woods would be killed or die of broken hearts. He said that from the moment of birth everything is in decline, and to appreciate life we must be aware of this, holding onto the joys, letting go of the sorrows, understanding that we make our lives what they are. There was a hint of sadness in his voice, as if he wished it were not so. Then he wished me luck on the hunt and asked me to leave.

All through the night as I lay awake next to Aspen, his words came back to me, and I carried their heavy burden through fresh snow in the sage the following morning as we rode out to kill the buffalo.

We came up with the herd, making its way downstream out of the valley, as day was breaking, and it stretched as far as I could see. So thick were the buffalo that it appeared the land itself was alive, shifting and rippling like covers on a bed. We brought our horses to a halt and stared for some seconds at the most animals I have ever seen in one place. I pointed to a small knob where I could set up my Sharps, not willing to test its heavy recoil from my saddle. At the spot, I dismounted, shooed my horse away, and lay down with the rifle steady against my shoulder.

Three Ravens raised his bow and with a whoop kicked his pony into a gallop straight toward the herd. The others followed, some brandishing bows, others rifles they had traded furs for, older .54 caliber breech loaders that were as apt to misfire as not. I took aim at a large bull and fired, hearing the bullet connect a full second after the blast. Shot through the shoulders, he went down in a heap and did not move. By the time I chambered a second shell, the other men were in the herd, riding hard among the buffalo, shooting from the bare backs of their ponies as well as most men would on solid ground. A dozen animals were killed while the herd stood in confusion, but soon it began to move, hooves sounding like drum roll, coming as one great, black wave, increasing speed as it approached until the animals at the front, stretched out like bounding deer, had all they could do to keep themselves from being trampled. I took a young cow in the chest as she drew near, piling her up at my feet, and as soon as she ceased kicking climbed on top of her. The buffalo crashed by on either side of me, so close I could not level the long barrel of the rifle, so for half an hour I simply watched them pass, nostrils flaring, eyes beady with fear, legs flailing, pounding the earth into a muddy mess. In the midst of so much noise, never knowing if at any moment one of the animals would be forced onto me, I found myself exceptionally calm, thinking over and over about Star Stepper's grim prediction for the buffalo. From what I saw in Kansas, I knew he was right, but I also thought about his belief about everything being in decline and that the best we can do is enjoy the moment. And so I did. I sat with a smile in the center of the stampede knowing that someday I would tell my grandchildren about it and they probably wouldn't believe me.

I had lost myself in thought, been carried away as pleasant conceptions of the mind have the power to do, when a volley of shots went up. The bulk of the herd was gone, leaving the wounded and stragglers to follow the swath of ravaged ground it left in its wake, and at first I thought that the reports came from men in the tribe firing to finish them off, but the second volley came too soon after the first. It came from repeaters: Spencers or Henrys, and the sharp crack of Colt's revolvers rang out between the rifle blasts. Across the prairie, with four hundred yards of trampled soil between us, the Indians were taking fire from ten men who'd come up from the river bottom. It was still early, and the sky was cloudy, but even without the benefit of the sun I could see they were soldiers. Their blue uniform shirts stood out only slightly lighter than the earth, and they crouched shoulder to shoulder as only men who have been trained in the military will do, working in stiff unison, shooting, reloading, and shooting again together.

I recognized Three Ravens by his pony, painted with black and white dots the size of saucers. He was coming toward me, hugging the animal's neck, and wasn't hit until I had a good view of his face. It was a scared boy's face, his eyes wide, lips pursed, his long hair streaming behind him, and when the ball struck him it all disappeared, an explosion of red taking its place.

Before Three Ravens's body tumbled from his horse, Nightspear, riding close beside him, was shot in the back, his chest erupting in a fountain of blood, his pony stumbling as the bullet tore into its neck. I stared for a second at their bodies, lying next to each other as limp as only corpses can be, then adjusted the vernier sight on the Sharps and, resting it over the cow buffalo, looked through the peep, down the octagonal barrel, over my two dead friends to the soldiers.

When I shot the man in Kansas if happened too fast for me to think. As I lined up my sights on a fat soldier close to the middle of their group, I had ample opportunity to consider what I was doing. I was choosing him, for no particular reason other than that he provided the largest target, to die, and a second after I touched the trigger he did. So did the next man I shot at, a tall, lean mean man who arced over backwards when he was hit, his arms flying over his head where they looked from where I lay like the arms of a doll, thin and small. At my third shot, a man clutched his stomach, stood up, his arms wrapped around his midsection trying to hold his intestines in, took several unsteady steps toward me, then sat down. His companions broke formation before I could fire a fourth time and began running for the river. I watched them go, saw the Indians wheel their horses after them, heard a few sporadic claps from their rifles in the cottonwoods along the water, and the whole time all I could think about was a drop of water working its way down the dead buffalo's nose. My eyes didn't move from the spot where it dripped off until the Indians were back, pausing only briefly as Buffalo Meat, an old man on his last hunt, cut the throat of the soldier I'd wounded.

Back in the village, as news of the deaths spread from tepee to tepee, first by the countenances of the men, then word of mouth, a dreadful silence fell over the tribe broken only by the wailing of Three Ravens's young wife and one of Nightspear's brothers. I sat alone with Aspen, who asked nothing and held me until Star Stepper entered the tepee. He asked only if more soldiers would come soon, and when I told him they would he said he had seen everything that had happened in a dream he'd had many years ago and that the winter meat must be cared for and the village moved before the sun set the next day. And so for the remainder of the day, and well on into the night, Three Ravens's wife, Nightspear's mother, and every other woman in the tribe worked on the prairie where their loved ones lay headless and chestless, crying softly to themselves, going at the skinning, boning, and fleshing with a vigor intense enough to keep their minds focused and maintain a weak hold on their sanity.

Toward evening a cold rain began falling, mixed at times with snow, and it came down as if it was trying to obliterate the day's events, gushing from the sky in sheets, drenching the earth, transforming the prairie into a bog of water stained with mud and blood. The rain and work continued all the following day, and scarcely had it been finished when Star Stepper, who had been stalking about all day, appearing one second at my side and the next one hundred yards away, gave the order to pack only what could be carried from the village and begin loading it into two dozen crude canoes, vessels that since my arrival had remained overturned near the river. He said that over the mountains south of Mistake was a small valley where game was plentiful even in winter and no white man had ever set foot. When he said it, I suddenly became aware that the recent grief had been brought on by people who, at least on the surface, were exactly like me. As Three Ravens's wife walked past, six months with child, I could not make eye contact with her, and even the gentle touch of Falling Elk's hand on my cheek, a gesture of understanding, embarrassed me, and I let her pass without speaking, watching her silver hair merge with the rain, hearing her soggy footsteps fade until I could not tell them from the thousands of drops falling all around me. Star Stepper and Aspen came last, but we took the first canoe, Star Stepper in the bow, me in the stern, Aspen kneeling between us.

The canoe was filling with water. Rain pattered down against its wooden gunwales, mimicking in miniature the buffalo's hooves from the previous morning. I took up my paddle, running my hand along its smooth shank, driving its head into the sand to push us away from the bank, unsure where we were going, wondering why my body and mind seemed on separate courses.

The river was up, clipping along, the color of strong coffee, and as we glided into its full force it swung us sideways so for an instant I could see the tribe behind us. Wet, muddy faces stared back at me, eyes half closed from grief and exhaustion, not a hand raised, then the river whisked us away, bearing us along on its wavy back like a huge snake, and when I looked over my shoulder the Indians were gone, swallowed by the rain, the night, and the wilderness. The current was heavy enough that we didn't need to paddle. It carried us quickly downstream, past the stand of cottonwoods where I was married, all the while picking up speed, sailing us along like an arrow shot with the wind behind it. The gorge came into view, the river whirlpooling around the rock I proposed to Aspen on, the cliffs jutting up into the sky, their tops hidden in damp, night fog. I paddled furiously, first on one side, then on the other, but the river did not allow us to turn. We crashed over a lip of white water as we entered the chute, and I reached for Aspen and slid from my seat. Icy rain and spray from the river soaked my face, and panic, as strong as the current itself, seized me. We spun crosswise to the flow and I looked away from the wave I was sure would swamp us, wishing just as I had in a dream that Aspen would turn so my last sight would be of her face. But she sat still as a statue, looking straight ahead at Star Stepper, whose eyes I refused to meet until he stood up. He rose swiftly, in one smooth motion just as the wave began to break over us, and as he did his sodden wolf skin seemed to conform even more closely to him, shrinking until man and pelt appeared one. From where I lay in the bottom of the canoe, peering up at him from behind Aspen, he looked as tall as the cliffs that rose above us, balanced as perfectly as an owl that sleeps away the day on a fir limb. He stood, and the pounding of the river, the roar of water on rock, the crash of the current against the canoe, subsided to a whisper, and we began gliding along as easily as thistle down blows over a frozen lake. In part from terror, in part from awe, I fainted.

When I awoke, the rain had stopped and it was growing light. I was lying on a sandy bank above the river, my buffalo coat with this diary in it and my Sharps rifle on top of me. The jagged mountaintops visible against the sky in the north I quickly recognized as those I had been able to see on a clear day from my cabin. Closer, all along the Big Hole, the air was dead and so full of mist that everything appeared blurry. Our canoe lay on its side, water draining from it, but no others were in sight. Meat, bundled in the skins from tepees, sat at the water's edge, and downstream, walking with their backs to me, I could see Aspen and Star Stepper. Through the veil of fog I watched them pause, embrace quickly without kissing, then turn from each other, Aspen toward me, Star Stepper away downstream. As the gray back of his wolf skin drifted in and out of view, vanishing behind curtains of fog that moved though there was no breeze, I was overcome with the belief that I would never see him again. I jumped to my feet, rushed past Aspen, and called to him to stop. I tripped over a log, fell into a pool of soft mud where he had left the heelless print of a moccasin, pushed myself up and began tracking him by his footprints, all I could see in the mist. They led to the river, down a sandbar that remained above the high water and seemed to continue into the current. I called several times, ran blindly downstream, slowing when I saw wolf tracks emerging from the water. They were closer together, staggered slightly, and even at the river's edge had not yet seeped full of the water that was running into them from the sand, pooling to round out their edges, washing the tiny flecks of stone back to their original positions, slowly filling the indentations.

The wolf tracks headed for a peninsula of trees that ran from the mountains like a tongue, and staring at them made me dizzy. The fog entered my head, filling it with silver as it does before I faint, I started to fall, then Aspen grabbed my arm. Her tight grip kept me conscious, her hot eyes shone clear, she pointed one finger at the track between my feet, now little more than a round dent in the sand, and as I stepped forward to follow said in an authoritative voice, "No."

December, 1865

Almost two months have passed since I last saw Star Stepper, Falling Elk, and the other members of the tribe. Aspen and I are living in my cabin, which we have recently finished fortifying for another winter. As I sit on my bed and stare at the round patches in my door, I have trouble believing less than a year has passed since I blasted holes in it, and even more trouble deciding what to make of the events that have transpired since that night nine months ago. I have returned to the site of the Indian village, six days upstream, on two different occasions, each time hoping to see smoke pouring from the sweat lodge or a young boy stalking imaginary buffalo in the willows beside the river, but it was as empty as the winter woods. On my last visit, I stood where my tepee had been as the sun set, watching the long range of mountains in the east, far downstream, wondering if somewhere beyond them Falling Elk was watching the same sky. A pair of stars appeared together, and I would like to think she saw them, but when darkness came, pouring into the valley from all sides, something told me she did not. I felt completely alone again for the first time since before I was married and walked as hard as I could through the night, through the next day, and the day after that, fearing with every step that something terrible had happened to Aspen. When I finally opened my door, so tired my dragging feet had collected several pounds of ice, and saw her sitting near the stove, I fell into her lap and refused to let go of her until I was asleep.

I am trapping again, running a shorter line than last year, trying to spend as little time away from Aspen as I have to. She is with child and tells me with eerie confidence that we shall have a son. I think about her constantly during the days I spend in the woods, always with a shadow of uneasiness hanging over me as if I'm in a dream too pleasant to be real and will soon be waking. I asked her only once about the night Star Stepper and the other members of the tribe disappeared, but she answered with a cutting look that forced my words to trail off into whispers. I don't know how much more she knows than I, but am certain it is more than she says. I could not even say if the other canoes made it through the gorge, and I do not let my mind ponder the whereabouts of Star Stepper. I have seen the same wolf track from the night he vanished several times since, always moving in a straight line, slightly larger than that of the other wolves, walking with purpose along the river, cutting across my path to ascend a mountain, or dotting fresh snow in a high meadow that offers a good view of the sunrise. For all I know, it is the same animal that drove me from my cabin last spring. All explanations for its mysterious appearance, solitary course of travel, and unusual size are as devoid of reason as these snowy woods are of song birds. I am left only with the conviction that there are forces at work beyond my comprehension and perhaps it is best that I do not understand.

The nights are long now, broken by cold, windy days of faint sunlight that seem to weave morning and evening together as if the world is eager for darkness. I have no more dreams of rivers, and my sleep is only disturbed when I wake periodically believing Aspen is not in the bed. These sensations are so powerful that it takes all my strength to turn my head to be certain she is there, and my relief upon seeing her is immeasurable. Sometimes I think I love her too much.

Today, as spring arrived in full force with bright sun and warm temperatures, melting the last of the drifts around the cabin, my son was born. He entered the world quietly, looking around as if he knew where he was, gazing at me through eyes that are distinctly his mother's, though without the intense fire Aspen's have possessed of late. She held him first to her chest, then to the bedroom window, and as his tiny hands touched the pane, mother and son both smiled. I have never seen anything like the way young William, a name Aspen insisted on more I think because she thought it would please me than from any real affection for it, stared outside. He looked at the woods: the fir that came down near the storage shed in a February wind storm, the stand of pine I hid in when I shot the wolverine, and away through a gap in the trees to the rounded, bald mountain his mother and I watched the sun rise over on the morning I asked her to marry me. His eyes moved slowly, taking in everything they saw, and the smile never left his face. He cried only when I lifted him away from the view, prematurely ending his first look at the world.

I am hoping our son's birth will improve Aspen's mood. She has been very sullen for the past several weeks, despondent, short with me, pacing from one end of our small home to the other like a caged animal, sitting and staring through the windows at the stars, often for half the night. When I ask her what troubles her she says there is nothing wrong, but her eyes betray her. Whatever is eating her burns behind her pupils like pools of coal oil, growing stronger by the day, glowing deep in her eyes, impossible to conceal. The only time she appears at peace is when she sleeps, and then her body grows so cold that I quiver when I touch her. She will hear nothing of seeing a doctor, and I have been given to understand that I should not broach the subject again. This evening she is relaxed, happily holding William, and with luck her good spirits will return with summer. Though she never mentions it, I know she is lonely. I preferred our days in the village together, too, and am not sure if she remains at my cabin because she does not know where the other Indians have gone, or because they are somewhere she cannot follow.

August, 1866

I am losing Aspen. She is slipping from me and the more distant she becomes the clearer I see she was never mine. She spends her days alone with William, taking him on long walks through the forest, speaking to him in Indian as if he understands every word. She is as possessive of him as a sow bear is of her cubs, all but showing her teeth in a snarl if I approach. It has been a month since she has spoken a word of English to me, and now her accent has become so heavy and she talks so fast that I rarely understand what she says, guessing from expression and intonation alone. Her change is maddening and has driven me to the limit of my emotions, tearing me because I cannot stop loving her, filling me with grief because it is obvious her feelings for me have weakened to something barely above tolerance. When she lies beside me at night she is clammy cold whether awake or asleep and draws away from my touch like a fawn from water. Most nights she sits by a window, gently rocking William, staring expectantly into the stars, remaining awake until dawn breaks.

She is so different from the girl I married that I wish her transformation was visible in her physical features as well. It is torture for me to look upon the same lovely figure I fell in love with and have her act so strangely. When I talk to her she looks at me as if I am speaking nonsense, shaking her head, stomping away, always going to our son, taking him outside to be alone. She is very gentle with him, as caring as any mother on Earth, and it is from this that I draw my sole comfort. Whatever has affected her has not taken all her senses, and while her actions may be as much instinct as intent, William clearly enjoys their time together. As awful as it is to say, I am as grateful to have him for the tie he provides me with to his mother as for any other reason. When I watch them together in the forest, I realize how much closer Aspen is to the wilderness than to me. She moves effortlessly through the trees, skirting deer and elk, which do no more than lift their heads at her passing. No animal is afraid of her, and I wonder at times if they see something about her I cannot.

I have considered moving back to Missouri. The war has been

over for some time, I miss my family again, and it might be that doctors there could help Aspen's condition. But even if she knew what I was thinking she would not go. She belongs here, that much I know. I fear I have already erred too much in taking her for a wife, and I will not ask her to make further concessions.

November, 1866

The mountains of the upper Big Hole reflect a blood-red sunrise this morning, shining like embers in a breeze, and the sky above them, scarlet in the east, purple in the west, seems to stretch forever, spanning the entire universe. It is an awesome sight and far too big a world to be left alone in. William and I will leave this wilderness by ourselves today, and perhaps by the time he is old enough to understand I will know what to tell him about his mother. Were he to ask me now, all I could say is that she is gone and I am heartbroken. My body aches for her, and I can no more imagine a time when it will not than I can comprehend where she is. I fear that wherever I go and for as long as I live last night will haunt me, slowly eating away at my sanity just as moss and rain will devour this cabin. I doubt I will know any more until time reduces us to the same matter, and even then, even if I have all eternity, I half suspect that the questions that well up in my head will go unanswered. Once more the Sharps is loaded, and as shadows shrink from the approaching day, drifting away like ghosts, I am writing in order to focus my mind. Penning much as Three Ravens's wife fleshed buffalo hides the day her husband was killed.

I woke in the early morning hours to a cold wind filling the bedroom and tiny flakes of snow on my face. Disoriented, I sat bolt upright and immediately saw the door open. I was alone in bed and knew also that no one else was in the cabin. William's cradle was rocking in the breeze near the stove, clicking back and forth with a hollow, empty regularity that caused me to call out for Aspen. No reply came, and it was not until I realized how hard it was snowing outside that I was able to move. When I saw the drift that had already formed in the doorway, six inches of fluffy snow that only accompanies severe storms, desperation replaced fear and I climbed from bed, my legs trembling so hard I was forced to place my hands on my knees to prevent myself from falling. I tied on my boots without socks, ripping both trouser legs when I shoved them inside, and staggered out in my nightshirt, unable to find my buffalo coat. It was too cold to be snowing as hard as it was, and yet it was as if the clouds themselves were falling, dropping so densely that the storage building appeared no more than a faint, gray shape as thin as smoke.

Aspen's tracks were nearly full. I ran on them, panicking wherever they disappeared in drifts, feeling an urgency I have never known. I screamed for my wife until my voice left me, at first stopping and waiting for a reply, then not daring to pause for fear I would lose the track. It led down a dry creek bed in a perfectly straight line, crossing boulders, blowdowns, and steep banks without missing a step. Where it broke from the forest and entered a sage meadow above the Big Hole, the strides increased to three of my own, so full of snow they were easier to see by looking off to the side as if they were very faint stars.

Across the meadow, less than half a mile from the river, the track entered a stand of old aspen trees, their bark thick and gray, scarred from elk antlers and moose teeth. It moved around the trunks, circling, crossing itself, and backtracking as if she had been looking for something. In the center of the stand, a spring bubbled from around the stump of a particularly massive tree, melting the snow as it fell in a soggy circle ten feet in diameter. The tracks led into this space of bare ground, and on the stump, wrapped in my buffalo coat, lay William. He was awake, smiling, staring at an aspen shoot that had taken root in the punky wood of its ancestor, and when I picked him up he grasped one of its slender limbs so tightly that I had to use most of my strength to pry his fingers from it. When I did, he looked at me with eyes that appeared far wiser than his age and fell asleep.

I tell myself that Aspen's tracks, where they left the spring, were snowed in. I tell myself the same thing about the wolf tracks I followed nearly two years ago, and I pray I am right about both. But prayers made in desperation seem rarely to be fulfilled, and if I place any faith in my eyes then I know both tracks vanished from the face of this Earth.

This truth is too horrible to face, for to acknowledge it would mean I could never look upon my son without wondering if he is real or if his flesh too can dissolve in air like ice in warm water, disappearing without a trace. He is all I have now to prove his mother ever existed, but I will not allow him to grow up in her country. I do not know how I shall be received when I come home with him, but it would be too much for me to stay. If I did, I could not help hoping that some day I would find Aspen, and each day that I did not would end in bitter disappointment. As it is, I see her eyes each time I close my own, can feel her hair on my face so vividly I am continuously lifting a hand to brush it from my mouth, and I know that I will never forget exactly how each curve of her body felt, every expression of her face, and I also know I will never experience love as I did when we were married in the cottonwoods along the Big Hole. If I had the choice of living forever as I am, or for a single day with her, the choice would be easy and my life short.

CHAPTER 19

ARAH WAS in her bedroom when I quietly slipped into the stairwell, and by supporting most of my weight with the railing I was able to reach ground level without a sound. I was taking William's journal back to my grandfather's house, prepared to leave it where it had come from. Under my shirt, it rubbed against my chest, and in my head it pounded away, throbbing worse than the blows I'd received from the man in Twin Bridges.

Ahead of me, over the Bitterroots, I imagined I could see flames from the fire rising up into the scorched, black sky. If it crested the mountains, it would rush into the Big Hole valley, and if it crossed the river it would destroy my grandfather's house. If that happened, the journal would be there waiting for it.

Cars must have passed me on the highway between the bridge over the Wise River and my grandfather's driveway, but I don't remember any. Perhaps the numbness I felt, the natural buffer my body was putting up to protect me from things I could not understand, blocked them out. The first noise I remember hearing other than the crunch of my feet in the gravel along the road was the buffalo, and to my great relief they didn't sound agitated. They were talking to each from the middle of the pasture, heads facing the driveway, some lying asleep, others poking around the clumps of sage for grass. Splinter Horn trotted to the fence and followed me all the way to the house, but for once he didn't seem bent on breaking through the wire. He walked with his head high, keeping up with me step for step, but his horrible bellows were absent.

In the light of day, the damage done to the kitchen didn't look as bad. It would need a new door and a couple of new studs for the wall, but nothing appeared in danger of collapsing. I started brushing the dirt outside with my sneakers, but that wasn't why I'd come. The door to my grandfather's room was closed, and as I stepped over the upside down coffee table in the living room, it suddenly occurred to me that maybe I shouldn't open it. I touched the cold, brass handle, turned it part way, then stopped, shaking with fear, afraid he might be in there. After a few seconds, not knowing was worse than whatever I might find inside, and I opened the door. The room was empty and smelled like dust. It drifted from the antlers of my grandfather's elk, catching the sun coming through the window, settling on the belt buckles, the bed, and the floor. I laid the journal on the small night stand, stared at the initials in its cover until my vision blurred, then turned away.

In my room, dust had collected on the whiskey bottle I'd found in the trapper's cabin. I blew the gray layer away, held it to my window and stared through the purple glass at a patch of fireweed. Through the refraction of the bottle, the pink flowers ran together like a swirl of paint. They reminded me of Katrina's lipstick, and thinking about her, the way she smiled, the warmth I'd felt sitting next to her, helping her fish in the Big Hole, how wonderful it was simply being near her, I knew I had to see her.

I was able to fit nine stems of fireweed into the whiskey bottle, and in the shade of a culvert along the highway found a single blue lupine that had not yet gone by. I set it in the center, its lavender petals surrounded by pink, filled the bottle half full of water from the Wise River, and carried it carefully in front of me, not caring who might see it, not caring if everyone who did knew who it was for. Most of what I was leaving in Montana, the things I felt slipping away from me, were beyond my control. But not Katrina.

At the head of her driveway I paused, looked down its length to the trailer, felt the coolness from the bottle run up my arm, took a deep breath, and started walking. It was two hundred and fifty-five steps to the porch, and when I reached it Cougar snarled from behind the door. Darla's station wagon wasn't in the yard, but I didn't think they'd leave the dog inside if no one was home. I rapped on the aluminum door, heard footsteps, placed the bottle behind my back, and hoped I'd be able to speak when I saw her. When the door opened, swinging outward fast, brushing the brim of my hat, I had no words. And when the bottle fell from my hands, breaking with a splash on the ground in back of me I still could not speak. Even running blindly up the driveway, charging toward the highway as hard as I could go, my breath would not come, my eyes did not open, and the image of Danny Twofeathers standing in the doorway would not leave me.

A log truck swerved away from me as I plunged into the road, its horn blaring and brakes shrieking, both sounds muted far away. I stumbled on the tar, fell face first, and did not think I could stand. The roof of my world was crashing down on top of me, crushing me like an ant below a boot, pushing me into the highway, and the only thing of substance I could resist it with was the enormous emptiness I felt inside; an emptiness so great that it didn't seem possible I could contain it all. It was seeping out, multiplying and growing, leaving me as hollow as the rotten firs my grandfather and I had cut on the Canyon Ranch.

"Kyle?" I recognized the voice from somewhere but couldn't place it. "You okay?"

The last thing in the world I wanted was to talk to anyone, especially anyone who would push for answers about what I was doing lying in the road or where my grandfather was. But Calvin Bulltail didn't do either.

"Looks like you skinned your chin," he said, easing me to my feet. "Took a nasty fall, huh?"

I looked down the road to his motorcycle, idling fifteen feet away. I'd never heard him pull up.

"Is there someplace I can give you a ride to? Maybe up to see Cole?"

I didn't want to ride all the way to Butte on a motorcycle. And I didn't want to admit that the world was going to go on around me.

"I don't have an extra helmet, but we could take your grandfather's pickup."

I shook my head, but Calvin was determined. If he'd come all the way from the eastern part of the state to see my grandfather, that's what he was going to do.

"Sarah called this morning. Kyle, I'm sorry. At least let me give you a ride into town. Won't get us killed between here and there."

I didn't particularly care if he did and was a little disappointed when we arrived at the Six Point. Calvin turned the key on his Harley, keeping the bike upright with his huge legs.

"Where's his truck?"

It wasn't until he asked that I realized I didn't know. The last place I'd seen it was in the parking lot on the way home with Sheriff Wilson.

"The Canyon Ranch, I guess." The world wasn't stopping for me, and I could still speak.

Calvin kicked the motorcycle back to life, swung into the highway, and accelerated rapidly out of town. It only took a couple of minutes to reach the gate on the Canyon Ranch, still open, and I closed my eyes when we passed Katrina's. My grandfather's truck sat in the landing where the skidder had been, and all the way to Butte I pretended to be asleep, not opening my eyes until we stopped at the hospital.

I remembered how to find my grandfather's room, and Calvin let me go in first. My grandfather sat in his wheelchair facing the window that looked out over the Highlands. When I approached he turned slightly, shifted in his seat, and whispered something. I bent over him, he grabbed my shirt, and said it again.

"Home. Goddamn it, home." With a jerky motion, he pulled the oxygen tube from his nose and threw it onto the floor.

I looked at Calvin in the doorway, standing with his hands on his hips, blocking most of the light from the hallway outside. From the expression on his face, a look of blank disbelief, he wasn't prepared to see my grandfather's condition.

"Cole." He mouthed his name, as much a question as a greeting.

My grandfather shuffled to the door, dragging me with him, coughing every step, and repeated the demand to take him home. His voice was hoarse but there was no question he knew what he wanted. Calvin shifted sideways to look down the hall, obviously not thrilled with the idea.

"Goddamn it, home!" My grandfather let go of me to stick a trembling finger in Calvin's face. "Now."

"Kyle, you walk on his left." He was going to do it. "Help him along and if we meet anyone don't look suspicious."

I wasn't sure how to follow the last instruction, but I believe if anyone had tried to stop us I would have fought them with everything I had. My grandfather's clean room with its single window and tiny bed was as much out of character for him as a penthouse suite in New York City, and if he wanted to go home I was prepared to help him. And so two days before I had to go back to New York, we walked my grandfather to the hospital elevator, took him down six floors to the lobby, waved politely at the receptionist, helped him across the parking lot to his truck, and went like a bat out of hell all the way to Mistake.

My grandfather sat in the middle, slouched under the drooping uphol-stery with his hands on the dash, his left tapping as if music only he could hear came from the square hole that once held a radio. I watched his eyes, and from time to time they seemed to focus, though when a buck antelope blurred across the interstate in front of us I don't think it registered.

Calvin said he'd follow me to my grandfather's from the Canyon Ranch, and I was surprised at how easily I drove the truck. It seemed like a different lifetime when I'd stalled it near the river. It was evening when I turned into the driveway, and the dark sky over the Bitterroots was turning blood-red. Part of me was surprised to see the skidder planted nearly inside the house when I stopped beside the canoe. The man next to me seemed so incapable of such destruction that I had begun to believe the entire episode had never taken place. As Calvin carried him inside and laid him on his bed, however, it came back to me clearly, and I could smell the diesel exhaust and hear the troopers on their loudspeakers.

I sat beside my grandfather until Calvin started his motorcycle, assuring me he would be back in the morning. Then I lay down close to him with my forehead pressed into the middle of his back the way I had with my mother after nightmares when I was very young.

The sun hadn't come into the house when I woke up, but my grand-father was no longer in bed. I could hear the rapid ticking of line being stripped from his fly reel. I sat up, glanced at my grandfather's belt buckles hanging above his bed, thought enough time had passed since he won them so that they could be considered antiques, and peered into the living room. He was sitting on the floor without a shirt on, his Winston rod held stiffly in his right hand, pulling line from the reel with his left. When I looked, I saw that there was nothing on the night stand where I'd left the journal.

It took my grandfather three minutes to thread the line through all the guides, and another three to tie on a leader. I didn't leave his bedroom until he began looking through his book of flies. The leather book, lined with something that resembled loose wool, held hundreds of tiny dry flies, pieces of old leader, big, brightly colored streamers, and dozens of smaller wet flies, some old and faded, others reflecting the iridescence of cock pheasants ex-actly as they had when new. He wanted a take-off on a royal coachman with extra red on its body, long white wings, and a hackle of gray thread wrapped liberally around a size ten hook, but his fingers couldn't extract it. He tried holding it close to him, then at arms length, then on the floor, and when he still hadn't removed the fly he kicked the book across the room. I fished it out from underneath the couch and plucked the fly from the fleece. I ran the leader through its eye, tied a simple knot, and clipped it into the cork handle of the rod. My grandfather's face was twisted with frustration, and the big vein in his forehead was throbbing. He looked as if there was something he wished to say but his mouth and brain weren't functioning together. All that came out was a puffing nosie, little breaths which further infuriated him. He snatched the rod from me, drew back his arm to throw it harpoon-style at the wall, but a strong series of coughs intervened. They doubled him over, forcing him to grip his stomach as I imagined the soldier William shot had done, then left him with a calmer look as though in coughing he had expelled his anger. He patted me on top of the head, and whispered, "Sorry."

It took us the better part of an hour to walk along the buffalo fence to the highway and across the meadow between it and Big Hole. Splinter Horn followed this time, as wicked-looking as ever, his nostrils clogged with thick mucus, his massive head swaying back and forth to show off its weaponry. I could hear him breathing, the air rushing from him as loud as the bellows my grandmother kept in her Gloucester home, and when we reached the end of the fence he gave the corner post a head butt sufficient to crack it lengthwise. Pleased with his handiwork, he trotted back to his herd tossing his head violently.

My grandfather stepped ahead of me before we reached the water, surveying the river where it ran over a rock bar into a deep pool then spread out and drifted away through a shallow set of riffles. He had to cast over his left shoulder, and a clump of willows behind him, bigger than his house, forced him to roll the line, flicking it into the current with short, circular motions of his wrist.

The river reflected the sky, clouding up from the north, with the mirror clarity of late-summer water. Gray clouds floated downstream as their three-dimensional counterparts moved overhead, and a cool breeze fanned the cottonwood leaves above me. The scent of smoke was stronger than it had been, harsh and thick.

My grandfather missed a strike on his retrieve, unable to set the hook in time, and sadness hit me all at once. For some reason, even before I'd left home, I'd figured that my happiest time with my grandfather, the event that in my mind would come closest to summing up my stay in Montana, would be fishing the Big Hole with him. The expectations of big trout and strong love had built up to the point where I took for granted that fishing the river together would be a pleasant, life-long memory. My grandfather missed a second trout and hung his line up in the willows. I untangled his fly and flipped it over the bank for him, but he didn't cast right away. He was looking upstream to where the river bent in from a hay meadow that had recently been cut, leaving brown stubble that stretched toward the mountains. They rose above the field, their summits hidden in smoke, the orange glow of the fire like a hazy sunrise behind them.

"Grandpa?" I brushed my hand in front of his face. "Cole?" When he looked at me I realized he hadn't been looking at anything in the mountains. His mouth was open enough to expose his upper teeth, and blood trickled from the corners of his lips. His eyes were glassy again, and when I wiped the blood away, flicking tiny ruby drops into the river where they slowly blended with the water that washed downstream, he sighed heavily and began reeling. A vulture flapped its ragged wings over me and soared off in such perfect time with the river's flow that they appeared somehow connected. I watched it until it disappeared among the leaves of a cottonwood, thinking of the buzzards William Richards had seen and how this one, though not feasting on rotten buffalo or slaughtered settlers, might herald something equally awful. The wind picked up and grew colder, cutting through my clothes, bellying my grandfather's line, pulling the fly upstream into a backwater. It fluttered near shore, skirted a large, red rock, and vanished in a silver swirl.

I could see the trout shaking its head as it swam out into the current, twisting back on itself like a snake, its entire body throbbing in an attempt to throw the hook. It hit the end of the slack line, jerking the rod tip toward the river, and my grandfather looked over his shoulder with a start as if the fish had materialized from behind him. The trout jumped once, then again, tracing a semi-circle arc in the air, took two clicks of line off the spool and was done. My grandfather swung it up to me, and I unclipped the hook from where it had lodged in the trout's lower jaw. It was only seven or eight inches long and had not yet lost the rings of blue along the pink stripe on its side. I knelt to release it, but my grandfather stopped me.

"Let me," he said, motioning with his hands for the fish. I gave it to him, watched it fall through his fingers and become coated with sand at his feet, flipping on the ground as brown as the spider that scurried out of its way. It wound up a foot or so from the bank in a patch of blue asters where its red gills trembled and its golden eyes saw nothing but grass. My grandfather leaned forward, slid his right hand under the trout's belly, and gently tossed it to the water. It was gone in a streak, leaving circles from its splashdown to spread slowly out from the middle of the backwater. As the last ripples merged with the current, my grandfather put his arm around me. I felt as if a part of me was drifting away like the rings of the trout, growing further from me, diminishing as they went.

"Look." He raised the rod tip and pointed upstream. Clouds had dropped over the Pintlers and were heading our way like shingles of slate, overlapping each other as they ate up the landscape. My grandfather took a deep breath, handed me the rod, and smiled. "Remember," he said.

I couldn't look at him as I reeled in the fly, and the only way I was able to hold myself together was by counting the number of clicks the spool made. It sounded ninety-one times, and then I began counting the guides on the rod, the number of trees on the bank, and my footsteps on our way back up to the highway and along the buffalo fence to the house. I counted, never losing track, to keep my mind occupied, sometimes saying the numbers out loud simply to hear my own voice, proving to myself I still held the power to speak. As soon as I reached the kitchen, I ran for my room and lay down on my bed, burying my face in the sleeping bag, spinning toward sleep. I was just drifting off when my grandfather shook me.

"Come on," he said. I walked behind him through the living room into the driveway, dragging my feet in the ground.

Bull thistles had grown up around the stern of the canoe and their pink blossoms tilted in the wind two feet above the up-turned bottom. My grandfather put the heel of his boot into their stalks to break them away, bent to lift the canoe, and coughed so hard it took him five minutes to completely catch his breath. When his chest stopped heaving in and out he straightened up, stared at the western horizon, now a solid mass of fire and dark storm clouds, pointed to where the Big Hole valley narrowed to a slit between the Pioneers and Bitterroots, and said, "Float."

It took me a long time to drag the canoe to the pickup, beat the tailgate open, clean enough junk out of the bed to haul it in, and the whole time I worked my grandfather gave me his half smile.

As much of the canoe hung over the tailgate as rested inside, and the knots I used to tie it to the back of the cab, pulling baling twine through rusted screw eyes, were poor. A building fear that I was acting against my better judgement had tightened all my muscles, doing its best to immobilize me. When my grandfather climbed into the passenger side of the pickup, it succeeded. I was frozen solid to the ground, feeling as if I was looking down on my body from a great height, watching the world move around me, sure I would not be able to blink so much as an eyelash for all eternity.

"Drive," my grandfather commanded from the cab as a bolt of yellow lightning forked down into the Pintlers. A raindrop as big as my thumb struck me square on the bridge of my nose, I gave what I believed could be my last look at my grandfather's house, and climbed into the truck.

I drove in third gear along the Big Hole, looking out a wiperless windshield, becoming increasingly opaque, at the swaying cottonwoods and frequent flashes of lightning that pounded down in front of us, appearing as yellow tears in the satin-black horizon. I drove past where we had logged, along the windy stretch of road where the river surged through the gorge, up by where we'd watched the moose to where the valley spread out and the river ox-bowed around peninsulas of willows and sage. With a jerk of his hand, my grandfather pointed to a single-lane side road that led to the water, and I began pumping the brakes, slowing just in time to make the corner.

The rain was coming down in earnest, falling hard enough so the drops exploded when they hit, rapidly collecting in the bottom of the canoe, when I pushed us away from shore. My grandfather sat in the bow, his paddle across his lap, his shoulders slumped, weighing enough more than myself so we rode nose down making it hard for me to steer. I kept changing sides with the paddle, shoving us away from a rock on the right, a sandbar on the left, trying to follow the deepest course, but with so much rain it was difficult to pick out which ripples suggested sufficient water to float us. We scraped on a round stone, but my grandfather didn't turn around. His white hair, hair that had turned to silver in less than three days, stood in sharp contrast to the sky I could see on either side of him, and for an instant, as I looked at him through the falling rain, it became a wolf skin and the past hundred years narrowed to a period of time less than that between the drumming raindrops. I shuddered, felt the paddle slip in my hands, shrank away from a deafening thunder clap, then sat up straight, shook my head, and saw only my grandfather's hair. I watched him sink lower in his seat, his hat tipping forward, and it occurred to me that perhaps he had died. We sloughed off a submerged cottonwood, and when he lolled onto his side I was certain he was dead.

I picked my paddle out of the water, letting the river turn us as it wished, feeling the weightless bouncing of waves beneath my feet, watching the sky drop down around me, wondering if its great weight would push us under. We spun sideways, and when we began taking on water over the gunwales I slapped at the river with my paddle, striking the surface out of anger rather than with the idea of turning us. But we did turn, and for a long time glided downstream through the rain and thunder, riding higher and faster as the river rose under us, clipping along toward the gorge whose rumble I could hear even though we were still half a mile above it. It sounded like a jumbo jet taking off. We slid around a bend and were forced into a leaning cottonwood steadily losing its grasp on the bank. Half its limbs already danced beneath the surface, woven tight as a net by the current, eager to hang us up and drag us down. We crested a wave and rose up onto the trunk of the tree, teetered for a moment on its wrinkled bark, then slipped back and turned against the river, pinned between the cottonwood and all the water from it to the Big Hole's source.

My grandfather had fallen onto his back when we came off the tree and was lying face up in the bottom of the canoe with his nose barely above the water. His eyes were closed and there was a peaceful look about him that reminded me of a painting I'd seen in a New York City museum when I was young. It was of Christ after his crucifixion, done by some medieval artist who'd depicted Jesus wrapped in a white cloth lying on a rock with several women standing over him. I'd never seen a corpse, but figured when I did its expression would mirror Christ's on that canvas. My grandfather's did.

Water was rolling past us in heavy waves, trying to force the downstream side of the canoe under the tree, coming closer to succeeding every second, and we were taking on rainwater almost as quickly. I moved to the middle of the canoe to keep my grandfather's head out of the water. Even if he were dead I couldn't bear to see him beneath the muddy lake that was lapping at the bottom of his seat. I braced him up with one knee and tried to balance him there while I reached for the tree. A wave pitched us up onto the trunk, slamming fiberglass into wood, so close on the bank that the concussion from the thunder deafened me, creating for a few moments a complete silence, and my grandfather began growing lighter in my arms, his limp body floating off his seat, swaying back an forth as we continued crashing into the cottonwood. Water splashed over his lips, washing faint traces of blood from them, revealing a face whiter than his beard. I continued to hold him as we began to sink, still unable to hear anything, unsure whether to hold my breath or breathe quickly and deeply in order to get it over with. The gunwales dropped even with the water's surface, we rocked slowly sideways, I saw a tilting panorama of river, sky, and tree, and then the cottonwood came free from of the bank. A huge round mass of roots rolled skyward as the Big Hole poured into the new cavity it had eroded, yanking the tree away from the canoe, pushing it off downstream where it bobbed twice then sank.

There was enough air in the triangular pockets at the bow and stern of the canoe so that even though it was full of water if refused to submerge. My paddle was wedged under my seat behind me, but to get at it I would have had to let go of my grandfather. If we were going to come to shore, it would have to be without paddling because I wasn't budging.

The first sound I heard when my hearing returned was the water entering the gorge. The hiss of river on rock was as engulfing as the silence had been, and again I thought about reaching for my paddle. I looked over my shoulder at it, extended my hand behind my back, and felt my grandfather slip. His head bumped against my shins beneath the surface and I hauled him up by the front of his shirt. We were heavy enough so we weren't moving quite as fast as the current, but were still cruising right along and I could see the spray of the gorge one hundred yards ahead. It looked like a picture of Old Faithful in my picture book; a column of white mist shooting high into a dark sky, going against the rain, pushing the drops back toward the clouds.

The river was rolling over a pair of boulders at the entrance of the chute, and as we drew even with them, slipping through the current, feeling the river's push against my thighs, straining to keep my grandfather's head above water, I wondered which stone had played a key role in my existence. I decided it was the flatter of the two, a smooth chunk of gray granite that more directly faced where the sun would rise. As we passed it, the bow of the canoe breaking over the wall of water that had backed up where the river was forced to narrow, we pitched downward like a plane in a nosedive and I thought for the briefest of instants how ironic it was that my place of death and ancestral beginning would be the same. Then my grandfather twitched. His lips fluttered, his stomach convulsed, and his hands tightened on his seat. Shocked to see a dead man move, I quailed away allowing his head to sink. His face fell beneath the rushing water, for a moment I could not tell hair from foam, and then he sat up, pulled his paddle from under his seat as easily as an experienced swordsman draws his weapon, shot me a quick, piercing glance from eyes as dark as the blackest night when no amount of blinking improves vision, and said, "It's a pretty trick to try and drown your grandfather."

I dropped low in the water, letting the current running inside the canoe straighten my legs, and looked at him. The rock walls seemed to be rushing in on us, pinching the river between the cliffs, ready to crush us, but he was smiling. He drove his paddle into a sickle-shaped boulder to prevent our being cut in half, looked down the gorge, up into the rain, back at me, and over the Big Hole's roar hollered, "No fooling around now, Kyle, get your paddle and give her the onion on the right side. Full speed ahead and we'll make the ride."

CHPATER 20

THE RIVER didn't just push us, it pulled us, too. It shoved us up the crest of one wave then jerked it out from under us to create a bucking sensation, snapping my head down and back so hard it felt as though my eyes would pop from their sockets. I was vaguely aware of the storm raging around us, but most of my attention was focused on my grandfather. He sat straight, dipping his paddle first on one side then on the other, riding the river as if he were on shocks, shifting only slightly as the torrent battered against us.

I hadn't been scared of dying. Either I never actually believed I would or I had resigned myself to the fact that there was nothing I could do about it. At any rate, the fear never overtook me, not as we were trapped against the cottonwood nor as we entered the gorge. I'd figured my grandfather was dead and it didn't look that bad. I wasn't afraid until we rounded a bend, brushed the opposite shore, and barely dodged a railroad tie washed down from somewhere upstream. And even then I wasn't afraid of dying, I was afraid the past and present were on a collision course, building up to my grandfather rising in his seat to quiet the river. Each time he moved, my windpipe contracted and my eyes blurred.

"Paddle, goddamn it!" he screamed, but my hands remained in my lap. "On the right. Now on the left!" He switched sides faster than he spoke. "Straight ahead now. Steady. Steady." He looked back at me and his eyes were even darker. They looked like tiny tunnels that went on forever.

We bumped into something under the surface that pushed below my feet like hands on a coffin lid, and I jammed my paddle into the river as hard as

I could. The current wrenched it from my hands, stood it up on end as if daring me to reach over the side for it, then slammed it down on a hog-backed stone shattering its wide palm into dozens of pieces. Up ahead the river cut in close to the highway and fell drastically to a cauldron pool where the water foamed around a tangle of trees that had caught up as the spring high water receded. The cottonwood was waiting there, ready to have another go at us, spanning all but a couple of feet of the river's width. Its limbs whipped in opposite directions as the current and wind fought each other, and its massive trunk pounded against the jam, splintering smaller pines and firs.

The nose of the canoe plummeted, my grandfather leaned back in his seat, ready, I was sure, to stand up, I felt the Big Hole yank us downstream, and was certain this time there was no escaping the tree. The distance between it and us shrank to feet, then to inches, and then I watched my grandfather, paddling for all he was worth, disappear into its leafy bulk and felt its trunk swell the fiberglass beneath my seat as we rode over it. A limb slapped me hard enough to create an explosion inside my head, and as we emerged on the downstream side of the cottonwood I believed for a second that we had passed through a forest. A few toothed leaves danced in the current next to us, twirling like pinwheels, lightning struck a utility pole on the highway and sent a shower of sparks out over the river ahead of us, then we were free of the gorge.

My grandfather caught hold of the bank, leaped onto shore, and pulled me out of the water. He wiped at the red line across my temple where the limb had struck me, looked me up and down to see it any other damage had been done, then hugged me.

"Done manfully, Kyle," he said. "Fine piece of work to get us down through there."

My brain had taken in too much that was too hard to make sense of. As I jogged behind my grandfather up the highway, running to keep up with his long, effortless strides, I found myself counting my steps again. Each time one of my feet met the pavement, sending a jolt up my leg, I was sure it was real. The rest: my grandfather's miraculous recovery, the ride through the gorge, William, Aspen, my entire family history, the sensation that the temperature had dropped down around the freezing point, I didn't know about. I wanted to grab the back of my grandfather's shirt, pull him to a halt, and if I'd been able to catch him I would have tried. Sheriff Wilson stopped him for me, pulling his car in ahead of us, activating the light bar on top of the roof to add beams of blue and red to the yellow lightning still coming down close by.

"Kyle took us through the gorge, Jack," my grandfather said as the sheriff opened his door. "Never missed a beat. Steady as a rock. Boy's got the balls of a mule."

"What the hell's going on, Cole?" Wilson asked as if he hadn't a word my grandfather said. "Doctor said he didn't figure you'd ... I mean they said you were in real bad shape."

"Fuck the doctors!" my grandfather bellowed.

Wilson put a hand on my chest and my grandfather whirled around.

"Cole, I've got to take you back to the hospital. Christ." Wilson dropped his hand from my shirt and extended a finger toward my grandfather. Realizing almost as quickly he'd made a mistake, he changed his tone from anger to pleading. "Shit, Cole, it's the hospital or the clink. Troopers are gonna press charges."

"The hospital or the jail, huh? Weren't ever in a man's best interest to give Cole Richards an ultimatum. Reckon you ought to know that."

"Then do it as a favor. A favor for a friend. Come with me, please." Wilson opened his door wider, letting rain spill in onto the seat.

"In the morning, Jack. It's Kyle's last night in Montana."

I wondered how he knew that, but it was too low on the list of things that puzzled me to think long about it.

"I ain't gonna have him spend it in a hospital or jail. I'll answer for my actions, and you know it, but I won't do it tonight. Might do the gorge again though. Wait till dark and see if it ain't even better."

Wilson settled back into his seat and shook his head. "You're gonna kill yourself, Cole," he said. My grandfather laughed and started jogging.

At the truck, I was out of breath. I was drenched with rain and sweat, and as soon as I stopped moving I began to shiver. My teeth clicked against each other and my hands trembled wildly. My grandfather had to open my door for me, and when he saw how cold I was he turned on the heater, which, even after we began flying down the highway, hydroplaning through deep puddles, didn't blow hot air. I sat in the truck while my grandfather loaded the canoe, a job I felt bad about letting him do alone but knew I wouldn't have been much help.

It wasn't quite eight o'clock when we started down the driveway, but we had to use the truck's one headlight. It shed a pale beam onto the soupy road in front of us, dimly illuminating a ten-foot path before the rain pounded it to pieces. It was so dark I couldn't see much past the forest on the other side of the pasture, and the trees looked more like stains on the windshield than softwoods. I stared at the smudge of timber until we came to stop beside the skidder. Beyond it, the fire had been extinguished, leaving the air smelling more of smoke than when it was raging.

"I take it you finished your great, great grandfather's journal," my grandfather said as soon as he'd killed the engine. I was still watching the forest and only half heard him. "Found it enlightening, too, right?" His eyes were so black I couldn't look into them. I'd seen them before somewhere but couldn't put my finger on where. "Not to worry my man, you come from very good stock. Very good." As he shouldered open his door, I started to ask him exactly what I'd read . . . what it meant anyway . . . but sensing the question he waved me off. "Soon enough. You'll know it all in good time."

"Grandpa?" I touched his wet shirt sleeve, and at the gesture he became attentive.

"Don't call me that, Kyle. We've discussed it before. Ain't my name and it don't fit me."

I was shivering so badly that the words came out broken, as if I had a severe stutter. "William's journal. Do you have it?"

"Of course." He slapped my legs, turned toward the house, stepped into the kitchen, snapped the water off his hat, and for a moment I could have convinced myself that it was early June and we were wet after a day of fishing.

As I was getting undressed, the phone rang.

"That's no one we want dealings with, Kyle."

It rang for a full two minutes, stopped, then began again.

"Please tell that persistent son of a bitch to go and fuck himself, Kyle. Tell him if he ever calls back I'll kill him."

I waited for my grandfather to disappear into his room the picked up the receiver.

"Oh, Kyle." It was my grandmother. "I'm so sorry, honey. And I'm so glad you'll be home soon. This can't be easy for you."

I glanced toward my grandfather's room, hoping to hang up before he came out, but it was too late. He glided into the living room, wearing wool pants and a his denim jacket.

"I believe my instructions were clear, Kyle." He was striding toward the phone with a hand extended for the receiver. "We'll be bothered no more."

"Is that Cole?" My grandmother's voice grew shaky. "I thought . . ."

"Who is this, and why by God do you insist on disturbing us?" my grandfather boomed into the phone. "Ah, Boston. Calling under the pretense that you're concerned I bet. Kyle," he covered the phone. "Shall we speak to her?"

I didn't answer.

"Very well." he sighed heavily and put the phone back to his ear. "Yes . . . yes, Kyle's fine."

I turned away to finish dressing, and my grandfather let me go. He stayed on the phone longer than I had expected, and when he hung up he didn't seem terribly upset.

The buffalo were running from one end of their pasture to the other half an hour later as we started down along the fence for the second time in less than a day, dressed in winter clothing, our pants tucked into wool socks.

Splinter Horn didn't see us until the fourth or fifth trip by, and when he did he brought his bulk of a body to a stop, digging his hooves into the wet prairie, allowing the herd to charge past him so he could face us. He stood motionless twenty yards away on the other side of the fence, and although it was dark enough so he looked more like shadow than the mud-caked beast he was, in my mind I could see his eyes fixed on my grandfather.

At the highway, we turned and walked up to where the pasture ended and woods began. The wind was out of the north, and it came singing through the trees, carrying something between rain and snow that bit at my face.

"Can it snow now?" I asked my grandfather.

"Reckon she can if she wants. Certainly not unheard of."

I hung back a few steps as he dipped off the road into the forest, picking up my pace when I saw how completely the trees hid him. It was as if he'd stepped into a black curtain, and as I ran to catch him it occurred to me he might be gone.

We walked up a ridge among mature lodgepole over one hundred feet tall, paralleling the fence back toward the house. The sky above the trees, where I could see it, had acquired an orange tint like the light that escapes through the back side of a jack-o'lantern, and it was snowing.

"Kyle." My grandfather's voice startled me. He hadn't spoken for fifteen minutes, and I'd lost myself in the silence of the forest. He leaned up against a boulder whose top was already collecting snow, transforming the stone from gray to white. "Do you remember me telling you I spent six days in an outpost camp on the upper Big Hole when I was a young man?"

I remembered everything he'd told me and nodded. "Without food, right?" He smiled and his eyes grew hot, burning into me, forcing me to look down at my feet.

"That's right, without food."

The snow began falling harder, the flakes spreading in size, reminding me of spring lake-effect storms in New York.

"What I didn't tell you, Kyle, is that I wasn't alone."

I started shaking as adrenalin mixed with my blood, unsure whether to throw up or ball my hands into tight fists and accept its energy. I couldn't stand still, and when my grandfather saw this he started walking again.

"My father was with me," he said without turning around. "And he was seventy-four years old and in as good shape as you or I."

An elk drifted through the trees ahead of us, apparently unconcerned. His velvet antlers were gathering a haze of snow, I heard his hooves sink into the damp earth as he ambled away, and realized I was counting his steps, straining as hard as I could to hear them.

"When William Richards, Junior was nineteen, he left Missouri and retraced his father's steps."

My grandfather's words filled me, surrounding me more than the trees, pressing into me, rekindling my conviction that something terrible was drawing near. The wilderness grew hungry, eyes everywhere, and my head began to pound.

"He was an old man when I was born, and I have no memories of my mother."

"What happened to her?" I asked, believing whatever it was couldn't be as bad as what had taken place on the river.

"She died before I was one, and as I understand it, it wasn't something my father liked to talk about, she'd been sick a long time."

"Was she an Indian?"

My grandfather turned around. "No, her name was Anna Rawlings, and she was a midwestern farm girl on her way to visit an aunt in California when she met my father." He winked at me. "Guess she never made it to the coast."

A gust of wind lifted my hat, but I caught it before it came off my head.

"That's as much as I know about her. Now pay attention."

We started walking up a long creek bed, one I'd seen before, and I began looking for my boulder. The rain had filled the stream and the current was swift, solid white water upstream and down.

"My father and I sat out the blizzard in our lean-to for five days. The snow kept piling up, and I wondered if it would ever stop. Felt like there was no end to it. I remember lying awake at night listening to the wind blow and our stomachs growl. Neither one of us said a whole lot . . . course he was quiet anyway. Did more watching than talking. Kind of like someone else I know."

I turned away when he looked back at me. The eyes were too much. I expected them to melt the snow like lasers.

"On the sixth morning, we woke up to sunshine. Amazing how that works. Just like that."

My grandfather's back was to me, but I felt his eyes close. It was as if a great weight had been lifted off my chest.

"Nothing more beautiful than sun on fresh snow." His eyes were still closed. "Makes the world look all new and fresh, and you kind of hate stepping onto it and messing everything up. But we were half starved and goddamned ready to go home."

I felt the eyes open.

"Kyle." We were even with the boulder I'd seen the wolf from. "Kyle, that Big Hole River should have been frozen plenty hard. We'd had lots of cold weather before the storm, and where we crossed it there wasn't much flow. When dad dropped through the ice I figured he'd just busted through a drift. We'd been doing it all morning, taking turns breaking trail, and I didn't know he was in the water until I saw it seeping up around him. He was out ahead of me twenty feet or so, and for a second I couldn't move."

We jumped across the creek and turned into the forest where the wolf had come from. The trees grew close together, small and densely-limbed. I followed the dark swath where my grandfather had knocked the snow from their branches, walking close enough to him to listen, afraid to lose sight of his coat.

"The river was deep." His voice came from all around me. "Way over his head, and the ice was bad all around him. Every time he tried to pull himself up it broke away and he went under. I finally started toward him, not realizing what I was doing, my legs working on their own. I don't know how he knew, his back was to me and all I could see when he surfaced was the top of his hat and his hands, but he knew I was coming."

The little trees gave way to rock as we neared the top of a ridge. The snow was coming hard enough to cake an inch thick on the brim of my grandfather's hat.

"My father never cussed much, Kyle. He didn't have to. He got his point across just fine without the use of profanity. But when I tried to help him, he swore at me in good shape. 'Goddamn it, Cole, stay the fuck away from me!' He didn't want me breaking through, too. I heard him, but I couldn't stop. He wasn't fighting as hard as he had, and I didn't figure he'd come up but a couple more times. We were wearing lots of clothes, and they'd soaked through."

We crested the ridge and my grandfather stopped. The back side dropped steeply, and in the snow appeared to be the edge of the world. All I could see were falling flakes.

"I was almost to him, looking down at the widening pool of water forming on the new snow, when he turned toward me. He had long hair, and it was down over his face, stuck to his eyes, so I couldn't tell if they were open. I figured they were because he tipped his head right toward me. I reached for him, heard the ice start to pop under me, and watched him push himself under as hard as he could. He never came back up.

"There were some rapids a hundred feet downstream where the river hadn't frozen. A merganser was working them for fish, and I sat on the bank, must have been in shock, and watched him for an hour waiting for dad to float down. Course he didn't."

We stepped off the ridge, and I was surprised to find earth under my feet. I had prepared myself to fall forever.

"The river broke up early that spring, and I must have walked it a thousand times looking for him. I pried apart log jams, poked long poles into the deep water around bends, and covered every inch of quick water."

I felt my grandfather's eyes close again. "Did you find him?" I asked. He stopped, extended a hand behind his back as if he knew I was scared to look at him, and when I took it he squeezed one time. I knew he hadn't. "He wasn't in there, was he?" My grandfather squeezed my hand once more then let it go.

My feet pushed long furrows of snow ahead of them as I slid down the slope. The trail I left, two lines of dark earth against the white hillside, filled in so quickly that when I looked over my shoulder it appeared that I'd been set down from the sky. I wondered if I stopped whether the snow would obliterate more than my tracks. I felt as if it was chasing me, pushing me somewhere I didn't want to go.

There were more trees at the foot of the ridge where the ground suddenly rose up to meet me, causing me to stumble. I reached out to catch myself on my grandfather but he drifted away, moving without walking it seemed, and I fell. I tried to get up too quickly and my feet went out from underneath me again. When I stood up, my grandfather was out of sight and the forest was watching me. Watching the same way it had when I'd seen the wolf. Among the snowflakes were thousands of eyes.

A shadowy figure glided in front of a leaning fir, so fast I wasn't sure if it was really there, seemed to turn toward me, and stopped.

"Cole!" The snow deadened my scream, and I ran toward him, fighting to keep my balance. The limbs behind him, palm-like and heavy, swayed as the snow slumped off onto the ground, hitting with a dull thud. As the branches rebounded to their horizontal positions, my grandfather vanished into them, and when I arrived at the spot I thought he'd been standing there were no tracks. I began shaking, strong spasms yanking my body in too many directions to go at once, the tree and snow swam together before me, and I dropped to my knees.

"Ain't no time for prayer, Kyle." I recognized the heavy weight of my grandfather's hand on my shoulder. "I tend to doubt that gentleman," he glanced up at the sky, still orange above the snow, "would be too inclined to answer them while you're in my company anyway." He helped me up and brushed the snow from the back of my pants. "Come on now, we're about there."

My legs weren't operating as well as they should have been. They kept wanting to slide out to the side, and I had to walk slowly, looking down, picking exactly where I wished my feet to land. I tried to set them in my grandfather's tracks, but they were too wide. I counted sixty steps before he stopped, and by the way he widened his stance, let his arms drop to his side and his shoulders relax, I knew we'd come as far as we were going.

I didn't need to ask him what the two buildings, one twice the size of the other, both caved in around the edges, listing to the south, bowed outward and roofless, were.

"I always liked beginnings, Kyle."

When he said it, I couldn't help thinking the ruins in front of me were closer to some sort of end than any beginning.

"I like spring more than fall, dawn more than dusk, and buds more than leaves." His eyes didn't look so hot. "I expect it's something that has come partly with age. The older I get the better I like beginnings. And this here's a good one. I don't guess it looks like much now . . . a few fallen-in, mossy timbers in the middle of the forest . . . but it's where an awful lot got going. And it's a spot I like. Can't quite put my finger on why, and I don't spend much time trying to figure it out, but it's special to me. Not a whole lot more to it than that." He coughed and drops of blood fell fast and dark onto the snow around him.

There wasn't much left of William's cabin, and looking at it, watching it fill quietly with snow, I remembered what he'd written in the journal about time reducing it and him to the same elements. I tried to picture him running out into a storm like the one I stood in, desperately searching for Aspen, and although I had seen it clearly when reading, I couldn't visualize it again. Perhaps my mind had removed it to the area of dreams I remember when I first wake up but soon forget.

My grandfather brushed enough snow off a log that had separated from the wall near where the door had been for us both to sit down. There were only a few steps between us, but it seemed to take a long time to reach him. When I sat, he put his arm around me and it was colder than the snow that seeped through my pants.

"What do you think, Kyle?" he asked as if some marvelous view spread away before us. "Lovely here, isn't it?"

I didn't think it was. It looked as dilapidated as William's spirits must have been when he lost his wife. I wished time would hurry up and allow the earth to absorb it.

"Cole, what do you think happened to those people?" It seemed like the right time for questions.

"Who?"

"Aspen, Star Stepper, your father? What happened to them?"

"Same thing that happens to all of us," he said with a casualness that made my back tighten and eyes water. The thought of everyone in my family either vanishing or assuming some other life form was disconcerting to say the least. "What I mean is that their time came and went the same as it will for you and me. Same as it does for everything. That old Indian gave your great, great grandfather some good advice when he told him to enjoy life every day."

My grandfather removed his arm from me, stretched his legs out straight, and leaned back. I watched the snow pile up on his pants, the flakes landing on top of each other, never in exactly the same place, and thought of more things I'd like to ask him. I wanted to know why he never showed the journal to my father, and if I could tell him about it when I got home. I wanted to ask him how much of it he thought was true, and I wanted to know where he got it. These were questions I wanted to ask, but I didn't. I kept thinking of the time he'd come east to visit and the way he'd held me up to look into my eyes. I wondered if he knew something about me I didn't, and the way he looked at me then, through the snow that fell between us, made me afraid he did and that our eyes were the same.

"Kyle?" He gave me his hand. "Kyle, yank this old man to his feet, will you?" I helped him up and he patted me on top of the head. "You're a good man, Kyle. A very good man."

My grandfather walked to the first layer of forest, giant, dark fir trees whose limbs joined half way up their trunks, and though he didn't look back, as I followed I did. I couldn't help looking over my shoulder, watching the snow drift in around the remains of the cabin until I could no longer see it. Like the last call from a high-flying flock of geese, I couldn't attach a precise moment to its disappearance, but when it did I had no trouble imagining William running through the night without his buffalo coat, driven with the same urge to find Aspen that my grandfather had felt to find his father, that drove me to find some sense in it all.

We didn't walk back the way we'd come. We stayed close to a creek for over a mile, cut away through a sage meadow where the snow clung to the plants more than the ground, entered a stand of old pine, and were soon seeing headlights on the highway and could hear the swollen Big Hole across it. One hundred yards from the road the earth grew damp and spongy, soaking my feet with cold swamp water. My grandfather never looked at the lone, enormous aspen he walked beneath, and by the time I reached the tree and wanted to ask him, he was calling for me from the road. Like William's cabin, I watched it fade into the snow until its uppermost branches, delicate limbs bent close to the trunk, washed into the night sky.

CHAPTER 21

PLINTER HORN'S MOOD had not improved any with the storm. His breath was condensing on his shaggy head, turning to ice to give him the appearance of something from the Pleistocene. He bellowed at us the entire length of the fence until my grandfather, walking ahead of me, stopped abruptly and faced him.

"My good sir, the time has come when all accounts are to be paid in full." The buffalo stood still and cocked his head. "I've got something for you."

We walked quickly the rest of the way to the house, carving a path through close to six inches of snow, stomping it off our boots in the kitchen, watching as it slowly turned to water on the floor.

"Look around and see if you can't come up with a flashlight, Kyle. I think there's one in the gun cabinet somewhere."

My grandfather headed for his room, I heard his bed springs squeak, then footsteps in the attic above the living room and a loud thump as something tipped over.

"I can't see a fucking thing up here. You find that light yet?"

I had and handed it up to him through the square hole in the ceiling. My grandfather bumped around a few more minutes before he appeared above me again. The flashlight was off, and it was dark all around him. Too dark to see more than his silhouette, but I could see his eyes, darker than the blackness, darker than the night, darker than anything I had ever seen.

"Take this for me, please." Before swinging down onto his bed, he lowered a roll of canvas, and by standing on my toes I was able to reach it. The cloth was oily, covered with spider webs and the small, irregular stains left by mice. It smelled old and had been rolled long enough so my grandfather had to fight to open it. His patience soon waned.

"Miserable son of a bitch!" He hauled on one end, shaking it like a bed sheet, and slowly it relinquished its grasp.

The first thing that amazed me about the Sharps rifle was how big the opening in the barrel was. The octagonal steel had a hole in it wide enough for two of my fingers. And it was long. Half again as long as my grandfather's 30.06. At the end of the barrel was a narrow post sight, and back by the stock was a peep that folded down in front of a large hammer set slightly off center. The stock was dull and worn, cracked its entire length, but the brass butt plate was shiny. On it, etched in small, neat letters, were the initials W. H. R.

My grandfather flipped me a shell as long as my hand and grinned. "She'll kill a buffalo as far as a man can see one."

I worked the casing along my fingers, staring at the blunt, gray bullet that protruded from it.

"That lead's backed by blue cordite. None of that smokeless shit. It'll carry a solid mile." My grandfather's chin was bloody. It came steadily from his mouth, and though he wasn't coughing, his breath was choppy. "We'll go hunting now, Kyle. It's time to send those buffalo home." He slung the rifle over his shoulder, I heard more shells click together in his coat pockets as headed toward the kitchen, and then his room was quiet, the only noise coming from the wind outside, moaning under the eaves.

I didn't want to move. I wished I could crawl into my grandfather's bed, pull the covers over my head and sleep, but I didn't have a choice. Something was at hand, more than the killing of buffalo, and I had to see it out.

We slipped under the fence, first my grandfather, then me, packing the snow under us, feeling its cold touch on our stomachs. The whole time we'd been at William's cabin I wasn't cold, but as soon as I stood up in the pasture, the hard north wind in my face, I began shivering. A chill crawled up my body, in from where the snow had worked its way over the tops of my wool socks, and lodged in my head, pressing like ice in the crack of a rock. The tips of my ears burned and it hurt to move my eyes.

The buffalo were against the far fence, near the woods, and we couldn't see them until we were within fifty yards.

"Not exactly sporting," my grandfather said as he dropped to his belly and sighted down the barrel.

There was only a second between the time he took aim and the gun went off, but it was long enough for me to see vividly all that rifle had shot at, and I believed there was more connecting my grandfather to the past than the three initials pressed into his shoulder.

As it had my first night in Montana, orange flame poured from the barrel of a rifle. The Sharps threw a thick cloud of smoke, from both the muzzle and the action, and cracked across the block. I heard a bullet connect and one dark shape among the buffalo sank into the snow. The smoke hung in the air, prevented from ascending by the barrage of flakes, but as soon as it dissipated enough to see, the gun went off again, throwing more smoke and sparks from the action, rocking my grandfather's whole body. He opened the chamber without taking his eyes off the sights, dropped in a third shell as smoothly as if he'd shot the gun every day of his life, calmly waited for the smoke to clear, and touched the trigger again.

My ears were ringing, my throat was sore from breathing the acrid smoke, and the pain in my head was mounting. I wasn't sure how much more I could take before my skull split. The herd wouldn't move. It was locked in place and the dead kept piling up, another falling each time the Sharps boomed out a bullet. I watched them huddled together waiting to die and thought that they were a far cry from the last buffalo the rifle had killed.

As my grandfather continued shooting, the ringing in my ears subsided, but the rifle blasts grew fainter. After ten minutes, I could barely hear it go off, and after fifteen had to watch for the smoke to know when another animal had died. The Sharp's action was splitting, shooting its own streak of fire at a ninety degree angle to the barrel. The steel was getting hot, expanding and cracking, but the shooting finally stopped.

My grandfather dug out the last shell, held it to his lips, and closed the gun around it. Then Splinter Horn emerged from the irrigation ditch less than twenty yards away, in full charge, his horns cutting through the snow like scythes, his hooves carrying him much faster than something so big should be able to move. I was between him and my grandfather, and I remember fixing on an icicle of mucus that hung from the buffalo's left nostril down over his lips. Attached to the thick hair on his chin, it bounced as he ran, swinging like a fast-moving pendulum, and I couldn't take my eyes off it. I watched it rocking crazily back and forth, closer every second, felt my grandfather's hand around my ankle, realized I was falling, slowly it seemed, a long way to the ground, and was barely aware of him rolling over me, firing the Sharps from his hip. There was a flash of light, as much inside my head as out, as the rifle blew apart between the stock and barrel.

Lying on my side, my face buried in snow and sage, I watched through one eye as the buffalo materialized from the smoke, hooked my grandfather under the ribs with one of his wicked horns, and tossed him high into the air as if he was a paper doll. Anyone who didn't know Cole Richards would have believed the expression on his face when he landed sideways on the buffalo's back was one of pain rather than mild amusement. His eyes met mine as Splinter Horn turned, and for the first time that evening they were his own, the flaming darkness replaced by a knowing stare. The buffalo wheeled in front of me, spraying blood from a hole in his chest, and my grandfather looked away, toward the forest where they headed.

I heard Splinter Horn break through the fence on the other side of the irrigation ditch, snap one low limb on a pine at the edge of the woods, and realized I wasn't deaf. Then he and my grandfather were gone. I lay in the sage watching snow begin sticking to the pile of brass casing now growing cold, breathing silently, waiting for a sign to get up. None came, and I don't know how long I lay there. I don't remember standing, following the bull's tracks to the fence, or entering the woods, but I do remember the first place the tracks blended with the snow. It was over a fallen fir where a drift had blown in against the back side, washing out the trail as neatly as it covered the dry needles on the ground. The eyes of the wilderness were on me, much closer than ever before, as I went on a dead run along the track up a ridge toward the creek where I'd seen the wolf. In some of the tracks there was blood, and where the snow covered it I kicked it up, dark and soft.

I crested the ridge, felt the wind pick up, and stopped. Splinter Horn was sprawled out ahead of me, lifeless and limp, his neck broken, bent over his shoulder so his head faced the way he'd come. His eyes were open, and they were wild with fright.

I ran past him to the creek, then back to the top of the ridge, circled, and fell down. There were no other tracks. Branches and snowflakes merged above me, I began to spin, then sat up, my senses sharp, and listened. I heard it once more, so far away that it could have come from the other side of the universe. At first I thought it was the wolf, and then I thought it was the wind, and then I wasn't sure.

CHAPTER 22

M Y GRANDFATHER'S CANOE didn't seem as heavy when I unloaded it at the head of the gorge as it had when I'd wrestled it into his truck before our trip down the river. And the rocks that I lifted over my head to smash through its hull, sending shattered pieces of fiberglass twirling downstream, appeared to defy gravity, rising in my hands like the mist off the water. No one, not even my grandfather, could negotiate the gorge at night, but after announcing to Sheriff Wilson that he might try, no one would doubt that he'd attempted it. That would be the story I would tell: my grandfather vanished in the gorge in his canoe. Vanished in the river. I looked upstream, in the direction of the Bitterroot Mountains, far across the Big Hole valley, and thought about the story I would not tell. My story.

The wind was swinging around, beginning to blow in warm breaths from the south to restore summer, and what stars I could see above the fog were especially brilliant, glowing blue, white, aqua, and red. I stared at them a long time, surprised I did not begin to count, and before I climbed back up the riverbank to where I'd parked my grandfather's truck, the eastern sky over the rounded mountain on the horizon was silver. Night was ending and the day would be clear, and all around me, even over the rush of the river, I could hear snow melting. It dripped from the guardrails along the highway, trickled over the stones near shore, and eventually became part of the Big Hole. I thought about everything snow had covered over the past century and a half and how over time it had all wound up in the river. Perhaps that was what had given the water sufficient impetus to cut through the mountain and form the gorge. Perhaps what I would tell about my grandfather had more truth in it than I realized.

In the numbness of shock, walking from the forest to the house, skirting dead buffalo, averting my eyes from William's journal lying on the kitchen table, working like a machine to get the canoe back to the river, I had been able to force thoughts of my grandfather and upcoming journey home from my head. But waiting beside the river, near the pull-off where I'd slept in my first night with him, for parts of the canoe to drift by so I could get Sheriff Wilson, so I could tell what I had to tell, I could no longer keep the images away: my grandfather's laugh, the odor of softwoods that clung to him, the way he'd silently watched me catch the big cutthroat in Firewater Lake, his intense love of the forest, his friends, and of me. These images flooded me, cutting it seemed as steadily as the water in the gorge, and in an instant I realized how much I had loved him, too, and also that I didn't, and never would, quite know why. There was both emptiness and fullness inside me; a sense of loss and understanding, as if I was leaving someplace wonderful, taking something wonderful with me. As much was beginning for me as was ending, and I knew recognizing that would please my grandfather.

The corners of my eyes grew damp, and the tears that ran from them down my cheeks were hot. So hot I wondered if they dripped from black holes of fire. I was thinking about it when the sun rose and blinded me with its reflection off the new snow. I cupped my hands in front of my face, and as my vision gradually returned, I leaned over the river where the current ran gently upstream in a backwater. The tears that splashed down to dimple the surface ebbed, my reflection became clear, and with my breath held and body trembling I looked at the eyes staring up at me. They were my own, perhaps a bit sharper than they had been; nonetheless they were still mine, and in them were reflected the cottonwoods behind me. Snow clung to their branches, diffusing the sun's rays into a million beams of light that were coming down all around me. Behind the trees were the tops of the Pioneers, where the snow was deeper, red in the day's first light, and beyond the mountains was the sky. The endless blue Montana sky, which even in the refection of my eyes seemed to go on forever, spanning the entire universe, pressing down upon me with all its great weight. And somehow I was holding it up.

COLOPHON

T̶HE LAST BUFFALO HUNTER has been set in Bulmer, a digital version of a type first cut in 1790 by William Martin for W. Bulmer & Company's Shakspeare Printing Office, established during the reign of George III for the purpose of producing a new edition of Shakespeare's works. The type was revived with great success by ATF in 1928 and was soon made available for machine composition on the Monotype. While Bulmer draws from the tradition of Caslon, it is, like Baskerville, a transitional face, graced with characteristics that point toward the types cut in Italy by Bodoni some decades later. Though it has been said that English printing suffered a decline in the decades following Bulmer's death in 1830, the types that bear his name retained their luster to such a degree that no less a critic than Daniel Berkeley Updike would write, "They were very splendid of their kind."

Design, typesetting, and digital imaging by Carl W. Scarbrough